Books should be returned on or before the
last date stamped below.

HEADQUARTERS

0 8 JUL 2003   15 MAY 2008   - 9 NOV 2010

18. 02. 05.   1 1 JUN 2008   2 2 MAR 2013

                                            2 2 MAR 2013
01. APR 05.   1 2 SEP 2013

                      - 3 JAN 2009
                      - 5 MAY 2009
12. FEB 07. 44   19 JAN 2010   3 1 OCT 2014
                      2 1 OCT 2010   2 8 NOV 2016
0 8 MAY 2007
                                            2 4 SEP 2017
- 3 SEP 2007
- 7 NOV 2007
                      ABERDEENSHIRE   2 8 MAR 2018
                      LIBRARIES

                      WITHDRAWN
                      FROM LIBRARY

ABERDEENSHIRE LIBRARY
AND INFORMATION SERVICE
MELDRUM MEG WAY, OLDMELDRUM

Binding, Tim

In the kingdom
of air / Tim
Binding
                    F Pbk

1403555

D0316134

ALSO BY TIM BINDING

A Perfect Execution

Island Madness

On Ilkley Moor

TIM BINDING

In the Kingdom of Air

ABERDEENSHIRE
LIBRARIES

WITHDRAWN
FROM LIBRARY

PICADOR

F PBK
1403555

First published 1993 by Jonathan Cape

First published in paperback 1994 by Vintage

This edition published 2002 by Picador
an imprint of Pan Macmillan Ltd
Pan Macmillan, 20 New Wharf Road, London N1 9RR
Basingstoke and Oxford
Associated companies throughout the world
www.panmacmillan.com

ISBN 0 330 48749 3

Copyright © Tim Binding 1993

The right of Tim Binding to be identified as the
author of this work has been asserted by him in accordance
with the Copyright, Designs and Patents Act 1988.

All rights reserved. No part of this publication may be
reproduced, stored in or introduced into a retrieval system, or
transmitted, in any form, or by any means (electronic, mechanical,
photocopying, recording or otherwise) without the prior written
permission of the publisher. Any person who does any unauthorized
act in relation to this publication may be liable to criminal
prosecution and civil claims for damages.

1 3 5 7 9 8 6 4 2

A CIP catalogue record for this book is available from
the British Library.

Typeset by SX Composing DTP, Rayleigh, Essex
Printed and bound in Great Britain by
Mackays of Chatham plc, Chatham, Kent

This book is sold subject to the condition that it shall not,
by way of trade or otherwise, be lent, re-sold, hired out,
or otherwise circulated without the publisher's prior consent
in any form of binding or cover other than that in which
it is published and without a similar condition including this
condition being imposed on the subsequent purchaser.

For Celia
who waited
and
for Paul
who also met the boy

The title is taken from the poem

'Lithuanian Nocturne' by Joseph Brodsky from the volume

To Urania (Selected Poems 1965–1985)

One

RECENTLY I HAVE DISCOVERED that I am attractive to women. Not more than any other men, but more than I ever thought I could be. Sometimes I wish that this realization had come to me earlier rather than later in my life, when there would have been more women available, when they would have been younger and freer (when *I* would have been younger and freer). Nevertheless this ability to attract, to get women to take their clothes off and fuck me is something which gratifies my senses and occupies my thoughts and actions for much of the waking day.

I am not sure when all this started. Certainly when I was younger I did less well with women (girls then) than most of my contemporaries. While I managed (eventually) a couple of unsatisfactory and short-lived love affairs I did not have the confidence or nerve to go out and fuck. This was partly due to the fact that other men of my age (boys then) seemed so more obviously adult than me. I was a transparent boy with a boy's manner and a boy's touch. But it was more to do with my perception of what women wanted – or rather what they did not want. I am not sure what women want. I am not sure what anybody wants. I am not sure what I want (Yes I am). But when I was younger I believed that women did not go for sex in the same way that men did and that therefore they did not like it as much, that either they had to be in love or they had to be tricked into it, 'conning the cunt out of them', as one of my contemporaries so delicately put it. What I failed to understand was that women for whatever reasons – love, passion, boredom, indulgence, hatred, revenge, drink – want sex quite as much as men, though probably (but not in all cases) not quite as often. Women prefer quality to quantity, but when they are faced with a combination of both they are perfectly prepared to pig at the trough with the rest of us.

Curiously enough the place which ought to have brought me to my senses, university, did little to remove the inhibitions I had. Despite the cheek-by-jowl student dwellings, despite the weeks of heavy drug taking and long drinking sessions, and despite the fact that many of my acquaintances spent a fair proportion of their academic hours sitting in the clinic waiting for Dr Black to disinfect their genitals, I was too unsure of myself to take part. Even the enticing offer of being attended to on a regular basis in return for writing Fiona Macintosh's thesis on Canadian Meteorology in World War Two did not alert me to the fact that it was all there for the taking and that, believe it or not I could be as good and successful as the next man.

The realization that I had a strong sexual appetite which could be fed and indulged, came, like learning to drive, late in my life. Does that sound crass? So be it. I never thought I would be good at driving and was afraid of it. Driving was for grown-up people and I had had enough of them. I never thought that I would be good at sex either and I was afraid of that too. I never had any intention of learning to drive and it was only because of my sister and her pitiful husband that I embarked on that long and humiliating series of lessons in the first place. Now of course I love driving and look forward to those long solitary trips on the motorway, when I drive for hours in the dark, with no idea of where I am going, nearly as much as I look forward to booking into a hotel room with Fleur or ringing the bell to Monica's flat or simply quickly fucking the Woman from Spain. Of course the motorway coupled with sex holds almost unlimited pleasure, and though it has happened only rarely, fingering Fleur as she attempts to steer a course down the M25, watching out of the corner of my eye while she languidly exposes herself are what memories are made of and Kleenex made for. I look forward to road journeys (you bet I do). I prepare for them. I open all the doors and take my small portable vacuum cleaner to the seats and the blue carpeted floor. I stroke it backwards and forwards, listening to the air being sucked in through its small eager mouth. I wash the windows and the windscreen wipers with warm, soapy water. I wash the headlights and the fog lights and the bright brake lights above. I soap its silver skin. My hands grow pink and clean. I fill the side door pocket on the driver's side with tapes of my favourite songs, songs of the Rhine and the Black Forest, songs of lost childhood, songs of anguish and regret. I sit down behind the wheel, adjust the side mirror, check the radio station and hold myself still. I reach out to the passenger seat. It is empty. The car is waiting. It is much the same with this sex. In Fleur's case, if it is at all possible, I will often go to the hotel bedroom in advance. I will take a portable stereo and I will set it up on the dressing table, the speakers facing the bed. If it is going to be one of those long evenings I will bring some food, a melon, some cold asparagus, a dozen oysters, some bright fleshy fruit. I will arrange it all like a picnic, sometimes on a table, sometimes on the floor, complete with linen tablecloth. Occasionally I will add a gift – a necklace bought too expensively at a Saturday market stall, some unusual bath salts, a length of wildly coloured material. When all is in place I sit in that room and hold myself still. I reach out to the bed. It is empty. The room is waiting. Quite often, although all we want to do is to go to that room and fuck and suck and fuck again, we will meet first at a wine bar or some quiet pub on some convenient corner, where she will tell me of her day and I will tell her of mine, where we will watch each other talk and laugh and drink and where we are conscious of only one thing – our desire to fuck. We will watch each other's mouths, the way our hands move, the way we touch our faces. Our legs will touch, first fleetingly, then naturally, then urgently. One of us will stumble over a perfectly ordinary word while the other looks on with wry amusement. We will start to take thick, indiscreet kisses. She will see my cock hard beneath my trousers every time I get up to buy cigarettes or to go to the lavatory (I have to piss through an inflamed erection. Most of it lands on my shoe or down the front of my trousers, or more dangerously shoots suddenly sideways on to my next-door neighbour). In the midst of one of her stories I will ask her, apropos of nothing, if her cunt is wet, and she will reply that it is, that she wants to go to the hotel *now*, and we will finish our drinks and pay the bill and lurch there together, grabbing each other in doorways and around corners, we will go there and walk through the lobby and take the lift, and we will fall out of that lift and lurch down the corridor and I will take out the plastic card and insert it into the slot, and the door will open and we will fall in, and in the moment she has put down her bag and I have taken off my coat, before the music or the picnic, before the champagne or iced beer, I will hold her and push her back on to the bed where she will raise herself up, so that her skirt slides over her hips, so that I may kneel by her side, both hands busy, one hand beneath her buttocks while the other dips in, and I will hold her there for a moment, pressing hard, watching her watching me, holding her cunt still, looking upon it before I lift the whole apparatus higher, to where my mouth is ready to greet it.

Does this all sound mechanical? Yes, it does. And so it should. That's the way to do it. That's the way it should be done. Ah, but where is the tenderness, where is the affection, where is the love? Well, to all you hopefuls out there, affection, love, and a certain amount of detachment are not incompatible. When it's like that, when it's long and cold blooded and bloody hard work, that's when it takes off into the stratosphere, when you almost die for the lack of oxygen. When it's like that you fuck forever. Fleur and I fuck forever. Her body is a beast of secret whispers and I a trembling ear. I listen to all it says. I note it down and use those confessions to catch her out, to have her gasping like a fish out of water. What she does to me I cannot say, but *she* knows. She knows *exactly* and when we are finished it is only a matter of time (and a short time at that) before one of us will stretch out and touch the other again and that instant, be it on my back or her neck, wherever, we will groan and turn ourselves about, to come and fuck, to fuck and come.

I have driven in my car with Monica many times but only twice with Fleur and it is she, I am afraid, with whom I wish to drive more. (I have no desire to drive anywhere with the Woman from Spain. She is purely a release and is only attractive to me – and that rapidly less so – in situ.) Monica's principal drawback is that she has no means of contraception planted within her, so that much of our sexual activity has to take place outside the main arena as it were. The possibility of external protection has never been broached and is understood by both of us to be out of the question. Our actual congress then is without doubt reckless and foolhardy, with ejaculation taking place (one hopes) only on her stomach, her breasts, her face, or over some third party – the carpet, the horsehair sofa, or, when times are hard, the balcony overlooking Marine Parade. Of course we are both intelligent and informed adults and are perfectly aware that this unscientific and often indecent use of the withdrawal method is unreliable even at the best of times, and our times are not the best of times, but simply the times which are available. But nothing has happened yet. I have a feeling that nothing will. Perhaps neither of us are very fertile. (A likely story.) Fleur on the other hand, who does not smoke (except joints), who goes to dance classes and who has recently given up meat is quite content to remain on the pill, although she is now in her early thirties and has been using them, so she tells me, since her teens. There are then no constrictions where Fleur and I are concerned (Oh yes there are) and we are able to do whatever we want in whatever order we want, without the fear of unwanted events, barring infection, which presupposes another unacknowledged arrangement; that we don't fuck around. Given the rather uncompromising nature of our first encounter this is a surprising commitment. I don't think she does. I do of course, though I do not consider screwing Monica or the Woman from Spain as 'fucking around'. I sense too, although this is unfair to Monica since we are unwilling, at the last resort, to conduct ourselves in the time-honoured manner, that Fleur is better at it than Monica and that even if we were able to stay glued, Monica's hit rate, or rather our combined batting average would be nothing compared to the tally that is rapidly mounting on Fleur's score-board. So I am content to jerk over Monica, to fuck Monica slowly, to lie on top of Monica motionless. I like it best when she holds me thick and desperate in her hand and tries to catch it in her mouth. It is a shameless and heathen posture and, thank God, it nearly always makes a mess.

I suspect by now there are many out there horrified by the tone of all this. What a debasement of women. What a debasement of language. I can see you all ranged against me, ready to use my words as your weapons. This is the truth though. This is how I think. This is how a lot of us think. Actually at some time or other, this is how *all* of us think, for in the case of the male of the species, sex is in the head and if we *don't* think about it, we're fucked.

I am prepared to concede that as far as the Woman from Spain is concerned I am open to criticism. I use her. I do not like her but I use her. She is near and when I am in the mood (I am nearly always in the mood) and if it is logistically possible, I go downstairs (or entice her upstairs) and get rid of it. She is tough and hard and ungainly. I distrust the sound of her voice. I am irritated by her faltering vocabulary (though what would I want to talk to her about?) and the strange acidic smell that emanates from her body repels me. When Mrs Delguardo is out, she likes us to cavort on Mrs Delguardo's bed, a pink thing in a pink bedroom and after we are done she likes nothing better than to wipe herself clean on Mrs Delguardo's pink curtains. This, I think is her prime reason for fucking me, for neither of us enjoys it very much. Wiping some sort of excreta over Mrs Delguardo's soft furnishings is much more appealing and if she could get away with it I am sure she would like to leave more concrete examples of her feelings. She stands there with her legs apart, grinning. 'All gone,' she says and I turn my head in shame. No it's not bloody all gone. I despise myself when I see the Woman from Spain standing before me with a corner of Mrs Delguardo's curtain in her hand because I know it is me who is the guilty party but I cannot, as yet, envisage a time when I would no longer wish to use her for my (not our) advantage. I place my hands on her and raise my eyes to the ceiling, as if to ask 'Is she there? Is it safe?' Actually I no longer care if it is safe or not. Indeed my sense of purpose is heightened knowing that Mrs Delguardo is downstairs preparing some canapés for her next round of guests, wondering why the Woman from Spain isn't there helping her out. Lately I have sensed that the Woman from Spain does not want to comply, particularly if Mrs Delguardo *is* around. She turns her head away and raises the palms of her hands, as if to warn me off. No use of course. It's far too late for that. I cut off her retreat. I take hold of her hands. I calm her down. I act quickly (which is all I want to do anyway). Only after it is over does she feel safe. Then her agitation ceases. She watches me nervously, waiting I suspect for some sign of betrayal. I like it when she is helpless like this, like it better than when she grins and kisses me and wipes herself on those curtains, for then we are partners, conspirators, and I have conspirators enough in Monica and Fleur. Under these conditions however every move is mine. So I lift her leg against the bath. I push her down into the armchair or on to the floor. 'All gone,' I say. 'All gone,' she replies. She does not believe me and I know her to be right.

There was a time, not that long ago, say a year, when I thought that if I had to choose between Monica and Fleur, I would have chosen Monica. I like Monica. She is a funny, intelligent and quick woman. She is good to talk to, and when there have been occasions when I have wanted to talk, it is to Monica that I have turned. Monica knows me and I, in truth know her. I am slightly (I *was* slightly) in love with Monica and she was (she is?) slightly in love with me. It is, I know, as far as both of us are prepared to take it. I know too, or rather I think I know why Monica enjoys my company. I am slightly dangerous, unpredictable, wild. I get drunk with Monica, smoke Monica's dope, make Monica laugh. Monica likes my bitterness, my bad manners, the fact that she is not responsible for me. Like others in my life Monica would like to cure me of my bad habits but unlike others who have attempted and failed, Monica knows better than to even try. She likes the sex well enough (she likes sport in general damn her) but she likes better to pit her wits against me, to have a sort of wild pet that she can let out of her cupboard every now and again. I am a sort of adventure for Monica, though when she chooses her claws can be as sharp and as cruel as mine. Naturally enough Monica has someone else, a sailor friend, and she likes to tell me stories about him, stories that are intended a) to make him appear ridiculous and b) to make me feel sorry for him. At the beginning of our little tryst category a) stories were very much in the ascendancy, but recently too many category b) stories have been breaking through. What Monica does not seem to realize is that I am interested in neither type, but if she must tell me one or the other then quite understandably I would rather hear eight of the former than one of the latter. No matter. I can take it. At least, when I throw back my head and ape laughter, or search my brain for a suitable rejoinder I know why Monica and I are still together, or rather I can surmise. With Fleur it is much more difficult, for while I can remember every detail of how it all started (and a great many of the subsequent events), the reason for it all, or rather the reason why it has gone on for so long evades me. It cannot be for the same reason as Monica, for whereas Leading Seaman Oates (for that is his name I believe) is rock steady, and as straight a man who ever sucked on a pipe, Jago, the man who Fleur is manacled to, is, without doubt, the most dangerous man I know. That could explain perhaps why *I* am attracted to *her*, and it could explain why *she* is attracted to *him* (for Fleur life is *the* drug and she the most eager of addicts), but it does not explain why *she* is attracted to *me*. I am not safe, nor sorry. I do not have power. Nor do I have presence (and he has both). I can only assume therefore that it is because of this. That she thinks of sex like a man and that when I see Fleur and when she sees me, we recognize in each other a part of ourselves. I know how its power holds me in its thrall. It is the idea, the articulation, the speech of sex as much as anything else. I love those words almost as much as the deeds themselves and I love the beauty of the misshapen mouths that recite such language. It is the same with Fleur. The words strike at her heart. They lie on her lips. I catch them running down her face. I gorge myself upon them! How wonderful they taste! I seize them, I grab them, I cram myself full. I chew them, I swallow them whole, I splutter with greed. How I devour them! I press my mouth against hers and push them back with my tongue and we feed upon them ravenously. This is the spell which holds me and it holds her. It does more than hold. It *possesses* me. It *possesses* her.

You have probably seen Fleur on television. She is becoming more famous by the day, though when I first met her she had only just started out on her climb to fame (though she rose rapidly enough). I don't know how many of you are familiar with the children's programme 'Planetrain' but that's the Fleur I'm talking about. Mondays, Wednesdays, and a big bumper programme on Saturdays. It is a very physical programme (surprise surprise) though Fleur maintains that it is educational as well. (It is not.) Nowadays I watch it all the time. Thanks to Clare I watch nearly all the children's programmes. Clare is educating me and I in turn am entering into a world which I had long forgotten and which has changed out of all recognition in the years I have been away. Childhood is not the same anymore. Childhood changes from day to day. When I was young it never changed. Childhood was like the Berlin Wall. You got shot trying to escape. Only dead children survived. Only dead children got to the other side. Now the wall is down and childhood is a world which is, curiously enough, as much a source of wonder for the parent as it is for the child (though no parent me). Childhood can be fun for the parent too. Parents can be children. Parents are *expected* to be children. The children they never were.

For all her talent (and I suppose it is a talent, or is that merely professional jealousy talking?) Fleur is not star struck, neither is she ruthlessly ambitious, although given her recent success she is more demanding than she was before. Clare of course adores Fleur although she has never met her, and dresses up in miniature versions of Fleur-type apparel. I have not told her that I know Fleur. Clare insists on watching 'Planetrain' every day it's on. She is not alone in this. 'Planetrain' and its star are enormously popular (which gives added spice to our meetings) and Fleur is, I suspect, by now extremely well paid. Clare insists that when she is at school and cannot get back in time I video 'Planetrain' so that we can both watch it when she gets back. I am not averse to this. I have my own selfish reasons, though I must say it is odd, sitting in front of the television with my arm around my niece, watching Fleur crawl around some playground with three or four children on her back, when seven or eight hours earlier, high above the domestic roofs of London, in a room with a Teasmade, a small colour television and a mechanical waiter stocked with gin, whisky, vodka and coke, Fleur was on all bloody fours with *me* hanging on for dear life. Clare would like to clutch at Fleur's hips too. She asks me why Mrs Galloway, her headmistress, has not invited 'Planetrain' to come to her school. I tell her that I don't know why. She asks me in an excited voice why don't I tell Mrs Galloway to invite 'Planetrain' to her school, that it would be simply *great* and I reply that I don't know Mrs Galloway well enough to make such demands, and that for all I know Mrs Galloway might well have invited 'Planetrain' already, that the chances are that every school in the country has invited Fleur's show and that it will take years and years for 'Planetrain' to visit even half of them. The truth is of course that I don't want Fleur to go to her school, that the last thing in the world I want is for her and Fleur to meet. I want Clare to be completely separate from Fleur (though paradoxically it is through watching her programme that we began to draw closer). I want Clare to be separate from Fleur and I want Clare to be separate from Monica (the Woman from Spain is a different case), for these two lives of mine do not mix. Fleur of course knows about Clare and the circumstances which brought us together, but she has never asked to meet her or offered me any advice. I am not surprised by the latter for it is clear that Fleur is completely ignorant of the needs of children apart from those which relate to skin and muscle. It is I feel a deliberate choice on her part and accounts in no small way for much of her success. The child as hedonist. And though I find the former oddly selfish it is probably an understandable act of self preservation. It is a job for her, not a vocation and if she were an accountant and I her lover she would not expect me to ask her to go through my tax returns. This suits me fine, for I do not want to bring them close either. When I am with Fleur I am not myself (yes I am). I have lost control (no I have not). So Fleur and I meet on neutral ground. Not on her territory, not on mine. When the going gets rough we meet once a fortnight. That is the least we can do. When the course is clear we meet once a week. That is the most we can do. There is no in between. The rest of the time, except for the occasional night in Brighton with Monica, or a quick dip into the Woman from Spain, is devoted to Clare (and of course, the weather). I used to go out. I used to go to restaurants and pubs. I used to pick up women at publicity parties or BBC functions. I used to go out for an evening with friends and lovers and even people I didn't like very much. Now of course I can't. Now there is Clare. I do go out sometimes just to get drunk. I ring up Eric and ask if he wants to come over and join me in the large anonymous pub down the road and drink too much. Mrs Delguardo is good about that. She is strangely supportive. (How quickly she would change her tune if she knew how I treated her young and helpless relative.) I tell myself (I tell Clare too) that everything will be all right, that soon her mother will get better and that everything will be back to normal. It's wrong of me I know. Things are not going to get better. Things are going to get worse. Mummy will die, I just know she will. I go to the hospital, I hold her hand, I tell myself that I am sure I can detect some flicker in those fingers, some dart of life behind those eyes but each time I am let down. I walk out into the cold air thinking that she will die and I'll be saddled with Clare forever. Clare's mother will die and I will continue to pursue Monica and Fleur and use the Woman from Spain. That of course is why I keep my lives so rigorously apart. That is why Fleur has never come to the flat or Monica for that matter. To keep Clare I have to keep my act clean. If the authorities knew what I got up to, what I *really* want, what I am *really* like, what I muse upon throughout the day, they would whisk Clare away from me before the ink had dried on the court order. They would be right of course. I am unsuitable for her. The trouble is I am all she knows, and she needs to know someone. I am not dead, nor dying, nor do I lie in a coma on a hospital bed. I don't push her away or send her to her room or get some woman to do it all for me. I read her books at bedtime and brush her teeth in the morning. I cook her breakfast, an unhealthy one of bacon and eggs I am pleased to say, eggs sent up from Kent, courtesy of Dickey Dove, and when I can I collect her from school. Colleagues at work have rearranged their shifts, have changed their lives so that I may do this. I cuddle her when she's afraid. (She's afraid every night. She's particularly afraid on the nights when I am not there, when I'm with Fleur or Monica, when Mrs Delguardo or the Woman from Spain step in.) I climb into Clare's bed in the unbalanced hours of the morning. Sometimes I have to hide myself, to wait embarrassed and cold beside my own bed before it is safe for me to move. I am irritable and stumble in, asking her what's the matter (as if I didn't know)? I lie next to her and stroke her head, her breath sweet and troubled, her little legs crossed over mine. She puts her face to my cheek and finds it wet. Why are you crying? she says and I tell her For no particular reason, Just a sad dream I had. She knows better and tries to comfort me. 'Mummy will get better soon,' she says, 'I just know she will.' I pat her head and agree. I don't believe her and she knows me to be right.

*

ON OCTOBER 15TH, the day this poor life began, when Fleur was in place, when I was still seeing Monica (The Old Shipmate,

13

as I was beginning to call her), *before Clare* in other words, The British Isles, according to the March 1988 edition of *Weather*, 'lay in a slack gradient in a complex area of low pressure'. The pressure was highest out over the North Sea, squeezing down upon the Shetlands, while a huge chute of sliding, freezing air, running from Iceland, was streaming south (as air from Iceland so often does), covering the north and west of Scotland and all of Ireland, in a bitter chill.

It was not so everywhere. It never is. As Belfast shivered and hugged its battered coat, a very different sort of air, born in the neighbourhood of the Canary Islands was moving as a matter of some urgency towards the land mass of western Europe, blowing over Spain's huge central plain and racing across to its adjoining foe, France. This was a warm, wet wind, a wind in a hurry. Its mission was to cover us with its damp heat, to rise up over the waters and give bounty to the comfortless creatures of the north. It wanted *to change our lives*.

Not surprisingly, with waves of such hot, moist air hurrying one way, and with an equally determined body of hard, frozen air moving in the other, a series of confrontations were forecast. Some had taken place over France, some had been fought over the north west of Spain; there had been skirmishes over the Head of Kinsale and outside Falmouth. But on this day the battle lines were being drawn up out over the sea, and a particular isolated and unobserved part of the sea at that. To be more specific, the Bay of Biscay.

It had been a volatile month, with depression after depression sweeping over Britain. Rain had come across in thick, heavy continuous cloud. It landed on the roofs and ran down the chimneys and fell upon the backs of sheep. It washed the walls and soaked the pathways and laid siege to flights of steps. It hammered on the tops of buses, it beat against the sides of houses, and slid unwelcome under front doors. We fell asleep to rain's dull lullaby, we woke to rain's urgent whispers and in the hours between it was rain's dreams, rain's wet dreams which we dreamt. We hurried from rain but we could not escape. It bubbled up from drains and soaked our shoes and stockings. It gushed from gutters and drowned our hats. When we dipped into our pockets we found rain had got there first and when we jumped from doorway to doorway we found rain lying in wait. The roads were constructed out of rain, and at nights it appeared as if our cities and towns were floating on a brilliant black sea. And still the rain came. It ran from the fields into the ditches. It ran from the ditches into the streams. It ran from the streams into the rivers. And from the rivers and the streams and the ditches it looked out upon the land from which it had come and determined to return. Britain was under water.

Seven inches had fallen by the fifteenth of the month (one inch less than the record for double that time back in 1960) and more was on its way. Every day I would wake up, look out of my cold wet window and see a cold wet world before me. Every day I would get up, dress, have breakfast, and drive to work, knowing that the wheels of my car were growing cleaner by the mile. Every day I would park the car, and slosh my way through the puddles and shaking umbrellas of Holborn to the concrete steps and the office, to see what the weather had brought, to see what the weather would bring.

I am a weatherman. I have been all my life. When I look upon my childhood and my younger days, I remember them for the clouds which covered me or the simple rays of sunshine that shone unwanted into my frozen home. If I recall my existence, or invent possibilities for its pitiful future, it is under the sky where I must move, hopeless moments of craven sentimentality which can only take place *in the right climate*. If I have any memories, if I remember anyone, it is my friend the weather, my darling companion, who is the principal player. It is the weather which has governed my life and if I think of what I have done, it is the taste of the wind or a vision of clouds fit for the hammer of God, which drove me to it. There is no friend like the weather, no one so sure, so true, so constantly fickle.

I am a weatherman and I know not which way the wind blows. I am deceived at every turn. There are times when I climb up on to the roof of the London Weather Centre and realize that though I have studied its swirling greatness, and I sit in a chattering world of dials and graphs and gauges, the weather has kept its mouth shut and told me nothing. If the world were still and never moved (as many people wish it to be) and if there were but one substance upon its surface (say granite, or iron, or even the stuff we are made of, *clay*), then it would be a simple matter, for weather's intention, *its long-term plan*, is plain: to obey the second law of thermodynamics and make the temperature the same the whole world over. To this end warm air moves from the equator towards the cold region, climbing as it journeys north, thereby creating a vacuum which the heavier, polar air is obliged to fill. If the earth stood still, if it would just rest up, the air would move in these two distinct and unchallenged directions and you could draw a map of lands and temperatures which would outlast all the ages of man combined. But it is not so. The sun has set it in a spin. The air, the atmosphere, is twisted. Dragged by earth's turn, it is forced to run *east* and *west* while still battling towards *north* and *south*. And it does not run over granite or iron and clay. It moves over all of these. It chases up mountains and down over seas, it sweeps across deserts and hangs above the endless green of the forest. It is in turn cooked and cooled and boiled and frozen until the very stuff just drips out. Like the great shark suspended in the ocean below, *it is never still*. Even on those sunny days when there is not a cloud in the sky, when it would appear that the weather has come to rest, in the outer reaches of its domain this peaceful weather system is battling for its very life – a battle which it will inevitably lose. This is what weather is. This is what we live under, this crashing, this turbulence, this treachery. Weather is a restless force. It bends your will (it bends mine). It lifts our spirits and sends us tumbling down. It helps us fall in love (not me, not me) and flies us into a rage. And at times it reaches out and reminds you that you are utterly alone.

I was alone that morning. I had driven down to Bath the night before, checked into the hotel out on the Chippenham road and waited until eleven o'clock before Fleur showed up breathless, her mouth punctuated by laughter and lust. By half past five I had left her sleeping on her stomach, closing the door on her bare back, rubbing my face awake for the drive to London. It was foolish of me to have gone to Bath in the first place, for I knew I was on the morning shift, but when Fleur rang me up the previous day to say she had to go down to Bath unexpectedly that night and why didn't I drive down so that we could fuck the night away, then reason did not play a major part in my decision. By a quarter to six I was back on the road, driving through the steady rain, glancing up at the heavy drenching clouds which hung above, immobile, sullen, and angry. There was a dull yellow cast to the light, a sickly colour which rose from the road, and though the traffic was light the air was thick with spray, a mixture of oil and dirty water and these solitary passing lives. It was greasy and dangerous and I drove luxuriating in the blue interior of my silver car, settled upon its wide moulded seat, protected by its quiet comfort, soothed by its gentle tone. I drove fast. I looked into the mirror and saw the blur of the evening recede. I thought of the rain beating down outside our hotel room and how Fleur would rise to its sound, how she would get up and tie a towel round her waist (it is something she does even when alone I am told) and walk across to run a bath. I thought of her body in the hot water, her strong wet shoulders and how she would lean back to wash her hair. I heard the splashing sound as she got out, and thought of the one time I had gone swimming with her at Camber Sands. I thought too of that red swimsuit of hers and how I first saw her suspended in the midnight air, with Jago and his pack of sure-footed friends prowling in attendance.

Unlike this floundering age I now found myself in, it had been a sweltering time. If it had not been for the appearance of Fleur on to the stage (an appropriate metaphor under the circumstances) my strongest recollection of that summer would have been lying comatose with Monica on the beaches of Brighton, far away from the city heat, drinking Cointreau and smoking a succession of fat bleached joints, eyeing Monica's tantalizing nipples, calculating the time when it would be appropriate for us to float back to her flat and the luxury of her thick brown fitted carpets. It could be argued (and I am the first one to lay the blame fairly and squarely on someone else) that had not Monica's breasts been so well oiled that summer, so continuously *on parade*, then I would not have been in the state I was. I might well have regarded the red swimsuit as an object (I use the word advisedly) an *object* to be looked at, commented on and no more. However Monica and her soft furnishings had ensured that this was not to be. It was a royal time for fucking and I was about to meet my queen.

On that particular day, the day which preceded the Night of the Red Swimsuit, I was not with Monica. In fact I had not seen Monica for several days and was not likely to for some time (hence the dishevelled appearance of the Woman from Spain). Monica's man, him of the Senior Service, had returned unexpectedly from Portsmouth (where he spends many long and dutiful hours, praise the Lord) and though he intended to troll up to London to see his chums and what-not, had every intention of putting his feet up on Monica's balcony to watch the sun go down for the next couple of weeks. Normally I would have had no complaints. However I had before me the bleak prospect of a fourteen-day shift, with no break in sight, and as I began to work through it I was only too aware that an hour away Monica was still slowly cooking on the beach, still returning to her flat when her lazy days were done, still snapping the top of her bikini off before stepping into her narrow, tiled shower to let the cool water run down. Perhaps it was this, the image of Monica's discarded bikini trailed across the sitting-room floor which gave this bathing suit, so sculptured, so complete, so unbelievably *red*, its great power. The suit seduced me and gave me strength.

I was, I have to admit, getting a little tired of Monica anyway. For one thing I did not care for the ever shadowy presence of the Royal Navy. Although we both acknowledged that we were perfectly free to do whatever we wanted, and indeed that our affair (begun rather unwillingly in my sister's bathroom) was but an interlude in our real life (*her* real life), I did not like the way Leading Seaman Johnny Oates was parked permanently offshore. She had a picture of him in some of his ceremonial headgear up on the mantelpiece and I had spent many an hour studying his tri-angular face while Monica was down below manning the pumps, and as far as I could make out there was very little to recommend him. Everything was there, ears, eyes, mouth, etc, but there was no sense to it. It was the sort of face that needed a pipe to give it character, with evaporating smoke a substitute for thought. I had seen him once in action, and if anything the photograph was more animated. He was carrying one of those ridiculous briefcases with brass combination locks, the sort of security device that would give one of Jago's mates fifteen seconds of work, and was striding through the town as if he had stepped off some patrol boat in Singapore. I followed him for a little while to see if I could glean anything from this sighting. He was veering towards Monica's, slightly off course, *and*, more disturbingly, slightly ahead of schedule. One thing Monica and I had laid considerable store by was Johnny's penchant for punctuality. When Johnny said six bells, six bells it was and not five and a half, but now it appeared that four bells would do just as well. No it bloody wouldn't. If Johnny turned up at four bells we could all find ourselves in some very choppy waters indeed.

The coolies of Brighton parted before his bow. I was a smaller vessel in his wake. We ploughed our way through the Lanes, we steamed up the road to Kemp Town, we span the wheel and ran down to the Promenade. And there he cut engines and idled. He drifted up towards the Marina and weighed anchor. With Monica's balcony clearly in view, he sat down on one of the municipal benches and looked out from whence he had come. The dear man had arrived early *and was going to wait*. Four bells would *not* do. Six bells it was!

I inspected this paragon at my leisure, cruising past him at regular intervals. What on earth could Monica see in him? A stupid face and a physique that from outward appearances seemed to have gone out with the ark – though I had not seen it in the flesh, and I knew from experience what a multitude of sins clothes can conceal. Monica herself is a prime example. She is slightly smaller than average with indiscriminate, rather ragged fair hair and the wearer of large unfashionable glasses. The sheer excellence of her body, first revealed in the mirror of my sister's medicine cabinet, came as something of a shock to me (which is why I suppose the vision of her dazzling bosom had stayed with me for so long). And here was this pantaloon waiting on his chosen hour before venturing into her sanctum. What sort of man is it who sticks to such rules? Why, he could be with her now! *I* could be with her now. I had half a mind to go back to her there and then, just to teach him a lesson. What secret pleasure I would get from that encounter! What a fool! What a complete bloody fool! Yet this was the man with whom Monica chose to spend most of her time. Why? What could he do that I couldn't do? Juggle? Dance the hornpipe? It was this I couldn't understand. Not that there was another man (there has to be another man) but that it was *this* man. I didn't get it, but it was beginning to get me.

Monica's curious combination of plain and plenty is reflected in other aspects of her life. For instance, she plays a lot of sport, tennis, squash, *football*, and when she and her beau go on holiday, they spend their time windsurfing or scuba diving or shooting some rapid or other. As long as it's in or under water, they don't mind. Her hallway is littered with their swimming gear, masks, snorkels and black flippers, and her wardrobe is filled with various fetching sports outfits which I see fit to despise. This is a side of her I do not understand, and to be frank, do not like. It is outside my province. I have no place in it, and from what I see of her, neither should she. Monica is unhealthy. She smokes thirty to forty cigarettes. She likes drinking corrupt alcohol, brandy, Chartreuse, rum, and she likes drinking lots of it. She is something of a dope addict. She doesn't care for men much and she certainly shouldn't care for men from the armed forces, especially ones weaned on the Falklands. And yet she sees Leading Seaman Johnny Oates whenever she can, and even drives down to Portsmouth to spend the odd weekend with him. What I was beginning to resent was not the fact that she still saw him (yes I was), but that on every occasion when she had a choice it was me who had to make way for him, *steam* before *sail*, which is, if memory serves me, the way it is on the high seas. There was no doubt in my mind that I was more entertaining than him, quicker witted than him, a more rewarding physical partner than him, but for some reason Monica refused to acknowledge this. 'Kiss me,' she would say, and I would kiss her. 'Hug me,' she would say and I would hug her. We would sit on her bed smoking joints and talking through the hours and I would kiss her and hug her again. Sometimes, on walks along the front, we would hold hands and our faces would touch lightly, affectionately, and I would hold her face in my hands and kiss both cheeks, one, two, three, four times. We would sit on the terrace of the hotel near her flat, looking out over the sea, our eyes bright from dope, and I would think of her and she would think of me and I would turn and lean across, wanting to kiss her, wanting to touch her gently, and I do, I lean across and kiss those cheeks as tenderly as I know how, I place my hand upon hers or her freckled arm and tell her how fond I am of her and how much I enjoy her company, how she must tell me if things get difficult, how I will understand, in other words how she can *trust* me, and she moves her head back to take a good look at me, and kisses me smiling, her lovely breasts resting on the table, and says, 'Oh Giles, I wouldn't trust you as far as the other side of the road,' and we laugh over it and kiss again and return to the flat to erase the memory of that unsettling truth, but this stubborn refusal to draw me in closer was beginning to annoy me. Her world, the world I ignored or at best scorned, her *sports* world, her simple healthy world where everything happened out in the open, was encroaching upon *my* world, and I found myself thinking about all those times when I meant nothing to her, when she lived a life which was none of my doing, one her watery companion shared, the world she liked (and liked me to mock). To put it bluntly, outside our relatively few hours together, Monica and I had nothing in common *and it was all her fault*.

Monica's perversity was well illustrated by the last time I saw her before the Night of the Red Swimsuit. I am afraid this is going to be another story concerning sexual matters, but bear with me. The Age of the Buttock is passing, and it will not cover the land-scape so generously again.

I had spent the night with her, and it was morning. I lay in her bed watching her getting dressed. She was off to some social event at her tennis club (to which I was *not* invited of course) and I was to pick her up later, sometime after lunch. Monica is self-employed. Like my sister, she runs an employment agency (they have a pooling arrangement I believe), and there was a possibility that she might have to 'pop into her office', on the way back. I had only visited this haven when her part-time secretary had been there and I was pleasantly surprised by its appearance; two passable walnut desks, a chaise-longue, two comfortable arm-chairs and an open fireplace. More drawing room than office. More home than place of work. It struck me, watching her get ready, that we could spend an entertaining hour or so there ourselves that very afternoon. I contemplated this while she sat at her mirror. Should I tell her now of this idea, I thought, or should I spring it on her when we got there?

The very idea made my tongue thick. Monica was now fully dressed in little white socks, a short pleated white skirt, a fluffy white blouse and a white bow in her hair. It was all rather too self-conscious and Heidi-like and although I did not exactly like it, it did make me want to fuck her again. As she moved out of the bedroom I asked her where she was going. No reply. You look wonderful in that outfit, I told her. It really makes me want to fuck again. Why don't you come back in here and fuck me? There was silence. Monica? She told me to be quiet, that she's busy setting the ansaphone, but I could tell from the tone of her voice that she liked the idea. Unlike Fleur who loves talking about sex but who does not appreciate compliments about dress or good looks. Monica responds well to such treatment. It was all perfectly true anyway. She *did* look highly fuckable in that outfit.

Monica returned and climbed back on to the bed. She smiled and kissed me, almost professionally. She sat astride me and I ran my hands up her legs. She had already taken off her pants. This was a very good sign and I expressed my approval. Everything was going according to plan. We both raised her skirt so that we could get a good ring-side seat of the proceedings. I was right. It looked bloody marvellous. I had half a mind to unbutton her blouse and watch her there, but I decided against it. There was something supremely erotic in what we were doing, she all dressed up as if butter wouldn't melt in her mouth, with her dainty white socks and her lipstick and her eyeliner, everything in place, everything *just so*, just her skirt lifted gently so that we could both watch.

Then, out of the corner of my eye, I saw the photograph of Johnny Oates on the bedside table. I hadn't noticed it the night before, but there it was nestling down beside the clock. She'd taken his bloody picture from the sitting-room mantelpiece and stuck it by her bed. What on earth for? So that he could watch? For an insane moment I heard their next conversation. 'Marvellous to see you again darling,' he says, unchaining his briefcase. 'And what have you been doing?' 'Well,' she replies, snuggling up to his three-sided form, 'As a matter of fact last Wednesday I was fucked absolutely rigid by that nice man on the radio I've told you

22

about. My, he is a caution. First he put his hand up me as we climbed up the stairs. He had me practically coming against my own front door! We were both trembling with excitement dearest, because my skirt, you know, that nice flamenco one I bought down the market, was hitched right up past my hips and anyone walking in could have looked up and seen my cunt framed in the doorway. He worked me into such a froth sweetheart that the moment we turned the lock we fell into the hall and started to suck each other, and we were in such a frenzy, such an undisciplined state of excitement that both of us found it impossible to come. Though I tell you, half an hour later, after a joint and a bottle of champagne, it was quite a different story. *And what have you been doing? Wanked into any good handkerchiefs lately?*'

We continued on apace, but by now pleasure was not my purpose. I wanted to goad Monica, to push her over the edge, to get her to admit to her own duplicity. I began by repeating myself, telling her that this looked wonderful, that it *was* wonderful, that I could do this all morning. I lulled her into agreement. It was wonderful wasn't it? Didn't she agree? Of course she did. I asked her if she didn't find it exceptionally erotic, with her so neat, so tidy, so prim, with this thick wet fuck slopping out underneath. Just listen to it! And we listened and we looked and she agreed. And on we went. I told her how I loved her for it, and how she excited me and how I was going to pick her up outside the tennis club and be back at her, in her office, within ten minutes of our meeting. Nothing else would do. I couldn't last the morning thinking about her unless. I told her how she would sit at her desk and how her skirt would be arranged. I presented her with a prospectus in which nothing was overlooked. I spoke of her blouse and her buttons and the white brassière underneath. I spoke of her ankle socks and her bare legs and the deep recesses of the patterned armchairs. How carefully I chose my words! How lewd and luscious they were! She began fanning her stomach with the hem of her skirt, as if the work down below were a furnace, but in reality it was the words that were setting her alight. She began to join in. *Now I had her*! The phone in one hand and you in the other, she said. That's right, I replied. The phone in one hand and me in the other. And all because of this wonderful outfit of yours. So demure, so sportif, so white. *Navy white you could say*.

Monica jumped up. A moment later I heard the front door slam. Although I did meet her after lunch, we did not go back to her office. After an hour or so on the beach I took the train back up to London. We did not speak of the morning then, nor have we since, but there is something there unfinished, for both of us. Which is why, I believe, during those first nine or ten days of separation (no telephone calls, no hurried letters) I had been using the Woman from Spain mercilessly, and why, on that particular morning I had taken advantage of her yet again when Mrs Delguardo sent her up to ask me down to breakfast.

A word about the Woman from Spain. The Woman from Spain is a relative of Mrs Delguardo's absent husband (a crooked lawyer involved in selling dubious time-sharing condominiums on the Costa del Sol, and now himself a fugitive from justice). Although Mrs Delguardo is solicitous of the Woman from Spain, and takes trouble looking after her, it is clear that this is not a labour of love, but an inflicted duty from which there is no obvious escape, though she would dearly like to find one. It is equally clear that the Woman from Spain does not care greatly for Mrs Delguardo either, and would also like to be elsewhere. The Woman from Spain (dark-skinned, dark eyed, abrupt in her movements, and blessed with an abundance of dark hair everywhere, particularly attractive around her rather brutal nipples), is a lonely young woman, locked in a sad solitary world of her own. It is obvious from the way she stares out of the window and fidgets with one of her necklaces that she longs to get out, to find some people of her own age, and I can never understand why she doesn't. She likes dancing. She has demonstrated a blundering enthusiasm for quick, uncomplicated sex. I would have thought she could have found a catalogue of acquaintances without much trouble, but she rarely ventures out unless accompanied by her putative keeper. Odd too is her reluctance to learn English. Though she watches television and flips through the occasional paper her vocabulary has remained static. At first I thought that the meagre set of stock phrases she used were merely an indication of the fact that she was a beginner, but the more I see of her the plainer it is that they are in some way a set of anchors for her, and one she will not give up readily.

How the Woman from Spain and I started I do not know. I can only remember coming home from Brighton one evening, drunk from an hour's gin on the train, and the smell of Monica still fresh on my face. I remember opening the front door and seeing her struggling up the stairs with her bicycle. I remember sitting astride it in Mrs Delguardo's kitchen, making her laugh. Then I was riding round the kitchen table with her balanced in front of me. My hand was on her waist and I remember thinking *Why not?* Then we were no longer on the bicycle or indeed in the kitchen. When it was all over she put her fingers up to her lips as if to say, This is our secret. We will say nothing about it, not even to each other. I nodded and there was a moment in our eyes and we fell to it again. 'All gone,' she said, and glad to get away I nodded and went upstairs to my own flat. This is as much as I know of the Woman from Spain. It is all I want to know. There were times when I tried to discover more. I would ask her how long she hoped to stay, or if she had thought about finding a job. I would show her articles in newspapers about her home country or try and explain the news to her. I would talk slowly and simply for five or ten minutes and she would appear interested and form simple replies, and I would sense that it was a beginning, that the real woman locked inside another language was beginning to come out, but then she would fall back, laugh and toss her head, or pout and pull at her clothes, as if deliberately jumping back before the door closed on her altogether. I had lost her again.

To return. This particular morning I had had breakfast with them. There was, I seem to recollect, a dispute over the Woman from Spain's boiled egg. The colour and texture were not to her liking and though I fully expected her to sulk and stomp off into her room I was not prepared for the kicking and screaming and banging on the table that ensued. I left quickly, walked out to the car and drove to work.

*

THE INSIDE OF our office is much the same as other weary places of work. A grim, open-plan design, instituted many years ago and showing distinct signs of wear, governs our lives. It looked unpleasant when it was new and it looks more unpleasant now, grey and scuffed and tatty round the corners. We smell of cheap coffee, old radiators and wet paper. Our lighting is thoughtless, hard and bright here, in the darkest shadow there. There are no blinds for the summer, and though the metal windows are impossible to open when the sun beats down over the length of the building, in the winter it is as if the architect had perforated every window with a thousand minute holes, so that the cold air whistling down Holborn infects our cuffs and collars and laddered stockings.

That morning I walked in to find Eric Lightfoot, my opposite number, perched on top of our desk dressed in a bilious green Hawaiian shirt and with his bare feet dangling over the edge. In his hands lay a small pair of gardener's secateurs with green plastic handles and a cruel curved beak. Eric was cutting his toe nails and muttering to himself. Eric is a tall, bent man with spare, shedding hair and thin agitated hands. He has a superb broadcasting voice, quite at odds with his ramshackle appearance (not as unusual a combination as you might think), clear and melodious, full of pace, range and control. Were he not handicapped by his curved spine, his falling hams, and his clumps of unruly hair and his fear of other people, the Met Office at Bracknell (where lies our headquarters and the Director General) would have sent him across to our better paid relatives at Television Centre and trained him to become a Little Droplet (which is what we on the radio call our cousins in colour). But fame and fortune and the opening of garden fêtes is not for Eric, not for any of us poor mortals stuck in Holborn. We just carry the country. And the blasted sea which surrounds it.

I walked over and took a good look. A cluster of gigantic nail clippings, thick, opaque, horny slices lay scattered on top of the contents of our waste-paper basket like almond flakes upon a meringue. Despite my presence he continued with his recital.

'He loves me. He loves me not. He loves me.'

'You should be doing that with rose petals,' I told him. 'Toe nails aren't quite the thing.'

'Too unpredictable,' Eric replied, without looking up. 'I practise the safe method.'

Eric had recently moved in with his new love, a man by the name of Michael Mulligan and by all accounts life was not easy. Eric met him some weeks ago when the Mulligan in question had written in congratulating Eric on his rich and cock-throbbing speaking voice and asked him whether he would be interested in discussing the theoretical and socio-erotic properties of the law of thermodynamics. Now as you already know the law of thermo-dynamics is bread and butter to your average weatherman, and anybody, *anybody* who shows the slightest interest in, and knowledge of, such a law arouses, if nothing else, immediate curiosity. In Michael's case, as Eric later admitted, curiosity was the first in a long line of arousals. Michael had some wild theory about how to live his life which entailed reading a lot of old newspapers. Eric had tried to explain it once but the reasoning had evaded me.

'I take it then, that he is still pursuing his ideas with as much vigour as ever.'

Eric waved his hands in anguish. 'Michael is impossible. Lovely but impossible. I never know what he's going to be doing from one day to the next. Today he's waiting by the telephone for replies to his advert.'

'Advert?'

'He wants a change from London. London doesn't understand him. London is too bound up with what will be. He needs to go somewhere where time is still, more or less. Somewhere in the country.'

Eric pushed a copy of the *Daily Telegraph* across to me. There, ringed in Biro under the want ads, ran the following:

> Violent debtor seeks large unfurnished country house.
> Nearby pub essential. Positively no references.

'Not one to make a landlord reach for the phone,' I said. 'But eye catching.'

Eric sniffed.

'That's about all it will catch. A few eyes. Raised, most of them.'

I threw the newspaper back at him.

'It may not be quite the thing he is looking for,' I said. 'But he could always use the bungalow.'

I was the owner (I am, I am) of a small wooden bungalow on the Kent coast. Although I rarely go there (I do not care for its interior any more, or for the tidy appearance of the once neglected garden, nor do I appreciate the solicitous enquiries of my neighbours, who are all too ready with their lawnmowers, and who know more of my history than they should) on occasions I let it out to colleagues and tedious families found in respectable magazines, or find myself reluctantly propelled towards it for purposes of the flesh. Although I had never met Michael, from what I had heard about him he seemed an ideal candidate for the place, someone who might paint it a hideous colour, break its windows, bruise it and give it life.

'Your bungalow,' Eric asked, somewhat askance. 'Without, I take it, you in it?'

'Eric. What would I be doing in a bungalow with two rooms while you and Michael besported yourselves. Of course without me in it.'

Eric picked up the newspaper and stared at it for a while. 'I could always ask him I suppose. Though I doubt if he's to a bungalow born. Why couldn't I fall in love with someone normal, Giles?'

'You mean like me?'

Eric smiled. 'No. Not like you. Not like you at all.' He looked at the newspaper again and then flung it in the air.

'Look Giles, he's holding some gathering tonight in Jimmy James. Why don't you come along and see for yourself. I'll tell him you're coming about the advert. Erroll Garner is playing.'

'Erroll Garner?' I said. 'Are you sure?'

'That's what he told me. He's booked a table. Why don't you come along? It'll be quite a party.'

I went despite my reservations. I was feeling restless. I needed some stirring up. A long night, drinking heavily (and who knows what else besides) would do the trick.

*

JIMMY JAMES is to be found at the centre of Soho. The outside is painted black and lined with dustbins and young men in sheepskin coats. The inside is red and hung with a low ceiling. It is a nightclub where jazz is played. Tables ring the stage, and on one side, to the left of the stage, is a long bar where prowlers and henchmen and those with runny noses sniff whatever might be in the air. Each table has a lamp upon it, and when you arrive, and if you are with a party, Olga, a pale fat waddle of a man, who breathes heavily through his nostrils, and whose big fat fingers are almost permanently clenched around used bank notes, will show you to one of them (depending on what denomination you fan his fat knuckles with). If you want a drink after normal drinking hours (and there is no doubt that you will) at some stage of the evening you must order a plate of cold chilli or stewed pork ribs to accompany it, but it is understood that you are under no obligation to eat any of it. The food, like the drink, is brought to your table by one of the short-skirted waitresses who work there, university graduates the lot of them, who sleep with their out-of-work boyfriends during the day and who snort cocaine from the back of Olga's hand in the kitchen at night. This makes them work hard, and gives a certain forced glamour to their eyes, but it also makes them hasty and brittle and lacking in the most elementary sense of direction. On any given night, two or three of them will be sporting black eyes, dark shadows on their thighs and when things are really humming, a dirty bandage or two. They are hungry looking (they rarely eat) and the combination of their seductive bruising and Olga's rolling weight gives the place its resonance of smouldering violence and depravity. They are the key elements to its thrill, that and the type of money which finds its way into Jimmy James's pocket. Honest money will deaden any evening here. It corrupts. To enjoy a night at Jimmy James you must spend tainted money, money stolen, money squeezed, money passed over in a brown paper bag, money from blackmail, money from a horse or a dog, money earned by threat, money gained by favour, but never money earned by honest labour. The night must either cost you everything or be entirely free. To be a guest at Jimmy James you must be a thug, a celebrity or a nobody, otherwise the smell will rise off the floor and hang on your very skin. Though the music be sometimes fresh, there is an unholy staleness to it all.

I walked in to a choking heat. In the foyer there were bodies everywhere, bodies waving cigarettes in the air, bodies leaning up against walls, bodies crying out for alcohol, bodies with their buttons awry. Olga sat at his little table with his cotton shirt undone, one hand resting on his great beached belly, white and hairless, the other squeezing money into an untidy, half-open drawer to his right. By his side, next to his belly hand stood one of his young and only moderately damaged accomplices, her eyes large and bright, her T-shirt stuck to her skin. Every now and again Olga would push his free hand deep into his groin, sniff his fingers and then lightly run his hand over the back of her legs. Eventually I arrived in front of him. He looked me up and down with suspicion.

'Fifteen quid,' he informed me. 'Thirty for a seat. Are you alone?'

'I believe my friend has a table,' I told him. 'Am I right in thinking that Erroll Garner is playing here tonight?'

Olga's right hand came to an abrupt halt. The girl beside him stiffened. A man behind me laughed. Olga leant forward.

'Who are you meeting then?' he said evenly. 'Vera fucking Lynn.'

'I'm sorry?'

'They do tell that Glenn Miller's playing at the Savoy tonight. If you're lucky you'll catch him before his plane crashes.'

'I am meeting a party by the name of Mulligan,' I told him. 'Has he not arrived yet?'

'Oh, he's arrived all right. So you're his latest flame? Just the job for Mr Mulligan.' He handed me a ticket. 'You'll find him at his usual table up the front. Sometimes I wonder why I bother. No I don't. Influential friends has Mr Mulligan. Are you an influential friend Mr . . .?'

'Doughty. No I don't believe so.'

'Pity. Well, we mustn't keep Mr Doughty waiting, must we Charlotte. Mr Doughty wants to hear Erroll Garner.'

This time the whole crowd laughed.

'Speedy Bec is playing tonight,' the girl said.

'Mr Bec plays the saxophone,' Olga said venomously. 'I suppose you know what a saxophone looks like, don't you?'

As I ducked into the thick swim of things and made my way to the front I heard a great roar go up. Speedy Bec was about to appear. The parties at the tables turned from one another to face the stage. The men at the bar, dark suited, rings soaking on their fingers, turned round from their drinking and held their glasses in the air. In their midst, a young woman with naked shoulders and naked lips, dressed in a red swimsuit, was raised above them by an enormous pair of hands. The man was a head shorter than his companions, with hair like a stiff brush arranged over his square-shaped face, but what held my attention was the way he held this body so effortlessly, a body which was to all intents and purposes nude. His hands were the biggest I had ever seen, with hair down to the very fingernails. His thumbs met up in the small of her back and his fingers delved knowingly, spreading themselves across her stomach. Above us all, held towards the stage, she wriggled on the hook of his hands, warm and slippery to his touch. She was not delicate, but as wild as he was strong, her big lips laughing in the dirty air, his hands stroking every muscle. I was glad I had Eric to meet that night otherwise I knew I would spend all night looking at those two and get in all sorts of bother. The man turned for a moment, and looked quickly in my direction. He had done that curious thing. Out of a crowd of men moving hungrily in the dark, he had sensed my interest, picked me out and noted me. I told myself I must not look at them again, for if I did he would want to play with me later. There was nothing he and his friends would have liked better than a little mauling after the show. I began to look for Eric.

He was easy to find. To the left of the stage, some three tables down I spied another of his hideous shirts. Next to him, sat a man hidden by a wrinkled copy of *The Times* which he held ostentatiously in the air. In front of them both stood a bucket of ice, a collection of glasses and an untouched bottle of whisky. Eric rose to greet me.

'Giles. I thought you'd given up on us. Michael, say hello to Giles Doughty won't you?'

The newspaper was lowered. An anguished looking man, with an expression of perpetual worry appeared. His hair was spiky, and his skin was pale and he had the air of someone on the run. He looked round the room several times.

'If you will excuse me for a moment. I just must . . .' And the paper rose once more.

I had only seen him for a moment but it was enough. While everyone else was wearing as little as possible Michael Mulligan was covered by an enormous army greatcoat buttoned to the neck, tied up with a boa constrictor of a scarf. On his hands he wore a pair of woollen mittens, with the fingers poking out at the end. Sweat was running off him like melted butter and his tongue hung out like a Spanish dog's. Eric looked at me in helpless despair.

I sat down. Speedy Bec was halfway through his first number, an early composition of his called 'Don't Flirt With Me'. I pretended to listen while all the while sneaking glances at Eric's preoccupied boyfriend and yes, that red swimsuit and the woman swimming within it. She was on the ground now, moving through the men like a fish through water, breaking the surface with her clean looks and her leaping energy. I could feel her slippery in my arms. I knew the texture of her skin, how damp, how cool it would be.

It was only after Speedy had completed his first set, closing with a dutiful version of his magnificent 'Hilton Balcony' and had left to prolonged but uninspired applause, that we three settled down together. I wanted to get loudly but attractively drunk. I was in the mood to fuck too, to seriously drink and to seriously fuck (the heat affects me this way) and I told myself that I would have to watch out for opportunities. In the meantime I would enjoy Eric and his strange companion. Michael Mulligan tilted his chair forward and held his hands out over the candle.

'I don't know if I like this place,' he declared. 'It's too full of strangers eyeing one another. Don't like it one bit. Your friend for instance.' He pointed at me. 'He's been unable to take his eyes off that woman over there ever since he sat down.'

I half turned in my seat and studied the bar. Her back was towards us. Her bare back and her bare legs and her bare shoulders. Her legs were moving to little beats of my heart.

I pulled out a packet of cigarettes and stuck one in my mouth.

'She is a very striking young woman,' I said.

He sniffed. 'There is always one in such a gathering as this,' he said. 'But beware Mr Doughty, those are a lively bunch of playmates she has with her. Nick Knack Paddy Wack and all that. I'm sure Eric would not like to see them rolling you home.'

'Well, she does not make it easy for us. She is not, over-dressed shall we say.'

Michael Mulligan looked at me with some irritation.

'And who *exactly* is this?' he asked Eric.

'This is the man I told you about,' Eric indicated. 'The man with the house to rent.'

Michael's face brightened.

'Ah yes. Eric warned me about you. You have such a property for rent you say?'

'Not exactly. I do have a property. I do sometimes rent it out. It's nothing elaborate. But it is near a public house, and if you like that sort of thing, it's near the sea.'

'And where would this be?'

'Near Rye in Kent. Camber Sands. A very pretty spot. Parts of it, if you care to walk a bit, are quite secluded. But it may not be quite what you're looking for.'

'Oh?'

'It's a bungalow. A wooden bungalow. Quite a small one. But only sparsely furnished.'

Michael wriggled impatiently in his seat.

'You read my advertisement?' he said. He lowered his voice. 'The one in *today's* paper?' His leg began to jiggle up and down.

'I did.'

'Well then I find it rather odd that a man who has a small furnished wooden bungalow should try and pass it off as a large unfurnished country house.'

Eric stretched out a placatory hand. Michael waved him away.

'It's all very well Mr Doughty enticing people to part with their money and explaining it away in the name of *friendship*, but some us, some of us would call it *deception* and *fraud*.' I opened my mouth in protest, but he went on. 'I know. I know. You did it from the very best of motives and I am not holding you completely responsible.' He glared at Eric. 'It's just typical that's all. Take this establishment for instance. The number of times I have presented myself at the door, expecting to see Lester Young or Charlie Mingus, only to find that they have been replaced without a word of warning is nothing short of scandalous. I have written to Mr James on a number of occasions, but do I get a reply? I do not. I mean what sort of man advertises Erroll Garner and then foists this has-been upon us?'

I looked to Eric for guidance but he had his head sunk in his hands, a man at a loss to know what to do. Michael sat there defying us both to say anything. I did not want to hurt Eric, but nor did I see why Michael should get away with all this nonsense.

'Eric has told me something of your habits,' I said. 'And I am not exactly sure what to make of them. We can talk about it if you wish. But for the moment let's talk about jazz and Jimmy James. Jimmy James is dead. He has been dead for thirteen or fourteen years, shot in the mouth with a twelve-bore shotgun. What's more to the point', I continued, unscrewing the cap to the new bottle of whisky that had appeared on the table and helping myself to a fresh measure, 'is that *anybody* who knows *anything* about jazz knows full well that not only Jimmy James is dead, but more importantly, so are Lester Young, and Charlie Mingus. And Erroll Garner dammit.'

Michael looked disturbed, almost upset. He nursed his drink for a moment then tossed it down his throat.

'Dead!' he repeated. 'Charlie Mingus dead! And to think I should have heard it in a place like this. How can they act so with Charles not yet cold in his grave? Excuse me.' He pulled out a handkerchief, and left for the lavatory.

'Eric,' I said, 'what in God's name is going on?'

'Michael has given up the present,' Eric explained. 'He does not trust it. He won't read today's newspapers. Not unless he has to.'

'Why?'

'Because that way he hopes to keep things at bay.'

'Things? What sort of things?'

'Births, marriages, deaths. Deaths mostly.'

'You mean . . .'

Eric put his hand up.

'Please,' he said. 'He does not trust this world nor those who speak for it. This world has done for him and will probably do for me too. So he has chosen to live in it as little as possible. He lives with this vast collection of old newspapers, and every morning he dons his cap, goes out into this sea of print and plucks one at random. Armed with whatever newspaper he has chosen he goes back to his hut, reads it, and constructs that day around it.'

'He must live in a continuous state of disappointment.'

Eric shook his head.

'On the contrary. Three weeks ago he came across an advertisement for a machine-hand at a sweet factory in Acton, in a 1958 edition of the *Evening News*. The money was not good, but being unemployed he went there, presented himself to the personnel manager, and found the post still vacant. He got the job immediately.'

'Are you talking about me and my soft centres?' Michael had returned without our noticing. For some reason he seemed in a better mood. 'It is not pleasant work for I do not like wasps. I drown as many as I can in a bucket of sugary water and mash them into the butterscotch. I have already been promoted to machine foreman. Did I tell you that Eric? Machine foreman. What do you make of that?'

'What could anybody make of that, Michael,' Eric said, pouring himself another stiff drink. 'Anybody would think you are off your rocker. Isn't that what anybody would think Giles?'

A sudden laugh, low, but rising in pitch and speed broke into his question. A pair of hands came down and covered Michael's face. A red swimsuit pressed against the back of his chair.

The man with the hairbrush head and hands stood directly behind her, one hand on her back again, his fingers squeezing her waist like a living snake belt.

'Fleur,' said Michael. 'And about time too. I have told you before about the importance of punctuality. Punctuality is the enemy of unpredictability. This is a five-seater table and as such was booked for five. I know,' he leant against her and looked up, 'I know it means nothing to you, but bribery and corruption does not come cheap these days and the fat man on the door has not been slow to point out the discrepancy in numbers. Are you joining us now? Have you brought that brute Jago?'

The man with the hands stepped towards the table, his arm still trailing round the woman's waist. He wore a pale blue shirt and a pale yellow tie and his light grey and extremely expensive suit was finished off with a pair of delicate black shoes. He was big. The backs of his fingers were covered in thick black hair. As I looked at them and at their proximity to this woman's belly, the closeness of her body, the sheer display of all of its parts, covered or not, I had a sudden vision of those fingers in her, of him sitting on a sofa watching a football match, pushing his fat fingers in and out as casually as he would take a sip from his can of beer.

'Mulligan,' he said in greeting. He wagged a finger at his petulant host. 'Now don't you tell such lies. Olga's been taking on cargo at the bar for the past hour. Lace *and* brandy. Three large helpings of each to my knowledge alone. So none of your yarns Mr M.'

Eric held out a glass for him.

'Honest to God, Jago,' he protested. 'Michael practically had to hand over his mother's golden locket to safeguard this table. And the mustard pot in the cruet. Now come and sit down and entertain us like a sensible man.' He turned to the woman. 'For mercy's sake Fleur, does this man of yours trust no one?'

Fleur laughed again and bent down to kiss him. She looked over to Mulligan who was hiding behind his newspaper again.

'I didn't know we had any jewellery in the family. Perhaps I should get Jago to find out what else he's been keeping from me.' She leant forward and pulled the ice bucket towards her. Turning her back to us she said, 'Quickly Jago, I'm desperate in this heat.'

Jago dipped his fingers in and with his hands dripping with iced water began to administer what was obviously a well-rehearsed cure. Her swimsuit was cut away at the top of her buttocks and her muscles shivered and twitched as he ran his hand up and down. After four or five passes he plunged his hand inside, where the suit covered her stomach, passed it once across and once around and withdrew, leaving the ice to trickle down. She turned back and splashed water on her face.

'That's better,' she said. 'A few more minutes and you would have had to drop me in the Serpentine.'

'I wouldn't do that to the dirtiest dog in town,' the man replied. 'And you'd have to find somewhere else to rest your head. I gave a lot of money for that bed. Wouldn't be worth a ship's candle after you'd splashed around in that tar.' He held out his hand and looked down.

'Come on Mulligan,' he admonished, looking at me. 'You're the captain on this table. What do you think you're playing at. Trying to hide him under a bush or something?'

Michael rattled his paper and nodded in Eric's direction.

'Ask him,' he said. 'He brought him.'

Eric held out his hands in surrender.

'Jago, I'm sorry. Please shake hands with a friend of mine, Giles Doughty. Giles, this is Tommy Jago. His business associates have christened him Woof-Woof, on account of his ferocious appetite. Jago is in the unenviable position of being something of a lawyer. If you've suffered from neglect, transgressions, wrongful dismissal, damages, then Jago, sorry Woof-Woof here, is your man. You just feed him the money, slip him off the leash and off he goes. Snap! Snap! Snap! Straight for the throat. His jaws never open.'

'You should be my PR man,' Jago suggested, with a satisfied smile on his face. 'I've just installed a new telephone message too.'

'And what would that be?' Eric asked.

The man with the hands pulled his chair back and climbed into it like a boxer entering the ring. Holding his nose between thumb and forefinger, he squawked. 'This is 081 198 4617. You have reached Jago and pack. BITE MY HAND.'

We all laughed. Then there was silence. I looked across the table, waiting. Eric instigated the proceedings.

'Giles,' he said. 'I don't believe you have met Michael's sister, Fleur.'

'Well then, hello Fleur,' I said, and held out my hand to touch her for the first time.

*

WHEN I LOOK BACK on that evening (and I do, naturally enough, it's a favourite pastime of mine) it is precisely this time, from the moment I was introduced to her to our chaperoned arrival at Michael Mulligan's riverside fortress, that glittering hour spent opposite her, drinking in the luxurious promise of her face, when all my senses were on full alert, which my memory so sensibly fails me. There is of course nothing abnormal about this, for there was nothing of any consequence to remember. All good and proper conversation, all the talk that was going to count for anything, was already raging in my head (and hers too), much more entertaining and, not surprisingly, much more to the point. Conversations shall we say of a direct and uninhibited nature, exploratory, informative, speculative, a sort of Gardeners' Question Time of the genitals. What went on in the public arena mattered little. I was already at her breast and when I looked at her face (and when did I not) I could see my wet cock pressed against her cheek. I knew too that this was no fantasy. There was not the slightest doubt in my mind that this was about to happen, and that it would take place sooner rather than later. It was clear to me also, as clearly defined as her succulent swimsuit, that Fleur held a similar script in her hand and was, to her heady joy, devouring its contents.

There were portions I do remember. It was here I learnt of Fleur's trade (told to me in a somewhat fatherly fashion by Eric) and where I first displayed my complete ignorance of the world of children's entertainment. It was here too, Fleur later told me, that I passed a vital test, by treating her as an adult.

'You would not believe,' she once admitted, 'the number of people who start talking baby talk as soon as I walk into the room. They think, Oh God, here's that woman from the kids programme. Better keep the subjects nice and simple. So I get a diet of animals and flowers and what I did in my fucking holidays. How many fingers have you got in now? Three? Only three?' It was here too that Fleur learnt the secret of my trade.

'You know,' she said, halfway through the proceedings, when we had exhausted the talk about Speedy and jazz and her brother's peculiar habits, 'there is something familiar about you, something that is within you but not exactly here. Why do I know you like that?'

I could have told her why she knew me of course. I could have told her that she knew who I was, what I was capable of, because she was of the same build and character. My familiarity was simply her foreknowledge of what was to come, but I would tell her that later, halfway through one of those long complicated ones, when you have to stop every now and again to have something to eat and drink and generally freshen up, one of those ones you should take a pack lunch for.

'It's my voice,' I told her. 'You probably recognize my voice.'

She leant back and let me take a good look.

'I don't think so,' she said. 'I don't think I recognize your voice at all.'

It was practically the last time we spoke that evening, and, like her previous question, there were two distinct replies. But this was a public performance. I drew myself up to the table, gripped the edge (as is my broadcasting habit) and put on that ridiculous sing-song voice that is the mark of our trade.

*

WE LEFT JIMMY JAMES soon after. Eric picked up the last bottle of whisky, stuck it in his pocket and announced it was time to leave. 'Come back for a nightcap,' he suggested. Eric and Michael took one taxi. Fleur, Jago and I followed.

'What day is it for the dear boy today then?' Jago eventually asked her, staring out of the open window.

'Twelfth of February. Some time in the early fifties.' Fleur drew her feet on to the seat. 'Apparently the south was hit by a sudden and wholly unexpected frost. He's been wearing woollen vests all day and arrived wearing ear muffs. Olga didn't care for that much.'

Jago looked across at me. 'Do you know all about this?' he asked. I nodded. 'He should be put away,' he said, without a trace of humour. He patted Fleur's knee. 'No bloody use to anyone. Frittering all that money away.'

'It's his money,' Fleur told him firmly. It was a conversation they had had before, but it was difficult to tell whether it was spoken in earnest or played out in jest.

'Could be your money,' Jago replied. '*Our* money,' he added, smiling. He turned his attention to me again.

'You haven't got any relatives you want taken out of circulation have you?' he asked. 'Nothing I like better than clearing the decks of surplus cargo.'

Fleur kissed one of his pitted cheeks.

'You're not a cab driver now Jago. You're not allowed to tout for business. It's against your ethics.'

Jago put his hands across her lap, rubbing her bare legs.

'I haven't got any ethics,' he declared. 'And you haven't got any clothes. Come on. Out we get.'

I followed them both down the dark and narrow alleyway. We were by the Thames on the south side, a little way down from Tower Bridge, walking alongside a red brick warehouse with thick pipes running the length of it, with booms and cranes cut out in front of the night sky. They ducked into a flight of concrete steps and started to climb. In the pitch black I could hear Fleur revelling in the delicious cold air.

'Just keep turning left Giles,' she called out. 'We're nearly there.'

'Just wait until you see this,' Jago added, sounding surprisingly out of breath.

We stepped into a vast open space that was some fifty feet wide and at least three times as long, a great airy cavern of a room with two huge open hatchways at either end. Running from side to side, high above me hung yard upon yard of stout washing line, all attached to stout wooden frames and pulleys, identical in design to the washing arrangements much in evidence in my youth, when in wintertime the daily wash would be raised and lowered in the only warm room in the house, the kitchen. But no clothes were to be found here. No socks or shirts or thin frayed collars waiting for their starch. Newspapers. Row upon row of newspapers, hanging like an army of pennants arraigned for battle. They ran in fluttering avenues from one end to the other, and in the middle of it all, like a clearing in a settler's forest, stood two creosoted wooden huts with little gingerbread windows and flowered curtains. Set before them was a long wooden table, a collection of canvas chairs and an old fashioned primus stove welded on to a filmmaker's tripod. On the table stood an antiquated coffee grinder with brass handle and wooden drawer, an uneven assortment of chipped mugs, a tin of evaporated milk and an airgun. Seated on one of the chairs was Eric, rubbing his newly polished feet. From the primus stove came the unmistakable smell of coffee on the boil.

'Giles!' Eric rose from his chair, and with a sweep of his hand introduced me to his new living quarters. 'Now you see why I am such an eager beaver at work these days. This is Michael's safari park.'

'You could give guided tours around this place,' I said. 'They could pop over from the Bloody Tower. Mulligan's Folly. Where is our host, by the way?'

'He's having a rest,' Eric informed us. He walked up to one of the huts and banged on the door.

'Michael, Michael,' he called. 'Do you want to come out?'

There was no reply.

So Eric took me round. Michael had spent years buying up cash-starved library stock and now had complete collections of *The Times* since 1945, the *Daily Telegraph* from 1950 and great swathes from the *Manchester Guardian*, the *Daily Mirror* and the *News Chronicle*. The layout was based upon Manhattan Island, with a criss-cross of broad avenues all named and signposted. We returned to the clearing. Jago was pouring coffee and Fleur was topping it up with what appeared to be dark rum. Mulligan had emerged and was huddled over a calor-gas heater.

'Home sweet home, eh Giles,' said Eric as we settled down.

'No complaints now Eric,' Fleur admonished. 'You two have a high old time here. Bicycle rides, sack races, nude roller skating.'

'I've never seen a place like it,' I confessed. 'I don't think I've ever seen anywhere quite so . . .'

'Quite so . . .?' Michael asked.

'Unpredictable.'

Michael beamed. 'Exactly,' he said. 'Exactly.' He patted the seat next to him and bade me sit down. 'Look at all this before you Mr Doughty. This is my world and with my pulleys I can change it at will. I can rearrange these papers and have a different view every day. Sometimes I will have them floating just above the floor. That is my marshland, my reeds and rushes-oh. They blow and move and rustle in the wet breeze from the river. They grow damp and a mist forms which swirls around us and hides us from the outside. On other days I mould them into a pastoral setting, with rolling hills and valleys, while there are days, grim days, when I need a cityscape and then their lines become more regimented and I see a host of chimneys and crowded roofs and the stern majesty of skyscrapers. And when I am at my clearest I raise them to the very roof, where I cannot see them, but only hear their murmurings, and then I have real company, for then they whisper and cajole, and confirm my thoughts.'

'A Hut with a View,' laughed Fleur leaning across and ruffling her brother's hair. Her shoulder blades moved wonderfully under her skin and I could smell her upper arm and every inch of her neck. Michael caught her hand and held it to his cheek.

'Why don't you take him to the roof and show him the Thames?' he suggested.

Fleur looked at us both, reached down into her canvas satchel and threw a tobacco tin at him. 'Not unless you roll us a joint first,' she said. 'I want my sensibilities heightened.'

So Fleur took off her shoes and led me to the roof. It was the absence of footwear, her bare feet in fact, which tipped us over the edge, for it seemed to both of us that with one swift action she had removed, quite consciously, the last opportunity for self-denial. As we climbed the ladder, and as I watched her walk across the flat surface to lean against a balustrade wide enough to sit on, with her white heels raised, her forearms resting on the warm brickwork, I knew I was under a moral obligation to strip her further, to have that swimsuit of hers hanging loose from her stomach, to have her leaning into me, the length of her neck stretched out against my shoulder, her breasts calling to the moon, her pelvis arching for my plunging hand. Which is what I did. I waited for a few moments for the two of us to establish where we were and what we were doing, to take in the stars and the lights and the smell of the river, and then I placed my hands on top of that thing and *peeled* it off, watching everything bounce into life, her body, my hands, our tongues and secret whispers, the very air around us. And at that moment I knew our present and I knew our future. I could hear it on her breath and see it clutching at her belly. We both knew it. We knew when we would meet and how we would meet and what we would do when we closed the door on the world. It would be a door we would close many times and each time we would close it a little faster than the time before.

This is what happened, by God. I have lost count of the

number of doors that have since closed, but we became very practised at shutting them. It is where we have lived our lives. It is where I have lived my life, my real life, the only part of my life (before Clare, that is) that seemed to require *me*. And that is how I drove up on that dismal October morning, looking back on that first encounter and thinking how appropriate it was that such an institution as the hotel guest-room should afford me so much pleasure, that only when confronted by an anonymous double bed, a small frigidaire, a hand-controlled television set and some brightly patterned pictures did I feel truly at home. There and in that wonderful car of mine, so silent, so dry, so confident in its ability to deaden my senses. And as I drove and thought of these meaningless matters, and as I overtook Fleur's lingering kiss and headed towards the heart of London, the deadly gloom that hung over us all shook me awake. There was a weight in the air that bore down upon me and impelled me to drive with studied abandon. It wasn't simply that it had been raining for days, or that the light was poor or that I was bone weary. It was as if this rain, this lowering sky, was the prelude, that matters were moving about in the world of which we knew nothing, *but that we would soon*. This was the softening up process. I felt as if we were living in complete ignorance, that we were nearly blind. And as I drove forward, my eyes blinking against the constant stream of this peculiar water, I thought back on the winters we had never had, the migratory birds which no longer left, and now the drowning of our southern coast. It is a truism that you never see what is closest to you. Sonia never saw no killer, the Titanic never saw no icebergs, Neville never saw no Adolf. And yet, and yet. I drove on, uneasy, with memories of Fleur mingling with bleak visions of this grim land.

*

I WAS FORTY MINUTES LATE by the time I finally arrived at work. I was greeted by a chorus of disapproval from the remaining members of the night shift. Forty minutes, without the excuse of a major road accident or family tragedy, was a long time overdue. I apologized.

Eric stood against the radiator in his fawn mackintosh (twenty years old with its belt missing) talking to himself and the world outside. I tapped him on the shoulder.

'You can go now Eric,' I told him, draping my raincoat over the edge of the partition. 'Sorry I'm late. The traffic was worse than I expected.'

Eric smiled his I-know-where-you-have-been-smile. While I have told him very little he knows that something is up.

'Not to worry. I'm in no great rush. Unlike Lady Bracknell. She's been on the line twice this morning asking for you, and she is not best pleased. She's very het up about all that,' he said, nodding in the direction of the rain. 'I think she wants to call out the lifeboats and inflate the rubber wear. She thinks we're going to drown. Tonight if we're lucky.'

'The Ark Syndrome,' I said wearily. The D.G. (Lady Bracknell to his admirers) believes himself to be a direct descendant of Noah. All of us believe in signs and portents, it is part of our calling, but only he thinks they should be handed down to him on an exclusive basis. Hence the courtesy title.

'The Ark Syndrome exactly,' Eric sniffed into his scarf. 'Mark my words he'll have us manning the Thames Barrier by lunchtime. He's got water on the brain.'

I ignored the pun.

'And?' I asked.

'And he's probably right,' Eric admitted. 'Wales is already lost, most of Kent seems to be going under and with a bit of luck Sussex will follow suit.'

'Couldn't we save Brighton?' I urged. 'I'd quite like to keep Brighton.'

'We could try.' Eric pulled out a handful of charts. 'The trouble is no one knows what's going on. We've got the two UK charts predicting fire and brimstone over the south and east, we've got the European charts telling us not to worry, that all the real trouble is going to happen well south of Ireland, and we have the latest forecast promising dances round the maypole in our shirtsleeves.'

'Eric!'

'Sorry. I exaggerate.' He picked up the last reading, taken at midnight. 'As you can see, it's still moving around a lot. There's a nasty looking trough here, north of Corunna with one centre here north west of Corunna, and the other here, 43 North, 19 degrees South. Strong pressure on the warm side, not much on the cold. Either of them could give us a run for our money and whatever happens to us it looks like the French are going to get it in the neck. However, to return to the matter in hand, the last report, the fine mesh, what Lady Bracknell likes about that is that it makes no mention of any storms at all. What it does promise is lots and lots and lots of . . .'

'Rain,' I said.

'Continuous, *heavy* rain,' Eric corrected. 'And that's what's uppermost in our leader's mind.'

'It's a shame . . .' I began. Eric put up his hand and stopped me.

'I know what you're going to say. If only we had something out there.' He raised his hat. 'Bring back the boat people!' he cried. 'Romeo, Romeo, wherefore art thou, Romeo!'

An old joke for which I duly admonished him, but an apt one. Scuttled by the Ministry of Defence nearly a year ago for economic reasons, *Romeo* had been one of three ships stationed in the North Atlantic for the Met, its location in the very area over which Eric was now waving his hands. It would have been invaluable at this hour and this was not the first time we had mourned its passing. Eric drew a crude boat upon a crude ocean in the condensation, inscribing the picture with a rude message to our masters.

'Still,' he admitted, 'we can't blame Lady Bracknell for that. Nor for this.' He nodded to the watery view outside.

Eric slouched off and left me to the weather. By twelve o'clock, the broad trough which he had showed me had advanced north-east and lay from north France across to Finisterre. The central pressure in the trough had dropped some fifteen millibars, and there seemed to be three distinct and separate centres to it. The strong pressure on the warm side remained but there was no evidence of any significant increase of wind coming from the cold. As Eric had predicted it was difficult to know what was going on. I did the usual broadcasts, the national forecast at lunchtime, and later some odds and ends for local stations. As usual I put a little something in for Fleur, an innocent enough sounding phrase, but one which had special meaning for us. (Fleur does the same for me, only when she does it I can see her mouth move, see her lips part, see the pink words form inside. Sometimes she speaks so slowly and deliberately that it is as if she were sucking me off in front of the camera.) By four o'clock, with our last conference of the day coming up, the picture was, if anything, even more uncertain. Our main problem lay in the fact that the two forecasts which serve as the basis for our analysis, the fine mesh model and the UK global, suggested different patterns of behaviour. The morning's fine mesh (which like breakfast coffee one devours in large gulps and which, as its name implies takes a narrow but detailed look at our *local* world) agreed with the earlier findings, tracking a low centre across the south-east of England during the day, keeping the strong winds away from land and ensuring that once again Britain was in for another soaking. Although the fine mesh is run early, with an early cut-off time, it has gained a reputation over the years as being extremely reliable when it comes to figuring out the behaviour of intense low-pressure systems, such as this one over the Bay of Biscay. The UK global, which takes a much broader view, disagreed. That indicated that the front was moving more slowly than anticipated and was therefore gathering strength, deepening earlier, holding off longer, *waiting* until the time was right for it to move across and greet the west coast of England with an unpleasant goodnight kiss from its great windy lips. Out of these two fictions we formed our own story, put together by the lads and lassies from Bracknell, the Little Droplets over at Television Centre and ourselves and which said that in these cold and fearful October days, the men and women of this land must button up their overcoats and put on their galoshes, for there will be rain, rain and more rain to come; that banks may burst and bridges may be washed away; that councils should prepare for sandbags and pumps; that Wales, Cornwall, Sussex and Kent will be sluiced up and down; that we will splish and splash and splosh, and if that isn't enough, where the wet is wettest, the rain thickest there will be a wind too, a wind that will howl up and down the Channel and knock Frenchmen off their bicycles and which might, if we are especially unlucky, take a brief excursion into the exposed tip of the south-east coast.

And that was that. Eric returned to relieve me a little early, around half past five. The six o'clock broadcast came and went as agreed. No change, no panic, no sweat. And then the phone rang. Not the direct line to the D.G. (the red phone) nor the duty phone (the blue phone) but my phone (and Eric's too), the one used for business and *pleasure*. I looked at it ringing on the desk. It could be a weather station or someone from an RAF base. It could be Monica or Fat Patrick or Michael Mulligan. It could have been Fleur about to say something provocative down the line, congratulating me on my latest little radio treat. 'Guess what I'm wearing?' is one of her favourite openings – a nice wide opening as Max Miller would have said. I stared at it not wanting to find out. Eric picked it up and held it out to me.

'You answer it,' he said. 'It's still your bloody shift.'

Whoever it was, was using a public callbox and having great difficulty in getting it to work. Every time they pushed the coin in it dropped straight through. The pips seemed to accelerate at each attempt, adding to the sense of urgency. The wind had started up again, lashing the rain against the windows in a burst of fury. It was dark and nasty out there. No time to be in a phone booth. Finally the coin held. It wasn't Fleur at all. It was my sister and she could barely speak.

'Giles. Giles. Is that you?'

'Of course it's bloody me. Whatever's the matter. Where are you for God's sake?'

*

EVER SINCE her husband died about a year ago, an aloof man who had something to do with passport control at the Home Office, Carol and I have become closer than either of us would have thought possible, or indeed desirable. Ian's death was an unpleasant, drawn out, exhausting affair, made worse by his own inability to cope. He treated her cruelly and abominably, showering her with bitterness at his imminent departure and at her (in his eyes) undeserved, continuing life. Carol turned to me for support, and I, reluctant relative that I had always been, obliged, not principally for her, for Carol was something of a wire brush, hard and abrasive, but for their little daughter, who became so disturbed by this vicious correction to her life. Let me make it plain that it was not something I wanted to do, for it meant entering into that loathsome thing, a world of emotional upheaval, but it was, alas, something I felt obliged to do, and though I cannot have brought them any true comfort (for I am incapable of providing such a naked commodity – or even wanting to) it gave them some sort of solid base. I could listen to Carol's heated outpourings concerning Ian's latest atrocity, his relentless humiliation of her, his impossible hatred of his three doctors, each of whom he held personally responsible, the horrible diary of death she found, tucked under his mattress, outlining the relentless decline of his failing body, his determined attempts to humiliate her sexually, comparing his wasted body with her healthy one, asking her to do things to him she never much liked doing anyway, asking her halfway through when she intended to do it with someone else, implying that she had already begun; how he would demand that photographs be taken of him in his shorts, garden photographs of disease and how he would prop them up around his bed and totter downstairs to stick them on the refrigerator door; how he would insist that he be taken down to the seaside and carried down to the water, to the distress of everyone, including himself; and how, cruellest of all, he all but refused to see his daughter, practically banishing her from his room.

What change can come over men and their affairs (I could have phrased that differently). Here was a man who went to work with the governmental signature on his black briefcase, who returned home to a loving and eager child, who lived with a woman, who, though like himself not capable of passion and often rather scornfully clever, nevertheless loved him and on occasions would treat him with affection. Not much perhaps but more than many (more than me). And there was this same man, an educated man, who must have thought of death in his life, who must have read of death and pondered religion and the universe and his tiny place in it, and considered his child and her future, who faced by his single awful circumstance turned his home into a ghastly family mortuary of the spirit where love, life and happiness were dissected and found wanting.

It nearly destroyed Carol. It was she who had taken care of our mother in her last year and it was she who insisted on keeping in touch with father long after I had deserted him. We have had quite enough deaths in our family, what with one thing and another, but those in the past were random blows, kindly bestowed by the Almighty, while these were aimed by the one man in the world who had professed to like her more than most. And so it fell to me to lay an occasional arm on those cold shoulders and to wipe those scornful eyes free from tears – tears that none of us would have presumed Carol to possess. Seeing Carol so distraught almost softened my own heart. There were times when I nearly asked after our own father, not in any desire to find out what the miserable man was doing (he was doing nothing, even I knew that), but merely to divert attention from her misery. But wiser counsels prevailed. It could have led I know not where – somewhere I have no wish to go. So I listened and made noises of sympathy and let the two of them stay overnight in the flat (no Woman from Spain for me then) on occasions. When Carol despaired of Clare ever developing into a normal child, I would chide her with tales of her own worth and would add, rather glibly, and probably unconvincingly, that when it was all over and she had settled down, it would only be a matter of time before she 'met someone else'. Not that I believed it for a second. I would not have described my sister as attractive in any way. She had decent enough brown hair but it looks as if she chops at it at night with a pair of scissors. There is a nasty fringe over her eyes when there should be an aspect of her clear eyebrows. She has good hands, good fingers, but she wears thick ostentatious rings on her wrists, ugly heirlooms from Ian's family. She has, if memory serves me, and if she has bothered to look after it, a perfectly acceptable body, but she dresses it in expensive and unattractive wear which accentuates her angular character, her stubbornness, her wish for confrontation.

Curiously enough though, after Ian's eventual death, from this tough and rather aggressive woman came a soft and astonishingly caring mother, who radiated a sort of gentleness (towards her daughter at least) that no one would have thought her capable of. It was as if her husband's treatment of her had warned her how little time there is for us all and how circumstances can strive against us. Not surprisingly this new turn of events bewildered her daughter, who up till then had sided with her father, for he was, before his illness robbed him of his senses, more tolerant, better fun, better looking, more at ease. This then was the father who had suddenly shut the door in her face, abandoned her, and died, and here was the mother, who now wanted to be cooed over, who wanted those kisses and those looks of adoration, which for so long had been the province of the other parent. Clare, torn, heart-broken, uncomprehending, would submit to her mother's protest-ations, but found it difficult to respond. There was for instance the time they took a bath together in my flat, something which in Ian's day would have been unthinkable. When it happened, at Carol's suggestion, said in a rather too bright and too hopeful voice, it was Clare who was clearly embarrassed, six-year-old Clare, who, though she went to the bathroom with her mother and held her hand as she went, did so not out of a sense of fun, or just ordinary pleasure, but because her mother had suggested it, asked for it, and her mother was not someone you crossed lightly. No laughter came from the bathroom on that occasion but, like me, over the following weeks Clare realized she was seeing a side to her mother she had rarely witnessed before. A new Carol was developing, a Carol which had been kept shut up, closed, trapped by her years as a young girl and later as a working, married woman. So here was Carol gulping down the phone, feeding handfuls of money into it. I could see her, those efficient fingers in that brown purse of hers (the only thing of our mother's she ever kept) pulling out the coins, pushing them through one after the other with that impatient thin look of hers. Coin after coin after coin. What was going on for Christ's sake? I half hoped she was drunk and had picked up a man and was going to take him home and would I look after Clare for the night? Not that she'd prob-ably want something like that after Ian's behaviour, but she still needed someone she could touch, and not a brother's touch. Nor a daughter's. Nor, I suppose, necessarily a man's. Actually a one-night stand is the last thing Carol needed. What she needed was warmth. With people like me around of course, she might have to fuck to get it.

'Carol? Carol? Can you hear me? Where are you for Christ's sake? Are you all right? Nothing wrong with Clare is there?' The dreaded question, oh the dreaded question. Nothing wrong with your daughter, your child. Selfishly, of course, I quickly prayed to God that there was not. I could do without that. I've got quite enough on my plate without that, thank you very much.

'Giles, listen carefully. I might have to run suddenly. God these phone boxes. Listen.'

'Carol, where are you for God's sake? And calm down.'

'Shut up Giles. Thank God you're there. I tried to reach you at home but only got the ansaphone. Can you leave now? You've got to leave. I'm at Charing Cross.' She paused again and fed some more coins in. Trust Carol to have the right change in her purse.

'Charing Cross? Why for heaven's sake? *What's the matter?*'

'Listen Giles. Oops. Wait a minute.' There was a short break, and I could hear the tannoy system and the noise of other conversations nearby. The phone crashed in my ear, a series of sharp metallic sounds, once, twice, three times – bang, bang, bang – as if she had laid it down suddenly and the phone had slipped off the edge, banging itself against the coinbox.

'Giles? Are you still there? It's all right. She's still there. For a moment I thought I'd lost her again. She's nearing the front of the queue, so I don't have much time. Listen, I've seen her. You'll never guess who. I saw her an hour ago. I've followed her here. It's her I tell you. I've found her Giles. I've found her for you.'

Carol's voice was high pitched and fast, bordering on the hysterical. I could picture her running her hand through her hair, bending low over the phone, twisting the strands through her over-decorated fingers.

'Seen her? Seen *who*?'

'Your little friend. The one who gave you so much trouble. She's standing not twenty yards away. It's Stella, Giles, Stella Muchmore as plain as I'm talking to you. I've found her Giles. I've found her for you.'

I looked at Eric, hearing the words but not believing them. Found Stella Muchmore? My sister? The world was closing in on me, the wet world was beating at my door.

'Giles? *Giles*. Are you there for God's sake?'

'Carol. Yes, I'm here. It's OK. Are you sure? Sure it's Stella? I mean it's been a long time.'

Carol brought her intelligent scorn to the fore. The Carol I knew, the Carol I lied to, the Carol I hid from. The Carol who was a relative, but no sister of mine. No brother, no father, no sister, no mother.

'Credit me with something Giles,' she was saying. 'Have *I* changed that much? Of course it's Stella. I used to walk with her to school practically every day if you remember. It's her all right. She's hardly changed at all.'

The line went abruptly hollow, as if the phone had been torn out of her hand. Now it was my turn to lose control. I began to shout down the phone, shout my sister's name, imploring her to come back. Carol, Carol, don't leave me in the lurch, for pity's sake. Then she was back.

'Giles. I've got to go. She's being served now. Buying one of those cartons of fruit juice. God, if only you'd been with me. She was in the wine bar, just around the corner. Drinking champagne. Half a bottle. On her own. I couldn't believe it.'

'What the hell are you doing in a wine bar at this time of the evening. Where's Clare?'

'With a friend. She's perfectly all right. They're off on a school outing tomorrow. That's why she's staying overnight. It was pure chance. I was having an early drink with Monica. We thought we might have dinner later on. She wanted to talk to me about something.'

'Never mind about Monica,' I said (though in truth I did mind about Monica). 'What about Stella? What are you going to do?'

'I'm going to follow her Giles. I've got this far and I'm going to follow her.'

'But you can't do that. You don't know where she's going. Why don't you go up to her, introduce yourself . . .'

She snorted with impatience.

'Use your head Giles. She *disappeared*, remember. She'd run a bloody mile if she knew I was on to her. She looks fit enough. I've found her Giles and I'm not going to let her go. And I *do* know where she's going. I heard her asking the ticket office when the next train was due. She's going to Wye.'

'Rye?'

'*Wye*. I think you have to change at Ashford to get there. Anyway that's where we're going.'

'And then what?'

'How the hell should I know? Follow her as best I can, I suppose. See where she's living after all these years.'

'She could be staying with friends.'

'*Friends*? Can you see Stella with friends? No, this is a journey home unless I'm very much mistaken. She's done this all before.'

'But she may be going miles. You can't chase her all over Kent.'

'It won't be all over Kent. It's a local station. And even if I do lose her . . . listen. There's a modern hotel on the outskirts of Ashford. On the London road. The Coach House or something like that.'

'The Post House,' I said, a little too quickly. Generous bathroom, moderately decent-sized double bed, some pond or other out the back. 'Planetrain' had visited the area last spring and I had followed in its wake. How on earth did Carol know about The Post House? Surely not . . .

'That's it. The Post House. Ian once stayed there for a conference on international policing. He'd broken his leg and I had to drive him down. Just before Leeds Castle. It's there on your right.'

It is indeed. So Ian had spent a couple of nights down there too had he. Thank God it hadn't coincided with my little jaunt. Fat Patrick lived down that way too, down on the marshes overlooking the military canal. Now that *was* Rye. Carol was still talking, giving me instructions.

'What you must do Giles is drive down there now, take a room and one for me. I'll meet up with you there later on. Don't worry if I'm late.'

'They may not have any rooms Carol. What if . . .'

'On a Thursday night in this weather? Of course they'll have rooms. If they don't you can leave a message where you'll be. I'll find you. Just get down there.'

'OK. OK. I'll have to go home first and pick up the car. Listen Carol, don't do anything silly. You don't know what she's been up to. It's a filthy night out there and it's going to get worse.'

'I won't. I've got to go Giles. I've found her, I've found her for you.'

And the line went truly dead and I was left standing there, holding on to God knows what. I suppose I took my leave of Eric, though I cannot remember, but I do recall struggling with my mac as I clattered down the stairs. I took a taxi back to the flat. The house was empty. All the downstairs lights were off (something I have told Mrs Delguardo never to do) and their bicycles, usually propped up in the hallway, were gone. I was glad that there was no one there, that there were no signs of life. It seemed so reassuring. I sat down on the sofa and called Brighton to see if Monica had returned. It would have been interesting to hear her side of the story, but of course she hadn't had time to get back. I called Fat Patrick down on the marsh but there was no reply from him either. I packed a small suitcase and went back out. It was truly a night for being on one's own. The whole world was crashing and banging and tearing at my sleeve. I went out to the car. I switched on the ignition and turned the windscreen wiper regulator up to full speed. Ashford then. When I was young I used to steal rides into Ashford, hopping off the trains when we thought no one was looking, ducking into the loco sheds, sneaking round the works yard, jotting down numbers, climbing aboard unattended engines. Rochester, Halling, Snodland, Aylesford, through East Farleigh and Wateringbury to change at Paddock Wood for the straight run down, Fat Patrick and I with our notebooks and pencils and packets of ten, leaning half out the windows, drawing nudes on the condensation, feet up in the first-class compartment, giggling in the corridors. No loco sheds now, no works, no sparks in the dark. When I was last at The Post House with Fleur I told myself that this was the closest I ever wanted to get to home. Now Stella Muchmore was dragging me back there whether I liked it or not. Home. Where the heart lies. Well, here's the beat of mine.

Two

THOUGH IT IS a long time since they have sat upon those waters, and the years in which I looked upon their form have lengthened, those boats still float before me with a grace and an insistence which is hard for me to forget. Their bodies have long been cut, their propeller blades long since stacked and hawked on a bargain pavement, their tubular seats found in dishevelled and discarded wayside cafés, but their presence is as acute and as powerful now as it was then, when the five of them rode so hugely on the river that is called the Medway. I remember them, dark and lovely, five Flying Boats moored up above the bridge, drooping slightly as if peering into the water that held them down so fast and which passed them by so swiftly. Their colour was grey and they were of peculiar bend. They seemed to me then as beasts raised up from the ocean's floor, blind and ill at ease, rather than creatures brought down from the sky. Two of them had been shorn, their wings cruelly torn, and although they turned no more or less than their companions they appeared to be in greater pain; their ropes were tighter, their bodies more susceptible to the stings of their internment. Theirs was the greater indignity, but the anguish could be seen on all of them. Five Flying Boats imprisoned in the open air, tied to the river bed as we were tied to them.

We lived in Rochester and we were an aircraft town. In the time of my childhood much of the factory that had made the aeroplanes had shut down and moved to Belfast, but I could still wander down to the Esplanade and hear the echoes of the hammering workshops or the shrill blast of the factory whistle. If I had been asked what I knew of Rochester I would have shut my eyes and entered into my elders' tales, for the past was strong and hung about the streets as fast as any fog swirling up from the sea. The past was the peeling paint of this town; there was nothing fresher.

If I had been asked I would have shut my eyes and remembered those high days of excitement when the doors of Number One Hangar would be rolled back and a new and fabulous creation would emerge for the first time. This was the age where we lived in the air, for what we made we set free. We were an aircraft town and we looked to the sky. For us the aircraft had flown. We had seen the *Singapore* and the *Calcutta* and the *Valetta*. We had seen the *Sarafand* and the *Scion*. We had seen them all as they were led down to the water's edge, each craft a new attempt at fiction. We had seen them run and rise, taken up out over the coast by one of the famed and envied test pilots, whose lives we led in our dreams. We had seen them rise and taken up and then disappear from view. Then the waiting time came, when the whole town stood on its heels. Families and classrooms, uncles and aunts, children with hoops and kites and grubby bags of humbugs, workers with black box cameras aimed to produce tiny, useless, wonderful pictures, all would wait, watching the empty air above, hands on hips, larger hands on smaller heads, hands clenched, hands held to the eyes, hands describing arcs, hands rolling tobacco, hands fidgeting, hands beating time, waiting for the moment when the first dot would appear, when it would be disputed, when it would disappear, when it would re-appear accompanied by the first doubted drone, when the dot and the drone would merge and take form. Look there! No *there*! Here she comes! Caps thrown, children shrieking, kisses on the street. People running, hooting their horns, whistling and clapping their hands. Those who had built such craft would bang their fists, smack each other on the shoulders, turn, and hurry down to witness the descent, while calmer shopkeepers would brush down their aprons and return to the cool of their trade.

We were an aircraft town and like all cities and towns where great industry flourishes there was a power and an imagination which marked us. Inside those factory sheds was a landscape in which we all lived, a landscape of molten beauty, of crackling dazzling energy, a landscape which could chill our bones and melt our fat, which could give us birth and serve us death, a landscape into which we could fall as easily as one on which we could walk, and which, as it enveloped us, inspired our love. It could rise and kill, it could maim and disfigure, and yet, through its eloquence and mystery it could soothe and inspire. We were an aircraft town and we lived in a world of hope and adventure, where skill reigned. For true skill is true hope and true adventure. To fashion, to shape form, is a great art. It is the consuming art and it informs everyone. It transcends nothing. Such towns and such cities are great towns and great cities, and the memory of such times is the memory of a great people.

I never saw those planes. For me and for those who grew up with me, those famous factory sheds were silent. Only minor operations remained. The slipway was thick with weeds, the water uncomfortably bare. I never stood at my mother's side watching a first trial, never charged out of the school gates on a corporation afternoon off. Only the Flying Boats remained, Rochester's finest and boldest experiment, now our abandoned offspring. When they had thought to build such beasts they had to erect especially large sheds in which to contain them. New men were hired, new skills taught, different procedures learnt. They emerged from drawing board to production line without a single prototype being made. Those who hauled themselves up the production ladders and walked upon their giant wings were walking on the moon. They were called the Empire Flying Boats and they flew in the age of the white saxophone. They flew the Empire routes, in the dress circle. They flew to South Africa and to Australia and to India. They flew, pale grey and humming, laden with the Empire's mail and the Empire's emissaries. They flew over everything, they were watched by everyone. They dropped out of an unbroken sky on to a lightly cooked lagoon. They circled over strange cries and unfamiliar chants. They flew low over huge herds of elephants (Lean out! Play hoopla! Try tossing your hat on one of those thousand thundering tusks!), they flew low over Kilimanjaro, looking into its black plug heart.

This is the Flying Boat moving. It has you seated within, lest motion should move you a muscle. See it rise, this flat-bottomed beast. See the windows, strange and low. Smell the whipped salt, imagine the huge angles that mark its height, that speak for its breadth. Now it races, now it speeds, charging past the warehouses and the gathered allotments that surround its place of birth. Now it thunders, washing the men standing in their boats, soaking them with this great spray of their future. Now it lifts, now it roars. It rises through the drifting smoke of the town, as if this brown air will choke it, as if only above this dirt and this mean aspect and this common field will it find an air fit enough to breathe. Ungrateful monster!

The Flying Boat moves lazily. The Flying Boat moves in curves. We drift in its cushioned shell. It is time to sleep, it is time to dream. When we awake we are flying over the Nile. There is a clean noise in the air. It is familiar. Outside there is nothing but heat. We eat iced melon and chicken. We turn over a slice of translucent York ham. A white-jacketed steward leans across with an enormous tureen of white soup. We watch him carefully, with oval eyes. Later we arrange the crystallized fruit into a flowering star, a sparkling bloom resting on white linen. The captain comes forward and invites us to look to our left.

Outside are the very eyes of Osymandyas. We are flying into his vision. We see nothing but stone. Palm trees flourish below. To us they are nothing but feather dusters. Alexandria is a place in which to get drunk.

The war comes. We land, maybe at Southampton. The passenger seats, the bunks, the cabins, the luggage racks and the kitchens are ripped out. In their place are mounted guns and extra fuel tanks. Wires are looped along the length of its interior. We are in danger for the plane has a soft underbelly and we must fly close to the water, but we know that one day the danger will pass and we will be safe again. We think that when this is all over there will still be a *Cairo* and a *Calcutta* and a *Durban* and they will still be our *Cairo*, our *Calcutta* and our *Durban*. We think that those who watched at the water's edge will always watch at the water's edge, and will be content to view the spectacle of our wicker dinner baskets, our franked letters, our feathered hats and our exclusive mooring buoys. We think that the Flying Boats will always inhabit this exotic state. But when at last both we and our planes had landed, we found that the world had turned. It was a different place. Our beautiful aeroplanes were the wrong shape, they ran at the wrong speed. They even landed on the wrong substance. No matter that they had held the world in their grasp, their time (their swift time) had gone. So they would take off and land, take off and land, and one by one they would be seized and hauled to the shore, some to be broken up on the spot; some crated up and lost, a forgotten jigsaw on a forgotten wharf; some left to sink slowly in shallow, unknown waters; and these five, flown back home, to be bound and held without reprieve, captives on the very river which had first given them flight.

Yes we were an aircraft town, but by the time the Flying Boats returned we too were broken and delivered of our wings. Our factory had left us, only its hull remained. We had empty skies and empty skies led to empty hearts. Oh, it wasn't as if there were no good times in our town. We still went to dances and queued up for the cinema. We still drank in pubs and kissed in doorways. We still fell in love and celebrated the births of our children. But even on those days of hope, even on those days of change, when the long winter would take its leave and a stronger sun would fall upon the water, before we could forget, our eyes would turn to where those five planes lay, dark and restless, as if lying in a troubled sleep. It was impossible to avoid them. Wherever we went we would see them strung out on the river, from the main street, coming back from work, on our way to school, from the top of the bus, from the windows of a train, there they would be, our unhappy reminder of what we had been and what we had become. For like those aircraft we had learnt that we were shapeless too, that we were ill informed and behind the times. Perhaps a few more German bombs might have helped to clear the ground. But this town had enough craters in its heart.

Other businesses came to Rochester. Some men got work in Chatham dockyards, some moved away altogether. But our purpose had gone. When those who had worked there became drunk they would hang their heads in their beer and talk. They would drink and become morose. What a hold they thought they had on their world! How quickly, how easily was it lost! And when they had drunk enough, and if the walk took them that way (and quite often when it didn't), they would take to the towpath where they would rest and look at those boats. Many men have sat there with their friends and wished for one moment that the night might be broken by the sudden noise of an engine turning over, that out of the stillness a great falling wall of spray would leap out of the dark and stream down their faces. Wouldn't that awake the town! They would look across the water and think of the cold and the current and their beloved aeroplanes, and wonder whether they should not kick off their shoes and swim across, just to climb aboard again, just to say hello, just to break their own drunken heat and stand on a wing-tip float and shout at the shoreline and the sky and the great world that grounded them all. But though they were drunk they were not fools. They knew the power of the river, and they knew too that what they might find at the end of their swim would be worse than their sour need. So they would sit and they would talk, and when it became too cold, or when they had said enough, they would rise up unsteadily and make their way home.

And so we went and so we came and so we lived our lives. In those days I thought the earth stood still, that the motion of the air and all that it touched (for it touches everything you see) was constant, that the world was *just so*. I thought the clouds moved one way and the sun in another, that old men gathered in the green club house down by the river, that young men threw up in darkened alleyways and fought outside the dance hall. I thought that men smoked cigarettes and that women carried shopping bags and that buses were best in winter, when the windows were wet and you squashed three to a seat. I thought that fish and chips would always be good for me, that the man in the black beret at the end of the High Street would always chop them long and thick, that they would always come wrapped in newspaper and that I would always lick my fingers on the way home. I never thought that someone else might like to lick my fingers. I never thought I might not know my way home.

We lived, my mother, my father, my sister, my brother (my dear dead brother) and I at the end of Gladstone Drive, on a small rise overlooking the river. It was a wide comfortable road, lined with lime trees and light green wrought-iron lampposts. The lampposts had a T cross sticking out just below the lamp casing, and in the winter it was not unusual for one of the residents to turn into the street, look up and see a line of us children perched on top of every one, bobbing about like fairy lights, chanting and gaily shouting, rather in the manner of Ubi Iwerks cartoon.

'Mrs Briggs approaching!' we would sing out. 'Here comes Mr Fisher! Unknown car! Stranger in sight!'

It was a safe and quiet street, where we could ride our bicycles and walk on our stilts without fear of passing traffic. Like the animated exploits we saw down at the Rex Cinema, any danger we came across had to be invented. The bicycles had to be ridden backwards with three passengers wobbling on board. If you wished to cross the road on your stilts it were better if you hopped across on one, better still if you asked, no insisted, that you be blindfolded first. Sightless happy days!

I can recite their names, the young inhabitants of this dreamland, this world that was never there, but I am not going to. Let the boy recite them, let him do it. Let me ask *him*. He is used to interrogation, this boy. He has been questioned by experts. But beware, he is used to evasion too. He lies easily. It comes naturally to him. He likes lying, if for no other reason than for not telling the truth. Sometimes this boy thinks that there is nothing *to* tell, and that there is no one to tell it to anyway, that it is *all* lies. But I know this boy. He will talk to me.

'Can you recite their names, this lamppost lot?'

'I can.'

'And what were their names?'

'Their names were Grey, Deering, Cramphorn and Fisher, Liddle, Muchmore and Doughty.'

'They had other names these children? Christian names? *Nicknames*?'

'Jack, Henry, Nigel and Poker, Fat Patrick, the SS girl and —'

'And?'

The boy frowns. He cannot remember what he was called. He shrugs his shoulders. Looks up at me.

'No matter. This SS girl. Why so?'

'She was', he pauses, digging out the word he only learnt recently, 'an *emphatic* walker,' he lowers his eyes. 'It was what my father called her. The SS girl.'

'You are referring to the Muchmore girl?'

'Yes. Stella.'

'And Stella was your age?'

He corrects me. It is so easy to forget.

'My sister's age. One year older.' He looks at his hands and adds, 'But after a while she was my age too.'

'And your house?' I ask him. 'Tell us about your home.'

He takes a deep breath.

'Each house was set back from the road, though not all at the same distance. Stella's house stood well back, on a steep incline, with a garage drive that cut through a very deep rockery. My mother thought it unattractive. She used to say she wanted to throw stones at it. We had only a small garden at the front before the path began which ran right around the house on both sides and which led to the big garden at the back. I do not know much about the gardens on the other side of the road . . .'

'. . . except of course the dark fir trees which lined Muchmore's lawn,' I remind him.

'. . . except the dark fir trees which *surrounded* Muchmore's lawn, but all the gardens on our side, on *my* side, ran down to the disused allotments, and then', his eyes grow bright, 'to the pillboxes, and the river.'

'You liked the pillboxes and the river?'

He nods.

'There were wild raspberries the other side of our fence and when I pushed the plank aside I would pick a great handful of them before going down. The first pillbox was the best, it was there you got the best view of them all floating on the river. Fat Patrick's father promised to take us alongside them in one of his friend's boats, but he never did. Anyway the pillbox was just as good. I would sit there and watch them . . .'

'. . . through the slit eye of war,' I add, recalling a phrase of mine he might not like.

'. . . through the slit,' he agrees, 'and I would be their captain and I would sit in the cockpit and start them up, and take them through the weeds and rusty buoys, past the stumps of black timbers and fishing nets, and out into the clear, when I would pull open the throttle, pull back, and up we would go, the lot of us. Then the play could begin. Then the passengers could come forward.'

Strange words for a boy. There is something unreal in this recollection, something missing. A boyish manner perhaps, a sense of friendship, of *games*.

'You would be with your friends I take it?' I ask him. 'With Jack and Nigel and Poker Fisher?'

'I would be alone,' he replies, staring at me with wide brown eyes. 'For most of the time I would be alone.'

'But not all the time?'

He is reluctant to agree with me, but eventually he does.

'Not all the time. But it was more fun on my own.'

I put him back on the path. I do not wish to know about his fun, yet.

'And when you were not alone, when you had passengers, who were they?'

'Fat Patrick mostly. His father helped build them. He had a cap, a pilot's cap from the airline. He'd let me wear it. His house was filled with Flying Boat stuff. His father was potty about them.'

'Anyone else?'

'Sometimes my sister and Stella. They would be air stewardesses or passengers. Stella liked being sick into a bag. Sometimes she would steal a tin of fruit cocktail and pour it into a bag and over her legs so that it looked like sick. Sometimes she would put her fingers down her throat to try and *be* sick, but my sister discouraged this. It made the place smell.'

'And this was all. No one else?'

'Cramphorn and Poker on occasions, but they wanted to be bombers or fighter planes, and I didn't like that.'

'And that is all?' I persist. I look at him gently, telling him he has nothing to fear.

'My brother,' he says simply. 'My brother would play with me. Before he died.'

Ah, his brother. Before he died. And after? The boy frowns again. What do I mean after? I tell him I mean that after his brother died, did he still play?

'Alone,' he says deliberately. 'After he died I played alone. Carol was getting too old for it anyway.'

This was a point I must clear up.

'Your brother was younger than you was he not? Four years younger? He was ten when he died?'

'He was ten.'

'And you were fourteen?'

'Yes.'

'How did he die? Your younger brother, your dear dead brother.'

'He drowned. He went down to the river one day and slipped in and drowned. He should have waited. He should have waited for me.'

'But surely,' and this is the point I want to make, this is where the boy must reveal himself, 'surely *after* he died your parents would not wish you to play on the very spot where he fell in? Surely you would not be allowed to go there? Surely perhaps *you* might not want to go there?'

He does not attempt to answer the second question, but says with complete honesty, 'I did not tell them when I went. I made sure they did not know. After he died none of the children were allowed down there, so it was easy for me to go alone.'

'But you would be seen,' I argued. 'Or rather you would be not seen. Your parents would wonder where you were, they would look out for you, catch you climbing back over the fence, send you packing off to your room, keep you indoors as a punishment.'

He looks at me as if I am a complete fool, this boy, as if I haven't a clue about mothers and fathers and brothers and sisters, and the world of families.

'I went at night,' he says, 'when everyone thought I was safe in bed. I went out the back door, ran across the lawn, down through the vegetable patch and out to the allotments. If it was very dark I took a torch. But I didn't care what the weather was like. In fact I liked it better when it was bad.'

I picture this boy running across a dark green lawn with the wind blowing at his face, one hand holding his jacket together, the other clutching a silver torch. I see him jump the stone steps down to the vegetable garden, hurry along the ash path to where the broken plank, now fixed, lies. He climbs the fence does this boy, he climbs it easily. He jumps over the fence and lands running. A minute later he is sitting on top of his favourite pillbox, staring out across the river.

'And how often did you do this?' I ask him.

'As often as possible. *Every night* if I could.'

'I see.'

So there he is, this boy, alone in his room, alert, nervous, impatient, waiting for the moment when the house settles down, when it is safe for him to emerge again. I have another thought.

'Tell me,' I say. 'I am interested to know how long this went on for?'

'How long?' He looks at me as if he can barely understand the question, and yet he is not a stupid boy. Perhaps it is something he has never thought of before.

'Yes,' I repeat, 'How long? You were fourteen when you started doing this. How long did it go on for? For six months? A year? Two years? Surely by sixteen, seventeen, you no longer wanted to play at being a pilot? Surely there were other things on your mind by then?'

He looks away from me as though he is trying to conjure up a picture of himself.

'I did not start at fourteen,' he says, 'though certainly after they banned everyone, going out there at night became more of a necessity. I do not remember going out there quite so much later on, perhaps when I was sixteen or so. Sixteen or seventeen.'

'When Stella disappeared?'

'When Stella disappeared,' he confirms.

'But being a boy,' I tell him, 'you would not know of this. We will come to Stella later, when you are a little older. Let us return to your home for a moment. You have told us about the outside, but nothing of the *inside*. You remember the inside very well do you not. It was very important to you, the inside. The inside *made you what you are.*'

He does not disagree with this, but waits patiently for the next question. He is very passive, this boy, very calm. There is a cold quality to him that is unusual in a boy of his age. It is not an adult trait, but it is a self-possessed one.

'Tell me about the house,' I urge him.

'It was a compact house,' he begins, 'made out of red brick. Looking at it from the outside, at the front, on the right-hand side you had the living room, a long room which stretched from the front of the house to the back and which could be divided up into two rooms by means of an ugly wooden partition. In the centre, directly behind the front door there was the hall. Halfway down the hall, plumb in the middle were the stairs. To the right of the stairs was the corridor which led round to the back porch and the back door. This corridor was rarely used. On the left-hand side, at the front, was the dining room. Also leading off from the hall on that side was the downstairs lavatory, and next door to that the kitchen. The kitchen, like the other end of the living room looked out over the back garden, and also, on the right-hand side of the kitchen was another door which also led into the back porch and the back door. The two front rooms had bow windows at the front, with flat roofs jutting out from the frame. Upstairs formed three sides of a square, with a landing at the back, halfway up. On the right lay my sister's room, next to that, facing the front, over the living room, my parents'. Next to that a tiny box-room, next to that the spare room, which lay over the dining room. On the left-hand side, the upstairs lavatory, the bathroom, and finally, me and my brother's room. My room.'

I study this for a moment while he gets his breath back. He has reeled it off as if the house had been nothing but a plan, as if it had been bare of everything, no furniture, no pictures, no colours, nothing. I humour him for a moment.

'This living room,' I say, 'when the partition was in place, how did one gain access to the back half? The half which overlooked the back garden?'

He answers quickly. 'There were two doors leading off from the hall into the living room. When the partition was in place both could be reached independently. There was no door in the partition, though of course one could always leave it slightly open.'

'I see. So these two doors led into the right-hand corridor, which in turn led down to the back porch and the back door.' He nods. 'So, according to you, it would be possible to go down the stairs, into the hall, through to the kitchen, turn into the back porch, walk past the back door . . .'

'. . . and the cupboard under the stairs,' he adds, catching my drift.

'. . . walk past the back door *and* the cupboard under the stairs, turn right, open the door and walk up the right-hand corridor back into the hall . . .'

'. . . and up the stairs,' he adds triumphantly. 'I had two ways of getting out the back. Through the kitchen or through the back corridor.'

'But there was still the upstairs landing. You still had to go past your sister's room. And what if the kitchen *and* living room were busy, particularly the *back* half. Surely it was quite dangerous for you then?'

He grins and agrees. It was quite dangerous sometimes. That only made it all the more fun, creeping down the stairs, listening intently, bolting back upstairs at the slightest sound.

'Of course,' he says, taking me into his confidence, 'coming back was much more dangerous than going out, for you had no idea what had been going on in the meantime. Sometimes it was quite impossible to use either way. That's when the third way came in handy.'

'The third way?'

He has a delightful smile this boy. He has been told this many times (he will find this useful later on) and now he uses it to full effect. It is gloriously mischievous.

'*The bay window,*' he says. 'The dining-room bay window. On to the windowsill, foot on the drainpipe, up on to the flat bay roof and through to the spare room. Six quick steps and I was back in my room. And remember I could always get out that way too. Only I didn't climb down. I jumped.'

The boy is pleased by these revelations, but they do not satisfy me. It is the act of leaving, of escaping which he dwells upon. Once inside the house, he's jumping out of it, once outside he's sneaking back in. I light a cigarette and blow the smoke carefully around the room. He looks as if he would enjoy one too, as if he is a practised and serious smoker. If we climbed upstairs and searched his room or, more probably, if we examined one of the sheds or lean-tos in the garden, I am confident that we would find a packet or two, alongside the money he has stolen from his father's trouser pockets. But I am not interested in which brand he favours or how much he has managed to lift from his slumbering dad.

'I am pleased to know the layout,' I tell him. 'The layout gave you the *means*. But I would like to know more about the interior, *the rooms*. The rooms propelled you did they not? The layout provided you with the opportunities, but the rooms furnished you with the desire. You could have done no less, faced with rooms such as those.'

'You are forgetting the Flying Boats,' he reminds me. 'I would not have gone out, were it not for them.'

I lift my finger to my lip. I could grow fond of this boy.

'Shh!' I admonish him. 'We will speak of the Flying Boats later. But not now. Their time has not come. They will hold the stage soon enough, but not now. Speak to me now of those rooms, of the rooms you grew up in. Speak to me of their quality, of their proportions, of the light that filled them, of the memories they contain.'

The boy is about to begin.

'Do not tell me lies,' I warn him, 'for I know this house. Your house had secrets. Your house told lies. Your house was redecorated once a year *and nothing changed*. So do not tell me of the dog's basket and the friendly Aga in the kitchen. Do not tell me of the mutton stews and piping waffles your mother would make, do not tell me of Sunday lunch and parlour games and chestnuts in the fire at Christmastime. I am immune to such deceptions. I do not even want to know of the pretty lampshades that adorned your sister's room, or of the patterned shawls she would find at jumble sales to drape over her bed. Your sister's room had nothing to do with the rest of the house. They had long been estranged. Your sister's room was a museum to her future life, a life of dead, pressed things. Tell me of the other rooms, of the kitchen, and the living room, and the hall.'

He looks at me in surprise.

'*The Hall.*'

The boy begins, 'The Hall is where the coats are hung and where the doors open, the doors I have already mentioned, the front door and the dining-room door, the doors to the living room and the doors to the kitchen and lavatory. The Hall is our favourite room, the room to which we all aspire, for within it there is no place to rest. We can only pass each other by. We are a house of doors and we love them all, but it is only in this room that they are set before us like immovable sentries faultlessly on parade. We stand before them and inspect them. We bend down to find a flaw in their facade, but these doors, so tall, so sturdy, never give ground. At night voices carry through the Hall from one room to another. The Hall distributes them and we lie awake listening to its orchestration, the stumbling footsteps, the clatter of plates, the sudden splutter of language. We hear low voices, sudden laughter, we await the false dawn of the television. Music comes up from the Hall, empty chords played upon an empty piano, snatches of broken songs siphoned off from where Father sings them in the darkened garage. *Sitz' ich allein, wo kann ich besser sein? Wo kann ich besser sein?* or, for levity's sake dance music from the overweight radiogram that hides in the recess on the other side of the fireplace. Our Hall pulses with life and yet no one is ever there. It is the centre of our home, its dynamo. It is empty and raining and dark. There is nothing in the Hall but a brass bowl upon a rickety table and whether it be day or night the bowl lights up the Hall with its dull glow. Sometimes, when I am passing, I tap the bowl lightly with my fingertips so that it sends a long low note humming through the house, turning our home into a temple, and our Hall its sounding bell. We worship in the Hall. When any of us are alone in the house it is only a matter of time before we are drawn towards the Hall, to fall down on our knees in its sanctified air. When we are together we take turns to look down upon the Hall, to pop our heads round the corner, to check that no one is disturbing the Hall's calm, and when we are outside, there is no greater pleasure than to unlock the front door and stand before it, to see if anything has changed, if anyone is there, but of course there is nothing. Only the Hall and the brass bowl and the sound of a family moving about its precincts.'

'*The Landing.*'

'Is where Father stands looking out over the Medway. He looks out in the evening when he has returned from work and he looks out in the morning before he sets off. At weekends he can be found there at almost any time, at first in his loosely tied dressing-gown, later with his hands folded into one of his pale, afternoon cardigans, and at night holding on to the curtains, after a few hours down the road. He stares out across the river and feels it lapping at his lungs. He breathes slowly as the waters fill his heart.

71

'Father is a flooded man and his mouth leaks his cold past. He lives alone in the small box-room and he drinks alone there too, little bottles of green and little bottles of brown. His legs are thin, his legs are cold. His lips are thin, his lips are cold. Father has a voice and it is flooded too. It speaks a slurred and forgotten tongue.

'Years ago, in this same house, on this same Landing, Father spoke differently. He was sharp then, quick witted. Years ago Father did not live in the box-room, nor did he sing in the darkened garage. Years ago Father drove around the town in his brand new Wolsey, the cock of the walk, his window rolled down, his elbow sticking out, a cigarette dangling in his hand. Father had a home then, but it was not here on the Landing, or even down there in the Hall, but across the water, on the Esplanade. Father found life on the Esplanade, and lived it there with all the other fathers, like Fat Patrick's.

'Fat Patrick's father was a practical man, fit for dreaming. He had a full awkward body, good for nothing Father would say later, topped with a restless mind. The interiors of the Empires were his creation. He would take his plans, drawn in the suspended hours of the night and take them to Father. "Here is my seat," he would say, "here's where I'll stretch my legs and look out of the window. You see if I don't. You might be paying me now, but when this is done, I'm going up there. You see if I don't." And Father would put a cold arm across his back. "Just see you don't put too many springs in them," he would tell him. "Too many springs and you'll find yourself in dreamland. We want these plane and we want your eyes upon them, but we want your feet on the ground." He would put his lips to Fat Patrick's father's ear. "They're going to be good planes all right, make no mistake about that, but in my opinion, and I only do the bloody sums around here, these planes are a luxury only the English would want to afford. Herr Hitler is building cars for everyone. He calls them *Volks Wagens*. We build planes for the few. They're grand planes all right, but some of us think they might be a bit *too* grand. The government likes them, the Royal Mail likes them, Imperial Airways likes them, *everybody* likes them. The trouble is, what happens when the Royal Mail finds something cheaper, or faster, or no one writes letters anymore? The simple fact is," Father would tell him, "that I just don't like water. You can't get hold of water. Water runs away. Dry land is what I like. You can't control water the way you can land." And Fat Patrick's father looks at him strangely and says, "I want to fly in her. It means more to me than anything. I would sell the house to fly in her. I'd live in her if I could. I'd even bloody die in her." Fat Patrick's father walks away and watches them being built. He works and dreams and sees them fly. He watches them crated up for assembly abroad and wishes himself a mechanic by some other water. He travels to Southampton and wishes himself a steward or cook. He sits in the Departure lounge and watches the passengers disembark from the long and stately Daimler coach. He sits by the Medway and waits for their return.

'Father climbs the stairs and looks down upon the water. He looks down upon Rochester and there is malice in his heart. He sees a slipway which is too small, he sees sheds which are wrongly placed, bridges which should not be there. Even the water is suspect. There is not enough! An outdated world! He looks upon Fat Patrick's father, sitting by the river, as slow as his machine, as sluggish as the water, as narrow as the paths between the sheds. "Get out now!" says Father. "Start afresh! Go to where you can have more space, where you can teach new dogs new tricks! Go where there's water if you like, but go! Forget the Flying Boats and Rochester! Get out now!"

'So they get out, and in the getting they leave not only Fat Patrick's father and all the other fathers, but mine too. They leave Father with a part-time consultancy and a place at the Long Service Dinner, held in January 1948 in the Masonic Lodge in Chatham. The planes are gone. The *Cairo*, withdrawn from service the year before. Gone! The *Cleopatra*, parcelled off to the breakers' yard. Gone! The *Centurion*, stalled while setting down in Calcutta, the *Connemara* burned to death while re-fuelling in Hythe. Gone! Gone! The *Challenger*. The *Corsair*. The *Ceres*! Gone! Gone! Gone!

'Father climbs the stairs and looks down upon the water. He dresses for Dinner. Down at the Lodge the toasts are made. To the King! To the Queen! To the salvation of the nation! To the prosperity of the town! To the future! On every table, carved in ice, there is a replica of one of the planes. By the end of the evening they will all resemble the same form, a muted, embryonic plane, the shape of what a plane, growing in the womb of this town, might have been, but when the men first sit down, they are cold and chiselled, with shining lines of a deep and dazzling blue. Wondrous icebergs! On Father's table sits Fat Patrick's father, Jim Liddle. Between them stands the first of all the Flying Boats, the *Canopus*.

' "That was your favourite was it not Jim?" he says. "You should have grabbed it when you had the chance. Taken it out to Egypt and buried it in the sand. You won't see it now. You should have flown it down to Australia and watched the Abboes hop around. Gone to Durban to strut amongst the kaffirs."

'And here Father leans over and whispers into Jim Liddle's ear. He laughs and Jim Liddle looks at him and tells him not to talk like that, how *dare* he talk like that, and Fat Patrick's father jumps up and grabs hold of the *Canopus* and presses it to his lips. He kisses it! He bites it! There are tears in his eyes! Fat Patrick's father is crying, sobbing, breaking the wings off this lovely creature. He kisses it again! He bites it again! He rubs it against his cheek. He carries it to the centre of the room, stroking it, talking to it as if it were a wounded bird. He runs his hands down its spine. He holds it aloft, kisses it once more and dashes it to the floor.

'Father climbs the stairs and looks down upon the water. It is here where he will end his days, standing on the Landing, looking out upon the *Durban*, the *Kalakala* and the *Galway Bay*. It is not his wish to be alone, but now he is as abandoned as they are. But how beautiful they were, and how mean his spirit. Yet they were loved and he is not. And in my imagination this is the moment when I am made, when Mother is pulled awake, when Father falls on top of her, his heart bitter, his thoughts raging with pity, and with his secret whisper to Jim Liddle still fresh on his tongue.

'All these things have I learnt on the Landing. It is where I hear of my history.'

'*The Living Room.*'

'Is where Mother stays. The front half is cheerful. There is a gas fire burning, there is a comfortable sofa, and along the windowsill of the bay window are her pots of *Cyclamen mirabile*, with their pale pink flowers and purple-stained mouths. The closer you get to the back of the room, where the unloved piano stands, the bleaker the room becomes, for outside the french windows, which open on to the back garden, stands my brother's climbing frame, a grey and lonely structure which drains the room of much of its warmth and comfort. It is on this climbing frame that he broke and lost his front teeth, and it is from here that he jumped that day and sauntered down to the river. Lately Mother has taken to the climbing frame herself. For the first week or so she perched awkwardly on the top rung, unsure of what to do next, looking like some strange bird blown off course, waiting to regain its strength. But gradually she has learnt to use its many hoops and rungs and ropes and now spends many hours there, swinging from hand to hand, hanging upside-down like a monkey, pulling herself up and slowly somersaulting through the afternoon. She grows fitter and more agile every day. I sometimes feel that if she could, she would never come inside again, that she would leave the house to us and spend the rest of her days vaulting effortlessly from bar to bar, preparing for the time when she will stretch out and leap off into the air, to fly up into the clouds and, like a fabled albatross, never set foot on this land again.'

'*Your Room.*'

'Is where I practise the art of not remembering. Learning this skill is the most crucial task a young boy faces, and to begin with it is best done in the privacy of one's own room. On shutting the door, and after insisting that disturbances are kept to a minimum, you first sit on the edge of your bed, or any other uncomfortable surface, and one by one erase all foolish or fond memory that ticks away in your head. By *erase* what I mean is the process by which you keep it there in endless tableaux, but give it no colour, no shading. Only form. The form must be exact. Every detail is to be learnt, but *nothing* remembered, for memory plays tricks on you, and you are the conjuror now. Near your room will be the bathroom, and it is here, where the mirror hangs, where you discover what a perfect liar the face can be, and what strangers we all are to our own. A boy concerned, a boy contrite – it is but the flick of a muscle. And what a lovely smile still hangs there when you have long closed the door.'

'And which of these', I ask him, 'was the most important room? Your bedroom no doubt.'

He shakes his head.

'Oh no. Strategically, the most important room was not a room at all, but a cupboard. *The cupboard under the stairs.*'

'How so, this cupboard?'

'I could hide in the cupboard. When I came back, if I had to, I could hide in it. It would keep me hidden until it was safe to go upstairs.'

There is something peculiar about this. Keep him safe? Safe from what?

'I do not fully understand,' I say. 'Why would you wish to hide?'

The boy looks at me in exasperation, as if I haven't been paying attention.

'Because I might be seen in the kitchen coming back, or seen in the Hall. I had to be certain that the coast was clear before I chose my route. I didn't want to be caught out.'

'But caught out doing what? You are in your own house. True it is late at night, and perhaps you should be in your bedroom, but you are a boy of sixteen are you not? It is not unusual for a boy of sixteen or thereabouts to be seen about the house late at night is it? Even if it were midnight, it would not be a crime. If no one had heard you go out, what could they possibly infer once you were back in?'

He thinks for a moment.

'One would not normally approach the kitchen from the right-hand corridor. It would appear that I had arrived from the outside.'

'But you could run into the Hall and in an instant be at one of two, three doors. Who could tell then where you came from? And why would anyone ask such a question? Why would they be so suspicious?'

He thinks again. He does not like these questions, this boy. There is something about them which unsettles him.

'They would be if I was wet, or had grass on my feet,' he says.

'Then they'd know. Then they'd know I'd been outside.'

'True,' I agreed. 'But then it was not always raining was it?'

'And I did not always use the cupboard under the stairs,' he retorts.

I fall silent for a moment. I am tired of following this boy, of watching him run from one foxhole to another, crouching in every nook and cranny that takes his fancy. It is time I took a hold of this boy's ear and led him.

'Let us imagine,' I say to him, 'that this house of yours, with its doors and drainpipes and routes of escape is also your home, where you live, where you find comfort and security. Let us imagine that in an hour or two you will be walking back to your home, perhaps with Fat Patrick in attendance. The two of you may even decide to walk along the river path, even though the school and your parents forbid it. It will give you an opportunity to look at the Flying Boats and talk about them. Fat Patrick is so very knowledgeable about them, and though you take care not to show it you are envious of Fat Patrick having a father who was so close to them, who so obviously loved them, loves them still, who is so proud of them and his association with them. You wish your father had an Imperial Airways cap, and a Flying Boat paperweight, and pens and pencils and postcards and a thousand other mementoes. But he has not. You wish too that sometimes Father was not your best friend, that he didn't like the Flying Boats so much, that he didn't know so much, that you could do something to him that would make him never talk to you again. You know that there is something wrong with Fat Patrick's father, just like there is probably something wrong with Fat Patrick and though you do not take part yourself (for you too are not a very popular boy) you are secretly delighted that Fat Patrick is so very thoroughly punished by the other boys for being so overweight and for having such a dad. One of the things that annoys you most about Fat Patrick is that he does not seem ashamed of his father, who does no work and has been "ill" for as long as you can remember. You have heard your father talk of Jim Liddle in the most contemptuous of tones, and of Fat Patrick's mother too, who he once described as "not only vacant upstairs but more than ready to take in lodgers in the basement", a remark which drove your Mother into an inexplicable rage, accusing him of indulging in filthy bar-room talk of the most obnoxious kind, beer-induced speculations with not the slightest grain of truth in them. You have speculated on the nature of Jim Liddle and Mrs Liddle and Fat Patrick yourself. How is it that such a beautiful woman (for you can distinguish beauty now) could produce such an ugly and ungainly child? And what could have attracted her to Mr Liddle in the first place? You have tried to imagine him as he must have been, as the photographs on the mantelpiece and in Fat Patrick's bedroom demonstrate he was, but it is hard when all you see is a man who spends all day at home in a pullover and a pair of loose grey flannel trousers and who has been known to drive around town in his dressing-gown. If you were Fat Patrick you would *never* bring anyone home. It would be bad enough having to come to school every day knowing that everyone knew of your father's strange behaviour, that the whole town referred to him as "poor Jim Liddle", without putting the evidence out on display. Like most of your contemporaries you are well versed in the sad tale of Jim Liddle, and your father, who was one of the principal witnesses, not to say participants, relishes his history and loses no opportunity in telling it to whosoever he can. Indeed, this very winter past, although the tale is almost as cold and sad as the Flying Boats out on the water, it seemed your father did very little else but hop from one Liddle indiscretion to another, barely concealing his delight over his former colleague's misfortune. That Boxing Day for instance, the day when Stella first took any notice of you, any real grown-up notice that is, your father entertained the company with a whole string of Liddle follies, starting with his embarrassing outburst at the Long Service Dinner and ending with the extraordinary episode some two years back when, under cover of darkness, he swam out to the best preserved of them all, the *Galway Bay* and hid in the cockpit for five days before the police came and hauled him off and sent him to the sanatorium. On this point your father claims to have played a major part in his rescue, insisting that it was while he was looking at the Flying Boats one evening (from the *Landing*), he suddenly thought that *that* was where old Jim Liddle could be found, not floating face down three miles out to sea, or working his passage on some passing tramp steamer, but scuttling about out there, catching his death amongst the cold wet rust of his beloved craft. The more he looked, your father said, the more he became convinced that he could practically *see* Jim Liddle, staring out across the darkened water to the twinkling town ashore. You are not sure whether you believe your father (which is nothing new. You don't *believe* anybody), whether he really did ring up the police and put them on the right track, as he would have everyone think, or whether this angle to the story is just another manifestation of your father's eagerness to take part in Jim Liddle's deterioration. You know that in the early days he played a part in his downfall, you know that your father and Jim Liddle had a falling out and you know that your father does not approve of your friendship with his son, (which is one of the reasons, one of the *principal* reasons, why you go to such pains to maintain it, despite your occasional lapses into a certain wilful meanness of spirit). You also know, and you can remember this quite clearly, that when Fat Patrick's father came back from the sanatorium, some eighteen months ago, he was a changed man. He was, in a word, *happier*. Unlike your own father and Fat Patrick, Jim Liddle has always welcomed you into his home (though it is clear he has never liked your father, more significantly perhaps that he has never trusted him) ever since you were a small boy, but since his return there has been a sort of bustling contentment to the man where previously there had been an unsettling emptiness. In fact, contrary to all expectations (and contrary to the several untruths you tell at school) Fat Patrick's home seems a rather pleasant environment (though you know it has no right to be), the incongruity of Mrs Liddle's misplaced good looks set against her husband's weak and aimless life notwithstanding. Even though Mrs Liddle is forced to go out and earn a living teaching at the local infant school and Mr Liddle spends most of his time cooking, emerging from the kitchen with kedgerees and curries and freshly baked bread, in a peculiar sort of way (and this unsettles you the most) it seems almost a *normal* sort of household, one where you can feel at home, although it is like no other you have ever known. Certainly with its strange taste in music, its bulging collections of souvenirs, plates and trophies, its propensity for bright chatter and, in Mrs Liddle's case exotic clothes, it is not at all like your own, nor indeed, from what Stella has told you (and she is telling you more and more these days) is it like the Muchmore's across the road. Your father does not sit around all day doing nothing, poring over plans of obsolete aircraft, nor have you ever seen him wearing an apron (you have never seen your mother wear an apron come to that), nor has Stella ever suffered the humiliation of having her father drive her to school in his pajamas (she gags at the very thought. How you both laugh!). Nevertheless, the apparent harmony which seems to be part and parcel of Fat Patrick's home annoys and angers you, much in the same way as your father is annoyed and angered by the sight of Mr and Mrs Liddle together. If you kept a diary (which you do not, for you are a sensible boy and you know that an honest diary would only betray you) you would find, on turning back its pages, that the times when you are cruellest to Fat Patrick, when your heart is seized by a cold fury at his very being, when your only wish is to hurt him, come immediately after your happiest hours with him, when you have bathed in the comfort and pleasure of his home. It is your reward for having to suffer so, and like you, he has come to expect it. You have performed many acts of unkindness over the years, for which you are duly ashamed, and to which neither of you refer, though there is one which haunts you, for its living reminder is with you every day. But that episode took place some years ago and for the moment you bear no grudge against your friend. Indeed his importance is receding. Though you will walk back from school with him later this afternoon, maybe even sit upon your precious pillbox and smoke a cigarette or two, the Flying Boats, and his obsession with them (very different in substance, you will agree from your *own* obsession with them) do not hold quite the same attraction as they did – or rather, more particularly, the Flying Boats cast a different spell over you now, a brooding spell, a spell of ropes, of bursting free, of secret things lapping steadily at your feet. The Flying Boats know you in a way that nothing else does, except perhaps Stella.'

The boy looks at me quickly, but I do not give him the opportunity to question my luck.

'This winter,' I continue, 'a passing time now, but no less potent for that, this winter has been the season of Stella

Muchmore, and it is she, is it not, who has impinged upon your lonely life and brought to those boats out there a new, dangerous beauty? You still sneak out at night, you still shin down the drainpipe or open the back door on to that dark solitary universe, but now, at least on some occasions, on orchestrated occasions, you land upon a terrain where another soul roams. There are times to be sure, the normal times, when you leave with her to go to parties or set out to join others at the cinema or the detestable bowling alley, but there are other times, which you still refer to as the Flying Boat Hours, which are no longer yours alone, and in which the risk of being caught has been heightened. You like the risk of being caught and to your fear and delight you have been introduced to someone who shares your passion. The detective who will interview you some months hence, when the name of Stella Muchmore is to give title to the lurking dread of every mother and father, will sense in you the need of a boy who wishes to be under suspicion, but will be unable to find out what it is you are hiding. Try as he might he will not be able to catch you out, and both of you will lie awake at night running through the day's interrogation, you delighting in your intransigence and evasive skill, he looking for the loose thread which might unravel your equilibrium. He is not a fool this detective, indeed you will come to regard him with an odd degree of affection, but though he can see quite plainly that you are a quick-witted boy, and thus perfectly equipped to pull the wool over his eyes, for a time at least, he cannot begin to guess the depths of your duplicity, the ease with which you lie, the maturity of your solitude. The long hours you will spend in the interrogation room, facing an empty table, a bare notepad and the florid features of Detective Sergeant Weatherspoon leave you quite unmoved, for you quickly discover, to your inner joy, that he, like everyone else you know, has not an inkling of who you are. There will be nothing to fear, only a momentary panic halfway through, when he will ask you, almost as an aside (though you are well aware of *that* particular little trick) how "well" you do at school, when you recall, while feigning the stumbling, frightened innocence that has been your trademark, with horrible clarity that damned exam paper that could expose you for the treacherous child you are. In later years you will recall too the words that Detective Sergeant Weatherspoon left you with, that though he does not believe you are a guilty boy, neither does he believe you to be an innocent one and that he knows in his heart "that one day you will come to me and tell me what you know, for though you do not know it now, you are too young a creature to keep silent forever" (and you went out *that* night didn't you), and you will hear also the intriguing rumour that Detective Sergeant Weatherspoon, now retired, returns every year to that pillbox where they found Stella's abandoned raincoat, and sits, as you used to sit, on its grey uncomfortable surface, looking out over that empty stretch of grey water, imagining the hour in which Stella Muchmore vanished. You will, in the early years, be worried that you might talk in your sleep, crying out this, and, God-forbid, other secrets, but on reflection you will recognize that even if this were the case, there would be no one there to hear, not your father, heavy with drink, sleeping in the cold dining room or singing grotesque love songs in the back of his Wolsey, not your mother, looking intently at the overgrown garden where your brother used to play, and where his climbing-frame and swing still stand (and which of course you have laughingly used yourself over the years), and certainly not your sister, who has no interest in you, much in the same way that you have no interest in her. Like you your sister has no friends to speak of, but unlike you, this isolation causes her some distress. One of the things you liked about Stella (a very minor attraction it must be said) was the way that she, a supposed friend of Carol's, took every opportunity to belittle her, scornful of her dreary looks, her thin talk, her ungainly walk, her tears, her ugly mouth, her general weakness. Not in fact an accurate appraisal of Carol's character at all as it turned out, but music to your ears. "What's the point of her?" Stella would ask. What's the point of her indeed. What was the point of anyone, Father, Mother, Dead Brother, even, as it turned out Stella herself? There was no point to your family, no point to the Muchmore's. This is the point that Detective Sergeant Weatherspoon will fail to grasp, that there is nothing within you to unsettle, *apart from the danger of being caught*. It is the house that has made you this strong. It is the house you have to thank for these gifts. You are its most sympathetic occupant and though it cannot offer you happiness or even comfort, it is the house which has brought you up, cared for you, sheltered you from the storm. It offers you a security, an understanding, which nothing else has ever come close to.

'So, to return to my original request, let us imagine that in an hour or so you will return to Gladstone Drive, via the towpath and in the company of your fat friend. Let us imagine too that before you enter your real world, a world which exists only when you close the front door and mount the stairs to your bedroom, there is, in front of you, a schoolboy task for you to perform. This is the Easter term, the closing week of it, and this afternoon you have set before you on your desk, an end-of-term exam, English Composition. Although you are an accomplished cheat and take pride in this ability (you would rather cheat than learn, even though your memory is perfectly good), this is not an exam which lends itself to such talent. Even so, there is no cause for alarm and you regard the back of the paper with equanimity. However, unfortunately, and in the circumstances understandably, you are not equipped to give this matter your full attention. Your mind is on other matters, matters which whirl and reel in your head, the warmth of the sun outside, the twisting craft on the river, the dark lapping water, the dark pillbox in the dark of night, the moon and Stella Muchmore, even, dare I say it, the fir trees which line the Muchmore's garden; in other words, a world stripped of your school uniform, a world waiting outside. As you turn the paper and read the instructions and act upon them accordingly, it is as if you do not notice what you are writing. It is the diary you have never written, the words you have never spoken. For the first and last time you drop your guard. Later on, when Detective Sergeant Weatherspoon asks that little question, "How well do you do at school?" you will realize how lucky you are that he has not thought to investigate your background more thoroughly before warning you of the danger, luckier still that your insipid, hairless English teacher, for whom you have the greatest contempt but on whom you practise your most potent charm has not seen fit to hand it over to him, for it will be known to all, in the days after her disappearance, that you are a prime suspect. For two days after his quiet aside, and to which you answered truthfully, with your heart careering inside, that English and Physics were your best subjects, you lie in your bedroom, your hands behind your head contemplating the best course of action, whether it would be best to leave it alone, to treat Detective Sergeant Weatherspoon's remark as wholly innocent, or whether, unwittingly he has revealed to you a fatal weakness in your defence which you would be idiotic to ignore. Naturally you look to your house for guidance, for it has always supported you in your endeavours, and this time, as always, it is emphatic in its conclusion. Thus it is, two weeks after Stella Muchmore disappeared, while you are under grave suspicion, while the forensic team is examining her raincoat, as the police scythe down the allotment once more and crawl over it on their hands and knees, while they move from house to house asking their fruitless questions armed with an unlikely school photograph that suggests nothing of her personality, you act decisively and boldly. You have lost none of your skill, none of your nerve, although to be sure the circumstances are different. As usual you announced your retirement for the night at about nine thirty, and as usual, as soon as you have closed your bedroom door you prepare yourself for your forthcoming excursion. A black polo neck sweater, an unpleasant present from Carol, your father's driving gloves (which he believes he lost six months ago), an old pair of corduroy trousers and a battered pair of gym shoes which you plan to place on the feet of Poker Fisher's Guy Fawkes and watch them burn the following night. How fortune has marked your card! You wait two hours, until all the rooms are occupied and all the doors are closed. Then quickly, without hesitation, you open your door, close it again with infinite patience and move across to the spare bedroom. In a moment you have closed that door too and you stand for a minute, looking out of the window, listening to the sounds of the house before committing yourself. The window opens easily. You lower yourself on to the bay-window roof and then jump down on to the garden below. There is a light snow upon the ground. The air is cold, very different from two weeks back when the nights were unseasonally warm. You had planned to go out of the back garden and down along the towpath but reason tells you that though there might be fewer people there at this time of night, there are also fewer places to hide, whereas the streets and alleyways leading to the school are replete with drives and hedges and parked cars. Gladstone Drive is white and still and you feel perfectly safe. Instead of hugging the pavement, instead of darting from one safe haven to another you walk down its very centre, revelling in memory. You pass bedroom windows where you know Jack Grey and Henry Deering and Nigel Cramphorn are sleeping, or perhaps listening to Radio Luxembourg under the bedclothes. If only someone were watching you, if only . . . Leaving Gladstone Drive you quicken your pace into a light trot, down The Lees, crossing Harbour Road, moving down towards the centre of town and the school. Now you are not so certain of your plan, for the nearer you get to the centre and your destination, the more difficulties you encounter. There are people abroad at this time of night, more than you expected. There are pockets of young men, drunk, unpredictable, looking for something to do, a brick to throw, a dog to kick, a boy to bash. The traffic is heavy and slow and the lights are brighter here than you ever imagined. You have no idea who might be lurking in such a vehicle, driving back late at night from work or a party – a schoolmaster, a parent, *Sergeant Weatherspoon*. Worse still are the couples, often secreted in the very places you choose to duck down into. In one particularly nerve-racking episode you dive into a side alley in order to avoid one oncoming pair only to find that they have followed you in there and seem in no hurry to leave. As you crouch behind a dustbin at the far end you are horrified to discover that the girl pushing herself so articulately against the wall is none other than Fat Patrick's beautiful elder sister, who is rarely seen in Rochester these days (she left home the same time as her father was introduced to the sanatorium) but who knows you only too well. You have no idea who the man is but you sense from his build and the tone of his voice that he is an older man, perhaps someone who you know. You daren't look too closely but neither can you hide completely, only watch and listen as Fat Patrick's beautiful elder sister lifts her sweater to her chin. The talk is quick and hurried and drunk. He pushes himself against her, she pushes back. Of course he is pleased to see her, can't she tell, he wasn't expecting her that's all, he's missed her so much, he wants to make love now, he's practically coming in his trousers, why don't we make love now, standing up, we haven't made love for such a long time, your nipples are so hard, no wonder they're hard, they're fucking freezing, I'm hardly wearing anything, a bit different now, a bit different from my school uniform, oh I don't know I rather liked your uniform, rather liked getting it off you mean, not always, I didn't always take it off, no and you bloody should have done, all down my front it was the first time, I'll catch my fucking death like this, why couldn't we have used your bloody car, looked all right to me, yes, well I know a jolly good way to warm you up, not here you don't, not in the bloody High Street for Christ's sake, oh that's nice, oh that's lovely, can you feel how wet I am, God if only mum had gone out too we could have had the place to ourselves, come here, *kiss me*, oh, if only mum had gone out you could have sneaked in and we could have done it in front of the fire, fucked and fucked and fucked, getting your baby brother out of the way first I think, that wouldn't have been a problem, not for an hour or so, *fucked and fucked and fucked* George, God it's been so long, and when they got back I'd be sitting there all prim and proper, watching "Come Dancing" or something, having fucked and fucked and fucked all evening, *very* discreet, that would really further my career, *no* George, not here, I know, have you got any matches, *matches*? what do we need matches for? matches, a lighter, *anything* . . . great, I know where we can go, no one will be there at this time of night, especially not now, kiss me again, oh Julia, oh Julia, it's so wonderful to see you again, I love your breasts, just one more kiss, that's enough, you can kiss them in a minute, come on, let's get out of this wind and have some of that whisky, and they leave, Julia's breasts momentarily returned to the warmth and comfort of her brassière, the alleyway still now, their footsteps fading. For a moment you cannot move. You have been distracted from your course. You have seen Fat Patrick's beautiful elder sister's breasts, you have seen Fat Patrick's beautiful elder sister lift up her sweater and brassière so that she might expose her breasts to someone who is vaguely familiar to you, so that he may hold them and run his hands over them and tell her how beautiful they are. You have seen this older man bend down and apply his lips to each one in turn, you have seen him *smother* them in kisses, before Fat

Patrick's beautiful elder sister pulled his head away and returned them from where they came, leading him out of the alleyway to somewhere more to their liking. You watch them now, hurrying down the High Street, the wind, which had not been there when you started out, blowing at her skirt, the two of them, like you, avoiding car lights and other nocturnal intruders. You wonder where they might have come from, wondering like her why she is not demonstrating the beauty of her breasts and the hardness of her nipples in the comfort of his car, and you are tempted to follow them, perhaps run ahead of them to catch the face of the older man who is vaguely familiar to you in the glare of the fluorescent street lamps and discover their secret, for you know a secret when you see one, and you have seen one tonight, brought out and stroked and made hard and stiff in the safety of the dark. But you do not follow them. You watch them turn the corner, and then you too turn, and continue your journey. It is not far now to the school, to the second-floor window you jammed shut with a wad of paper this afternoon while at art class. Although the ledge and the pipe and the lip of the metal window are cold and slippery thanks to the unexpected snow, there is enough light in the air for you to see what you are doing and you do not need your torch, your companion on so many other occasions, until you have climbed up, prised open the window and dropped down on to the floor. Suddenly you are terrified. There is no one else here, of that you are sure, but you are terrified. You have spent the last six years of your life in this building, there is not a classroom you do not know, a study you have not entered, but now the very walls seem bent upon your destruction. You move forwards carefully, shining your torch down just ahead of your feet and immediately your elbow catches something and sends it careering across the floor. It is almost human the way it totters and slips and bangs into desks and chairs. An easel, a fucking easel with paints and brushes and drawing pins spilling out of its guts. It crashes to the ground, pencils and charcoal scattering before it. They roll away in the spotlight of your beam. You snap the torch off and stand perfectly still. Gradually the room grows lighter and your ears begin to pick up on sounds you have not heard before, the thin hiss of a radiator valve, the drip of a nearby tap, the chime of the school clock sounding clear over the square, half past twelve already. You move across to the dais and place your gym shoes on the art master's desk, where you know you will find them on your return. In your stockinged feet you pass through the doorway and down the stairs, into the long corridor that turns at right angles some eighty feet ahead of you and which will take you to your destination. You pass your classroom, the room you were in the year before and the room you were in the year before that. You pass the noticeboard and the entrance to the main hall and the master's common-room, down to where the studies are: Mr Cooper's, Mr Lee's, Miss Taylor's, Mrs Bradshaw's, *Mr Cooper's*. As you expected it is not locked, though you were quite prepared to kick the flimsy door open if it were, to play vandal instead of thief, but no, it opens, revealing the pitiful domain of the senior English master in all its empty banality; the cheap desk, the uncomfortable armchair, the motley collection of stained mugs and half-used coffee jars. For a second you are tempted. How wonderful it would be to play the hooligan, to hurt and wound this puzzled man, to tear up the picture of his wife and daughter he so coyly parades on the desk and leave an enormous turd smack in the middle of it all, the torn features of his family stuck strategically in place. It is but a passing thought. Quickly you move across to the filing cabinet, Form 3A, Form 3B, Lower Sixth, Upper Sixth. Why can't he give essays back like any normal master you don't know, but no, it is always, May I keep this one Doughty for my little library, or I hope you don't mind but I have decided to keep your last effort for future reference. Well not this one he wouldn't. It didn't take you long to find, four pages, your hand-writing getting progressively worse as usual. You pull it out and push the cabinet shut. You sit for a moment on the edge of Mr Cooper's cheap desk scanning the pages. You were right. You should never have written it. You were a bloody fool. What were you thinking of? (You can remember only too well.) Even he found it odd. What was it he had written, ah yes, "Not quite what the doctor ordered but it does show your imagination at work. To be on the safe side in future I would stick a little more to the question if I were you. We're not all free thinkers!" Fatuous idiot. Well, it's in your hands now, safe and sound. You get up to go. As you do you turn towards the window and see to your consternation the caretaker standing in the middle of the square shining what looks to be a portable headlight on the open window as it bangs to and fro in the wind. You can hear him curse, curse the damned kids and that useless poofter and his poor feet. You watch him play his searchlight over the rest of the floor, to see if any other bastard has left a bleeding window open. Only that one. He shines his light upon it again, watching it swing backwards and forwards, like the door of a monstrous cuckoo-clock. Why didn't you shut it properly? How could you be so careless, so stupid. He fumbles in his pockets for his keys. How many times have you seen him do that? A key for the storeroom, a key for the darkroom, a key for the cellars and the cricket pavilion. He has one in his hand now, an enormous brass monstrosity. It glints in the moonlight like some warped Excalibur, a harbinger of your doom. He coughs and moves towards the main door. You have about twenty seconds to run in your stockinged feet, out of the study and down past the studies to the right angle turn. You slide into that, hoping to grab the corner of the noticeboard and swing yourself round, but you lose your grip and crash into the wall. You push with your hands, your feet take grip again, you pick up speed. You can hear him stamp his boots outside, hear him muttering and swearing and blowing on his hands. There is a desperate hope in your mind that the key will jam in the lock, that his hands will be so cold and the lock so stiff that he won't be able to turn it, but as you hear it rattle in the lock, wriggle its way into its obscene fit, you know that's an impossibility, he's always oiling locks and hinges, checking the boiler temperature, the oil gauge on his precious grass mower. Everything always works. You run straight down the centre of the corridor, your essay flapping in the air, your feet pushing desperately against the wooden floor, past the main hall and the classrooms and up the stairs, oh God, up the stairs, your left hand pulling you up and round the landing, up again, up and up, leaping and gasping into the darkness of the Art Room. You can hear the door open now and the hollow sound of his torch on the floor. You are at the desk. You cram on your shoes. Light floods up the stairs making your final journey easier. Keys jangle. Footsteps come slowly forward. No pretence now. No shadow

boxing, no ducking, no diving. Up on to the windowsill, out on to `
the ledge and jump, jump and land, land and steady oneself, grip
the sheaf of paper hard, squeeze it tight and off, across the quad,
pass the science block and down the passage. Who cares about
the footprints or the glimpse of a fleeting body, who cares about
the indignant face surveying the room, it's down the street, and
down the path, and down the narrow steps, one, two, three at a
time and out on to the towpath and the way home. Only then do
you slow down, only then do you hold yourself against the railings
to catch your breath. You're out. You've done it. You hold in your
hand your salvation, your protection. *Nothing* can touch you
now, not Carol, not your mother, not your father, not Sergeant
Weatherspoon or the caretaker, not hairless Mr Cooper or Fat
Patrick's beautiful elder sister, not even Stella. You are alone and
it is your world, your room, your street, your river, your essay.
Although these four sheets of paper could have placed you in the
greatest danger, you are somehow proud of them, proud of what
they made you do. They tested you, they called to you. They said,
come and rescue us, come and take us back, away from the
sycophantic pawings of that hairless stumbling man, away from
the prying eyes of Sergeant Weatherspoon, take us back, reclaim
us, set us free. You were going to destroy them, you were going to
burn them along with your gym shoes in Poker Fisher's Guy
Fawkes bonfire, but you know now you cannot do that. They are
too precious, too much a part of you. You know this is foolish,
you know that you should burn them or tear them up and scatter
them to the wind, but you have gone too far, displayed too much
nerve, too much skill, to play such an ordinary game. You will
take them home to your room and plan what to do with them.
You walk slowly now. You have your breath back. There is no
great hurry. Soon you will reach the pillbox and the allotments
and the mended fence. The wind has dropped slightly, and the
moon is up, shining on the white and speckled path. It is an
illuminated world you are in, a huge reckless world of white
shadows and hidden movements. It is the wind on your face, the
sound of your feet on the snow, the breath that leaves your body
and floats, with the waters of the Medway, out to sea. You look
across the empty river wishing that you could be so flat and so

deep, wishing you could move with such relentless power, that you could be so empty, so calm. *So empty*! You look again. There is nothing there. The Flying Boats are gone! The river flows, the moon shines, the clouds pass. The Flying Boats are gone! There is nothing there. You strain your eyes, looking up and down the river to see if you can catch sight of their shadowy bulk elsewhere, but no. The Flying Boats are gone! Once you get to the pillbox you will be able to stand up and get a better view. You quicken your pace, forgetting for a moment the need for stealth and secrecy. Small wonder. The Flying Boats have gone! As you round the bend though, your pace alters abruptly. There is a sort of flickering glow coming from the pillbox and the sound of voices, low voices, high voices, quick voices, slow voices. You cannot detect any outside movement, no other presence, so you move cautiously forward. The pillbox grows brighter, the voices louder. You move to the very edge of the path, so as to give it as wide a berth as possible, and move right up opposite it. To the right, by the side of the entrance burns a small fire. On the concrete roof, caressed by wisps of smoke stands a bottle, nearly three-quarters empty. The voices are quite clear now in their meaning, sometimes giving explicit instructions, sometimes praising a particular move, sometimes musing on the delights to come. You move forward and peer through the slit eye of war. It is much as you expected. With her legs tucked under her and her elbows resting on the lining of a heavy overcoat, Fat Patrick's beautiful elder sister has once again lifted her sweater and her white patterned brassière to her chin, arranging herself in such a manner to give the older man who is vaguely familiar to you another opportunity to assess her beauty. She has also raised the level of her pleated skirt to her stomach, so that the older man, who is without trousers and underwear, may obtain easy access to her pale brown buttocks which he lifts with such urgency into the air. As he raises them up and down, as he places his lips yet again against one of her unimaginably hard nipples and marks it out of ten for both rigidity and pliancy, as he begins his report of the spotless terrain of her stomach, the dexterity of her hips, her unfathomable capacity for lubrication, etc., etc., you realize that though he is still the pathetic man you have always thought him to be, desperate to please, he is by no means hairless. There is ginger hair on the back of his legs, and some darker material on his back. If only you had a camera, you could take a quick flash of them, develop it at school and slip the result into that precious picture frame of his. That would give him something to think about, a nice little picture of him and Fat Patrick's beautiful elder sister stuck on his desk. Both of them have grown quiet, and although you would like to witness the completion of their endeavours you sense that this is the moment to back off, before they become aware of their surroundings. As you do so, you take with you the near-empty bottle of whisky and settle down behind the thick tangle of briar bushes that form the allotment boundary. They have started up again, but all conversation, all commentary has ceased. Oh George Oh George, Oh Julia Oh Julia, Oh George, Oh Julia, George, Julia, George, George, George. All is quiet again. You unscrew the top to the whisky and drink it in one draught. You have never drunk it before. It feels wonderful. You raise the bottle to catch the few remaining drops. Soon George and Julia emerge, brushing leaves and sweetpapers from their clothing, scuffing the fire out with their shoes. Where's that bloody whisky gone? he asks, looking around, I could do with some right now. Never mind about that, she tells him. Take me home. Mum will have a fit if she catches me out this late. So George George and Julia Julia hurry back up the path to her home. Once again you are alone, once again it is your world. You clamber back out of the allotment and up on to the pillbox. Part of it is quite warm, where the fire has burnt against it. You sit down, your legs hanging over the edge, looking out on to the water. Now you know what to do. There it is in front of you, the River Medway. It has taken your younger brother and it has taken the Flying Boats. Fat Patrick's father lost his mind on this river and most likely Stella Muchmore lies somewhere in its arms. It takes everything from you and yet it is the source of your greatest strength, for unlike the house, which is your other home, it moves and murmurs and lives before your eyes. Now you know what to do with your four-page essay. Now you know where it belongs. Taking it out of your pocket you roll the four pages into a thin cylinder and push them into the warm bottle. Your fingers are cold and it takes you a minute to screw the cap back on properly. There it is. You hold it up to the fearless night, up to the white shadows and the moving moon. Therein lies your curled-up life. Leaning back, you throw the bottle high into the air, out to where it will join the Flying Boats and Stella Muchmore and your dear dead brother. It twists and tumbles in the chill air. Oh that you could reach out and catch it! Oh that it would return to you! But no. It falls into the river and is quickly lost in the gloom. It is done. You are safe now. After standing quite still for a moment you turn and make your way home, back through the cleared allotments, back over the fence, across the lawn and round to the bay window and the bedroom above. Within the minute you are in its protective walls. You look across to the Muchmore house, silent and partly empty. You look over to the solid front door and the blank windows, to the steep concrete drive leading to their garage where you have seen Mr Muchmore struggling with his car, scraping the doors against his wife's beloved rockery, stalling the engine on the impossible incline, hurtling up the ramp in a determined effort to reach his goal. How many times have you seen the whole Muchmore family stretched out along his route. Stella standing aloft beckoning him on, Martha, his wife, heroically placed at the back of the garage, all offering advice to this furious father locked in his bull-nosed Rover. You can hear it now; "Am I straight? Are the wheels in line? Look at the *wheels*!" while they in turn would cajole him with "Forward! Forward! Straighten Up! Straighten Up!" You will never see that pantomime again, never see Stella standing there, her dark skirt and dark eyes and dark hair bent to the task. Stella Muchmore is gone. Perhaps the Flying Boats took her.'

He looks directly at me, something this boy usually avoids. He does not like looking at people, leastways not when they are looking at him.

'Do you think so?' he asks. 'Do you think they really took her?'

'I don't know. *Somebody* took her, don't you think? Or do you suppose she simply sneaked out of the house and vanished into thin air, all of her own accord?'

He shakes his head vigorously. It is as if I have almost insulted him.

'No,' he says. 'She would not have done that. She could have done it, but she would not have done it without . . .'

I smile. '. . . without telling you first?'

'It was something we talked about,' he admits, 'running away, deserting, disappearing without a trace. Most children do.'

I do not deny him the pleasure of this delusion. Most children don't. Even I know this. Some may consider running away, some may threaten to run away, some may even go so far as to tie the knotted handkerchief, but not many talk of disappearing without a trace. I let him continue.

'The Flying Boats taught us, the *Durban*, the *Kalakala*, the *Galway Bay*. They wanted to leave as much as we did, they turned as we did, they tossed as we did, always on the move, never going anywhere. They called to us, you understand, to Stella and me. No one else. Not Father. Not Fat Patrick. Not his daft dad. That's why I spoilt his party piece, not because I was jealous and cruel as you have said, but because it was all wrong. He was so pleased with them, so grateful to them. He acted as if they belonged to him . . .'

His voice trails off. He is quite wrong about this of course. He spoilt Fat Patrick's party piece because he *is* a cruel and jealous boy.

'Remind me,' I ask him, 'of Fat Patrick's party piece, the one which demanded such cruel and jealous behaviour. Remind me, before we return to Stella.'

The boy sits forward, quite willing. He is in full flood now.

'You know,' he says. 'You must remember them, those cigarette cards of his. Ogdens Birds Eggs of 1908 with their wistful red and green colouring, W.H. Wills Fish and Bait Collection; Strange Craft; Railway Engines of the World, and above all others . . .'

'. . . above all others, the Ardath Flying Boat of 1938 . . .'

'. . . a set of forty-eight cards, which when assembled depicted a complete vessel, cut open in a cream and brown cross-section flying against a sea of bright blue and a sky of green.'

Ah yes. I remember. The Ardath Tobacco Company, manufacturers of State Express and Ardath cigarettes and their bewitching set of cards, made all the more wondrous by Fat Patrick's own performance. I can see him now clearing his desk and putting a schoolbook underneath it to make it flat. Smoothing out a sheet of white paper (for desks are grubby things and have grubby things upon them) he would take out the pack of cards from his satchel, remove the rubber band (it was the only collection that lived *outside* the album) and deal them out, supposedly at random, one here, one there, looking at each one and placing it on its unmarked square, and all the time delivering his sermon. 'Look at that hull,' he would say, 'see its pointed smoothness and its playful shadowy colour. It flew above blue seas and green skies. It flew over the Mediterranean to Egypt. It crossed the yellowness of the sands and the ultramarine of the jungle. It flew via the Sudan and Uganda to Kisumu and from Kisumu to Mombasa and down the coast to Durban. It was eighty feet long and had Smoking Cabins before the engines, Promenade Cabins to their rear and Midship Cabins directly below them. The volume of the hull was nine thousand eight hundred cubic feet, equivalent to four double-decker buses. The total number of rivets needed for each hull was approximately two thousand, and the number of blows from any hammer to rivet one such hull would have been in excess of one million. The thickness of the hull, the seal by which it kept the blue and the green and the ultramarine out, was point-o-three-sixth of an inch.' He would hold up his fat thumb and forefinger. 'About *this* thick.' How it angered me to hear all this, how I hated seeing all the other boys crowd around Fat Patrick's desk (when they too despised him for the unsightly manner of his deportment), how I loathed seeing those pink fat fingers deal the cards so cleverly, so that when finished there would not be a gap between any of the cards, no matter what order he placed them down, how unfair it was that he should have this set, and that father, and a house full of flying boats and caps and polished insignias and badges, when all I had, a better boy than he, a cleverer boy than he, a quicker boy than he, was a Bare Landing, a spare room and the empty night. *His* flying boats? Not likely.

'Bring them down,' I said one day. 'Why don't you?'

'You can come home and see them,' Fat Patrick had replied, looking at me in a long hard manner.

'I don't want to see them at your home,' I told him, suggesting somehow that showing them to me there would taint them. 'I want to see them here. I want to make a picture of them for art class.'

'It is already a picture,' he told me. 'Better than you will ever do.'

'I want to copy it,' I said. 'Just once.'

So Fat Patrick brought the Empire collection down and spread the sheet before him. The class gathered round as I knew they would. He began. First a section with the words 'Ship's Clerk' and 'Mail Compartment' written upon it. He placed it at the top, slightly left of centre. Then came the picture of the ship's chef, with his back towards us, which he placed some four inches directly below the first. Then came the man with binoculars ('What is he looking at?' Fat Patrick would ask. 'Is he looking out on the Persian Gulf or is he sensing the approach to the island of Bermuda? Is that a tropical suit he is wearing, suitable for Burma or Siam, or is it a suit of heavier material, made for northern climes?') Backwards and forwards, up and down he dealt the cards, until he had but one space to fill.

'The Pegasus Engine. One of four. Air cooled. Built by Bristol Aeroplane Company. Top speed of two hundred m.p.h. Each engine was of seven hundred and forty horsepower, with a take-off power of nine hundred and twenty.'

I leant over.

'I'll take it off all right.' I picked it up and held it at arm's length, as if it disgusted me. Fat Patrick turned and looked up at me.

'Put it back,' he said.

'There's a hole in your picture,' I told him. 'It's no good. What if there is a hole in the engine?'

He looked quickly at the others circled around him to see if this was a collective effort. When he realized I was on my own he turned to me again, pushing his glasses back, holding his gaze steady.

'There are four engines. It could fly with a hole in any one of them.'

'There are not four now.'

'It could fly on three.'

'It should have a spare,' I insisted.

'It's fourth *is* a spare,' he said. 'The designers allowed for that sort of thing.'

There he was bringing his loony father in. I was quick to cut him off.

'Don't give me that. It should have a fifth.'

He sighed. He sighed as if he had known all along that this would happen. He looked back at the incomplete picture as if to say This is how I will have to view you now. This is the price you have to pay for being so perfect. He turned his back on me and traced the outline of the vessel.

'See the white greyness of it Giles, see the hugeness, the circling hugeness of it. It flew before everything. There was *nothing* flying before these. They floated in perfect liquid. It wasn't a question of feeling comfortable. You were embalmed.' He turned back. 'Give it back to me, why don't you?'

There was a mutter of approval. His quiet tone enraged me. How had he guessed my purpose? How had he fixed me with those steady blue eyes of his? I had expected a shrill bleating. I had hoped he might take a run at me, to charge in blind anger. I had wanted to hold his head and jab at his fat stomach. I had wanted him to plead with me, to cry out so that others would hear, so that I might throw him down, fling the card at his feet and cross over to the other side. Now I was as alone as he was.

'It should have five,' I repeated and tore the card in two. 'Here. It has now.'

I handed him the two halves. He was almost cheerful. I could have burnt it. I could have made him eat it. I could have thrown it into one of the outside lavatories and shat upon it. But I had ripped it up and given it back, made a present of his misfortune. There were a few laughs and everybody wandered away. It had been nothing spectacular, no blood spilt, no cheering, jeering throng. Already Fat Patrick had placed the two pieces face down and was busy sticking them together with tape. We did not speak to each other for a few days, but such is the nature of friendship in such a place, and such is the value placed on such expected acts that it was only a matter of weeks before Fat Patrick and I fell into the habit of talking and I could enter once again into his entertaining and soothing world. But though he brought the Empire set down again, and would willingly perform his party piece to others, I could never bring myself to look over his shoulder and see him trace the great greyness of it. I did not want to see his finger falter over the thin jagged scar that marked one of the four Pegasus engines, nor could I bear to hear his voice take on the tone of a man whose rounded wonder at the beauty of things had settled upon him as easily as that huge hull had settled down upon the movement of the sea.

'I can see him now,' the boy begins, 'clearing his desk, putting a schoolbook underneath it to make it flat. Then, taking out a sheet of white paper . . .'

'That's enough of that,' I warn him. 'I am not interested in your version of events, particularly *those* events. I needed only to be reminded, that's all. We have passed that age some time ago. We are older now. As you have already admitted Fat Patrick is no longer so fixed by those beasts upon the water. Indeed even his fractured father no longer seems torn by their presence, appears less obsessed by them than was formerly the case. The drawings, the plans, the endless photographs that were constantly strewn across the coffee table and the dining-room table and a fair proportion of the living-room floor, have all been moved away. Even Fat Patrick's fourteen-inch telescope, permanently trained upon them from the vantage of his bedroom window (and how you envied that restless view) has been relegated to the attic where no one ventures. Only you and Stella Muchmore kept the faith, only you and she (so you thought) kept long vigils around the pillbox, staring across the water, aching at their ache, turning on their ropes. How you both would shiver, even on the warmest nights. Oh that you could touch them, stroke them, lie upon their silver wings. This much, and this much alone did you admit to Detective Sergeant Weatherspoon, for that is what you had to admit. That is where Stella's raincoat was found and that is where the two of you were often seen holding court upon its pitted surface, smoking cigarettes, ignoring the rest of the world. But now Stella Muchmore is gone! The Flying Boats are gone! It is time you returned to your bed.

'The next morning you awake to a house in turmoil. Father is dancing up and down the landing in high agitation, scanning the river for any signs of the missing craft, ringing what few cronies he has left to tell them of the startling news and speculating on the nature of their disappearance. It is true then. The Flying Boats are gone! For a moment you forget last night's escapade and join him by the window to look out on the bare water. What could have happened you ask, with genuine interest, has someone taken them away? But this only drives your father into a more furious routine, his bony white feet treading the carpet as if he were a small boy ready for the lavatory, his pajama bottoms flapping about in a thoroughly obscene manner. How the hell should I know, your father answers angrily, putting the binoculars to his eyes again, and you wish that you had stayed in your room, that you were back in your bed examining the events of last night, instead of by his side, forced to watch his genitals jiggle up and down. How repulsive you find them! They seem larger and darker than your own and possessed of an overpowering menace which you can practically smell. Small wonder that your sister is still in her room. Anyway, your father continues, you'd better get moving. You've got visitors. Again. You run to the spare-room window. Outside, the stubby black car that has already taken you from your house to the police station some six times over the past fourteen days is standing patiently by the side of the road once again, while its occupants, Policewoman Andrews and her sleeker and less comfortable companion, Police Constable Savage, sit on the edge of the settee in the living room with cups of tea balancing on their knees waiting for you to eat your breakfast and comb your hair. As you eat your bacon and egg and fried bread (a most unsuitable preparation), with your mother hovering over you, examining your fingernails and the state of your collar, your father berating the air with his theories, you are struck by the fact that neither of your parents are at all concerned over your imminent removal. It has become a commonplace event. It is almost as if they truly believe you *are* helping the police with their enquiries. (Only Carol will show any sense, leaning over the banister in her blue flannel nightdress with an awkward thumbs-up sign – an unexpected act of solidarity which surprises you.)

'Policewoman Andrews and Police Constable Savage greet you like an old friend of the family, which in some respects you are. Although you know that they are trained not to give anything away to a suspect, there is nothing in their manner to arouse your suspicions. They are the same firm and friendly couple they have always been, and they take you to the car as nonchalantly as if they were giving you a lift to the railway station. However as you approach the rear door, with Police Constable Savage already settled into the driver's seat, the police radio suddenly bursts into life and in a moment Police Constable Savage holds up his arm, signalling you to go no further. Almost at the same time two more police cars come racing down the road, pulling up outside the Muchmore's house. While Policewoman Andrews confers with her partner, and while you stand alone on the pavement, four policemen walk quickly to the Muchmore's front door. Two are in uniform and two are in plainclothes and the four of them are let in almost immediately. By the time the door has closed Policewoman Andrews has come round to your side again and opened the car door, ushering you inside. As the car speeds away you look back through the rear window, just in time to see Dr Morgan hurrying up the drive.

'What's going on? you ask, have they found her? but neither Police Constable Savage nor Policewoman Andrews will reply. You twist and turn in your seat, you address the motherly bulk of Policewoman Andrews, you lean across and inhale the cheap aftershave of Police Constable Savage, Can't you tell me what's going on? but every question only strengthens their resolve. Can't you keep that kid still? he snaps and she pulls you back sharply. How their faces have changed! How set they have become! The car is moving faster than strictly necessary, you can sense it in the way he changes gear, the way his mouth turns down, the way he leans forward as he pushes down on the accelerator. Next to you, Policewoman Andrews is unable to keep her hands still, she fingers the buttons of her tunic, she straightens her skirt, her peaked cap is examined for loose stitches. Oh that you were home and buried in your mother's breast! Oh that you could call to her and put your arms around her waist! The car moves swiftly to its destination but this does not prevent you from noticing everything that is yours, everything that is familiar and dear to you, every window, every door, every driveway, every dog and cat that you have ever known. There is Nigel Cramphorn's bedroom, with his model aeroplanes, and his cricket bats and his boxing magazines and there is his brother nosing about in the front garden. There is Henry Deering's father's car, the one he drove through the back of the garage one evening, there is still a dent on the roof and scratches down the side. You pass the piece of scrubland where the three chestnut trees stand, where you used to spend hours throwing sticks into the thick leaves, filling your satchel with smooth-smelling conkers, and in whose branches you would settle a year or so later to watch the Spencer twins bathing in their private swimming pool in the garden across the road. As the car races down the hill you catch sight of Fat Patrick's mother and Fat Patrick's beautiful elder sister walking back up from town, carrying a shopping basket between them. There she is! you want to cry out. She was out last night! I saw her! Why don't you talk to her? Why don't you take her down to the station? but she is gone. How long ago was last night, what a different place this town was then? Here is the High Street, so plain and mundane, with its traffic lights and pedestrian crossings, camera shops, chemists, and dry-cleaners. How wild it was, how the colour glowed, how the air swirled! There is the alleyway with its two black dustbins, its dull crumbling brickwork, its mean narrow aspect revealing nothing. What a transformation has taken place! Where are the moans and kisses and breasts now, all tucked away safe and sound for another time? Did Julia's eyes linger this morning on the crumbling wall, which she leant against so eagerly last night? Oh, if only you could just be a boy again, still happy to sit upon your pillbox and look out upon the town's misfortune, those cursed planes, who have spoken to you so eloquently over the years. Oh if only you had not listened to them, had not been mesmerized by their endless motion, not seduced by their relentless beauty. Yes, you wish you were a boy again, just an ordinary boy, but you are not. You are a man, a young man, but a man nevertheless, and, for the first time in your life you are what you thought you always wanted to be, alone. There is no one to touch you now, no one to hold you, no one to try your friendship. You are alone and as cold as you will ever be. There is sunshine outside. It is one of those sweet winter's mornings that announce the arrival of a storm, calm and warm and filled with a radiant light. People have abandoned their raincoats and overcoats and woollen scarves and are walking about as if spring has come, but you are so chill, so alone, that you start to shake. By the time the car has driven into the police car park round the back of the station, and Police Constable Savage has positioned it facing the back entrance, you are barely able to walk. You lean against the car quivering. The yard is filled with cars, mostly black, but there are a couple of those new white ones that are used on the motorways. This is the last thing you will see, this is the last sniff of the outside you will ever have, this surround of authority. Policewoman Andrews takes your arm and eases you off the side of the car. Hanging on to her arm you walk unsteadily over to the door, like a man with the palsy. What a sign of innocence is this! You hang on to her, pathetically grateful. Her breast would do!

'Inside, the corridor that you have trod so jauntily down six times before stretches before you. At the end, lies the interrogation room and the florid features of Detective Sergeant Weatherspoon. As you walk along it seems that every doorway is filled with a watching uniform, as if they have all gathered to witness your passing. What do they know? you ask yourself, what has gone wrong? Is it something you have said, something they have found? Were you seen last night, did Fat Patrick's beautiful elder sister see you out the corner of her eye, did the caretaker recognize the soles of your shoes, did Mr Cooper return for his whisky bottle to find you standing on the pillbox with that essay in your hand? Have they found Stella? Have they found Stella with something of yours on her? Why was Dr Morgan going to the house? To sedate someone? *What has happened*? Oh that you had told the truth, had trusted them, but it's too late now. No one would believe you. You pass the men's lavatory, and as if on cue, your stomach begins to buck and heave. You swallow hard, tightening your grip on Policewoman Andrews, trying to force it down, but it only redoubles its efforts. You swallow, and then burp. You burp again and again, each one louder and more desperate than the one before. At each convulsion your mouth opens wider, and then, out it comes, eggs, bacon and fried bread, out on to Policewoman Andrews's pressed uniform, out on to her white blouse and her brass buttons, out on to the wall and your green cord trousers. Ah shit, you hear Police Constable Savage exclaim as he jerks back to avoid the second wave, losing his balance as he does so. Get him in the toilet! someone shouts, but no one helps you as you lurch back to the lavatory door, spraying your poison before you. By the time you are clutching the bowl, looking down upon the specks of dried excrement, swallowing in the air into which your tormentors defaecate, your stomach is quite empty.

'You are allowed time to clean up. Next door you can hear Policewoman Andrews's murmurs of disgust as (you presume) she removes her blouse and wipes herself clean. A young policeman, not a great deal older than yourself you suspect, stands in the far corner, leaning up against one of the urinals while you rinse your mouth out and bathe your face in cold water. After you have combed your hair and studied yourself in the cracked mirror, and sat down for a spell on one of the wooden lavatory seats, you are shown, once again, into the interrogation room, where Detective Sergeant Weatherspoon and a refreshed Policewoman Andrews are seated. Curiously enough, although you still feel weak and apprehensive of what is to come, you have to some extent regained your confidence. If the act of throwing up could be interpreted by them as an admission of guilt, the first chink in your armour, it has also turned you, however briefly, from suspect into martyr. They no longer have a healthy boy to assault, a cocky youngster to bring down. Instead they are faced with a pale and hunched boy, who approaches the table with a brave, but pitiful smile, a boy who apologizes for his shortcomings, who is most dreadfully sorry for what he did to Policewoman Andrews, and for the mess he caused generally, who doesn't know what brought it on, and who feels much better now. You sit down in front of Sergeant Weatherspoon who is forced by this abject humbling to wring his hands too, to push aside his notebook (thereby signalling that nothing yet has started) and deliver a long speech on the perils of the latest strain of Asian flu which is sweeping the Medway towns, on how the population is falling over like ninepins, on how doctors' surgeries are filled to bursting point, and even how it has affected his own family. You raise your eyebrows in astonishment. That it should come to this. His own family! You wonder briefly whether you should enquire as to which member of his family has suffered the most, and whether they are all right now, but before you can articulate your sympathy he has refocused his attention on his place of work, and the decimation that is taking place in the ranks. And of course, he admits freely, it couldn't have come at a worse time. Things are just getting impossible. Take last night for instance. Forget we have a major inquiry on our hands. Last night we had three car thefts, a punch-up at the C of E Youth Club, an attempted break-in at your school, and as if that wasn't enough, some lunatic got out on to the river and cut all the Flying Boats loose. I mean, I ask you, who'd want to do such a thing? Who'd want to row out, or God help us, swim out, and saw through two-inch steel cables? Would have taken them most of the night anyway. I mean what's the point of that? and you can think of one or two reasons, but you say nothing. Not that they got very far, he adds, nor luckily did they cause much damage. Most of them ended up on Limehouse Reach, one sank almost immediately and only one remains 'at sea'. His little joke. You laugh. You always laugh at other people's little jokes, especially if they are made by policemen, or schoolmasters, or anybody else who is in a position to do you harm, no matter how feeble and contrived they may be. It is the ingratiating quality of these rejoinders which you despise the most. Mr Cooper for instance is particularly fond of them, forever stroking that ridiculous moustache of his, sitting on the edge of your desk, trying to be one of the boys. How could some-one like him, someone so obviously pathetic, end up in a pillbox with Fat Patrick's beautiful elder sister? What could she possibly see in him? Like mother like daughter perhaps. It is one of the things that angers your father the most, the relationship between Mrs Liddle and her husband, and it was from his lips that you first heard the suggestion that the dark complexion of her skin might be part of the answer. Your father's, what's the word, jealousy? obsession? yes, that's more like it, your father's obsession with the Liddle family, has to be seen to be believed. Hardly a day goes by without him making some comment or other. How he would love to learn what their daughter got up to last night. How his eyes would bulge with delight. When you were younger you used to think that his principal displeasure was directed at Jim Liddle, but over the years you have learnt that Mrs Liddle too holds a special place in his affection. You have lost count of the number of times you have been sitting beside your father in the Wolsey when he has passed Mrs Liddle on her way back from town, or simply walking down the road with their dog. You can see him now, staring straight ahead, as if he could not see her, as if he were blind to her presence, only to give himself away by quickly looking into the mirror at her receding form. He could never help himself, and once done he would wriggle in his seat and become bad tempered. And from those early signs you came to appreciate that your father was always on the lookout for her, would stand in the front garden if he thought she was likely to pass by, would deliberately cross the road if he saw her walking on the other side of the High Street, and would if he could bring her name up in conversation, so long as it was in a hurtful or demeaning context. It was because of him that you first felt a pang of pity for the family and made you determined to stop your petty cruelty to her son (though of course you never did). In particular you remember your father, deep in his cups, driving back from God-knows-where, after talking to God-knows-who, slowing down and giving you a lift as you walked back late one night after a school chess match, and how the car passed Mrs Liddle hurrying down into the town, carrying a light coat, a bright turquoise dress flattened against her body. Your father licked his lips and looked at you and looked at her and said, Look at that mincing along with all her airs and graces, the little dark bitch. I'll never forgive Jim Liddle for that, bringing a piece of colour into the street. God knows what they get up to. Where's she going now? Jim doesn't know the half of it, the stupid pig-ignorant bastard, knows nothing about planes, knows nothing about women, knows nothing about decency. It's all right poking a bit of dark, but to marry one. Your father laughed. Marry it! he said, Marry it and bring it back to Gladstone Drive. Well that was that wasn't it . . . and the car swerves and mounts the pavement and he lurches forward and brings it back on the road. Sorry about that old son, he said, your father is a bit over the top today, it's been a bad day, that fucking factory, I've had it with them, had it up to here, after all I've done for them, God how they've let me down and now where am I, left in this Godforsaken town with all this shit and that fucking darkie grinning from ear to ear, and other places besides. Don't think I don't know what she gets up to, I mean where's she off to now, fucking *Sunday School*, and once again the car bangs up against the pavement and as he wrenched the wheel across and pressed his foot down upon the accelerator, your father leant back and howled into the night, leant back and let loose every sound and image he could summon. Oh you heard it all that night, all the words you would later love yourself so much, great gobs of beery saliva spilling out, forming those lovely words, but in what bitter profusion, how she loved it, how she couldn't get enough of it, how dark cunt always loves it, can never get enough of it, how the night shift would fuck her and leave greasy paw marks on her breasts, how every travelling salesman would fuck her and have her suck them off in return for a new home appliance, how she loves it from behind, they do you know, like it on all fours with their tits hanging down, and now she was off to the dockyards to get some Navy coq inside her, *which is where he found her in the first place*. On and on it went, every lurch of the car directing your father to a new avenue of exploration, his knuckles white with excitement, his hips bucking under the weight of his imagination. By the time he had turned into Gladstone Drive and roared down the road to your house, he had quite forgotten that you were by his side. Drink had quite driven you from his presence. He'd give her some cock all right, he'd have something for that mouth of hers. He'd have her gobbling it down and *still* have enough left to fuck her so she couldn't walk for a week. You watched him fall out of the car and stumble off towards the front door, his face flaming, his body bursting with hatred, and you knew that depravity was about to take place, either over a washbasin, or in the little box-room overlooking the front garden, or more likely, expended upon his reluctant partner. The next morning your worst fears were confirmed, for there was a silence at the breakfast table that had practically been imported from somewhere else. Your father had no recollection of last night's performance. He not only asked you how you got on last night (you lost) but whether you got home all right. Your mother fussed over your sister, not looking at him, and not looking at you either. Why should this be? Did she see you in the car with him? Did she think you know what might have taken place after he had negotiated the stairs and emptied his bladder?

You had deliberately stayed in the car for some time, so that you would avoid all sight and sound of it, but as you watched your mother moving about the kitchen, saw the shape of her mouth, and the way she moved, as if she was ashamed, you wanted to drag your father from the breakfast table, hang him over the climbing frame and beat the shit out of him, kick his teeth in so that he could never mouth those phrases again. Why won't she look at you? Is it because you are the same sex as him? That you are his son? You looked at your father and saw his thin little legs and his cold damp hands and his hair that was beginning to fade and you knew from that moment on you would never ever help him, never show him any affection, never support him, never, if you could help it, touch him. And you knew too, that although this resolution was made in anger, no matter how your father suffered, no matter how lonely he might become, no matter how sad or desperate, your resolve would never weaken.

'Who would do such a thing? says Sergeant Weatherspoon again, who would be stupid enough to set those things free, and for what reason, a dare, a grudge, I mean no one's going to try and steal them, I mean who? and you say, My Father, and the room stops. Your father? Detective Sergeant Weatherspoon leans back and lets a great laugh out into the air. Your father? That's a good one. Here you are brought in to help us with Stella Muchmore and within two minutes you're shopping your own father for something else. Why, *do you think it's going to put us off your trail?* he says leaning forward and you realize that Detective Sergeant Weatherspoon has just changed track and is quite serious about all this. What trail? you say, I haven't done anything. Haven't you now, he replies. Well that's very nice. A boy who hasn't done anything. Must be some kind of record that, eh Andrews, a Do-nothing Boy. I don't think we've had one of those in the station before, do you? Perhaps we should put up some sort of plaque. "Here sat Giles Doughty, who went out with Stella Muchmore and who did nothing." Does that seem quite right to you Andrews? Does that ring at all true to your feminine ears? A seventeen-year-old girl and a sixteen-year-old boy who go out together and *do nothing*? Is that the latest craze then? Let's all do the Do Nothing? He snorts contemptuously. What I meant, you say, after a moment's pause, not knowing quite what to say, but knowing you have to say something, what I meant was that I, we, didn't do anything that would . . ., you trail off into uncertainty. Yes? enquires Sergeant Weatherspoon. We didn't do anything that would leave a trail. Ah, says Sergeant Weatherspoon, thank God for that. A young man who cleans up after himself, the Kleenex Kid, and Policewoman Andrews sniggers into her hand. Your father, Detective Sergeant Weatherspoon says unexpectedly, is it your father you're worried about? Do you think he had anything to do with it? What, with Stella? you reply, panic rising. Yes, Stella, he says. She lives opposite. She came round to your house didn't she? You don't think . . . Of course not you say indignantly, remembering how he talked, poking some dark cunt, remembering Stella's lovely olive skin, Of course he has nothing to do with it, How could he, knowing all too well how he could. It's just that he seems to be in your thoughts this morning, and I was wondering why? The Flying Boats, you reply, you were talking about the Flying Boats and Detective Sergeant Weatherspoon writes on his pad of paper and looks up and says, Well, do you think your father had something to do with last night then, and again you say, Of course not. It was just that he was involved with them. He was working for the factory then. Detective Sergeant Weatherspoon nods. Yes, we all know of your father's involvement with the factory. Not the most popular man in Rochester your father. Got a lot of hate mail in the early days, when they were pulling out. Blamed it all on him, the move to Belfast. Not that they wouldn't have gone anyway, his plan or not. But that's long ago. We're not even sure whether these blessed planes belong to them anymore. They belonged to us though, and he draws one on his pad. So, he says eventually, when he has filled in all the windows and drawn the four propellers mounted on the four Pegasus 740 horse-power engines (he knows his Flying Boats all right) we can wipe his slate clean then on last night's business. He hasn't got one of them tucked away in your back garden or hidden away in the allotments, and you laugh and become bold and looking him straight in the eyes tell him no, we couldn't get it past the pillbox. Ah the pillbox, he says. That could tell us a thing or two. So it's your father and you now is it. Batman and Robin.

There was enough going on last night for it. I mean it wasn't your father on the water and you at the school was it? Sorry, you say. The school, repeats Detective Sergeant Weatherspoon. Didn't I tell you? Someone broke into the school. Vandals probably. Didn't do much. Old Lewis disturbed him before he could do any real damage. Made a bit of a mess in the Art Department getting in, but that's all he had time for. You haven't got a grudge against the school have you Giles, like your father's got a grudge against the factory. They got rid of him eventually, after all that didn't they? The school hasn't got rid of you too has it? You make no reply to these outrageous accusations. Sergeant Weatherspoon taps his pencil against his teeth and you wonder yet again what he knows and why exactly you are here. And then he says, Let's go through it one more time Giles. Let's go through it bit by bit. Stella Muchmore is still missing. We still have no idea what has happened to her. Apart from her raincoat we can find no trace of her. It is still my greatest hope that we may find her alive. Perhaps she has gone off on her own, run away. Perhaps she has run off with a friend, a friend we know nothing about. Perhaps she has been abducted. Perhaps she's being held prisoner, you know the sort of thing. And perhaps . . . She could be anyway, and we are all very concerned for her safety. It is fourteen days now and frankly we are no nearer to her than we were on day one. As I said, we have no idea. And it is that word Giles, which gives me the greatest hope, idea. For that is what I need Giles, an idea. So tell me again of your time with her, how you met her that Boxing Day, where you went with her, what you did with her, who you met with her, what you talked about with her. Take your time. This is not an interrogation. This is a pooling of information. So start at the beginning. Start on that Boxing Day. So you take a deep breath and you start on that Boxing Day, walking across the road with your father and mother and sister to have Boxing Day lunch at the Muchmores'. How did it begin? I saw you the other night Giles. You were running across the road. I was going to call out to see if you wanted to come to Jessica's party but you were too quick for me. You'd better come better dressed than you were then though. Jessica's most particular. Call for me at eight. And you called for her at eight and took her to Jessica's party. You tell Sergeant

Weatherspoon all you can remember about Jessica's party and you tell him about all the other parties you went to that winter. You tell him about the walks you took together, the films you went to see. You tell him that she became your girlfriend and that the two of you would meet down by the river after school to smoke cigarettes and kiss each other. You tell him how later on, if it could be arranged, sometimes under cover of other visits, other parties, school outings even, you would meet up by the pillbox after homework, or at the weekends. You tell him, truthfully, that actually neither of you had very many friends, that for the most part you kept yourselves to yourselves, which is why you liked the pillbox, because it was, in itself, a solitary place. Sergeant Weatherspoon's eyes open in some bemusement. Well, you know, he says, that pillbox is a comfy spot for courting couples. I'm surprised you didn't have to book it out in advance. As far as I know half the population of this town was conceived down by the allotments. It's very fertile territory. When we conducted our search we found lots of evidence of, what shall I say, activity down there. You understand what I'm saying Giles don't you, bits of this and that. From the way that you talk I can see that you got on with Stella, that you liked her a lot, that you were very fond of her. That's good. There's nothing wrong with that at all. What you haven't told me was how Stella was disposed, if you like. I mean would you describe her as an experienced young woman? Are you, thanks to her, an experienced young man? and you answer, which is partly true, that you didn't go *that* far, and Sergeant Weatherspoon leans forward again and says well then *how far* and you look at Policewoman Andrews, marking her discomfiture, and invent scenes which never took place. With the memory of Fat Patrick's beautiful elder sister still fresh in your mind you invent jerseys you never lifted, breasts you never (hardly ever) touched. Touching each other, you understand, but nothing more. (Nothing more! What lovely lies!) So you never ... and you reply, quite truthfully, no never. So, he says, as far as you know, there would have been no reason for her to leave, or for someone to get rid of her. No embarrassing scenes in the doctor's surgery. You didn't get her pregnant did you, and you jump up and say Of course not I've just told you we never ... and you stop. Why are you asking me this you shout, thinking that he has been lying to you all along. What has happened? Have you found her? Is that what all the police cars at her house were all about and Detective Sergeant Weatherspoon looks at you wearily and says No, she has not been found, and I have a feeling that she never will be which is why I beg you to tell me all you know. You lie and shout back that you *have* told him all you know, knowing full well that you cannot tell him now, the fear of incarceration is too great. Well, he says, rising too, if that's the case you'd better go. You are an honest boy, but for some reason you have not been honest with me. One day you will tell me everything, and then I might get to the bottom of it. One day you will come to me and remember what you have forgotten, for you are too young to let this lie quiet for the rest of your life. He motions you to leave, but you hang on to the edge of your chair. But what's happened you ask? Why are there police cars outside the house? The trouble with cases like this he says, The whole thing starts to fall apart. Everything unravels. No we haven't found her, but early this morning Mrs Muchmore hanged herself in the garage. That poor man found her. First his daughter and then this. Jesus.'

I paused for a moment. I have nearly finished now. I look at the boy opposite and hand him a cigarette. Let him smoke if he wants to. Let him inhale and wrap it around his lungs.

'So once again,' I tell him, 'let us return to that afternoon, to the classroom and the world outside. Let us read this triumph, why don't we? Fish it out from where you might have kept it over the years, fish it out and let us all take a look. What harm can it do you now?'

He shrugs his shoulders.

'When the Flying Boats went,' he says, 'a lot of people lost interest in Stella, though no one would actually admit it, least of all the police. And one of course was never found. It is so much easier to lose a schoolgirl than an aeroplane. If I'd known they were going to disappear like that I don't think I would ever have bothered to go out that night. Though if I hadn't . . .' He stops, remembering.

'You would not have seen Fat Patrick's beautiful elder sister's breasts, nor your English master naked on his knees.'

He shakes his head.

'I would not have been one of the first, perhaps *the* first to see that they were not there.'

'Ah yes, you prefer watching something that is not there to something that is. So very like you.' I stick out my hand abruptly. I have had it with this boy. 'The essay,' I tell him curtly. 'Hand it over.'

There is no evasion this time. He reaches into his jacket pocket and pulls it out. Four pages.

'Just a schoolboy essay,' he says.

The First Bad Tale of Mr Muchmore

Late one night Mr Muchmore steps off the train. It is an unusually long train which over-runs the platform by four coaches. Although the passengers have been warned of this Mr Muchmore is tired and has forgotten. He is in the second of four coaches. He steps out into the air and drops. He rolls down the grassy bank. His nose is squashed, his shirt is torn and he has lost a shoe and his car keys.

He feels vulnerable on the way home. He cannot decide whether he should take off the other shoe and get both his feet wet, or walk with a limp. He does not want to call a taxi in case the driver think him the worse for drink. In the brightly lit main streets near the station he can hardly bear to look down at his deformity. Whenever he hears someone approaching he stops, twists his foot round his good leg, plunges his hands into his pockets and looks up at the sky. 'Filthy beast,' they think as they hurry past.

The nearer he gets to home the more convinced Mr Muchmore becomes that he is being watched. Once or twice he thinks he sees a figure darting across the road in front of him, but up in the residential streets the lighting is too poor for him to be certain. There are a couple of times when he has the impression that there is someone behind him, hiding behind a tree or fence, watching his awkward progress with undisguised glee.

As he turns into Gladstone Drive, the street is lit up by a brilliant moon. He has never seen his street look so lovely, never seen it lit like this, solely for him. He would like to throw off his other shoe and dance down it. He would like to hurl his overcoat into the air and caper uproariously past his neighbours. Suddenly, at the far end of the street he sees this figure again race across the road, hunched and furtive and up to no good. Although it is too far away to be sure it almost looks as if it is his drive he emerged from. There he is again!

He watches as the figure dashes from one side of the street to the other in a wild zig-zag pattern, first crouching down behind a tree or parked car, then careering out into the open with feverish energy. Whoever it is, darting in and out like this from one post to another, appears to be hiding from someone, or worse, creeping up on someone, but there is no one else in sight.

Mr Muchmore moves forward carefully and slowly. There is something not quite right about this figure, something which would be only too obvious in the broad light of day. If only he had his torch he'd soon catch the blighter out.

By the time he reaches his drive however the figure has vanished once more, and Mr Muchmore is alone again. Although he stands perfectly still, listening, he can hear no one. He moves cautiously around the house with a large stick in his hand. The garden is black and quiet, the moon illuminating the dark expanse of lawn. The fir trees surrounding his property beckon to him. He shivers and walks inside.

Once in the kitchen he takes off his remaining shoe and puts on his slippers. He rakes the fire in the back boiler, and, with the glow calling him, places the solitary shoe in the centre of the burning coal. He shuts the doors and watches his shoe sitting there, motionless. Blue flames spring up. In a moment it lives before his eyes. He hopes his wife is not awake. It would never do for her to find him burning one of his shoes. His daughter too for that matter. But the thought appeals to him. If he made enough noise . . .

His feet are damp despite his slippers. Why shouldn't he take his socks off as well and put them on the fire? Why shouldn't he peel them back, sniff them quickly and place them inside, on either side of the weightless remains of his shoe? It is done! They lie quiet only for a second, then curl up quickly and are consumed.

He walks to the kitchen door and looks up the stairs.

'Martha?' he calls. 'Martha, are you there?'

He closes the door and moves around the kitchen in a curious circular fashion. His insides are agitated. He is devoured by heretical thoughts. He takes off his jacket and folds it across his arm. He looks to the fire and to the light above his head. He moves quickly. He cannot believe how quickly he is moving tonight. Once more the door is opened. He throws his jacket in and closes the door. It fills the fire, pressing up against the glass like a man trying to escape. It is he who is burning, it is he who is trapped. He cannot breathe.

There is no turning back now. He raises the blind and flings open the window. He stands back and looks out into the night. He can see nothing. He strips to the waist, his shirt, his vest, his tie. God, the air! The clothes go in. To be burnt! Destroyed! He can hardly contain himself. He runs his hands across his chest, underneath his nipples and then to his belly. There are thick hairs there and it pleases him to feel them. He takes off his trousers and his underpants. His jacket and shirt and vest are quite ablaze now, and when he opens up the fire door again, the noise booms out. Everything is burning. His skin is aflame. He could plunge into ice and burn forever. He is naked for the first time in his life.

Mr Muchmore runs upstairs to his bedroom. He is light on his feet, as if he has lost pounds. Martha lies fast asleep, oblivious to his state. He moves around the bed and opens the curtains. There, in the centre of his dark green lawn, illuminated, radiant, bathing in the light of the moon, stands the darting figure, his arms outstretched, looking up towards the house. Mr Muchmore looks at him transfixed. It is as if he is looking at a distorted mirror image of himself. Now he knows what was odd about him!

He is about to move forward, to open the window and to leap into his arms, when a noise from next door stops him in his tracks. He can hear the soft scrape of a reluctant latch, the slow yawn of a damp hinge, perhaps even the soft urgent whisper of a familiar voice. Quickly the darting figure moves forward and is lost in the immediate dark below. Mr Muchmore moves around to the other side of the bed. Standing over his wife he looks once more out over his empty lawn and his beckoning trees. Out from under them runs the figure again, only this time he is joined by another. Round the garden they race, leap-frogging over each other, running and skipping and tumbling over the soaking grass.

Mr Muchmore looks down as thick drops of liquid fall upon the sleeping form of his wife. He marvels at his own wetness. He wipes his hands on his stomach and on his haunches and climbs into bed. Outside he can hear them as they call to each other in the secret language of the night, hear their fading echoes as they disappear out into the street. He turns over and falls into a long and restful sleep.

'A very pretty piece,' I say, handing the four pages back to him, 'if not a little risqué in places. Why for instance, did you use the name Muchmore at all?'

'It never occurred to me that he would ever hear of the name. They were such a secretive family that I couldn't imagine him being known by anyone. It was also', he added, 'too good a name to ignore. That of course was not the risqué part of the essay. I don't think he did know the name of Muchmore at the time. It was the other matter he really liked.'

'You refer I take it to the "drops of thick liquid"?'

'Thick drops of liquid,' he corrects me. 'Indeed. At the time, *at the time*, it was simply a matter of taking things as far as possible without jeopardizing your position. One term to go with an English master desperate to understand, to participate in your creative process, to dangle you on his literary knee. He liked the potent imagery.'

'Yes, I can see that. But of course that is not why you stole into the school that night. That is not what you feared Detective Sergeant Weatherspoon might come across. No. It is not Mr Muchmore himself that is the problem. It is the other figure is it not, the running darting figure, dashing about in the street and in his garden . . . *looking up at the bedroom windows*. Looking up at what I wonder? Mr Muchmore in a state of undress? The stars?'

The boy looks down. 'You know who,' he says.

'I do. I know who. Stella.'

'Stella.'

'And I know who the darting figure is don't I? We all know who the darting figure is. It is the same figure who ducked and darted out of his house and down to the pillbox, a dark secretive figure who loves to hide and cheat and keep himself to himself, who is cruel to his only friend and distrusts his parents, who creeps out at night to run down to the river, but who has recently broadened his horizons. You are seventeen. Pillboxes, allotments, waste ground in general have, as Sergeant Weatherspoon pointed out, other uses than schoolboy fantasies, as we have already witnessed with Fat Patrick's beautiful elder sister, and Stella, dark Stella, with her moonlit eyes and midnight hair is only two years younger than her. Is that not right?'

The boy nods his head.

'And that', I tell him, 'is one of the odd things about all this, and something which puzzled Sergeant Weatherspoon as well. Most girls of Stella's age, eighteen, nineteen, seventeen, if they choose to have boyfriends at all, usually pick someone of their own age, or possibly a year or two older. It is not often they pick on a *younger* boy, a boy who looks younger than they do, who acts younger than they do, who moves in a different circle, a *younger* circle, than they do. Unless of course there is something very special about him. But Stella took to you quickly, almost instantaneously. There you were with your satchel on your back, walking along with your fat friend, sitting on pillboxes pretending to be an airline pilot, going in and out of the same house opposite her week after week without so much as a nod or a wink, and then, suddenly, on Boxing Day, she takes a shine to you.'

'She asked me out to a party that's all.'

'To which you hadn't been invited.'

'Of course not. They were all a good deal older, Carol and Stella's crowd . . .' He stops.

'Quite so. So there she is on Boxing Day, with a dreary lunch organized by her dreary parents, having to sit next to your mother and father, fielding a whole battery of tedious questions coming from all sides, when she turns to you, who she does not know and says . . . what was it?'

' "I saw you the other night Giles. You were running across the road. I was going to call out to see if you wanted to come to Jessica's party but you were too quick for me. You'd better come better dressed than you were then though. Jessica's most particular." '

'And?'

'I said OK. I went.'

'So you did. And I never thought you to be much of a party goer.'

'It was the party season.'

'So it was. So you went to that party, and you went to other parties, and you and Stella became quite the thing, didn't you? You'd meet up after school, down by the river, you'd go out together in the evenings when both your parents thought you were each doing something else, and sometimes, in the midst of all this activity, you'd still find the time to get out of the house late at night, when everyone thought you were in your room, and run down to the pillbox, sometimes with Stella waiting there, sometimes on your own. Is that right?'

He nods. He is beginning to tire.

'So the bay window, and the spare room, and the cupboard under the stairs still had their uses eh? Still the house and you in cahoots.'

He smiles at the thought.

'I am pleased at that,' I say. 'I am pleased that you have not abandoned them altogether for, like you, it is the house to which I wish to return. Particularly one small portion of it. It is this cupboard under the stairs nonsense. Why should you wish to hide there so much, keeping so still, not moving, barely breathing, terrified lest someone should open the door and spill the light upon you?'

'I have already told you,' he replies. 'I would be found out.'

'Found out doing *what*,' I ask. 'What was there to find out when they came upon you under the stairs?'

'They never found me under the stairs.'

'No. No one ever found you under the stairs did they? But you were "found out" weren't you? Someone "found you out", didn't they?'

The boy is silent.

'You could have been found out there if someone had opened the cupboard door and seen you crouching there in the dark. But you weren't. You were found out somewhere else. Let's return to that phrase you used when I asked you why you had to hide there. The reason you had to hide you said, was that if they saw you they might be able to tell you had been outside, for you might be wet, or have *"grass on my feet"*. Notice anything odd about that?'

The boy notices nothing.

'*Feet*. Most people would have said shoes, but you said feet. And it was true. You weren't wearing any shoes when you went out at night, were you?'

He agrees, reluctantly.

'But why should that be? Why should you go out in the dead of night, all wrapped up except for your feet?'

He looks down. He cannot answer.

'No matter. There is always your story to help us, the story you stole back from George Cooper's study, the story you hurled so bravely into the Medway, the story you wanted no one else to read. What happened there? Mr Muchmore had no shoes did he? He burnt them, or rather he burnt one of them in the fire. But that wasn't enough for him. He had to take off his socks and burn them. He had to take off his shirt and his trousers. He had to take off everything until he was naked for the first time in his life. And then what does he do? He runs upstairs and looks out of his bedroom window and sees *a figure* racing about in his garden, a figure who followed him the moment he got off the train, a figure who we know, by your admission is you and who is "a distorted image of himself". And what is the similarity? Why, that the figure dancing in the garden, the figure racing across the street, the figure that haunts Gladstone Drive, who runs down to the pillbox, who leaps from windows and hides in the cupboard under the stairs is as naked as he is. *That's* what Stella saw, and that's what she was saying to you that Boxing Day lunch. "*I saw you the other night Giles. You were running across the road. I was going to call out to see if you wanted to come to Jessica's party but you were too quick for me. You'd better come better dressed than you were then though. Jessica's most particular.*" That's what she was telling you, that she had seen you darting across the road without anything on at all, a boy of sixteen running naked in the night. As soon as she asked you, you knew that that is what she had seen. It must have come as a frightening shock, the embarrassment, the fear of exposure, but when you look back on it, it wasn't so very surprising that someday, someone would catch you at it. For that's what you used to do, *every night if possible*, steal out of the house when everyone thought you were safely ensconced upstairs, and roam about the world as naked as could be. That's why you had to agree to go with Stella that night, to find out what she intended to do. And that's why later you could never tell Detective Sergeant Weatherspoon what had happened, for who would not suspect a boy who exposed himself in such a manner, who prowled the streets nude, who delighted in the night, who enticed a young woman with such depraved bravura and who wrote such stories about the vanished girl's father? Who, for a moment would have believed that your hands were clean? And have you not always lived in fear that you would be found out?'

He is crying now. He is weeping as if his life has never known such tears. He raises his face and drinks them in. I pull over and let the engine idle as he calms down. I put my hand on his shoulder. I stroke his head.

'Ah, those Flying Boats. How you loved them. But as you grew older, running down to the Flying Boats was not enough. It was not simply the Flying Boats that held you in thrall, it was the time of day, *the night*, which urged you on. How else could you approach the night but unclothed. How else to greet its power and complement its mystery? But more than this. Running madly in the garden, your clothes piled neatly under the cherry tree, was not enough either, for the garden was your garden and the night's writ ran so much larger. There was no sudden rush of wind here, no moment of terror, nobody to outwit. So you began to leave your clothes in your bedroom, edging round the door naked, running down the stairs naked, closing the back door naked, everywhere in the house silent and unknown and unclothed. And when you stood in the spare room, naked in the cold night air and looked out on to the front garden and the pale road beyond, you knew you needed wider boundaries, to dare the street and the town, to run through it all naked, to be invisible and naked, to come across a daylight scene and remember your naked times, running madly, hot and out of breath. And this is when Stella saw you, opening that upstairs window, pausing for a moment to touch your stomach before climbing out. There she is, looking out of a dormer window. Across the road a naked boy appears, crouching in the window frame, jumping down on to the front lawn, moving stealthily up the gravel drive. He eases himself past the boundary of his home, his body half bent. He inches out into the open, looking right, then left, then right again (ah, the learnings of youth) before darting out across the road and out of sight. Was that Giles? Giles naked? Later she tells you that she wanted to run down the stairs, creep out the back door and hide behind the high front hedge to catch you coming back, but she knew that if she did she might miss seeing you again, so she waited, waited in the dark room, forgetful of the chill upon her clothes. Ten minutes later you reappear, running back home, no longer crouching but gliding with the moon upon your back. *I saw you the other night Giles. You were running across the road. I was going to call out to see if you wanted to come to Jessica's party but you were too quick for me. You'd better come better dressed than you were then though. Jessica's most particular.* So the next evening you present yourself at the Muchmore's front door, your hair still wet from the bath, ready to accompany her, sick, apprehensive, ashamed. She says barely a word on the walk there and during the evening you are left on the stairs while she scampers up and down talking to her friends, though even in your unsettled state you can gauge that this for her is not a normal activity, that her peers are somewhat embarrassed by her party performance. By twelve o'clock you are escorting her home along the silent road, and it is only when you both reach the bottom of her drive that she addresses the matter directly. *I hope you find time to go out again soon Giles. Tonight perhaps. I won't be going straight to bed. I like looking out into the back garden. To see if there's any wildlife around, badgers, foxes, you know the sort of thing. It's amazing what you see if you stand still long enough. In half an hour?* And she turns and disappears up the drive. Half an hour later you have climbed into her father's garden, moving anxiously behind the tall border of fir trees that surround the lawn. Such a dark oppressive lawn. Such a dark oppressive house. It is cold and windy and you know you cannot stay long. Heavy dark clouds move low across the town. A curtain is thrown back. She stands in a lighted window. You move out into the centre of the lawn and stand facing her. The shifting moon races across your skin. You are silvery and light, you are young and defiant. It is only the beginning. You go to other parties with her. She invites you to the cinema. You meet each other (sometimes in company) after school. At each meeting you whisper a time, a date, when she will witness your next performance, and each time you stand still before her and let the weather take its course. Rain falls upon you, freezing rain from the east, warmer rain from the west. You race through drifting snow, you appear dazzling under crystal stars. And then one evening, when it is warmer, when spring is turning into summer, she is not there. Her window is dark and lifeless, like the rest of her house, the curtains drawn back as if the room has been vacated, as if it were empty. You stand in the centre of the lawn, imagining an eye at every window, imagining your parents and your form master brought to witness this depravity, imagining the garden suddenly illuminated. Discovery and Betrayal! A noise has you back crouching behind the fir trees, fearful of your future. You look up. Stella's window opens and there is Stella climbing down the trellis. Her feet are bare, her legs are bare, from her calves to the arch of her back she is bare. She has an olive skin and her buttocks are milky white. She jumps down and turns to face you, your eyes on her eyes, her eyes on your eyes. She clasps you hard, hugs you close, and then, as if by prior arrangement you both break off and race around the garden, one, two, three times. You lean against the fir trees, panting, not daring to speak, not daring to laugh. She touches you on the shoulder and then retreats, climbing back up the trellis without another look in your direction. In the weeks that follow, as the nights grow longer, warmer, the two of you become more adventurous. Although you rarely talk (warnings, bursts of laughter, whispered exultations) together you move amongst the sleeping residents of Gladstone Drive, cartwheeling on their lawns, kicking up their piles of mown grass, running in and out of their garden paths. You meet at pre-arranged times. Sometimes you wait for her in her garden. Sometimes she is there when you open your back door. There are evenings when you both walk down your respective drives and stare at each other across the road before moving off. Together you have run through allotments and climbed upon the pillbox roof. Together you have sat aloft your brother's climbing frame and slid down her old slide. And that night, the night before she vanished, you did what you both always wanted to do, you walked down the centre of Gladstone Drive arm in arm. How dangerously happy you both were. How fiercely you kissed, how fiercely you hugged, holding each other's shoulders. *Walking down the Drive! Walking!* This is what held you two together. You were laughing heathens alone in the world. How could you tell anyone? And why should you? Would that have saved you? Or would it have imperilled you, fatally?'

The car pulls up and I lean across and open the passenger door. 'Out you go,' I tell him. 'You're on your own now,' and the boy skips out into the night.

*

I GOT TO the Post House around ten o'clock. The drive down had been bad, with strong driving rain and gusting winds pushing the car across the road, but to tell the truth I had barely noticed the conditions outside. I was still in the clutches of Rochester, the Flying Boats and the long leafy road where my youth had run out. That of course is what a car is good for (amongst other things). Cars in their perfect state, when they are quiet and dark and travelling, are vehicles for memory and indulgence and, if you are particularly fortunate, depravity.

Three months ago. In this very car. We are travelling down to

Kent, to the furnished wooden bungalow that brought us together. It is the first time I have been there in months (it will be damp and musty) and it is also the first time that Fleur and I have gone away together as a couple. Although I intend to use the place to its best advantage there are enough distractions, enough clues from an unwanted past, to unsettle me and, more worryingly, to unsettle her. In other words, although I am looking forward to our two or three days together, I am apprehensive as to the outcome. Consequently, in the weeks running up to our little outing, in order to minimize the risk, we have held full and frank discussions on the required agenda. We know exactly why we are going and what we are going to do. We are bringing a bottle of massage oil, a quantity of heavy succulent peaches, a bagful of grass and Thai sticks, a video camera, a bottle of brandy, fruit juice, mineral water and lots of champagne. Everything that we might need has been accounted for, so that this furnished wooden bungalow, with its tatty furniture and its small and suffocating loft, this bungalow with its dark creosoted front and its abundance of warped windows, this bungalow with its thin, brittle walls and its smell of long locked afternoons, this bungalow which means *nothing* to me, is finally and irrevocably turned into a hotel bedroom. This detailed planning has focused our minds wonderfully, so it is hardly surprising, given the environment, that we are behaving as if we are already there. It is early evening and we are in a high state of excitement. We are twenty minutes away and have been reviewing the prospect of forthcoming intercourse with some relish. We are both in agreement that something will have to be done the moment we disembark but Fleur is disturbingly vague, saying that as long as we fuck and fuck quietly, she doesn't care how we go about it. I question her lack of attention to detail, but of course she does not fully appreciate the risk we are taking. She thinks that when we disembark it will be as it always has been, *only more so*. My car, my beautiful clean car, is lulling her into a false sense of security. I try to pre-empt the proceedings but she will have none of it. The Highway Code, she tells me, does not allow that sort of thing.

Of course I was right. Once we arrived and unlocked the front door, once we gazed upon the cracked Bakelite radio and the faded curtains and smelt the smell of must and mice, the intensity with which we had approached this escapade (for that indeed was how we had viewed it, as an erotic adventure) evaporated. Hotel rooms are designed for the transient, the immediate, the gratification of now, and we enter and leave them as equals. But this stranded ark, abandoned after childhood, where every object reeked of my past, where the very view of the grass reminded me of bare legs and kites and rusty buckets, was mine, not hers, and when she crossed its threshold she had to give up some part of herself and this she could not do. It was not as intimate as she had imagined (it was not as intimate as I had imagined). It was bare and uncomfortable. I should have thought it through of course. I should have known that the bungalow was not a fit place for Fleur and perhaps, if I had been there more often beforehand, and remembered it the way it was, I would have realized that before we set off. (I knew it quick enough though. As soon as we drew up, I knew it.) After my baby brother died, summer holidays were suspended for the duration of our family life and later, when it came to Carol and me, neither of us felt much like going back. I had tried over the years, and had succumbed to its naive charm one fatal summer when I had the misfortune to fall for someone and was captured on that very beach. Carol too had felt obliged to parade her good luck amongst its precincts, particularly with the arrival of Clare, but Ian's illness had put paid to that. Towards the end, Camber Sands was where he asked to be taken, where he would rant and rave and behave most abominably, writing in his Diary of Death while the wind whipped at the pages, and after he died she vowed never to go there again. We were in half a mind to sell it there and then, but somehow we never got round to it, and there was a part of me (and perhaps Carol too) that wanted to hang on to it, despite the memories. So I would go down occasionally. Fat Patrick and his father lived just a few miles away. It gave me an excuse to drive over and see them once every six months.

Patrick and I had kept in touch throughout the years, though some years we were more in touch than others. When Stella vanished, and the rest of the town had shunned me, Fat Patrick's mother and father were the only ones who carried on as if I were still the same boy they had known, the only ones who would still invite me to their home, and though his mother had died I still enjoyed their company. I liked to drive down to Rye, give the bungalow an airing, pay the neighbour for any repairs that needed to be done and then drive over to Patrick's for dinner and a stop over. They lived in a small brick house, set back from the old military canal, where his father would keep himself fit by rowing up and down the flat surface in a scull, while his son sat on the grassy bank shouting encouragement. I once suggested that they should reverse the process, but Patrick pointed out that while his father could sit and dangle his legs as well as he could, there wasn't a scull broad enough to accommodate his own girth.

'You should slim,' I told him. 'Exercise. Diet.'

Fat Patrick had looked at me. 'I was born fat and I will die fat,' he said. 'It isn't fatness that has held me back.'

I used to wonder what he meant by that remark (unless he meant marriage), for Patrick was now an influential figure on some government education council, and had index-linked pensions and civil service perks coming out of his ears. Not that I had kept in touch with the Poker Fishers of this world, but out of all of us from Gladstone Drive, Patrick had come out on top. No one had thought at school that this shy, private, *lump* had harboured a keen, analytical *brain*. No one had thought him anything but his father's son. They had long left Rochester, but his father still had a small room downstairs which he called his own and in which there hung his trophies of those Flying Boats days, but now he was reluctant to talk about them, and spent much of his time watching birds with his old cronies.

'It's a social thing,' Patrick told me, when I once asked why his father seemed to leave the house every morning at the crack of dawn. 'He drives over to Rochester and Chatham, picks up Peter Jackson and a couple of others and they hightail it down to the sanatorium, where they spend all day glued to their binoculars.'

'The sanatorium?'

'That land he bought with his redundancy money when the factory closed. God, did my mother cause a stink about that. He called it the sanatorium. Where only rejects go.'

Naturally enough over the years we had often spoken about

Stella Muchmore. Being my only real friend, Fat Patrick had known Stella better than most, for though Stella and I held ourselves apart, inevitably there were occasions when the three of us were thrown together and it was Fat Patrick who bore witness to the only visible evidence of Stella Muchmore that I still have. My bent finger. In those early days, when we all went to parties, when for the first time for both of us, Stella and I felt the urge to dance, Stella would stand with her head on one side listening to the music, as if waiting to come to an agreement with it before she joined in. Then she would move, throwing out one leg, hopping on the other, kicking hard into the air. Hop and *kick*, hop and *kick*. It was a vicious dance for she took no notice of where she was going, and many people went home with black bruises planted down the backs of their legs. I would circle her, flapping my arms up and down, jumping from side to side, a kind of pilot warning everyone of her approach. We were an ungainly and selfish couple, easily the worst dancers in town, but that winter we dominated the floor. Round and round Stella kicked. Round and round I flapped. We were not a courting couple. We did not snuggle up in each other's arms. When the slow numbers came up we would move apart and spiral across the floor in awkward, solitary strides, and yet we were closer than all of them. We knew it and so did our compatriots. They had never seen such sympathy before.

That evening Stella's movements were particularly wild. It was as if she had been cooped up all day and could not wait to be let off the leash. The accident happened towards the end of the evening. We had been drinking beer and several bottles of illicit Martini. Fat Patrick was there, but not dancing. As usual he hung back, alone, nursing a half-empty glass. The room was dark. In one of my flapping circles, growing increasingly wider in order to avoid Stella's uncontrollable feet, I spotted a coin shining on the floor. Slightly drunk, without realizing the danger I was putting myself in, I bent down to pick it up. Hardly had my hand covered it when Stella gave one of her great hopping leaps and landed fair and square on my fourth finger. I jumped up, screaming. The back of the finger-nail had sprung through the skin, and the front was badly squashed. It was bleeding heavily. For a moment I stood still, half expecting Stella to come to my aid, but she had hopped and kicked a dozen times since then and was oblivious to what she'd done. Fat Patrick came to my rescue. He led me into the kitchen and bathed it in water. He took out a large white handkerchief and wrapped it round the broken nail. He pushed his glasses back and held my dripping finger in his gentle fat hands. He was wheezing slightly. I was struck with the thought that I had seen the same quiet intention on his face, the same unbothered care when he had been busy piecing something else together, binding another wound.

'You should see a doctor tomorrow,' he had said. 'The nail is quite broken at the back. It could go septic.'

'Patrick,' I said.

'Yes? Do you feel all right?'

'I feel fine,' I said. 'But I am sorry.'

'Sorry. Sorry for what?'

'You know. When I tore your card in two. I always meant to say sorry, but I never did. I didn't really mean to do it, it was just . . .'

'Oh that,' he said. 'It was only a card. It wasn't the real thing. I'd practically forgotten about it. Cards don't matter, you see.'

But cards obviously did matter. Over the years Patrick has, amongst other things, gathered a huge collection of cigarette cards, and every time I went down there my bent finger would remind me of the Flying Boats and Stella Muchmore.

'Do you ever wonder', I would ask him, 'if Stella's disappearance was somehow connected to the Flying Boats being cut loose?'

'You mean you think she had a hand in it.'

'I don't know,' I would say. 'She was as drawn to them as much as you or I. Perhaps she tried to copy your father. Perhaps she swam out there and hid in one of them. Perhaps it was Stella who cut them loose. Perhaps if they ever dredged up the *Galway Bay* they'd find her body amongst the wreckage.'

Patrick would sit forward. 'It would have been a lot for a young girl to do on her own.'

'She was strong, determined. She had the time to do it.'

'I thought the police went out there and checked them out. Is that not right Dad?' His father would look flustered. Just as I had trained myself not to think about Stella over the years, he too preferred to forget his Flying Boats.

'That's right,' he would reply, 'in the first few days. Though I don't know why they bothered. The Empires would never have harmed Stella. I could have told them that.'

That weekend I had toyed with the idea of driving over and introducing Fleur to Patrick, to lend, if you like, some legitimacy to our affair, to broaden its outlook, but I quickly realized that if anything, she wanted to narrow it down. It was clear from the start, from the way she ran her eyes over the meagre furnishings, that for all her carefree spirit, she would have much preferred to be back in one of our hotels, with everything laid on. Despite our plans and provisions, there was no escaping the fact that here there was no room service, no self replenishing drinks cabinet, no sculptured bath, no fluffy towels, no crass enemy to laugh over, no one to behave badly in front of, no full length mirror to fuck in front of, no extra ice, no clean efficiency to feed our needs whatsoever. But it was more than that. From the moment we opened the door and stepped inside, she realized to her dismay, that in coming down to Camber Sands this whole affair was in danger of changing course. It would be all too easy to lose our way, to wake up in the morning and walk down to the sea, to lie side by side in the late afternoon and listen to the grasshoppers, to stand under an evening sky and *do nothing*.

All my apprehensions about the trip came true. We did not fall on the floor in a frenzy and while I had thought that pushing the two iron bedsteads together would somehow be fun (bedsteads that my baby brother and I had played on so many years ago), when it came to it it was not. It was serious. The beds were uncomfortable. When eventually we undressed and drew close they came adrift and in the heat of the moment, in our attempts to be closest, when we tried to block everything else out, we always ended up apart. It was, I have to say, unpleasantly symbolic. The next morning was no better, and after breakfast she declared that she was going for a swim, *alone*. As if the sea were *hers*. As if I were not welcome in it. As if by being near her (watching? swimming?) I would somehow spoil it for her. I didn't understand. Why had she come down here? What did she want for God's sake?

What did she think *I* wanted? It wasn't *me* who was possessive. It wasn't *me* who was always handling her in public, balancing her on his knee, putting those great hands of his around her, manipulating her. That demand came from Jago, and she, always so outwardly free, outspoken and independent, was always acquiescent. At first I thought that she did this to reassure Jago, to lower Jago's guard, but it dawned on me that weekend, seeing her step into that red bathing suit and walk down to the sea alone, that those demonstrations were given for my benefit, to show me the exact nature of the territory on offer. The trouble was by showing me she was also showing Jago and Jago was no fool.

We left a day early, driving back up to Ashford and the motorway. As we passed The Post House Hotel, I never thought that I would be returning there so soon.

*

IT WAS ONLY when I pulled into the forecourt and switched off the engine that I realized what kind of night lay ahead. The sky was beginning to concentrate its efforts now, thick low clouds sweeping across, hard rain, wind drunk with power, unpredictable, violent. I switched on the radio just in time to hear Eric deliver the latest report: gale force winds, flood warnings operating in the south east and more to come. He sounded calm enough, but I could imagine the state of the place, Lady Bracknell dancing up and down over at HQ, everyone scurrying around, poring over computer forecasts and pressure reports, readings being phoned in from land and sea, three-way consultations with Bracknell and the Little Droplets as to who we should get out of bed. Should we alert the fire brigade? Should we alert the police? Whatever was going on up there, what was crystal clear was the fact that this weather system had picked up a lot of muscle since I'd left it some five years back. We were in for a rough night. I looked up. There was nothing to see of course, only a low sort of blackness surrounding me. The wind was steadily gathering strength, you could practically feel the system flexing its muscles, pounding away at us as if we were a punch-bag, softening us up for the knockout blow to come. I was glad to get indoors.

The Post House was much as I remembered it, empty and

unattractive. Bare brickwork in the lobby, a large open-plan bar to the right, a health club to the left and plate-glass windows everywhere. The building itself overlooked some recently acquired turf, a thin little pond round the back, illuminated in the evening by a ring of stone dolphins with fluorescent balls on their noses, and, barely visible through the rain, a nice set of beech trees ringing the grounds, now in full leaf and dancing furiously against the unrelenting sky. Carol had not checked in yet, nor was there any message from her. That worried me. She'd rung me some five hours ago. The train couldn't have taken more than two, which left her three hours to go chasing after Stella. Surely she could have found the time to make at least one phone call?

I did not get the same room as I had shared with Fleur but I might as well have done. It was just the same. The same wide double bed, the same prints on the same wall, the same deep bath with brass handles on the side, the same television in the same corner and the same questionnaire propped up on the pillow with a note from the management imploring me to fill it in. *What is the reason for your visit?* The rooms themselves were all on the ground floor, fanning out from the main body of the hotel in the form of little chalets. Each one opened up on to a small brick patio with steps leading down on to the newly-laid lawn. The last time I was here Fleur and I had refreshed ourselves by opening the window and walking across to the pond in the early hours of the morning. They were going to stay firmly shut tonight.

I put my shaving things in the bathroom (*Did you find the toilet requisites to your requirements?*) and went back and sat on the bed. Before me the television set and the drinks cabinet, the mirrored wardrobe (*How would you describe the furnishings found in your room?*) and a table with an illustrated guide to the health club. I rang reception to see if Carol had turned up yet, but there was nothing. I tried to call Eric on our own number to see if he could tell me how bad it was going to get, but not surprisingly I couldn't get through. I pulled back the curtains and stood looking at the outside. There was almost a tidal quality to the rain now, as if the hotel had been set down at the edge of the sea. It came rhythmically, angrily, wave after wave. I picked up my keys and went looking for a drink.

Apart from one couple looking despondently out of the window, the bar was empty. Walking into it and seeing the solitary barman wiping the glasses and fiddling with bottles at the back made me realize how I relished the prospect of sitting down before him and becoming the centre of attention. I was angry for Carol dragging me out here and until she had the decency to turn up I was going to get as drunk as I could. I was going to tell this barman my troubles (and anything else I chose to talk about) and he was going to listen. 'And have one for yourself,' I would say to him after my third or fourth.

'Filthy night,' I ventured, settling down and helping myself to some peanuts.

'I've known worse, sir.' He'd known worse. Marvellous.

'Not here though. Not in the Garden of England.'

'Not here,' he agreed. 'At least I don't think I have. The problem here is that it is so unremittingly bad most of the time that it's hard to differentiate one sort of awfulness from another. It all tends to merge into one long filthiness, if you understand me sir. So this weather leaves me very much as it found me. In Ashford.'

He was a small man, with his chin not much higher than the pumps. He peered through them with that woeful expression on his face that you find on animals in pet shops. You wanted to take him home and make a fuss of him. Put him by the fire and give him a biscuit.

'Not your favourite place, I take it. Ashford?'

'Not *quite* my favourite place, no sir. You are not familiar with it?'

'No. Not any more. Used to come here when I was a kid. For the trains.'

'Very wise sir. Not to be familiar with it any more. I am very familiar with it, and we all know what familiarity breeds don't we sir?'

The wind threw itself against the building followed by a wash of water that made the plate glass bend. The couple by the window moved back.

'Not to worry,' the barman called out. 'This is nothing. Just you wait until you go on that world cruise for your holidays. Then you'll see some weather.'

'You speak from experience, I take it.'

'I do indeed sir. Fourteen years in the merchant navy. Chief Steward for the last seven. The *Queen Elizabeth*, the *Queen Mary*, *Queen Alexandra*. I served drinks when the bar was perpendicular sir, when we were all standing sideways. People knew how to conduct themselves then. They knew how to spend money. Proper money. Not this stuff rolled up in rubber bands that you get touted about nowadays. Retired wrestlers is what you get nowadays, men who dress up in coloured shorts, women who read explicit novels. Not that it couldn't get a bit frisky at times, if you get my meaning. But drunk, lewd or sober, they all had . . .'

'Class?' I suggested.

'Not *exactly* class. Humour sir, a certain generosity of spirit. That's why I called it a day really. On the *Queen Alexandra*. It was well run enough, blew its own whistle well enough, but there was nothing there any more, if you understand me. There was no depth to it, just a desire to plough the water and forge ahead to the next stop. Then the wife died and I moved up here to be near my daughter. She runs the health club in the hotel here. Lucky really.'

'I've never been on a cruise,' I told him. 'The thing that always puts me off cruises is the idea of a *boat* full of *people*.'

He smiled. 'Very true sir. In the past I would have told you not to worry and that some boats are quite *big*, but nowadays . . . What will you have sir? Something nautical?'

'A gin and tonic. A large one. A very large one.'

He looked at me. 'When you say a very large one sir, do you mean a *very* large one, or a *very very* large one?'

'The latter,' I told him. 'I mean the latter. If I was on a ship in this weather I think by now I would be having a very very large one, especially if I had lost my sister. Don't you agree?'

'I do indeed sir. I would practically prescribe it for you. *Have* you lost your sister?'

'I have.'

'Forgive me for asking, but would that be lost as in "overboard" or lost simply as in "on the wrong deck"?'

'The latter again. I haven't lost her exactly, rather she is not where she is supposed to be. Which is here. Cheers.'

I drank the very very large gin down in one and set the glass back on the counter. He wiped the bar down and studied me for a moment.

'If I may say so sir, that was very quickly drunk. By the looks of things on an empty stomach too. When I was at sea sir, and confronted by a gentleman such as yourself, who intended to consume a number of very very large drinks on an empty stomach in a moderately short space of time, I often supplied a plateful of hard-boiled eggs for their use. If you eat one every now and again you will find that you will be able to deal with your succession of very very large drinks for a longer time, and remain on an even keel.' He bent down and produced a plate of unshelled brown and white eggs.

'My daughter sir keeps chickens. We have more eggs than we know what to do with. I take it that you will be needing another drink of similar proportions?'

I nodded. 'Possibly larger. And one for yourself.'

'One for myself. How very kind sir. If I may make so bold sir, being as it is late and with no other customers likely to hove into port, and while not wishing to impose on your goodwill or your pocket, but seeing how my daughter has brought home a young man of whom I do not approve, I am going to have a very very large one myself, though you must only pay for the first portion of it. Have an egg, why don't you? Get those sea legs working.'

I took one and started to peel it.

'I know someone else who talks in a sort of sea-faring language, though his is more river talk I suspect. Cockney. Bow Bells. You're not cockney though are you.'

'Not at all sir. I can't abide them cockneys. All that *leave it out* and tedious bonhomie. Meaning no disrespect sir, if you are a cockney yourself, but I have grown very weary of the cockney race over the years. Their no nonsense philosophy I find particularly grating. Actually sir, your average cockney knows bugger all. What? Leave it out.'

I nodded and pointed to the plate of eggs.

'Quite. These eggs are excellent. The yolks are so rich.'

'You should see what they eat. Them chickens eat better food than I do. The cook here sir, new he is, insists on making everything *fresh*. Well, who's going to come here to eat, apart from the odd customer such as yourself? Ashford's London's chuck-outs that's who and they don't eat *fresh*. They can't abide *fresh*. So Dibby, Sidney and Gob, that's her names for them sir, get the lot. Talking of which, she's out this evening, leaving me to lock them up. Another drink sir?'

'How many would that be?'

'Well, let me see. There's the first one you had and now there's the second. That's six gins sir, six very neat gins if I may say so. In my experience, in times of stress, six gins and two hard-boiled eggs is only just the beginning. *Twelve* gins is more like it to my mind. Shall we start steering a course towards the twelfth?'

He turned his back to me and held my glass up to the optic. Something caught my eye.

'Is that a trumpet?' I asked.

'It is indeed sir. A very good trumpet. Given to me by Max Kaminsky. Used to do a lot of touring in Europe did Max. Jack Teagarden. Earl Hines, the lot. Had a spell once with Speedy Bec. That's when I first met him, when he was with Bec. Bec had a small group working on the *Alexandra* at the time and I got to know them quite well, particularly Mr Kaminsky. Well I'm a sort of trumpet player myself. Not in his league mind, nothing like that, but we got on very well Max and I. So when I last saw him in New York, on my last trip over there he gave me that as a going away present. One of his very own. Been everywhere that trumpet. Sometimes I feel sorry for it, hanging up here with only me for company, but I do the best I can for it every now and again. If they go,' he nodded in the direction of the window, 'and when I've had another one of those very large gins, I might even be tempted to fetch her down. A damn sight better than that racket going on outside. Would you care for another egg sir?'

I don't remember getting into bed that night or indeed how I got back to my bedroom. All I know is that from that moment on we talked nothing but music, of musicians he'd met and known, of Frank Galbraith and Coleman Hawkins and Sweets Harry Edison. He was a trumpet man was my little bartender and I began to love him for it. Perhaps this is what the wind was doing, stirring up our memories, for just as my past seemed to be whirling around my ears, so he entered into a world humming with tunes. He told me many stories that night, his face was polished and shining as that instrument hanging up behind the bar. I can remember only one – that of Slim Bulee Gaillard, whose father had been a steward on a liner just like he had been, and who he had met one summer in San Diego, when Slim was managing a motel there. As a young boy Slim travelled with his father in the school holidays and once was accidentally left behind on the island of Crete – 'and stayed there *for six months sir*! There's not many fathers what would do that for their offspring is there now?'

It had taken some effort on my part, but by this time I had banished all thoughts of Carol, like the key to her room hanging in the foyer. Until she claimed me I was more than willing to not know of her existence. Sitting on the barstool watching the gin go down was much more fun. No tiresome messages, no emotional phone calls or tedious calls of duty, just a full bowl of peanuts, a friendly face and the clear rings of drink upon the bar. By the time I fell asleep I cared more for that barman than I did for my sister or indeed for anyone else. I was his friend. He spoke the truth to me. He brought drunken tears to my eyes. All his sorrows were my sorrows and when he laughed at a fond recall I joined in, for I had been there too. We understood each other, my barman and I, just as all barmen understand me and love me and see me for the troubled creature that I am. Oh to be a barman and have friends such as me! How many lives must they know. How many men must love them. They see us at our weakest, at our most foolish, when our hearts are tender, when we are flushed with hatred and contempt. They see us lustful, boastful, triumphant. They see us sly and deceitful, our eyes swimming with envy and despair, and every day they hear our commonplace wisdom, as stale and unhealthy as the smell of last night's cigarettes on our morning breath. Oh what would we do without barmen? Where else can we make the grade?

Then I was awake. I sat bolt upright, holding on to the bed like a man clutching at a raft. As a child I had been swept out to sea on a rubber dinghy and for a moment the terrors of the waters were upon me again. I was wet and cold and crying, desperately holding on while the waves tried to sweep me overboard. There was a mad scrabbling at my face and a roaring in my ear but I could not let go of the bed for fear of falling into the deep. Without warning I was lifted up and slammed against the wall. I began to shout. I had no idea where I was or what had happened to me. I could remember nothing. I could see nothing but there was a wind shaking the very life out of me. A sudden lash of water brought me to my senses. I understood what had happened. That little swirl on the charts that everyone had been tracking, that elusive depression lying out in the Bay of Biscay, fed by warm winds, hardened by cold, had decided to move. While I had been talking to my little barman, while Eric and the Boys from Bracknell had been sipping their cocoa, expecting a bad, but not untoward night, this little storm of ours had filled its lungs, gathered its strength and caught us on the hop. It had floated out between Cornwall and Brittany and, with barometers falling and with a warm night in prospect, had started moving towards England. It had lain off Plymouth covering Portland Bill with a cold front of heavy showers, and had then crossed the coast of South Devon, skirting close to Exeter. There it had deepened and had grown more confident. By the time it had reached the Somerset Levels it was ready to show its hand. There is a purpose to every storm. They have names bleating on their hungry lips. This was no exception, only it was darker and bolder than most. Now it would sweep the country, searching. It would lift off roofs, upturn cars, flood rivers and break down walls. It would throw up barriers, rip up railway lines, topple pylons, flood basements, flatten crops, tear the world into shreds until it had found me. And it *had* found me. It had smashed down my door and come bursting in bringing broken trophies in its wake.

I crouched down on the floor (a favourite position of mine) and moved towards the windows. My hands and knees were in a good inch of water and a steady rain fell on my back. Though I was aiming to shut the storm out of my room and bring back some sanity into the night, it was not altogether unpleasant. It was not a cold wind. The air was touched with a hint of the tropics. The rain was warm, the water beneath me cool. A thick layer of leaves eased my passage across. I was in my element! I was home! I remembered storms and the wind on my face. I remembered grass and leaves and wet things clinging to my skin. I remembered the night air on the back of my neck, my feet on the dark green grass, my body rolling on the earth. And here I was now crouching with this great swirling beast before me. It was as if I had never left. A hundred yards out the storm was dancing in its full fury, but here, in the relative shelter of the half square of cabins, it was entertaining me with its skill, its virtuosity, its implacable power. 'Here I am,' it was saying. 'I have come for you. Watch me now while I dance with this world, while I take it in my mad embrace. This is for you and me. I kiss your back, and trickle down your spine. I bathe your chest with lotions and cover you with garlands. Kneel on all fours before me and take me in your mouth. Let me wash over you, envelop you, lift you from this sedentary place. Watch me now.'

I managed to close the windows and held them shut by dragging the table across and wedging it between them and the foot of the bed. Feeling my way back along the wall I found the light switch. To my surprise it worked, but there was not much of Room 101 left to see. My bedclothes and suitcases had long gone and the wind had opened my wardrobe and stolen most of my clothes too. The bedside lamps were broken, one light-fitting was smashed, and the little drinks cabinet now lay on its side, bent but intact. All around the room, hanging from picture-rails, light-fittings, furniture, and gathered at the head of the bed, were great bundles of twigs and branches, their dark plumes still shaking from the rocking storm. I recognized aspens and sycamores and the dark sheen of the copper beech. Oak apples, cob nuts, acorns all bobbed at my feet. I was in an enchanted, wooded cave. I switched off the light and fell back on the sodden bed. My skin was covered with leaves, my hair was soaked, and my breath came in bursts, but as I lay there I discovered I was not frightened but excited. There was something hugely erotic about this storm. It had come to my room in the dead of night and covered me in its kisses. It had come whispering and raw and urgent, just like Fleur sometimes arrives, when I am half asleep, expecting her, when she climbs into the hotel bed wearing her black dress, or her red dress, or her green dress and lifts it up to show me what is waiting underneath. I knew what the storm was doing, the destruction it was causing, but at that moment I could not help revelling in it. If I had been with Fleur I would have turned her on her stomach and fucked her there and then while we both looked upon the world outside. I could hear the noises she would make. I could see the dull shine on her skin and feel her cold breasts hanging in my hands. I spread my legs and lifted my buttocks up into the air. Let the wind fuck me I thought. Let the wind find me naked in the dark, lying like this, waiting. Let the wind take hold of me, suck me, breathe on the crack in my arse.

A low wallowing moan made me sit up. It was not a human cry, nor that of any animal I have known, but it was a terrible sound, pulled from the very depths of something living. Looking out I saw one of the great beech trees at the end of the park come crashing down. It bounced and rolled and shook the earth, quivering for a moment before settling down, while the wind tore its long life to shreds. Another groan and another tree followed. Whether the cry came from the roots, wrenched out of the wet clinging soil, or whether it was the hole itself, sucking in raw fresh air, I could not tell but it was a sound I will not easily forget. The storm was pulling trees out of the earth as easily as one might lift a row of leeks. In the space of five minutes I saw eight trees go down that night, one after the other, groaning as they went. They were trees in full leaf and their shape was preserved, but they were dying now, torn from the earth and laid down side by side while the storm moved on, bending over the earth and pulling up its produce.

In the distance, through the hazy gauze of rain, a lone branch appeared, torn from its mother trunk as you or I might tear the wing off a chicken carcass, tossed out to sail heroically on the unrelenting wind. It bore itself bravely that branch, dipping head-long into the troughs, decked out in full sail, the rain lashing at its rigging. As a ship might seek a harbour in such times, it turned and moved towards this manmade sanctuary, its flags fluttering, its prow held high. No table was going to keep it out, no french window, no barrier of bed and broken furniture. Faster it came, faster and lower, pulled in by a great incoming wave. I jumped back as the glass cracked, and the windows flew open and the storm and the branch and the great sea burst in again. I fled to the bathroom. I sat on the lavatory seat. I was cold now. The room started to shake. Somehow the wind was louder here. I could feel it pulling at my head. I looked up to see the roof peeling back and the night sky pouring in. Everything in the room flew up, the flannels and the towels, and the hard curtains around the shower. My head was in a screaming shroud. All around me I could hear this howling, this tearing, this shrieking cry that rose in pitch, and never seemed to fall. It seemed as if I was at the end of the world, and I was merely waiting to be lifted out into the vortex of the night. Now I knew where my brother had gone, and into what world Stella had vanished. Now I knew what my mother looked for when she spent her hours upon the climbing frame. This was the world she would fly up into, where the Flying Boats roamed. It had come for me now, this weather world. I had played long enough. Now I would join the other lost passengers, Stella and her poor hanging mother and father I no longer saw. Perhaps his body would come crashing through, perhaps his limbs, torn and crushed would brush up against my face. And I would vanish into the night, just like everyone else.

It was then I heard the trumpet, wailing down the corridor.

'You all right in there?' he cried and started to kick down the door. He was through within the minute, his little head perfectly combed, still dressed in his white bartender's uniform. He had a tea towel hanging from his back pocket and in one hand he held his trumpet. Over the other arm hung some clothing.

'Sorry to wake you like this sir,' he said, 'but as these buildings are very likely to fall about our ears and as you are our only guest staying in here tonight, I thought I better get you out as quickly as possible. I've seen some trashings in my time but this quite takes the biscuit. Put these on why don't you sir. I got them from the health club. Put these on and follow me.'

I put the tracksuit on and he led me back up the corridor.

'Do you know,' he said, putting the trumpet to his lips, 'I feel almost inspired tonight, as if I could play anything I chose to.' He ran through a few notes. 'Do you see what I mean, sir? Hear how that scale *rippled*. My fingers too. Pure electricity. What shall I play sir? Something rotten? Eddie Calvert? "Oh My Papa"?'

We trooped back to the bar. It sounded endless that trumpet, echoing up and down the empty corridors, calling to guests who were not there, guests who never would be there. It was our night now. The hotel and everything in it was ours, and though the night would be long, and though we might be swept away in the course of it, we would be taken while riding the high notes of Max Kaminsky's trumpet, flinging tunes into the air.

The bar was still intact, the glasses polished and in their place, the mirror shining at the back. The plate-glass windows still bent to the wind's call, the empty tables were still perfectly arranged. Three chickens stood on the counter, glistening black creatures, pecking away at several packets of cheese biscuits that lay open before them.

'Dibby, Sidney and Gob, sir. Got them in just in time. Saw their chicken-hut go past not twenty minutes later. Soup, that's what they'd be now. Cold soup. Look at that outside sir. The Devil and Mary Poppins if you ask me. Good name for a tune that. Shall I play it sir, while you pour? Cocktails I think would be appropriate.'

And so I began to mix the drinks for my little barman. There was a greenish glow in the sky and the drinks we made were coloured too, shot with raspberry syrup and grenadine and maraschino. We drank Irish cocktails and Imperial cocktails. We drank Pernod and kirsch and apricot brandy. We mixed Tom and Jerries and Charles Lindbergs and had three Damn the Weathers on the trot.

'I don't know,' he said finally, 'if Dibby and Sidney really appreciate the trumpet, though they do look like they could do with some more eats. I wonder if they realize the peril I put myself in to save their feathery souls.'

'They do look a bit cut up,' I said. 'They're not walking very steadily.'

'That's because they're drunk sir. They were pretty miserable when I brought them in, a bit damp and battered, so I fed them some bread soaked with whisky. The truth is I wanted to make them drowsy, so that they wouldn't make too much of a fuss, but I don't think I gave them quite enough. Whoops.'

Sidney fell sideways off the bar and fluttered to the floor. He pecked at my leg a couple of times before stumbling off and settling into an armchair.

'We're in a whirlpool sir, have you noticed? Sitting in the very centre of it, watching it all go down the plughole. I've never seen the world go *round* before, have you? I've been to a lot of places over the years, but this is the first time that I can truthfully say that I, Dickey Dove have been at the centre of things. What say you make us a nice Nose-Dive, while I play another selection! *These are a few of my favourite things?* Was that a greenhouse I saw go past?'

Like an elemental Pied Piper the storm had skipped through the town crying, 'Throw off your domestic yoke. Come with me and dance in my midnight ballet.' And so they came, from churches and bungalows, from shop windows and supermarkets, from broken homes and broken garden sheds. We saw tea-chests and traffic-cones, dustbins and frying-pans, clothes' lines full of waving shirts, brollies and benches and barbed wire fences, armchairs and butchers' bikes, milk bottles, prams, crates and cushions and carpets and the blank faces of five truant televisions. We were trapped by a wild chorus of beer kegs and bean poles and the loose baggage of Kent. Round and round they went, cart-wheeling their way across the forecourt. Outside the rain poured down the surface of the plate glass, sometimes clear and alive with bubbles, sometimes cloudy, soaping our view with its dirty water. The world had had its ravished suitcase torn out of its hand and stuffed unceremoniously into the sky, and we were here to watch it turn. There were times when I thought that the shapes and images cavorting in the dark came from the coloured cocktails swimming in my blood, but Dickey saw them too, I swear. Indeed it was Dickey who first noticed the arrival of the books. They came late, a tumultuous regiment of them, rifling their pages in the midnight air. They rode in with their loose jackets flapping open, like a dusty cavalry, the legions of the lost library, coming out of the swirling past. There were textbooks and story books and books in foreign tongue, maths books and picture books and books that could be sung, dictionaries and mysteries, anthologies and histories, books of poems, books of plays, books of prayers and books of praise, books for the night, books for the days, books of priestly memories. There were lavish books and lean books, messy books and mean books, books on the stomach, books on the spleen, books for the languid, books for the lean, books on prison and parts in panto, books on the law and Esperanto, books that rhyme, books that reason, books for the cold winter season, forgotten books, rotten books, ugly misbegotten books, books for Dennis and books for Dave, books for the cradle and books for the grave, books for mum and books for dad and books that drive mad men mad.

'The bayonets of war,' said Dickey Dove, 'could not have made a sharper impression. Look at the whiteness of it sir, the hue of it. Almost makes me want to dive into it. Like Edgar Allen Poe and that man on the sea. Gordon Arthur I believe his name was. Have we had a Pimms, by the way?'

'Play the Hilton Balcony,' I asked Dickey, reaching for the lemonade.

Dawn was coming up and the storm was growing tired of us. It began to move away. Suddenly the forecourt was empty and silent. If we listened hard, we could hear it still, playing out over the sea.

'It's all over then,' said Dickey yawning.

'Not quite,' I said. 'Look.'

Moving steadily down the road, raising her head to the storm's dying breath came a solitary puma, as lightly golden as the dawn was grey. She was wet and sleek and quivering from the night's work and she came into the forecourt and stood there like a ship's figurehead, resolute and proud.

'Must have come from the zoo down the road,' observed Dickey. 'I wonder how many more got out last night. I wouldn't mind seeing a couple of giraffes strolling about Ashford, though they're not carnivores of course. Tigers would be best I suppose, tigers and some irritable polar bears.'

We had eggs for breakfast that morning, eggs stolen out from under the chickens in their armchairs and boiled on the gas ring in Dickey's room at the back. The puma stayed with us, sniffing at the window and staring at us with her curious pale eyes. It was as if she knew that she was safe, that the elements had returned and that man was not in control.

'Lovely thing, ain't she sir,' Dickey said. 'Must be starving, poor creature. Half a mind to give it one of these chickens, though my daughter wouldn't hold with that I shouldn't wonder. Do you think it would be safe for me to go out there and give it something to eat sir? It's the least we can do. Give it some strength so it can run off before some nosey bastard rings up and gets it shot or tranquillized or what have you. It would be nice to see a bit of wildlife going native. I could introduce it to a few sheep I know.'

We mixed up a bowl of eggs and took them outside. She watched us while Dickey opened the door while I stuck my arm out.

'You'll have to go further out than that sir,' Dickey insisted, 'she'll never come that close,' so I edged myself nervously out under her watchful savage gaze. Then we went back to clean up our mess. We washed up the plates, rinsed out the glasses and brushed the floor and by the time we looked again the puma had gone. The bowl was empty and everything around us was smashed. The sky was sodden and low, and ill content with its work. There was more rain to come. The great trees at the back had all been pushed over. In the middle of the artificial pond stood a mangled collection of ironware, and though the dolphins still frolicked at the side, every one had lost its head. My car had a small dent where something had flown into the back of it, but otherwise it stood unharmed.

I unlocked the front door, climbed in and switched on the radio. The heaviest storm to hit Britain in living memory had just passed over. Power lines were down from Wales to Kent. There was no electricity. The telegraph wires were down. There were no phones. Most of the Southern Region Railway network was blocked by fallen trees (there were an estimated four hundred between Folkestone and Tonbridge alone). There were no trains. All roads and runways were blocked. Flood warnings were still out in many parts of the country. People were being told to stay at home. Questions were being asked as to why the Meteorological Office had not foreseen it, why the country had not been warned. I switched off in irritation. No one is allowed to make mistakes these days, to overlook the obvious, to simply *not know*.

'I'm one of those,' I told him. 'I should have been there. I probably would have been if it hadn't been . . .' My face drained.

'I know sir. You told me last night. You sang the whole of that Dylan song to prove your point. I am not a Dylan man myself, but I was impressed by your memory. Johnny is in the basement, I believe.'

'Johnny's *in* the basement,' I reminded him.

'Quite so sir. And you mixed up the medicine. It was quite a night sir. If it wasn't for all that water sir, I would have sworn we'd been at sea.'

'I think I'd better try and find her,' I said. 'Though God knows where she is.'

'She might have tried ringing last night sir, but who knows when the telephone lines went down. She's probably safe in some hotel or other. There's a nice pub down by the river at Wye. You could try that for a start. There're some guest houses further up in the village too, though it's some time since I was last there. Tell you what sir . . .'

He left me for a few moments and came back with a chain-saw, and a couple of cans, one for petrol, one for oil.

'You might find you'll be needing this. There'll be a few trees in your way and no mistake. Bring it back when you've finished with it. And the tracksuit. I've found an old overcoat of mine which you can have too. I looked into your room to see what I could find and frankly, this is the better cut. Good luck.'

It took me the best part of a day to get there. Many of the roads were blocked, not all by great trunks, but by obstacles big enough to slow me down. The air was filled with the sound of chain-saws. It seemed as if the whole of Kent were using them that day. Whenever I got out to pull a fallen branch back from the road, I could hear their shrill whine all around me and catch the blue smell of petrol floating across the fields. I enjoyed it, driving round the battered countryside, rounding a bend to find another tree down, another group of people clustered round its branches. I was glad of the storm. I liked the fallen trees and the wet green and the excitement of normal things displaced. They did too of course. It was what we all imagined the war to have been like. Not simply because of the spirit of camaraderie, but rather the state of nervous excitement which abounded. Young men threw off their jerseys and leapt on top of trunks rather than climbed; they twirled their chain-saws as if in a circus, eager to demonstrate their skill and muscle. It was a physical morning, a time of ropes and pulleys and working together. There was no going to work, but there was plenty to do, plenty to push and pull, plenty to sweat over. There would be trays of sandwiches and mugs of tea, and the pubs would stay open all day. Soon it would be the afternoon and it would get darker quicker and more completely than we had ever known. There would be candles and hurricane-lamps and the glow of open fires and once they had been lit and the shadows imprinted themselves upon the wall, then those tired limbs would stretch and turn and find another strength.

I reached Wye around three. I parked the car by the tall brick station and walked up. Apart from a few lost tiles and some broken windows there appeared to be little damage there. The pub had not heard of her, and neither had any of the three guest houses up the road. I wandered about knocking on doors, wandering up and down the bruised lanes, asking questions no one wished to answer. There was not much to Wye, just a few streets, a few shops, and by the end of a couple of hours I had learnt nothing. All that was left was the Ridge, the steep hill that climbed up to the downs, and as one shell-shocked inhabitant told me, 'no one's come down there today, so you're unlikely to go up.'

I managed to get the car up to where the road started to climb but he was right. From then on the road was completely blocked. The track cut deeply into the hillside, with a high bank of bracken rising up on the left and a densely wooded slope of mature oak falling away sharply to the right. The majority of these had all been torn out of their sockets and thrown across to the other side, so that the road had a low solid roof of fallen trees. It took me an hour to reach the top, by which time I had called at four houses and found nothing. But what was there to find? From the top of the hill I looked down upon the Weald. The noise of the chain-saw had gone. The country was getting drowsy, nursing its recent wounds. From this distance the destruction looked orderly, even pretty, with the rows of flattened trees laid out in patterns. Had Carol come up here? Had she found Stella? She must have done. But where? Was I to search every house? Impossible tonight at least. And where was she now, this thoughtful sister of mine? Had

Stella confided in Carol, and did Carol now understand *everything*? Was she now sharing a cup of coffee with her old time chum, laughing together over some schoolgirl indiscretion? No that wasn't Stella. Perhaps the confession was followed by catharsis. Perhaps Carol was helping her clear some great forest tangle, freeing her house from the ravages of the storm just as she had freed her from the prison of her past. Whatever they were up to there was nothing more for me to do. I would go back to the hotel, spend another night there and then see about getting home. I would leave a message with Dickey to say that I had gone back. Perhaps Carol had tried to get back already. How I didn't know, but there was Clare to think of, of course. There was no telling what had happened. In a matter of hours all normal means of communication had been obliterated. I couldn't drive to London. I couldn't telephone. I couldn't get the police. I couldn't even go down to Patrick on the marsh, at least I didn't think I could. No electricity, no phones, no movement except of a peculiarly isolated sort. It was as if we had been thrown into the Middle Ages, where community life was the only thing which kept everything together. I started down the hill. It was going to rain again soon, just for a change. By the time I reached the roof of trees it had already started, as thick and relentless as ever. As if the storm had never come. I looked through the slatted window of leaves and branches and saw the Weald of Kent preparing to swim another night. It was a Balcony view, a Landing view and I felt myself slip into the darkening water. I began to sing:

> Oh Mein Papa
> So Funny, so Adorable
> Always the Clown
> So funny in his ways

A low growl interrupted me. I looked down through the bruised foliage. There, standing over the body of my sister, stood the puma. She stood with her great head low, next to my sister's, and her pink tongue was licking away the blood that had dried down the side of my sister's face. My sister lay head down in the dirt, and in her fingers lay the handle of her battered brown bag. The back of her head was dark and a great branch had crushed her. She was covered in the greenest leaves, and had the puma not spoken I would have passed on down the hill and left her to her death. But the puma had found her. The puma had left the hotel and sniffed my sister out. She stood there now, nudging her, trying to move her head with her wet muzzle. Oh my Puma.

'Go now,' I said. 'She is safe with me.'

I tried to lift the tree but I could not. I held her hand and kissed her fingers. Hold on Carol I said. Hold on my dearest sister. Don't leave me, don't go away. Stay here. Stay here and I'll be back. And so I was. And so we brought her to safety. And still she threatens to leave me.

Three

I AM IN LOVE. I am in love with the nurse with the flat feet on Fleming Ward. I love her when she opens the swing doors with her fat behind, or when she hurries down the main ward checking to see if her hair is in place, but I love her most when she turns the corner and lumbers into the small room set aside for the badly broken, the desperate and the dying, the room where my sister lies. She is not overly timid, nor excessively attractive, nor is she put upon by any of the others (there is no real reason for me to show her extra kindness in other words) but I am in love with her just the same. I sit by my sister's bed and wait for the sound of her heavy feet coming down the corridor. I watch her approach the bedside and marvel at her little watch dangling at her breast. I am bewitched by the way her fingers hold my sister's wrist. I long to put my arm around the nurse with the flat feet, to stand near her as she examines my sister's charts, to bend close, to mix my hair with hers as we examine the slow descent of my sister's life. I would like the nurse with flat feet to know that I too am familiar with such devices, that I too can hold a check board, examine graphs, plot movements, record the fall and rise of temperatures, that I too am susceptible to wild surges, unexpected breezes, and am woken by surprise and the breath of God.

When I look upon my sister, when I examine her face or study her undressed body, it is as if I am looking upon a landscape dressed as a negative, upon which all recognized form lies, all manner of light and shade, all gradations of contour and depth remain, but which has been drained of colour and lives, if you like, on the other side of life. My sister is in another world, close to mine but quite removed. There is a huge chasm between us of fathomless depth, and whenever I attempt to call her I know my voice is lost in its unimaginable gloom. What could it be that would wake my sister? A word? A song? A chance remark? What-ever it is, it is clear a vital ingredient is missing, which is why we surround her, in time honoured fashion with artefacts of her past. It is why Clare plays her mother nursery songs and recites the very stories Carol first read out loud to her. It is why Monica appears from Brighton and perches on the edge of the bed and pronounces on Carol's business, (Monica has taken over the day-to-day run-ning of Carol's enterprise. Monica travels up to London twice a week and travels back alone, on the same day. Monica has become brisk and businesslike with me and awfully attractive, but for some time has denied herself the benefit of my employ), which is why my wife, bless her cotton socks, surfaces occasionally when she knows I will be there and enquires after my health, asks how well I am coping, impresses upon me in other words what I have been missing all these lovely years, and why I appear, every day (or rather *nearly* every day), with that relic of our connected past, Mrs Briggs's Bag, out of which I pull bits and pieces of Carol's shattered life. My sister is in many respects much the same as she was. Not surprisingly her daughter recognizes this. For Clare, this mother on the bed, with her immobile face and awkward body is much the same as the mother she knew when her daddy was alive, silent, uncommunicative, and demanding. Although we fuss over her, bring in flowers, make the room look pretty, it is all one-way traffic as it were, just as it was in her family days. So Clare performs for her, demonstrates her worth, as of old. The old Carol has returned and when she is with her mother I see the old Clare surfacing too. She knows how her mother has been injured (she does not know why) and when she sees her in the hospital I can see her little face career around inside, bewildered, frightened, alone. Though she does not say it (though she *cannot* say it), it is clear that part of her believes that her mother did this on purpose, that this return to the Carol we all knew and did *not* love, is absolutely *typical* of her, a grotesque demonstration of how stubborn she can be, and that the open arms and bathtimes of yesterday were but as the twenty-four-hour blooms that appear so suddenly in the desert, an unexpected vista of delight which lulls the brain and deceives the senses and which is gone as quickly as it came, to be replaced once again by the arid landscape of the sand. So my sister has not changed greatly. Her limbs and organs are intact. Her brain is (almost) the same. Her blood is dark and red like mine and yours, and it still seeps out of her at regular intervals. Her hair grows. Last month an ingrowing toenail was attended to. However, the composition of Carol, the distribution of her weight *is* changing. Her arms are growing thin, the flesh on her legs beginning to hang slack. Her breasts too are sliding away, evaporating, leaving her two pale nipples stranded on the reef of her ribcage. Only her buttocks flourish. They seem to grow in size every time she is revealed to me. She is draining into her behind, her blood, her fat, her water, all are sinking into this adipocerous pool. When she is washed, when we take a flannel to her and turn her from one side to the other, I half expect to hear my sister slosh about, to hear all that has vanished from her surface as a sort of fatty liquid rolling around inside.

My sister sleeps but she is not dormant. Events chase over her countenance like racing shadows in the moonlight. At odd moments, clouds of comprehension, the warm flush of what, memory? run over her skin revealing the life, the colour, that *is* there, just as the rising sun awakens the shadows of the night. The veins on her neck will pulse, a rose dawn will creep up from her belly and brush her breasts and neck, but my sister does not wake. The colour passes over, the mouth slackens, the limbs lose their tension and she lies still once more. Carol is for the most part at peace with herself, though at times (when there is an emergency, when there is a severe shortage of staff, once or twice a month in fact) she is still strapped to her bed in case she has one of her fits and pulls the drip feeds from her wasting arms. She gives plenty of warning of these attacks. Her pulse rate rises, the heart monitor takes on a new urgency, a shrill precursor of the impending crisis, and if you examine her face you will see underneath her eyelids, her eyes darting about their dark prison. Then her feet will start, and suddenly she will sit up, throwing her head from side to side, ducking and weaving and beating her hands into the air. It is clear to all of us where she believes herself to be, and though we try to calm her down it is only after she has beaten them off that she sinks back upon her bed to have the drip reinserted and the monitors replaced. There is an argument going on as to whether my sister should be strapped in at all. True it prevents self-inflicted damage but it also brings much fear in its wake. So constricted she is unable to defend herself and strains against the straps with such vigour that she has been known to move her cast-iron bed several feet across the floor. Both the nurse with flat feet and I concur that she *should* be allowed to duck and weave and tear the tubes out of her arms. It just might wake her up. But doctors are doctors. They know best.

It takes me thirty minutes to bathe my sister, to wash her pale skin, but it only takes me fifteen minutes if the nurse with flat feet is there to help me. There are parts of my sister I do not care to wash, that I am embarrassed to wash, and they are of course the parts which need the most attention, those and the sores which we treat with handfuls of an unpleasant-smelling cream. It is on these occasions, when I am bending closest to her, when my sister is so slippery, when the textual accent is so familiar but the body so foreign, when the nurse with flat feet and I are at our most intimate, that my sister tries to speak to us, when the air trapped in her loose coils, escapes. It comes from the front and from the rear, a dark and horrid language full of uncontrollable rage. Moans of articulate anguish, cries for help we are powerless to answer. It distresses me more than I can say and when it happens I want to leave the room. It is a noise I cannot bear, a sound I would never have thought to hear again, a dreadful drowning sound, the sound of those trees as they were pulled out of the ground, the sound of my father conducting himself in the privacy of his garage, the echo emanating from our empty Hall. I never thought another human would utter such a sound, not to my ears at least. Now, in the safety of her hospital room, in front of the nurse with flat feet and anybody else she cares to choose, my sister regularly torments and humiliates me, safe in the knowledge that I will always have to come back for more.

It takes me three quarters of an hour to get to my sister in the morning and a little less than that in the evening, particularly if I am leaving from work. When I am there I wander in and out, talking to the nurses, the doctors and the other residents. I am a fixture now, not a patient but more than a mere visitor, as regular as the vicar and a lot more fun. Part of the staff almost. When I walk through the ward it is as if some of the authority exercised up and down the ward has rubbed off on me, that I hold within my power some ability to improve their condition. I joke with them. I exchange banter. I listen to their complaints. I bring them magazines, fruit, the occasional bunch of flowers. In return they listen to me on the radio and compliment me on my delivery. I am a ladies' man and for the most part tolerably well dressed. I am flirtatious with the older ones and utterly correct with anyone under thirty-five, and though my eyes might stray to the screened bed at the far end of the ward from which the succulent figure of a would-be suicide sometimes emerges dressed in very casually worn bed attire I keep my distance and make no attempt at intrigue. I am a minor celebrity and because of that have quickly become part of the pecking order. I have as much influence on the morale of Fleming Ward as the trainee nurse from Birmingham or the red-headed one who comes from Ireland, whose name I forget and who is a little too tall for comfort.

I spend about an hour a day with my sister, sometimes more. In the evenings, in the early evenings, after school, I bring Clare along. I park by the school entrance and what do I see? Clare at the railings. Clare waiting on the school steps. Clare in her green coat and green hat standing underneath the brick arch on which is inscribed the instruction BOYS. She does not run to greet me. She stands alone, waiting. Clare has few friends. Like her mother, and like her uncle, like all her family, she is unable to make friends, or rather, she is unable to keep them. It is all of our own choosing. We know what it is to have a friend and we can recognize the benefits accrued thereof, but no matter. Friends are not for us. Friends require something which we cannot give. *Friendship*! Each generation learns this at an earlier stage in life than the one preceding it, which is why I came to my senses when I was seventeen, my sister somewhat earlier, say fifteen, and why Clare has discovered her true self at the age of eight. (We were all worried of course that under the influence of her father, the hero of the Diary of Death, she might have thought otherwise, and gone through life accompanied by people she could count on, people she could turn to, but luckily she was spared such folly and now has a slab of Portland stone, with her father's name and age upon it to remind her where such vanities belong.) So there is Clare at the railings. She opens the rear door of my immaculate car and settles down upon that long upholstered seat, the seat which is never used, which has no memory, which is blank to me, places her satchel to one side and straps herself in. Let us go then, she says. *Let us go*, as if she were a biblical child, visited with wisdom, as if *she* were leading *me*. *Let us go* she says and I pull out into the traffic. There are times when I am loath to take her to see her mother, when Carol's sores are worse or I have a general feeling of foreboding that her mother will be in one of her talkative moods, and then I pray that the traffic will be bad, and that we will be late and can get away quickly, but there are other times when Carol looks almost well, when this routine of ours seems normal, almost healthy. Then we walk back to the car with our spirits raised. But it does not last. It does not last.

The days of Clare are long days and they stretch me back along a thin, trembling line. When she first arrived, with her books, and her animals and her lump of moon rock, which she prays to every night (Oh Moon that is so far from me/ Shine tonight that I may see/ Your lovely face upon my bed/ Your lovely rays around my head/ But though you are so far away/ I have a piece of you to pray/ You, the earth's gold watch/ The stars your chain/ Who winds you up?/ That you may rise again?) it was obviously I who brought comfort to her, but over the weeks I have noticed that if anyone is at *home* in my flat, if anyone brings it warmth and security, it is Clare rather than me. What a child is I do not know. It is little legs and a large head. It is running feet and jumping up and down. It is quiet and serious and the possessor of worlds which impinge on your own. On occasions it is the leaping into the dark, becoming what it *will be* when it *is not*. Like the painter who can anticipate age, who will impart to his young subject a look, a vision, an expression beyond the child's years, so too will a child dip into her adult past. To see Clare staring at her moon rock, to hear her touching it and talking to it, to hear her sitting in the back of the car saying *Let us go then*, makes me wish I could take her into my confidence, that I could take her aside and *tell her things*. For if she can talk to her moon rock so steadily, if she can say *Let us go then*, could she not talk to me? Who else is there? Let us go then she says, adding, *and what have you got in Mrs Briggs's Bag today?* What indeed.

My time is divided now. I never knew that the clock was so constructed. I thought telling the time was easy. I am used to its dictates. I can sit at the console at the Weather Centre and watch the second hand sweep up to the appointed time of my performance, safe in the knowledge that I am in charge. The red light will flash, the green light will come on and off I go, jiggling my right knee, broadcasting to the nation with only a brief notepad as my prompt. I do not resort to a full script like some of my colleagues, nor can I pluck it out of the air as can Eric, but I can introduce, pronounce, joke, reassure, summarize, fill in, link, sign off, right up to the last second of my allotted time. Only Eric, with his slower, richer delivery, is my superior. But now. There are the half hours and the quarter hours, the forty minutes and the fifty minutes. There is one minute *to* and three minutes *past* and they all cram in on my day, crying *Look at me! It's my turn now. Three quarters of an hour!* There are the times to take Clare to school and the times to collect her, there are times to run her bath and times to make her breakfast, times to read her stories, and times to cover the kitchen table with discarded newspapers and let the colours run. There are clothes shops and shoe shops, the laundry and the library and the spaghetti treat on Saturdays. There is the park with its swings and slides and a great rumbling round thing I have to leap upon. There is the skating rink half a mile away. I am conscious of time passing as never before, of how long I have *spent*, or how long I have *left*. I have no time for myself and I have become a nervous visitor in its presence. I enquire after it as if time itself were the patient strapped on the bed and I its hovering relative. I look upon its surface and wonder what it is going to do to me, whether there will be any time left after it has done with me. If I do *find time*, if I manage to sneak out on my own, I dare not look back just in case Clare should be looking out the window, should catch me hurrying down the path, deserting her for those secret hours of the night. I start the car and pull away fast and though I am put through my paces happily enough, I dread the return the following day, when I might hear from Mrs Delguardo of the times Clare woke up, the times Clare cried, the times her breath came in gasps. If her mother is on the other side of a huge chasm, where the clock has stopped, then Clare and I are on a tightrope balancing over the dark below. How long we can keep our balance we cannot guess. We dare not look down, we dare not examine our plight, for we know that should we falter we can only totter and fall. All we know is that our past was briefly glorious, deliriously light. Oh we were happy then, Clare and I, she on the beach collecting fossils with her father, me wrapped in the luxury of an anonymous bed, intensity filling both our hearts. Now those days seem so distant, so alien, that it is with great difficulty that we can recognize them as real. Most probably they were not. They are gone for ever. Perhaps it is the same for Carol, that this *is* her life now, all she knows and all she needs to know. What beauty that?

Every two weeks I pick up my sister's hairdresser from her salon and take her in to cut my sister's ugly fringe and to rub oils into her flaking scalp. My sister's hairdresser greets her like a long lost friend and treats her to a barrage of gossip, though like everyone else she is inquisitive as to how Carol got into this state. Telling them a tree fell on her is not enough, for then they want to know *what* tree, and *where* tree and how come she was under it in the first place. What *was* Carol doing there they ask and I lie to them as best I can. We were visiting I tell them, visiting a friend of ours, Patrick Liddle. Visiting? says Mrs Delguardo. You never told me you were going visiting. Visiting? says Fleur. I didn't think you and Carol were the sort to go visiting. Visiting? says Eric. Funny time to be visiting. You sure she wasn't, you know, *visiting* and I shrug my shoulders. What Carol was doing that night on that hill is a question I would like the answer to myself. I sit on the narrow chair opposite and stare at her through the thick green bars of her cumbersome bed. I take my place by her side. I hold her hand. I whisper into her ear, so that Stella's name may leak in. I stand up and let Stella's name ring around the walls. But Carol will not tell me anything.

The only person who knows the true circumstances of Carol's catastrophe, besides Dickey Dove, is of course Monica, for it was Monica who Carol left so abruptly that night and it was Monica who accompanied me to Carol's house, four days later, to collect

Clare's belongings, to sort through Carol's affairs, *to fill Mrs Briggs's Bag to the very brim*. I drove down to see her as soon as the roads were clear. I didn't know what I would find. I didn't know whether Sailor Beware would be happily ensconced, nor did I much care. I wanted to hear what Carol had done that night and I was quite interested to hear what Monica had done that night too. What for instance did she do after Carol ran out on her? Had she returned to Brighton or what? Question; why, when Carol *did* leave Monica did *Monica* not ring me? Why did she not try and make use of this golden opportunity to see *me*. Had she rung of course, I might well have been out when Carol rang. Carol would have gone ahead without me. She would have got on that same train, hurried up that same High Street, and been knocked on the head by that same tree. No one would have found her the next morning and Carol would have died. So I was glad Monica did not ring me that night, but still aggrieved at her apparent lack of initiative. Monica held the key to many questions. Our encounter however was something I am not happy to recall.

Leading Seaman Oates was not there, or if he was Monica had packed him up and tidied him away. She greeted me in a blue towelling robe (which I have worn on occasions), and smelt as if she had just had a bath.

'Giles,' she said. 'What the hell are you doing here?' And then, just as quickly. 'It's Carol isn't it. What's happened? I knew I should have waited.'

While I began to tell her I noticed that Monica had been ironing her way through an enormous pile of the Sailor's washing: shirts, socks, voluminous male underpants. What on earth I thought is Monica doing, ironing this fellow's underpants? What's she doing ironing *anyone's* underpants? I tried to remember if the Woman from Spain, who irons my clothes once a week, irons my underpants. From the look of things I concluded that the Woman from Spain probably did, for my underpants looked much the same as these exhibits, folded and pressed and neatly stacked on a nearby armchair. The only difference between his and mine appeared to be that his were exclusively *white*. The Woman from Spain actually likes ironing. Though she would prefer to perform this task downstairs, out of harm's way (out of *my* way), I have installed an iron and an ironing-board in the neighbourhood of my airing-cupboard, so that when I am there I can have the luxury of the Woman from Spain ironing up in my flat when the Time for Ironing arises. Mrs Delguardo thinks I am being needlessly extravagant. The Woman from Spain does not mind going up and down the stairs, she tells me. She is young. It is no bother to her. But No, no, I say. I will not have it. (Ah, Mrs Delguardo, but I will.) The Woman from Spain takes great care when doing my ironing and sings softly to herself while doing it. There are no pains which she does not take. She is particularly solicitous to my shirts, sprinkling the cuffs with water, going round all the buttons and that little area between the shoulder and the neck which is so easy to overlook, and attends to the crease in my collar with an intensity that borders on the religious. At first I thought that the inordinate lengths the Woman from Spain went to were a means by which the Woman from Spain avoided taking care of my other pressing needs, but practical tests have shown that she is no less studious at the ironing-board *after* than *before*. The sight of all this ironed washing going to waste set me along my usual predictable course and by the end of my dreadful tale I was half hoping that Monica would cast off her robe and comfort me. Instead she announced that she was coming back up to London. She left the room and shut her bedroom door. Shut the door. On me, who has handled her naked form once a fortnight for the last three years. I found this behaviour hard to credit.

'What *are* you doing in there?' I called out.

'What do you think I'm doing?' she replied.

There was no answer to that.

We were soon back on the motorway. The plan was to collect Clare's things, sort through Carol's belongings, look at her finances, and then drive back down to Ashford. Although Carol was going to be transferred to London as soon as possible to be near her friends and relatives, that wasn't going to happen until her condition had stabilized. Monica greeted all these arrangements with her usual degree of efficiency, but what was lacking was, if you like, the personal touch. There was something bothering her, something more than Carol's death (Ah, what a slip of the tongue. That is not the right word for it is it? Let us call it her *animated death*), some other thing. She was acting as if she wanted to do it all on her own, as if I was in the way.

There were not many cars on the road and I planned to drive so fast that Monica would have to talk just to occupy her mind. I assumed the police had better things to do than to harass the odd speeding motorist. If we hadn't left in such an abrupt manner I would have lifted something from Monica's kitchen to help me on my way, a flagon of brandy perhaps, or a refreshing bottle of bourbon. Something to get me nice and drunk between Marine Parade and the M23. I hadn't touched a drop since the night with Dickey Dove and abstinence was beginning to take its toll. I switched the windscreen wipers to maximum speed to increase the sense of urgency.

'You must understand Monica,' I said, lurching into the fast lane and putting my foot down, 'what this means to me. First the death of my younger brother and then Stella's disappearance. It was something that hung over me for years.'

'*Your* younger brother?' Monica questioned. 'Not Carol's I suppose.'

Fifteen love to Monica. As a matter of fact, I ruminated, looking across at Monica's increasingly nervous face, I had never thought of him as Carol's younger brother. Only mine. Carol never really came into the equation. I tried to remember how she had been affected by his death, but could bring nothing to mind. All I could remember was her sorrow over the death of our neighbour's dog. Nelson I think he was called. She held a funeral for him at the bottom of their garden, but for poor baby brother, not a tear could I recall.

'Carol was five years older than him,' I told her. 'Carol had long gone. Carol left the family earlier than any of us. Carol was the first to leave. By the time I made the break Carol had already gone. She'd turned her room into that tent of hers, which she recreated everywhere she went. You know what Carol is like. You've been to her house. You've seen her bedroom. That's what it was like everywhere. College, flat-sharing, that cottage of theirs in Wiltshire. Always a version of Carol's room. It wasn't a den, like the pillbox down by the river. It was solely for her, a retreat, where she could wrap herself in scarves and tapestries and odd bits of cushion. Strangers were *not* welcome. That's why we were all so surprised when she took up with Ian. For all his faults, Ian could be quite jolly sometimes. He liked parties. He liked going out. He liked *people*. How Carol got him in her clutches I never could work out. Carol didn't like other people very much.'

'Carol *doesn't* like other people very much,' Monica corrected. 'And you Giles. Do you like other people? Or just other women? Jesus Christ, do you have to drive so fast? What are you trying to do, kill me?'

I took a deep breath and increased the car's speed. We were now hovering around one hundred and five. Another ten would do it. I switched on the headlights and started flashing the car ahead of me. At least it looked like a car. Visibility, as they say in the broadcasts, was poor.

'Look Monica,' I said. 'Let's talk about that another time. I want to know what happened. You saw her. Why don't you just tell me? Whoops.'

I pulled the wheel over and took him on the inside lane, hand down on the horn. It wasn't a question of bad driving, simply of defying every rule of the road I could imagine. I passed him with an inch or two between us, cutting back in front of him even though the middle lane was empty. Wrenching the wheel back I started to cross all three lanes with reckless precision, rocking from hard shoulder to crash barrier and back again. Finally I straightened up. Monica was hanging on to her seat, her knuckles wrapped around the edge. I clapped my hands in delight.

'That's what I like about this car,' I told her. 'For all its pretensions to good taste, when it comes to bad manners it knows exactly what to do. A kindred spirit. Do you ever get the feeling Monica, that sometimes you can do *exactly* what you want, that somehow you're unstoppable, unbeatable, unbreakable. That's what I feel like this afternoon. Unbreakable. One hundred and twenty!'

Five miles later the steering-wheel began to vibrate. Monica was mouthing those little inarticulate screams, so reminiscent of happier times. I waited while she got into her stride then gently took my foot off. I put my hand on her knee and patted it.

'OK, OK,' I said. 'I'm just a little wrought up that's all. I need to know what happened, Monica. I need to know what you saw that night. If you can tell me what happened maybe it might help Carol. I won't go any faster, I promise. Look, *you* can drive if you want to.'

We had fallen back to about eighty. I had to look closely at the cats' eyes to check we were still moving at all. But it had done the trick. Monica went limp. All the air came out of her with a rush. She leant forward and pushed the cigarette lighter in. Monica was going to talk.

'So tell me about it,' I said. 'You were in some wine bar with Carol, having a good old chinwag, when bang, in walks Stella.'

'Wrong. It wasn't like that at all. It wasn't Carol who first noticed her, it was me. Carol wouldn't have spotted her at all if I hadn't pointed her out.'

'But why would you point her out. You don't know her.' I gripped the wheel hard and turned to her. 'You don't know her do you?'

'I never set eyes on her before in my life,' Monica replied.

'I don't understand.'

'It was like this. I had rung Carol up the week before. We arranged to meet outside the National Gallery at about five. There was an exhibition I wanted to see and Carol was going to be around that area anyway. So we met up and we walked down to this bar I know near Charing Cross. We didn't know exactly what we were going to do. Meal, theatre, whatever. We both needed it. After the first bottle it was clear that what we wanted to do was to carry on drinking. We'd got the taste for it. I think we were both looking forward to getting a little drunk.'

'Strange choice of drinking partners,' I said. 'Carol never gets drunk. Of all the people I know in London the last person I would choose to accompany me on a piss-up would be Carol. She disapproves of drink. I always made a point of trying to get Ian drunk. She would try and ration his intake. God how it irritated me. I'm surprised she didn't do the same to you. She was always warning everyone off it.'

'Well, she wasn't issuing any warnings that night. Carol has changed or haven't you noticed? Carol *used* to disapprove of drink. Now, under the right circumstances she's a convert.

Anyway, it wasn't her choice to begin with. It was mine. I wanted the drink, not Carol. It was bloody dreadful outside. All that wind and rain. No one was going anywhere.'

'I know what the weather was like, Monica.'

'I went up to the bar to get another bottle of wine. We'd gone to that rather dirty place behind the station, in the catacombs. Very crowded, rather smelly, rather damp. No service to speak of, just a lot of rickety tables, and a rather harassed barman. I can't remember the name. Lots of little dark alcoves all over the place. Candles in bottles. That sort of thing.'

'I know where you mean. It's got a shabby red door and steep stairs down. Haven't we been there ourselves?'

'No. A lot of men take their mistresses there, so I am told,' she added pointedly.

'Monica.'

'OK. I went up to the bar and ordered another bottle. There was this woman standing there, alone, drinking half a bottle of champagne.'

'Stella.'

'So it would appear.'

'What did she look like?'

'I can't remember really. Tall, dark, quite thin, not exactly muscular, but strong looking. Mid-thirties? I wasn't looking at her. But I had an impression. Anyway, on the other side of her, lounging up at the bar were these two men, drinking beer, both a little the worse for wear, but not much. I've no idea what they were talking about, but as I was paying one of them stepped back, drained his glass, and said, "Yes, it's a rotten old world all right, but nothing that a few pints of wallop won't put right." And he put his glass down and shoved it across the counter for a refill. It was then that this woman, who had taken no notice of them before, turned round, smiled and hung her arms across their shoulders. A one-of-the-boys sort of stance. You know the sort of thing. You could see their eyes light up. This is better than the pub back home, they thought. Strange women putting their arms around them. *Attractive* strange women putting their arms around them. "Well now," she said. "I know it's only October, but as it's nearing the festive season, and as you both seem in such high spirits, such fun loving boys, I've a suggestion to make." "Always open to suggestions sweetheart," one of them replied. "Always try anything once." And there they all were, smiling away at each other and she bent into them, so that the three of them had their heads almost touching and said nice and slowly, "Why don't you give us all a nice early Christmas present and go and throw yourselves off the fucking bridge. Or better still put a rope round your necks and toss yourself off. I expect you're used to doing that." And with that she kissed them fiercely on the lips, one after the other, picked up her glass and moved back to her place, staring at the bar walls as if nothing had happened. These two fellows didn't know what had hit them. They looked round helplessly for some sort of confirmation that it was nothing to do with them. "What was that all about?" one of them asked looking at me. I shrugged my shoulders and gave the barman my money. The men returned to their beer. "Too much to drink," said one. "Santa not giving her enough," said the other. "Too near a couple of arseholes," I whispered to the barman as he handed me my change. "She should be so lucky," he said, smiling broadly. He'd enjoyed it. He was one of those barmen who thrive on anarchy. I went back to our table and settled down in front of Carol who'd been reading the newspaper while I'd been gone. "See that woman in black, the one with her back to us," I told her. "She's just been wonderfully rude to those two men over there. For no apparent reason. Just didn't like them that's all. I wish I could be like that to men that got to me." And Carol said there weren't that many hours in the day and we both laughed, and just then the woman turned round and ran her eyes over the place. It was dark where we were sitting, so she couldn't have seen us, but Carol saw her. She went all stiff and started to crouch down behind her drink. "Jesus Christ, Monica," she said. "Quick, sit in front of me. Move *over* for God's sake." When I was directly opposite her she lifted her head up again and moved it to one side, so that she could look at her again. "Jesus Christ," she said. "It is. After all these years. Give me that bottle," and she poured herself another drink. She was shaking, whether from nerves or excitement I couldn't tell, but I'd never seen her so tense. "What's up Carol?" and she just gulped it down. "God Monica," she said, – "You. Have. No.

Idea.", like that slowly, a pause between every word "You. Have. No. Idea." And just when I thought I was about to find out, she crouches down again and buries her head in that big ugly brown thing of hers . . .'

'Mrs Briggs's Bag.'

'That's it, saying, "She's coming over, she's coming over," and there I am sitting with my back to this woman, not knowing what's going to happen, seeing Carol desperately trying to hide, feeling this dreadful tension building up, not knowing whether I'm going to get a knife in my back or at the very least half a bottle of champagne emptied over my head, when the woman walks straight past us, up the stairs and out into the street. Carol gets up and says, "I'm sorry Monica but I've got to go. I can't explain now, but I've got to go. I'll call you later. Stay in the house if you want. I'll call tomorrow." And with that she left with her coat trailing on the floor and that bloody bag of hers half open, leaving me with a full bottle of Rioja and no one to talk to.

'Ah,' I said. 'I was going to mention that. Why didn't you call *me*? It's not often you're up in London.'

Monica looked at me. 'I didn't feel like it. It was not what I wanted. I'd met Carol to . . .'

'I know all about that Monica,' I said. 'Carol told me over the phone. She said that you wanted to talk to her about *men*. Seemed unlikely. Carol knows nothing about *men*.'

'She knows something about some men. She knows something about married men who turn out peculiar, about divorced men who *are* peculiar. She knows something about you, for instance.'

'For God's sake Monica. What do you want to go talking to Carol about me for? I thought we'd agreed to keep this between ourselves. I thought we'd agreed not to tell anyone.'

'Ah yes. There's a lot of not telling in your world isn't there Giles. *Not telling* is your modus operandi. Can't tell, won't tell. Perhaps for instance if you'd told everyone about the bloody hurricane none of this would have happened. I'd have stayed in Brighton, Carol would have gone back home and Clare would have her mother.'

'For pity's sake Monica, it's not as simple as that.'

'Of course it is. It's just that you don't choose to see it that way. It's always much easier for you not to tell. Otherwise you might look a fool or make a mistake, or let your guard down. Another enclosure. Another fucking club. Another private world. So fucking typical. Locked briefcases, weekend conferences, secret affairs, this car of yours. Why is it do you think that every car built nowadays has to look like an office? I mean why can't cars have curtains or plants in them?'

'You mean so that they can look like your office?'

'That's right. Like the one you wanted to fuck me in.'

'I thought we'd forgotten about that.'

'Car, office, the steps of St Paul's. It's all the same to you. Any time, any place. As long as it's not in your home. Why is that I wonder? You complain of Carol's bedroom, but you're not exactly brimming over with hospitality are you. Why is that I wonder? Don't I match the decor or something?'

'Monica. What is this? It's got nothing to do with you. You know how fond I am of you.'

'Ah yes, Monica, you know how fond I am of you. Monica, you know how much I like you. Monica, you know how I enjoy your company. Monica, get your legs open.'

'Monica I don't know what's brought all this on, but calm down. I didn't come down because of that. I haven't done anything have I?'

'No, but it's crossed your mind hasn't it? Don't think I haven't noticed. Why the hell do you think I shut the door? God, after fifteen minutes of preliminaries, no matter what, Giles wants to get his end away. Your sister is in a coma, your niece might become an orphan, and Giles is thinking about his erection. I mean you've probably got one now haven't you? Would you like me to have a look?'

She leant over and started fiddling with my zip.

'Jesus Christ, Monica, don't . . .' I began to squirm in my seat.

'What's the matter Giles? Don't you want to? Wouldn't it help you concentrate if I jerked you off first? Come on. Let's get these trousers off.'

'Jesus Christ, Monica, would you stop it. Leave me alone.' Monica slumped back and stared out of the window. 'As a matter of fact,' she said, 'I did think of ringing you up, but thought better of it.'

'Why? What did Carol say?'

Monica smiled. 'For a secretive man Giles I've always been fascinated by the way you love other people to talk about you. That's what I was doing that night. I wanted to get Carol talking about you without her knowing. Not unusual. I imagine in most affairs the partners share mutual acquaintances. Wouldn't you say that's true?'

'You seem very *au fait* with this sort of behaviour Monica,' I said.

'My dear Giles. You're much more experienced in this sort of game than I will ever be, of that I am sure. Don't you think I know anything. Do you honestly think I believe a man like you would be content with fucking me once a fortnight. I don't know who the others are and I don't really want to know. I suppose you view it a bit like crop rotation, a bit of ploughing here, a bit of seeding there, another one lying fallow over yonder. With the right sort of fertilizer, another joke, another drink, the odd gift, you see no reason why this can't go on forever. That's just what you would like. You see no reason why anything should change. You can keep coming down to Brighton. I can keep on lying to Johnny and you can carry on screwing the other members of your secret service. Everyone has a good time. No one gets hurt. Why should it change? Why should anything change? Change isn't in your vocabulary. It's another word that's strangely missing from the Giles Lexicon of Life. You're like a dictionary where real meanings have been blanked out and substituted with definitions to suit you: *Honesty* – what Giles wants to tell us; *Discussion* – what Giles wants to hear; *Openness* – what Giles will let out. Well Giles, *I* don't want to talk about it this time, OK? Let's just get to Carol's and sort this mess out as best we can. I've told you what happened. Let's leave it at that.'

We were in the suburbs now, and I had half a mind to stop the car, haul her out and leave her stranded on the pavement. On the other hand, up ahead lay Carol's house and the bathroom and I wondered whether or not I could use this setting again to my advantage, perhaps while rifling through Carol's effects or reaching over Clare's bed to grab her stuffed animals. Although Monica was right, what she didn't seem to realize was that it didn't necessarily make it true. I loved the secret part. The secret part was what made it best. What else was there? It was the secret part that drove her to my sister's mirror, and it had been the secret part ever since.

'One last thing,' I asked her, 'before you clam up altogether? Did you tell Carol what Stella had overheard?'

Monica stared out of the window. Her voice was weary.

'I didn't have time. Stella was up those stairs almost as soon as I got back to the table. It was all over in a minute.'

'So Carol never knew what Stella had heard.'

'No. Not that it mattered. It was only some fatuous remark between two fatuous men.'

Of course it was not simply some fatuous remark between two fatuous men, but I was not going to enlighten my reluctant travelling companion of its significance. *Can't tell, won't tell,* Monica had said and I thought how appropriate, how bloody fitting, that Monica should have chosen this moment to haul me over the coals. So I wouldn't bloody tell her what those words meant. I would take Monica to Carol's flat and let her sort through Carol's effects. I would hand over the keys to Carol's office, her engagement book and list of clients, and if things calmed down, I might even make a move on her while we rummaged about in Carol's bathroom, opening that memorable wall-cabinet which had once contained in its white-framed mirror the sudden spectacle of Monica the Half-Undressed, soon to be transformed into Monica the Three-Quarters-Fucked. As to those other matters, I would keep her in ignorance, even if it meant forfeiting these pleasures. I would tell Monica nothing.

'I will,' says the boy.

I look in the mirror. There he is sitting in the back with his wet hair and his satchel full of water. Mrs Briggs's Bag with its large brown handles lies next to him.

'You will,' I say deprecatingly. 'What does a boy know about bars and men and the drinking of several pints of strong beer. What do you know of women and their strange reactions to perfectly innocent phrases. It *is* a rotten old world but a boy is not usually sufficiently practised to know just how rotten. Not most boys.'

He does not reply to this but looks across to the brown entity on his left.

'You have Mrs Briggs's Bag now,' he says.

'Leave it alone,' I tell him. 'It is not yours. It never was yours.'

'It was everyone's,' the boy reminds me. 'Except Mrs Briggs's. It could have been mine. Only others chose to use it first. I never cared for it much anyway. It smelt.' He sniffs it. 'It still smells. Why hasn't it been thrown away?'

Why hasn't it been thrown away? He knows perfectly well why it hasn't been thrown away, and knows too why it now sits dark and empty in the back of my car. Only the brass bowl had more potency. I had often thought of the brass bowl and wondered what I would do with it if I came across it unexpectedly in some ignominious junk shop. What an awesome responsibility that would be. Would I dare take it home? Would I dare hold it in my hands and start to rub its grimy patterned surface? What dread would await me? Father as genie? Brother as bottled slave? God knows what might rise out of its gaping mouth. What chants I might hear again. What cries. What songs. *Die alten boson Lieder, die Traume bos und arg, die lasst uns jetzt begraben, holt einen grossen Sarg.* The olden songs of sorrow, The dreams so wild are past, We'll bury them e'er morrow, Bring then a coffin vast. And though Mrs Briggs's Bag *is* such a coffin vast, and stores within its interior our very bones, I harbour no such fear in its presence. Indeed I am reassured by the sight of Mrs Briggs's Bag and it is only a sense of the ridiculous that prevents me from telling this boy to fasten the seat-belt around its brown circumference.

'Be quiet,' I tell him. 'Your recollections are not wanted here.'

But what would he tell Monica of that day? How would he begin? His friend Fat Patrick had, amongst other things, a collection of snow storms. The Eiffel Tower, the Empire State Building, the Golden Gate Bridge, blue transparent domes in which danced a thousand snowflakes, and in his mind's eye he often imagined one such illumination depicting his home, with the backyard, the bonfire and his brother's climbing frame caught forever in the falling snow, a frozen tableau of that Boxing Day where nothing moved except the swirl of the weather. There was no indication that that day would be any different from any other Christmas occasion. Although his baby brother had died some nine months back, drowned in the cold waters of the Medway, his forehead bruised, round pebbles in his pocket, and though this Christmas was their first Christmas as *four* instead of *five*, to begin with it seemed the same as any other, a cold draught of undigested cheer hanging chill in the stomach of his family life. In an improbable and futile attempt to enter into the spirit of things his father had arrived home late one night and stuffed a handful of holly into the brass bowl, so that everytime the boy passed by and set the rickety table shaking on its rickety legs, the holly would move and scratch inside. It reminded him of nothing so much as their holiday bungalow at Camber Sands where, late at night his brother would reach up and scrape his fingernails down the thin walls, making his very spine stand up on end. It sounded as if someone were trapped inside, walled and bricked in, their mouth agape. A prison sound.

Outside in the back garden, underneath the disused climbing frame, his mother had constructed a vast pyramid of cardboard boxes, their lids squashed and closed and tied down with lengths of knotted string. All that morning she had tried to set it alight. She had stuffed it with firelighters and torn bundles of newspaper and had even run out with a shovelful of glowing anthracite, but it would not take. The night had been damp and a light snow was settling upon the bonfire's rectangular folds. Quite what it contained he was not sure (surely not his mother's old clothes, for that was all his mother wore, old clothes, faded clothes, clothes with patches and darns in them, clothes which did not speak of poverty but clothes which revealed neglect), but his mother had been bringing out these boxes over the past few days with a fierce determination that precluded questioning. As he stood on the Landing recently vacated by his father, who had been instructed to mount the remaining stairs and prepare himself for one of his rare, almost legendary baths, he saw his mother emerging from the garage carrying a green can of petrol. By his reckoning, and he was not a child for cars and the working of engines, it was a large can, filched at some time from down the Esplanade. A five-gallon can he suspected. He had seen stacks of them piled up against one of the derelict sheds in what had been known as Five Gallon Yard. She carried the can with difficulty, but not because she was a woman. She was strong, his mother. The can was full. He could see how she strained to lift it, the petrol spilling out of the wide unscrewed top, running down her big brown arms. As she approached the bonfire he was horrified to see her shake the contents out over her reluctant monument, throwing ribbons of petrol across it with an abandoned vigour that appeared, even from that distance, almost unnatural. Tiring of this his mother then mounted the climbing frame herself, and holding the can of petrol on her shoulder, began to pour the petrol down from above. Although he was not familiar with the exact properties of a large can of petrol evenly distributed over a six-foot pile of rubbish, he was of sufficient wit to realize that he knew more than his mother appeared to, and he thought it appropriate at this juncture to warn her of the dangers involved. He was just about to tap the window when, as she jumped clear, a great sheet of flame appeared, taking his mother by complete surprise. It shot up a full twenty feet and struck towards the house, flaring up outside his sister's bedroom window in an uninterrupted wall of crackling heat. Although protected by the glass, he put his hands over his eyes instinctively. For a moment he thought his mother had flown up with it, that this was all a choreographed demonstration of her odd behaviour, that she was quite literally flying the coop. An idiotic refrain ran through his head, *Goodbye cruel world, I'm off to join the circus*, and he saw his mother shoot out from an enormous cannon, winging her way out over the horizon. When he next looked down he saw that his mother was partially on fire. She was standing with her dress billowing up around her and her big red legs exposed. Her frizzy hair was smouldering. She appeared engulfed in flame, but not at all perturbed. She stood with arms outstretched while all around her was fire, fire in the air, fire on the ground, fire on the tips of her very fingers. His mother was not of this world. She too, like his sister and his baby brother had already left. The climbing frame itself burned vigorously with flames running up the parallel bars and the ladder and the hanging steel loops. More importantly the explosion had revealed the true nature of his mother's bonfire, for spilling out of the boxes he recognized all the books, and the toys, and clothing that had once belonged to his younger brother. His mother was burning his baby brother. He had already been cremated (how she fell at the altar that day, how she fell and cracked her head, rolling and screaming and beating her hands on the stone floor. How he had watched her, how everyone had watched her, this mother with no dignity, no sense of place. How embarrassed he had felt, how embarrassed they had all felt, and how he had wished that he had rolled and screamed alongside her), and now his mother was burning what was left of him, his little drawing books, his bent six-shooter, his stuffed animals, his woolly hats, even the little shoes that had covered his feet. His brother's life was being consumed before his very eyes.

Before he could cry out Carol burst out of the back door and launched into his mother as if she were on the school playing field, bringing their mother down in the manner of an experienced rugger player. To his knowledge Carol had never been to a rugger match. She had never been one of those girls who appeared on Saturday afternoon to watch their boyfriends play (she had no boyfriend), unlike Fat Patrick's sister who, before her departure, was almost as permanent a fixture on the playing field as the goal posts. He could never understand why that should be. Fat Patrick's beautiful elder sister was too beautiful and too elusive for boys who played rugby, but until she left for London she would often accompany the two of them to the playing fields to watch the school team play. She would make more noise than the two of them put together, running up and down the touchline, waving her scarf, shouting improbable words of encouragement. Why on earth does she do it? he once asked Fat Patrick. It isn't her school. You're not playing, and after watching her for five minutes dancing about in her tartan skirt and white ribbed sweater, Fat Patrick suggested it was the opportunity of examining a wide variety of boys' legs that drove her to such acts of insanity. I don't believe she cares for boys' legs, he had replied after a further five minutes' study, and it was true. Jump up and down as she might, once it was all over, once the whistle was blown, she showed no interest in the collection of muddy young men who ambled over to exchange pleasantries with her despised and overweight brother. Perhaps in her spare time though, in one of those all-girl get-togethers they heard so much about, she had been coaching Carol in the ways and means of rugger play, for his sister ran up behind their mother and brought her down in a classic flying tackle that could have graced the turf at Twickenham. Steam arose from his mother's hair and as he watched them roll around on the wet ground it occurred to him that his sister was not rescuing his mother from immolation but fighting with her over his brother's life. He was sure that he saw her bite his mother's leg. Then there came the second explosion (who knows what else Mother had inserted into the womb of this fire?), lifting into the air all the curling and burning boxes, and out of every one of them came every little thing that had belonged to his brother, turned and sifted in the tender flames. And when the dust had settled, there hung on a blackened rose bush Mrs Briggs's Bag. The Indestructible Mrs Briggs's Bag, the brown museum of the age, thrown out by Mrs Briggs, snatched from the jaws of the dustcart by his baby brother and taken to his den. Mrs Briggs's Bag, a bag for conkers and apples and dirty snowballs, a stowaway's bag, a pirate's bag, a bag even for soot. Carol wrenched it from the rose bush and ran back with it to her room. Carol dried it and rubbed it and filled it with dried flowers and lavender bags and abandoned nests, *dead* things. Later it carried Carol's books when she attended her university lectures and protected her white nightdress from the westerly showers that accompanied her first weekend with her future husband. Carol's shopping bag, Carol's overnight bag, Carol's handbag, Carol's statement to the world. Carol doesn't care what you think of the disgusting old thing. And Carol had it with her that night.

'I believe,' I say, 'that on occasions, when Carol was not around, and sometimes when she was, you used it for your own ends, to pack *your* clothes away, to have *your* clothes protected from the westerly rains. If I recall correctly there were times, when you and Stella chose to disrobe al fresco, and would take Mrs Briggs's Bag with you, so that should the opportunity arise you could skip through the town safe in the knowledge that Mrs Briggs's Bag was keeping your clothing nice and dry. Perhaps if you look closely within its many pockets you might find a small memento of those activities.'

The boy buries his head in its dark, damp interior.

'There is nothing here,' he says. 'The bag is empty.'

Of course it is empty. When I finally got home I took it upstairs and shook the contents out on my bed. Now I intended to fill it again, to take Mrs Briggs's Bag to Carol's home and fill it with whatever I could find, to fill it and take it to the small room at the end of Fleming Ward and to sit by my sister's bed and bring her life out bit by bit.

'She is no better then?' the boy asks.

'It is early days,' I tell him. 'But the signs are that it could take some time.'

The boy smiles. It is a smile of the dark, a smile that is only seen in mirrors, or made behind one's back.

'Yes,' he says. 'It's a rotten old world all right.'

'You need several pints of strong beer to be in a position to say things like that,' I tell him. 'It is not a phrase to be used by boys at all.'

'It is not,' he says quietly, 'a phrase to be used in front of boys either.'

'It is not,' I agree.

'Or girls for that matter.'

'Or girls,' I repeat.

'*Especially* girls,' he affirms.

'Especially girls.'

'It's a rotten old world for girls,' he says. 'And boys.' We drive on in silence.

'By the way,' he says. 'I've written another one of those stories.'

'Why don't you read it to me?' I ask him. 'She's not listening.'

'Only if you go faster,' he replies.

I look at Monica and put my foot down once again.

The Second Bad Tale of Mr Muchmore

Mr Muchmore wakes. It is Saturday. He sits on the edge of the bed for a few minutes then crosses to the window. The grass is wet but there is already a warmth to the air. Across the fence he can see the Liddle girl setting up a deckchair. She is wearing one of those modern bikinis.

He has a momentary feeling of nausea. He turns to his wife and pokes her in the neck.

'I'm off to the garden,' he says. 'I'll have breakfast in half an hour.'

Downstairs he places his daughter's raincoat over his pajamas and pulls his wellington boots over his feet. Out in the garden he can hear the sound of more furniture being assembled. The Liddles are preparing for a whole day of lolling about. Mr Muchmore is seized with a need to push something, something that will make an unpleasant noise. He strides off in the direction of the garden shed. When he opens the door and smells the scent of old oil and faded grass, he settles down on the unused lavatory and thinks of his breakfast to come, of the four rashers of green back bacon, the carefully quartered tomatoes, the spoonful of fried potato, the neat triangles of fried bread, and above all his two fried eggs, their yellow heads covered with a delicate film of white. All this will lie on his plate, sensual and responsive to his desire. He is reminded of something and decides to look over into his next door neighbour's garden once again. At the very vantage point he chooses, he is disconcerted to discover Mr Liddle pruning one of his rose bushes. He decides to complain about the overhanging branches.

Twenty minutes later Mr Muchmore comes in from the garden. Jim Liddle has been telling him about his son's plan to go to college, and in his anger, for Mr Muchmore has no sons, Mr Muchmore has sliced off part of his foot with the electric lawnmower. The blade went clean through the sole of his boot. His face is quite pale.

'Martha,' he says. 'Thank God.'

'Breakfast is ready dear,' Martha says, and points to his seat.

Breakfast. Mr Muchmore blinks. I must pull my boot off, he thinks, but I must be careful or everything will rush out. He can still see his neighbour's daughter lounging about on a beach towel while he had to listen to all that prattle about further education. I should sit down, he thinks, and have some hot sweet tea. I could be in shock. Breakfast eh?

'Breakfast eh?' Mr Muchmore says.

'Kippers,' Martha tells him.

Mr Muchmore sits down and grunts. Kippers. He pokes at them with his fork and finds them quite free of bones.

'Where are their bones, Martha?' he asks. 'Where are their spines? Do you think that is what our stout fishermen brave the elements for? So that we may eat spineless kippers. I would be interested to learn the evolutionary process of such fish.'

He spears one on his fork and lifts it up to the light.

'How for instance do you think they get from one wave to another without a spine? What is it do you think that moves their fins from side to side? Willpower?'

He returns the kipper to his plate and starts to cut it into small pieces. He tastes it. It is rather good.

'I suppose they came in an attractive packet. What did they call them I wonder that attracted you so? Floater Paste?' He laughs.

A large puddle of blood seeps out from Mr Muchmore's right boot. When he has finished his kippers Mr Muchmore turns his attention to his side plate and eats three slices of bread and drinks three cups of sweet tea. After breakfast Mr Muchmore faints and slips down under the table. He holds his hands above his head as he goes down. He is sliding into deep water. He is enclosed. Martha bends down and lifts the tablecloth. Her husband is lying in a pool of blood. She cries out and pushes back the table. She loses her balance and slips heavily on the slippery surface. She hurts her back and has difficulty in getting up again. She climbs up on to her knees. Her hands are sticky and she is in pain. She reaches over and pulls off her husband's boot. It is like pulling apart a small seaside dam. She looks down at her husband's foot which is raw and red and pumping blood. She lifts up the boot so that the heel points to the floor and shakes the boot about. Three toes can be heard rattling inside.

'The thing is,' says Mr Muchmore in his hospital bed, 'what happened to my three toes?'

'It is a mystery,' agrees Martha. She turns her head away and looks out of the window. To her the light seems unnaturally bright, like a sudden burst of flame. It illuminates her every feature. She faces her husband with fire on her face.

'Perhaps they flew off into the garden.' She raises her fingers to her lips. 'Perhaps they were minced rather than chopped.'

'They were chopped Martha. The blade went in and chopped my toes off. I was pushing a lawnmower, not a Kenwood Cheffette.'

Mr Muchmore is lying with both his head and his sliced foot slightly raised. He lost three pints of blood and three toes. The blood has been replaced but the three toes remain unanswered for. 'Had your wife found them and brought them here in time,' the doctor had told him, 'we could have sewn them back on, but as it is . . .'

'Very odd my toes disappearing like that,' says Mr Muchmore. 'I'm sure I had them with me when I came in from the garden. Are you sure Dodo didn't have them?'

'The vet found nothing,' Martha tells him for the third time.

'Nothing at all?'

'Nothing you would be interested in.'

'Stomach clean?'

'Quite clean. He hadn't had anything since his evening meal.'

'What about his bowel. Did you tell the vet to take a good look at his bowel.'

'Nothing in his bowel either Leonard.'

Mr Muchmore scowled.

'You shouldn't have had him cremated Martha. I would have liked to have a good look at him myself. The dirty dog!'

Mr Muchmore falls silent. Trust Dodo to die under the anaesthetic. Mrs Muchmore remembers the expression on his face. Her darling Dodo. But what could she have done? He had insisted. And yet. There are tears in her eyes. Three of them fall on the back of her hand. She tastes them one by one. Mr Muchmore looks at her sharply. He has noticed nothing.

'And what about that blighter Liddle. Him and that daughter of his. They were there when it happened. Haven't come to visit me of course, not that I'd want to see that little madam. Did you get them to search their garden?'

'I did dear.'

'Well you shouldn't have. You should have done it yourself. Don't trust those Liddles. Letting her wander around the garden with no clothes on at all hours of the day. Her mother's no better. Should have taken a good look inside their fridge while you were at it. I wouldn't put it past him to have packed my toes up in ice, ready to ransom them off one by one. College indeed.'

Mrs Muchmore says nothing but stares at her husband. It is something he is not used to and if he could he would grab hold of her and stuff her under the bed. She folds her hands and asks simply, 'And when do you think you will be coming home?'

Mr Muchmore pats his pillow. The masterful weight of this institution lies easily upon his shoulders. What could his wife know of such things?

'A few days. Doctor says my balance is to be impaired. For your information toes, Martha, are an essential requirement of keeping upright. Doctor says I shall probably fall down a lot.'

Mrs Muchmore places a hand on her husband's shoulder.

'I'm sure you will dear,' she says.

Mr Muchmore is sent home after three days. He falls over in the driveway and he falls over again when he gets up off the gravel. He tries to use his stick as little as possible, so he falls over a third time on the way to the dinner table. Martha had suggested that he have his dinner on his lap, in front of the television, but he tells her that normal routine is not to be disturbed.

The food at the hospital had been excellent, but he had had no appetite. Or had it been quite the opposite? Mr Muchmore cannot remember. He only knows that he hasn't eaten for days and as he climbs up on to his chair his whole body is desperate for food. For his first dinner home, Mrs Muchmore has cooked her husband a giant steak and kidney pie. It sits on the table like something oiled and naked on a white beach. There is a shine to it that obsesses his eye. He can see it breathe, see it rise and fall, see it quiver in the heat. He would like to touch it, to run his fingers lightly over its surface, to bend low and hear it turn and murmur songs of praise. New potatoes and a bowlful of fresh garden peas accompany it, set discreetly on either side, but they are unimportant. This is a pie world, where everything is golden and perfect, where fulfilment comes to the man with the starched white napkin, the appetite, and the willing knife. This is a pie world and Mr Muchmore is the pie king.

Mrs Muchmore cuts the first portion. He marvels at the flood of smells that envelop his soul. I am strong again, he thinks. She cuts deeper. She lifts the crust carefully and places a portion of it on the side of his plate, then spoons a dark and glistening jungle of food into the centre. Three huge spoonfuls. He helps himself to vegetables and prepares to eat. He sees that his wife's plate is empty. She makes no move to eat.

'Aren't you hungry?' he asks.

'You eat,' she says.

He eats. The most splendid pie he has ever tasted. Good thick cuts of rump steak, a bountiful supply of quartered ox kidneys, a dozen or so oysters, sliced mushrooms, a sauce consisting of good red wine and a rich stock. He can identify them all. And yet? There is an extra ingredient which evades him. There must be, for no pie he has eaten has ever tasted as good as this. This is the mother and father of pies, the greatest pie in the world, the greatest pie ever made! Every pie that was a pie is in this pie, and every future pie that aspires to greatness will look to its shimmering magnificence. All pie knowledge and pie folklore lie beneath its lovely crust, but there is something else here too. This pie is personal. It is his pie. Only he can eat it.

'I must say Martha,' he says, after his third helping, 'this is quite the most wonderful pie I have ever tasted.

After a few more spoonfuls of this pie I could almost imagine myself sprouting wings! What do you say to that Martha? Imagine me, sprouting wings, flying about the garden! What in heaven's name have you put in it?'

'Oh the usual things.' Martha looks content. 'Nothing special. You eat up. Don't worry about me. I'm not hungry.'

Mr Muchmore does not worry about her. He eats as much as he wants. At one point, when ladling out his fifth helping he cannot see himself ever stopping. He turns the innards of the pie happily in his mouth and when he has to wipe a trickle of gravy from his chin, he grins the grin of a baby, helpless and happy. He is in heaven. His cheeks are lined with nectar. His tongue is diving into honey. His teeth are running and dancing around his mouth. He feels like a small child in a wood full of bluebells. Another mouthful. He balances it on his tongue, he throws it up to the roof of his mouth, catches it between his teeth, giving it a playful squeeze. He can feel his mother's huge swollen nipple squirting something sweet and sticky into his mouth. But what is this? He rolls it about his mouth again. He presses it against his roof, trying to determine the shape and texture. It *is* a nipple. No! It can't be. He places it nervously on his teeth, first on one side and then on the other. He bites it gently. Something horrible is happening. It is like the dream he has of excrement coming out of his mouth. His hands fly to his throat. He can feel himself gagging. He opens his mouth and a great stream of foul slime comes pouring out. How quickly it has all changed! He begins to retch. He looks at his dinner and examines it with his fingers. There it is! He has found it! He holds it up to the light.

'Whatever is the matter dear,' Martha asks. 'Something gone down the wrong way?'

'It's this bloody pie of yours. Nearly choked to death. Look at that. A piece of india rubber. What do you think you're playing at?'

He does not want to look at his wife ever again. He would like never to talk to her again. All he can think of is the feel of that hard little thing working away in his mouth but he knows he has to tell her. It shames him and drives him to great anger.

'Do you know Martha,' he says, 'that for one awful moment I thought I was chewing on a bit of my own toe. It felt just like it. For one ghastly moment I thought that somehow the remains of my toe had got into that pie and that I was eating a part of myself. What a terrible thought, eh Martha? What a horrible thing to think! Why, if it *had* been a piece of my toe it could hardly have got in there by accident could it? It would have meant that *you* had put it in there, quite deliberately. What a terrible thing to think, eh Martha? Take it away. I've had enough.'

Martha clears the table and turns out the lights.

'What the devil! Ah, cake!'

Mrs Muchmore enters with a large chocolate cake on a plate. There are three candles stuck in the middle, one for each day you were away, she tells him. Mr Muchmore looks uneasy. They are fat, squat candles, ugly and slightly bent. They are not fit for a cake, or for anything else. They are candles made in an asylum.

'Where did you get those candles from?' he asks her.

'I made them specially,' she tells him.

Mr Muchmore grows cold. His wife has gone quite mad. She is not fit for this house. Not as a mother. Not as a wife. He uproots the candles and snaps them in half. Ugly wax through and through. Pain shoots through his leg. He reaches over and grabs her by the hair.

'What have you done with them,' he cries, and pushes her face into the icing. When he raises her head he sees that she is wearing the clownish grin of an idiot and her face is covered in shit. Mr Muchmore puts his hands around his wife's neck and squeezes hard.

'What have you done with them?' he cries again.

'Put it in the bag,' I tell him, 'so that I may read it later.'

He rolls down the window and feeds it to the air.

'You should know by now,' he says, 'that I don't like to keep anything in writing. Letters, essays, diaries.'

'I wonder,' I say, 'if Monica here keeps a diary?'

'Why don't you ask her?'

I look across at my silent companion. I didn't want to know.

'Hand the bag over then,' I said. 'It's time it got filled up again.'

*

GOING THROUGH Carol's house took more time than I had anticipated and if Monica hadn't been there looking over my shoulder all the time, distracting me, deflecting me from my real intentions, it would have been a lot simpler and would have caused a lot less aggro. If I had been on my own, with just the Bag in tow I would have cracked open a bottle of Dead Husband's claret and gone through everything, Carol's letters, her finances, her clothes, the Diary of Death, *everything*. I would have spent the whole evening sniffing my sister out, and after I had arranged the best bits out on the carpet, I would have packed them all into Mrs Briggs's Bag and gone home to the Woman from Spain's ironing. I could have returned to Ashford knowing more about my sister than I had ever done before, sat down by her side and started whispering her little life in her ear (which is what I intended to do over the coming weeks, goad her, prod her, nudge her awake). But Monica was here with her notepad and I had no inclination to include her in the proceedings. I sent her upstairs to go through Clare's clothes while I snuck into Carol's office and rooted through her writing-desk.

It was, of course, in perfect working order, lap-top computer, filing cabinet, in-tray, out-tray, everything labelled and tucked neatly in its place. House, Mortgage, Insurance, Car, VAT, Clare, Father, Father? I bloody knew it. She couldn't leave him alone could she? She had to keep in touch with him from some misguided sense of what, loyalty? Love? Duty? How could she? Carol never forgave me for turning my back on him that day, on my way to the station. I saw him down the far end of the alleyway clutching at his stomach, gasping for air, slipping down the wooden fencing to lie against the gutteral bars of a municipal drain as he heaved into Rochester's sewage system. Seeing Father lie face down, his body jerking almost rhythmically, I was made aware of what the body could look like while effecting congress, splayed out, helpless, barely in control. Carol believed I should have gone to his help, that I should have picked him up and carried him home, so that all our neighbours, who I did not care about, could draw back their curtains and see the remnants of our family totter back in disgrace. Impossible. I had a train to catch, essays to complete, beguiling offers to turn down. How was I to know that that was to be the last time I would see him, that later that term I would learn that Father, like Stella had gone walkabout? Ah, I hadn't told you that. I have been unfair. It is a habit with me you see, this disappearing act. First Stella, and later, three or four years later, Father. I wave my arms and they all disappear. A phone call from Carol told me. Yes, another phone call. She had gone down and discovered the house quite empty. From the bills on the doormat it became obvious that Father hadn't been seen for some time.

'Why didn't anyone tell us before?' she wailed down the phone, interrupting my studies, 'Why didn't he call me. Where is he?'

'He's probably gone off somewhere. Germany. And he hasn't called you', I added, 'because he hates talking. You know that.'

'But after all that's happened,' she cried. 'I would have gone down to help.'

'How could you have helped? He's gone. You should be grateful. You don't have to see him any more.'

'You don't understand,' she said. 'They found him in the gutter.'

'The gutter?' I said. 'What again?'

'Giles. What do you mean, again?' and I told her how six weeks before I had seen him reeling and staggering and spewing his way home one afternoon, and how I had turned on my heels and left him.

'Giles,' said Carol, 'he wasn't drunk. Not especially. He'd been *beaten up*, by those thugs from the works. After all those years they set on him like a bunch of savages. They got who did it, one of them anyway. Father recognized him. Do you know who it was? That bloody Scotsman we saw up at Stella's. Gordon somebody-or-other. He'd moved back up north and had come down for the weekend. He saw Father coming out of a bar and just dragged him down to the river and beat him up. In broad daylight with half the town looking on! Everyone thought they were just a couple of drunken football supporters, celebrating. No one took a blind bit of notice, but as soon as he got him down by the river . . . It's so *horrible*.' She started to cry.

'It's all right,' I told her.

'It's not all right,' she sobbed. 'That's not the worst of it. They held him up and stuffed his mouth with sweet papers and . . .'

'. . . and what?' I asked.

'Dog shit!' she screamed. 'They stuffed his mouth with dog shit and beat him up! Poor Father. What did he do to deserve that? Luckily *somebody* took pity on him Giles, *somebody* helped him home, *somebody* called the doctor. It should have been you.'

'I thought he was drunk,' I told her. 'If I'd known . . .'

'Yes. Well perhaps you shouldn't always be so ready to think the worst of everybody. Luckily there wasn't much internal damage. A couple of suspected cracked ribs and heavy bruising, that's all. They kept him in one night for observation then sent him home. And now this. Where is he? I'm desperately worried. Nothing taken, no clothes, no money. Car in the garage.'

I could hardly bear this conversation.

'What about the Scotsman,' I asked, dreading the reply, 'they don't think he's got a hand in this?'

'No. Father gave the police his name and he was arrested getting off a train at Glasgow, drunk of course, and taken to the police station. When he learnt what he was being charged with he went berserk and smashed up the room. They're still holding him.'

'Well that's a relief. I wouldn't want him to have done anything foolish.'

'Foolish!' Carol almost had a fit. 'Foolish! What are you talking about? You almost sound sorry for the man. He beat up our father! An unprovoked brutal assault by a common-place thug. The infuriating thing is that with Father gone they don't think they'll be able to press charges. Except for destruction of property. Fancy him getting off scot free like that.'

'I wouldn't worry about that Carol. I'm sure the Glaswegian police don't take lightly to their decor being changed. I'm sure they'll have lots of little treats in store for Gordon Mackenzie.'

'Mackenzie. That's it. Fancy you remembering his name.'

It was months later, after I had made no attempt to elicit any further news that she informed me rather sniffily that she, or rather the Salvation Army, had found him. Would you believe it, Father had taken to the road, Father had packed all his troubles in his old kit bag and taken his sprained ribs to the highways and byways of Kent. Father was now a tramp! I put down the phone and laughed. How I laughed. And from that moment on I made it a point not to give money, shelter, or a mug of hot sweet tea to anybody whose circumstances appeared worse than mine, a resolution I have yet to break. As for our house and its contents, after various legal complications, claims, depositions, power of attorney, all that tedious stuff (which I believe he signed away in the privacy of a dormitory bed), Carol sold the lot and kept the money in trust. 'For fuck's sake,' I said to her, 'I thought the whole idea was to divide it up. My half would enhance my social standing at university no end.' But she told me no, it was to be placed in trust, where he could call upon it whenever it was needed. Now, according to this buff-coloured file, our father's trust, so carefully nurtured over the years had been redirected in early 1980 towards the maintenance of Carol's own daughter. The crafty cunt. Which presumably meant that Father had died. She could have told me.

As if that wasn't enough, underneath I came upon a bundle of postcards. Not signed but obviously from him. I recognized the spidery handwriting (Oh how I recognized it). Typically Carol had arranged them in chronological order, and by looking at the postmarks I could see where Father had been walking over these years. Up and down his corner of Kent; Gillingham, Whitstable, Herne Bay, Broadstairs, Folkestone, Ashford, Lenham, Maidstone. A sort of squashed circle. There were no more than one or two a year. The messages were as brief. My father had written about two things. The Weather and Nothing. Gillingham August 1971: *Heavy rain last night. Nothing for me here.* Sittingbourne March 1973: *Ice on the Road. Nothing that I can't cope with.* Margate June 1973: *Sun at last. Nothing to report.* Three or four words, and all denials. Maidstone, February 1974: *Bitter cold. I have a small foot problem. Nothing to worry about.* A gap, of over two years. Then a postcard of Pegwell Bay. July 1976:

The heat makes me very thirsty. Nothing cools me. On they went. Deal September 1977: *Warm evenings. Nothing keeps me awake.* Canterbury December 1978: *Snowed in. Nothing to do.* The last two followed in quick succession. Canterbury December 1979: *Rainbow. Nothing at the end.* Ashford January 1980. *Unbearably hot. In hospital. Nothing left.* I put them in my inside pocket. Postcards from home. I moved on to the other rooms. There were the usual sets of photographs dotted around, Clare at School, Clare in the Garden, Clare on the Beach, Clare and Mother, Clare and Uncle. But not one of Clare and her father.

Monica came downstairs with two great suitcases.

'It's all here,' I told her. 'All except her will. I can't find that anywhere. She must have made one.'

'There's a deed-box in the bedroom cupboard,' she said. 'I haven't opened it. Perhaps it's in that.'

It took two kitchen knives to break the lock open. Monica was right. On the very top lay the last will and testament of Carol Hayward, née Doughty. I rolled it up and stuck it in my pocket. There were other papers underneath. I tipped the lot out on the bed. There were the usual things, birth certificates, marriage licence, letters from Ian, another smaller bundle. But there was something else. With Monica looking over my shoulder I peered inside.

'Good God,' I said, quite involuntarily.

Monica strained forward, leaning close to me. 'What is it?' she said.

Had it been anything else I would have touched her, pulled her close to me, tried to resume normal service, but I did not. I stared into the dark and empty recesses of the deed-box. Sitting snugly on the bottom sat a brass bowl, a brass bowl that I had last seen playing tunes on a rickety table in a dark and empty hall.

Monica put her hand in to take it out. I grabbed her arm.

'No!' I said. 'Leave it there. I don't know if I can bear to touch it. This is the second thing that I have seen today that Carol has kept from me.'

I put my hand into my inside pocket and showed her. 'I found these downstairs,' I told her. 'They're from my father. That bowl is from my father.'

She knew about my father. Carol had made certain of that. She flicked through them. 'Are these all?' she asked.

'That's the lot.'

She got up. 'I think you'll find,' she said, buried in the depths of the bedroom cupboard, 'that there are more here. I found them earlier but I didn't think they were important. I recognize the handwriting. I'm sure they are from him.'

She brought out a bundle of letters held together by a couple of bootlaces. I took one out. She was right. It was my father's handwriting, addressed to a Mrs Mayhew in Croydon. A name I was not familiar with, though I knew well enough the soubriquet with which he addressed her. Mrs M. Even before I read *that* name I knew what I would find, for I recognized the notepaper, lined and jagged at one edge, as if torn out of a school exercise book. Carol must have found them when clearing out the house. I tried to stop Monica from reading them at all, but it was impossible once she'd read a few of the instructions. She took one look and grabbed. The words jumped off the page. Father and his little hobby. What he did on his holidays. The Barry Bucknell of the Scrotum.

Reading them in their entirety I was reminded of earlier times, in my days of heavy cocaine taking when, following Father's footsteps, I reeled along the corridors of the National Portrait Gallery trawling for something wet and slippery. Alone, in pairs, trailing behind their parents, sometimes whole parties of them, American, South American, European-all-sorts, not forgetting the highly efficient and technologically advanced Japanese variety, I would spend whole afternoons in pursuit of them. Student, tourist, mother, wife, the older woman, they all took their clothes off and gave me what for. Daughters were my speciality. Accompanied daughters. They didn't take so much time. They were in a hurry. If they wanted to fuck they wanted to fuck quickly. On a good week I could fuck two or three daughters and still have enough left over (if I was lucky) for something more substantial over the weekend. And here was Father all those years ago with *his* menu. His was a more organized approach. He paid for it. White girls with black girls, black girls with white girls, black girls with black girls, black girls FRIGGING themselves, rubbing their

TITS together, SUCKING each other while this Mrs M strokes his HUGE COCK. I could hardly bear to read them and yet I could not stop. Neither of us could. We passed them over in silence, backwards and forwards over the counterpane. They were hypnotic and shaming and quaking with a ghastly life. He had no right to talk like that, to think like that, *to put such words in my mouth*. I could see him now. A slave to ejaculation. Nothing else mattered to him. How he gloried in its wealth, in its erotic properties and its crude abundance. And how he thought they loved him for it, these black girls. He could satisfy their greed, stand over their animal ache, push his hips out and drench them all right. See the white man with the spindly legs! See his turkey cock, as red as his neck! Watch it jerk! Catch the white sperm! Who was I kidding? I could send one of those postcards. To Dad. London October 1987: *Vicious storm. Nothing has changed.*

When Monica had read the last one (and they did not take long to read) she said, 'Christ. What are they exactly?'

'I would have thought,' I replied, wrapping them back up, 'that it was pretty obvious what they were.'

'But if they were real letters, to a real woman, a real life madam, what are they doing here?'

I knew the answer to that. I had worked it out long ago.

'He collected each letter he sent on his next visit,' I said. 'That way he gave his instructions *and* created his very own pornography. There were no sex magazines in those days you know Monica.'

'You don't seem very surprised to find them.'

'No.'

'And why on earth would Carol want to keep them?'

'Things like that are hard to throw away,' I explained.

'I wouldn't have kept them,' she said. 'They're so ugly, so contemptible, so . . .'

'Racist . . .?' I asked.

'No,' she said. 'Familiar.'

We had a desultory meal at a nearby Italian restaurant, conducted for the most part in silence. I couldn't think of anything to say though there was so much I could tell. Every time I looked over I caught Monica looking at my mouth as if she could see my father's words spilling out. My voice, my words, my thoughts. I kept thinking of the brass bowl still sitting there. I wanted to go back and take it home. I wanted to look at it, hold it, touch its sides and hear it hum.

'Do you want to stay the night?' I asked her.

She looked at me in a strange, almost angry way, but that may have been the low lighting.

'Stay the night?' she said.

'Yes. In the flat.'

'Are you serious?'

'Of course.'

She reached for her cigarettes.

'You're welcome to use the spare room,' I added.

Monica looked around the half empty room and said, 'Giles sometimes I think you have no idea what you're saying, or what effect it might have. First you try to fuck me, then you try and kill me, then you shower me with your father's pornographic correspondence, which, apart from a few archaic expressions sounds *strangely* similar to your own little preoccupations. Now you invite me back to your flat for the first time in living memory and just to prove you haven't got any ulterior motive you say I can use the spare room. What would you really like me to do? I'm sure you've picked up some good tips from your old man.'

I winced. 'I'd like you to come back,' I told her.

'And?'

'And nothing. Keep me company.'

'That's nothing is it?'

'You know what I mean.'

'Indeed I do. And what about Clare? What would she make of it?'

'Clare's staying with Mrs Delguardo downstairs. She has this niece. They get on well together.'

Monica stared at me for a moment, then put her cigarettes away. 'No,' she said. 'I've made other plans. There's a friend's house I can stay in. I'll call for you tomorrow OK? Around ten? We'll drive down then.'

And so she left without even a kiss. I ordered another bottle of Barolo and pulled out Carol's will. I had to put the salt and the pepper and the ashtray on the corners to hold it down. It made bitter and morose reading. It appeared that I was not to be trusted with her daughter in practically any shape or form, that the trust money set up after the sale of our father's worldly goods, added with the money realized by selling her house and all her effects (except those which are specifically assigned in the subsequent pages) would be administered by Clare's legal guardians, the first of which was the lawyer who drew up this treacherous document, the second Monica, and the third of whom turned out to be, wait for it, Fat Patrick's beautiful elder sister! I didn't recognize the name at first. It was only when I read it again in anger, thinking how insulting it all was, how cruel, how unjust, how absolutely typical of my sister to treat me in this way, thinking who is this bloody woman anyway, that I took in the rest of the description. Julia Savage, *née Liddle*. I didn't know Carol still knew Julia Liddle. They had never been friends at school. How had they become bosom pals? Julia Liddle née *Savage*. That name rang a bell. Where had that come from? Was that another school name? (Grey, Deering, Cramphorn, Fisher, Liddle, Muchmore . . . I couldn't remember any Savage.) According to the following spiel, Monica and Julia Savage née Liddle (Monica I noticed with some relief was not née anything), in due consultation with Mr Brian Ryan (the legal wallah) would secure the best future for Clare in regards to domicile and education in accordance with the direction of the court. Clare's wishes of course would be taken into account, but, in regards to recommendations to the court *from the mother* it was hoped that Clare could live with Mr and Mrs Savage. If in the judgement of the aforementioned guardians a sufficiently stable environment had been established by her only remaining living relative Giles Doughty the guardians were at liberty to arrange for Clare to stay for extended visits but any attempt by the aforementioned Giles Doughty to apply for custody even if this were the wish of Clare herself would be treated with the utmost caution it is the view of the mother at the time of making her will that the aforementioned Giles Doughty is not and would not be a suitable guardian for her daughter. What a vote of confidence I thought. Thanks very much.

Then came the bequests. Another testament to Carol's

generosity. Monica was to inherit the business and all the files and hardware and material pertaining to thereof. Julia Savage was to have the china, her antique rings and the Turkish carpets, and I was palmed off with an old mercury barometer, some of the family photographs and was allowed to keep any family papers I desired *except* Ian's Diary which was to be handed over to Mr Brian Ryan who would promptly throw it in the fire. No mention of the brass bowl which she'd hidden away all these years. That presumably came under the auctioneer's hammer. Well not if I had anything to do with it. And what else had she got tucked away there? What else had she kept from me? I decided to go back there and then, to go through the contents of the deed-box, which still lay scattered on her bed, and to rescue the brass bowl. A large brandy later I was on my way.

Parking the car, I noticed that I'd left one of the bedroom lights on. Nor, I discovered upon opening the front door, had I remembered to switch on the burglar alarm. I was just about to walk over to the cupboard and check, when I heard voices, low voices, or rather, as I listened harder, one voice coming from upstairs. At first I thought it must be one of those clock radios that come on automatically, but as I moved towards the stairs it became all too clear what or rather who I was listening to, a voice I recognized all too well. Monica. Monica on the phone. Monica was staying here! I crept up the stairs as quietly as I could. Halfway up it is possible to turn round and, looking through the banisters, see into Carol's bedroom at the far end. Which is what I did. There she was, lying on Carol's bed, talking eagerly into the phone. Unlike the gloomy countenance she had presented me with all evening, Monica was now bright and alert, and instead of the tense, brittle statue which had sidled past me on this very landing not two hours back, here she looked relaxed and happy. She was laughing softly and taking large drags from what was a very fat and indulgent joint. One of the many she had neglected to offer me. Monica was enjoying herself in a restless sort of way. I could tell that she was pleased to be back in her blue towelling robe. Every now and again she would brush fallen ash from her breast. She obviously had not heard me come in.

'That's great, that's just great,' she was saying. 'I'll probably be back tomorrow. The day after at the very latest . . . No, I haven't seen her yet.' She took another drag. 'Yes, of course I am. Like a chimney. It's the only thing that's going to get me through the next couple of days. They're moving her up to London as soon as they can, to be near her family . . . Yeah, her brother . . . Not too bad . . . He's looking after her daughter . . . It makes you think, doesn't it? . . . I know I mustn't . . . I know you do. I do too.' I could hear a voice at the other end. She began to smoke heavily while she listened. Clouds of marijuana smoke were filling the room and drifting out on to the landing, bringing that rich sweet smell which so often had enveloped us in our pleasure. Monica always smoked excellent dope. Like me she preferred the strong sticky blocks of resin to grass. It seemed to soak into the body more, sweated like skin. Her free hand was under her robe now, stroking her stomach.

A sudden clatter at the window made her start. She got up quickly and went to the window, pulling the curtains together before she returned.

'Nothing to worry about,' she said. 'Just the weather. Hailstorm. Look Johnny,' she added, hunching over the phone, 'of course I wish I was down there, but if you want to look at it from our point of view, two days from now will be even better. I've just been working it out on that bloody chart the doctor gave me. Thursday or Friday. If I had seen you tonight, who knows, but you probably wouldn't have anything left when it really counted.' (Laughter.) 'This way you can come prepared.' (More laughter.) 'Eat lots of oysters or whatever it is that's supposed to be good for you. This could be our lucky month.'

Hail showers are not uncommon in the late spring and early summer in the British Isles and though we do not attract the monoliths which descend upon the southern hemisphere (a sudden hailstorm in Bangladesh once killed ninety-two people) they can be big enough to cause damage to cars, cold frames and I daresay, even alarm systems. The hailstone is a curious thing. Let me introduce it to you. It is not simply a collection of frozen rain made specifically for your inconvenience, and unlike rain there is no aerodynamic limit to its size. The hailstone is brought up in the roomy quarters of cumulo-nimbus clouds and when the time is right, when it is big enough, hard enough and cold enough, is shoved out with its brothers and sisters to the waiting world below. If you took hold of a hailstone and attacked it say with a breadknife or a meat cleaver or one of the smaller chain-saws on the market, you would find as the two halves fell away from your incisive blade, that the spheres rolling across the frozen ground were composed of rings or rather *layers*. However, unlike the rings on a tree, or the many layers of your skin, which is wood upon wood, or skin upon skin (as it always should be), the components of a hailstone are made up as follows: a layer of ice (which is clear), then a layer of ice-and-air (which is opaque), a layer of ice, a layer of ice-and-air, and so on and so forth, first the one, then the other. As it grows in strength, your humble hailstone will travel the length of its candyfloss home like a demented day-tripper out at the seaside, joy-riding on an endless whirl of updraughts and downdraughts, enjoying more bumps and loops on its journey than the most demanding of roller-coasters. Thus it develops, gathering water and air as it careers along and when it has fully grown, when it has matured and become responsible, a bruiser in other words, then the time is right for it to fall out of the sky and clout a few holidaymakers on the nose. Which is what a great many of them did that brave summer day when I met my wife (bless her cotton socks) upon Camber Sands. In my blind excitement at their unexpected descent, I did not look where I was going or, more importantly, who I was talking to, and by the time I realized that the young woman, whose hat I borrowed to collect as many as I could, and who returned some nights later to my little bungalow and removed everything *but* her little cotton socks, was a mistake, it was too late. I had married her.

You may in all fairness wonder why I am bringing my wife into all this at such a late stage in the proceedings. She plays no part in this sorry tale and unless you are very unlucky I doubt if she will appear again. But I bring her into the picture, albeit ever so briefly, to illustrate the poignancy of what I was now witnessing on the landing. Of all the weather they had at their disposal, the winds chose that night to bring on the tender little hailstone. Under cover of darkness, unbeknown to Monica or me, there drifted across the northern skies a party of huge anvil-shaped clouds, a gathering of cumulo-nimbus brethren ready to knock on our doors with the gospel of the hailstone. Hail at night is unusual in itself. Hail at the bedroom window of my stricken sister was an ill omen, but hail at my sister's bedroom window while I was standing on the landing listening to Monica pandering to her ovaries was inexcusable.

I am going to be brave now. I am going to use a much abused phrase, a phrase which trips out of the lips of drunken men at the twitch of a skirt. It is said in bars and over dinner tables and lying on a stranger's breast. It is said on unmade beds and in the stillness of parked cars. It is a phrase we use to betray and cajole, to smear one party and to flatter another. It has five (or six) words. I do not know it in German or in French but I daresay they say it too. I daresay they say it the world over. Here it is then, this little gem. I shall say it once. No, I shall say it at least twice and then I may repeat it a little later, for it is true you see. It has a truth embedded in it which is in all of us, and it gnaws away until it has eaten out our very heart. This is the phrase then. *My wife doesn't understand me.* My wife doesn't understand me.

Actually one could turn that phrase around, change the words and it would still retain the same meaning. Then the phrase would run, My wife understands me utterly. Or better still, My wife understands me *all too well*. That's better. My wife understands me all too well. She is kind and solicitous. She wants to keep in touch, to make sure I am all right, that I don't drug myself to death or fall off the London Weather Centre roof blind drunk or pick a fight with some yodelling lager lout and end up in hospital. Actually I have never picked a fight with a lout, lager or otherwise, but my wife who does not understand me, who understands me all too well, thinks that my ability to hurl a dinner plate or two around, or to pull the odd curtain clear from its moorings, automatically makes me a candidate for Pub Bruiser of the Year. She suspects that under the right circumstances I could find myself tearing my shirt front open and issuing invitations. She is wrong about that, but then she is wrong about so many things concerning my nature, even those things about me which she understands only too well. In fact of all the things my wife is wrong about, the ones which reveal some understanding of me are the very ones she is wrong about the most.

I don't like my wife. I never have done. From the moment I planted that first kiss on her lips I knew that I did not like her much (cotton socks or no), and the more she elbowed her way into my life, the more my initial impression was confirmed. By the time we walked up the aisle I found it difficult to stay in the same room with her, let alone clasp her to my bosom and set up a happy home. This glorious indifference to her worth, this strong aversion to her character, this disdain for her boundless chatter, her healthy good looks, yeah even the very way she held me in our wedded embrace, only confirmed my feelings, that here was someone ideally suited to me, someone who I could keep apart from but who would be on tap whenever the occasion demanded. She was a jolly happy soul, who liked the outdoors and dogs and the wearing of wellington boots and she mistook my interest over the hailstones as *enthusiasm*, which is not the same thing at all. She thought too that she could bring me out of myself. She should have read the signs. The great thing about the hailstone is that no matter how you treat it, no matter how many layers you peel away, when you arrive at its most private and personal section, its *core*, you find that it is of exactly the same consistency as its most exposed skin. There is no *inner* hailstone. The inner is as the outer, cold and clean and without guile. It is much the same with me and of course it was only after time that I discovered that it was much the same for her. It is my belief that despite everyone's protestations, it is much the same for everyone. Had my wife learnt of this, had she left me alone, never started up her prodding, had she *taken me for granted*, as I was only too willing to do for her, ours would have been a perfect marriage. I would have been serene and pleasant and tender as a church mouse and she too would have smiled upon married life. As it was she got out the tin opener and tried to get inside me, but only succeeded in cutting herself badly on the jagged edges. The soft, warm Frances on the outside turned out to be inadequate protection for the soft, warm Frances which resided on the inside. She nearly bled to death.

You may ask with some reason why, if I disliked her that much, did I get married to her in the first place? A good question with no discernible answer other than the fact that it seemed the right thing to do and Frances (the very name sends a glow down my spine) was there, willing and generous and full of good cheer. Of course the real reason why she seemed so suitable was that my sister found her as implausible as I did (particularly her penchant for chewing apples), and I was in a mind then to prove my sister wrong about all aspects of my existence. She regarded Frances as wholly unsuitable (which she was) but I was damned if I would let Carol stand in the way of my unhappiness. It started off well enough. Frances's simple charm, her willing naivety, her simple need for affection. She was amused and intrigued by my behaviour (both of which were put on for her benefit. There is nothing so seductive as charm) and when she clapped her hands in delight upon seeing the product of my Ice Fridge (which is kept at an exact temperature in order to preserve such precious items as the hailstones which had brought us together) I fell for her too. Two days later we made love for the first time, there on one of the narrow iron beds on which I had made so many childish journeys, with those faded curtains blowing in the evening air. Afterwards she got up and led me back to the Ice Fridge, where we sat illuminated by the light of the open door, feeding each other the remains of our hailstone harvest. 'Sugar never tasted so sweet,' she said, and I, poor fool, became enchanted too. The trouble with enchantment though is that spells are swiftly broken, and while I could preserve the hailstone it was beyond my powers to preserve her contentment. When time for dissolution came, it was only then, when Frances was presented as victim, that Carol relented and instituted a reign of condescending pity, but by that time it was too late for such pleasantries. It was all over. If only we had been more dishonest. But she would have none of it, she wanted no lies or deceits or evasions, when it was clear to me that was all that would help us through. She wanted to talk and to plan and yeah, produce children. Her goodwill defeated me.

Now the clatter of hailstones against the landing window began to drown the rest of Monica's conversation but I had heard enough. I stood there watching her lips against the olive-coloured mouthpiece, the way her stubby fingers held that fat, familiar joint, how seductively the wreaths of smoke curled around her head. I had known her thus equipped, and I too had been the recipient of such laughter and such marijuana chat, but there was more intimacy displayed on that bed than I had ever received. Her hands followed a mouth that could not be seen, her hands drew pictures for eyes that were not there, she waited impatiently for a voice I could not hear, and when she interrupted him, it was nothing more than an excuse for her lips to touch his. The Senior Service if you please. Monica had embraced me and kissed me and bundled me in and out of her flat for what had been a long and often flagrant conspiracy and yet all the time she had been playing Happy Families with the Bermuda Triangle. She had deceived me and lied to me. All the times she had been with me, smearing me across her breasts and wiping her mouth clean of it, all those times were interludes, decorations, *dried icing on the fucking cake*, while she waited to stuff herself full of her salty friend, to open her legs wide and ask him, most politely to fill her up *to the very brim* and get her reproductive organs going. Monica was planning to get pregnant. By him!

I stepped out from my hiding place and started up the final tread. She saw me of course and straightaway screamed down the telephone but covered herself up just as soon as she realized who it was. 'No it was nothing Johnny,' she said, giving me a furious look, 'just something banging against the window. Sounded like it was coming straight at me. Don't suppose it will happen twice though.' Nervous laughter down the phone while waiting my approach. What did I look like that night I wonder. Menacing? Weary? The Worse for Wear? She put her hand across the receiver. 'Giles, what the fuck do you think you're doing?' she whispered, but I was too close then and she was frightened that I might answer. She waved at me vigorously and beckoned me to sit down. I was used to such gestures. They had been employed from time to time in her flat, in more equitable circumstances. They meant *don't do anything to give the game away*. It was obvious that she had no idea that I had been eavesdropping and most likely was thanking her lucky stars (Oh the stars were out for her tonight), that I hadn't walked in when the talk of doctors and times of the month and fish-induced intercourse were being bandied about. She could handle it from now on. And why not? She had done it many times before. She was not best pleased to see me, but there was no fear or worry in her eyes. Why should there be? This was Carol's house not hers, and I hadn't known that she was going to stay the night here. She had deliberately kept it from me! Whatever had brought *me* to the house then, was not *her*. I sat down beside her (not too near). I waited while the conversation ran its full course. We looked at each other. We smiled. I even held her hand.

It may not seem much to you, this sitting-on-the-bed-and-talking-lark, but I am sensitive to these things. If the hotel is where I live my life (Why are you staying in this hotel? the questionnaire asked. *Because my wife doesn't understand me* I answered. We laughed. I was divorced by then. Fleur leant over and crossed it out. *Because we want to fuck*, she wrote in its place.) then beds, in one form or another, are where I do my talking. Sitting on a bed talking. Sitting on the bed talking to Fleur. Sitting on the bed talking to Monica. Sitting on the bed talking, even to my wife. The hospital bed is where I lean in now and converse with my sister, the spare bed is where I am closest to her daughter; the iron bungalow bed was where I played with my brother. Now Monica sat on Carol's bed, me in one hand, the phone in the other (remember that phrase?), not realizing that her luck was about to run out.

'Jesus,' she said, when at long last she had kissed the little charade goodnight. 'Jesus, you gave me a fright. I nearly had a heart attack.'

'You should have told me Monica,' I said, meaning one thing, but saying another. 'You shouldn't have kept me in the dark.'

'I know,' she said, putting the phone back on the bedside table. 'I should have told you. Carol and I swapped keys about a year ago. You don't mind do you?'

I sighed.

'No Monica. I don't mind. It's just . . .'

'I know. I'm sorry. I simply wanted to be on my own that's all and I remembered I had a key. Carol wouldn't object. What brought *you* back? Did you forget something?'

'No. I was driving past. I saw the lights on. I thought you were a burglar.'

'Ah, well that explains the stockinged feet treatment at least. I should have been more discreet.' She put her other hand on top of mine. 'Look, I know you wanted me to stay tonight. I just didn't want any more unpleasantness between us.'

I nodded.

'Who were you talking to?' I asked.

'Who do you think? I couldn't not. He was expecting it. Don't worry. I'll pay.'

I shrugged my shoulders. 'I didn't mean to interrupt,' I lied. She inhaled a particularly large pungent lungful.

'Nearly gave the game away there,' she said, coughing it out. 'Do you want some of this? There's not much left.'

I took it anyway.

'I could do with a drink too,' I told her.

'Just one,' she said. 'I'm tired.'

I went downstairs and fetched up a bottle of brandy. I could hear her humming to herself as she rolled another joint. She was in a good mood. The prospect of imminent impregnation had dispelled her worries over Carol, temporarily at least, though she remembered to sombre up a bit when I got back. For the next couple of hours we went over her sighting of Stella. The dope and the telephone conversation had lowered Monica's guard, and instead of the tired exasperated version she had treated me to on the journey up, now she was helpful and eager, and not a little excited. The prospect of the chase had awoken her senses.

What had been lacking from Monica's first description was any feeling of what Stella had looked like, what her manner was. Tall, dark, and thin she had said, not exactly muscular, but strong-looking. Well that fitted Stella all right, but then again it didn't carry us forward very far. If it was Stella, and I had to assume it was, I wanted to know what Monica's impression of her was. What she thought might have happened to her in the intervening years? I should have done this over dinner of course, when Monica was a little less stoned, but unlike then, sitting on the bed in her blue towelling gown, with the wherewithal for a succession of joints before her and a bottle of brandy being loosely passed, Monica wished to help.

Monica had studied Stella more than she had let on. She had stood next to her and not only heard the altercation, but had watched it carefully. The moment Stella had turned towards them she had sensed that something was up. Up to that point neither of them had noticed her at all. Carol had gone up to the bar to buy the first bottle.

'So we can assume from that,' I said, 'that Stella hadn't arrived when you first got there. What time did you get there?'

'About half five. It was just beginning to fill up.'

'And you didn't see her at all?'

'No. We had a look round to see what tables were free. The ones at the back were already full. We were lucky to get the table we did.'

'So Stella could have been at the back when you came in. She could have been talking to someone for a while and then gone to the bar later.'

'She could have been but I doubt it. We'd only been there about three quarters of an hour before it all happened.'

'Waiting for someone?'

'Possibly. But again I don't think so. Otherwise why should she have left when she did?'

'Irritation?'

'Possibly, but not solely. She might have left earlier than normal because of them, because she was annoyed, because she didn't want to be next to them anymore, but I don't think she was *driven* away. If she was meeting someone she would have stayed there. She wouldn't have let those two get the better of her.'

'Though they did.'

'How do you mean?'

'They got the better of her. They got to her. They made her come out of herself. Because she knew what she was doing, she was out of control. That's why she left. Not because of the train, not because of them, not because of Carol – though I'm sure she would have left just as quickly had she known Carol was there. She left because she had drawn attention to herself, and drawing attention to herself was the last thing that Stella Muchmore wanted to do. Remember what Carol said to me on the phone. I saw her an hour ago. An *hour*. She left that bar as soon as she regained her composure, even though she had to wait an hour before her train. Had she not lost her temper she would have stayed there until it was time. That's what she was doing, waiting.'

'You're right! So she loses her cool over some completely trivial remark.'

I might as well tell her now.

'Ah, well, that's not strictly true Monica,' I said. 'It reminded her of something.'

'What did?'

'The conversation. The two men. The wording if you like. It took her back. Christ, it took me back too.'

I took Monica's hand and led her to the cupboard. There it was, dull and gleaming, golden on the outside and dark within. 'You may not understand this Monica,' I said, taking it back, placing it between us on the bed, 'but this bowl, this brass bowl, with its fake Egyptian markings and its tarnished rim, contains my whole life. Outside in the car, there is a bag, Mrs Briggs's Bag, and inside that bag, curled up and utterly fearful is a small boy. He has been hiding in that bag for over twenty years and he had hoped he might stay there for the rest of his days. But there is one object more powerful than Mrs Briggs's Bag, which can drag him out, even against his will. It was thought lost, sold off, gone forever, but now I discover it here, in this house. Now I discover that Carol had it all the time, hidden away in her deed-box, far apart from Mrs Briggs's Bag. In the bedroom! No wonder Ian died. Were I to take this brass bowl and hold it so, and if I were to rub it gently, so, I assure you that the boy would rise, like a coiled and sleeping wraith, ready to grant me my one wish. And do you know what it would be? It would be to hear those words again.'

'Rub it then, why don't you,' she said. She leant in close to me and ran her fingers round the rim. 'Is that the way to do it? Is that the way it must be done?'

I took it from her and began. 'He is here,' I told her, 'here in this bowl. I will entice him out.'

But you did not come. I rubbed the bowl and you did not come. I used all my expertise, all my knowledge of things to rub, of things to entice out of their folds, when they swell and quicken and move in urgency, but you did not come. I waited for the bowl to glow, for the bowl to quiver, for it to buck in my hands and deliver you before me, so that I might exhibit you, so that I might demonstrate before Monica, Monica the Mournful, Monica the

Mouth Organ, *Monica the Mother*, what I had to contend with, but you did not come. You hid in my car, like a frightened boy, like a boy on the run, like a boy who had been up to no good. So it was left to me to tell Monica of your doings, your little exploits and your little foibles and the things that run around your little head.

It was of course deliberately wilful of you, for if any day were your day and named as your birth day, then it was that Boxing Day. Thinking back on it, it was a wonder, after the spectacle of your sister and your mother fighting in the back garden while a cascade of toys and clothing and broken books swirled around them, you did not foresee that this day was to be special, but you assumed, in your ignorance, in your childish way, that after the bonfire it would be all over, that nothing more *could* happen. It did not take long however for you to understand that the bonfire and the explosion and the biting on the motherly ankle, was but the beginning, that that day was crammed *to the very brim* with things to take out and examine over the years. The day before, *Christmas Day*, you had met with Fat Patrick for a few moments on your respective bikes and exchanged notes on the way the festivities were progressing. Fat Patrick had got the twelve-inch telescope he had wanted and was already looking forward to daylight fading and poking his third eye at the bright winter sky. As was his wont, he immediately set about bombarding you with endless information concerning the seventy constellations that were to be found in the hemispheres and began by reciting as many as he could remember in alphabetical order. It was hard to display real interest, for in truth you did not envy him (though you wished, just to silence him, that you had thought to ask for such a gift). While you had not received anything as remotely interesting, as you pedalled back home you reflected that in fact there was nothing much that *did* take your fancy, telescope or no telescope, unless perhaps your parents had presented you with a cardboard box full of cigarettes. Fat Patrick had invited you in to look at it but you had declined, saying that you would see it soon enough, that you had better go home, where they were 'waiting for you'. The truth was that they were not waiting for you, and you did want to see it, but you did not wish to appear over-eager, and anyway it would add just that little risk to the night's coming effort, for you planned to go out that night, and celebrate the only way you knew how. You had become very au fait with your surroundings and the habits of your neighbours by now. You had to be, for however quick you might be, and however late you might choose to go out, there was always the danger that the unexpected would catch you unawares. Knowing where all the hiding places were and which escape routes you had at your disposal, had become vital to your defence. When you lay in your bed at night, planning where you would venture next, you could picture in your mind the exact nature of your intended route, where the holes in the fence were, which walls were easiest to jump, what trees you could shin up. You knew who watched television until closedown, who took their dogs for late night walks, who saved the washing-up until last thing at night. Patrick's telescope therefore possessed a new risk, for though he might intend to aim it solely at the heavens, there was no telling that he might not, in an idle moment, stick his face into the eyepiece, and sweep up and down Gladstone Drive just as you had decided to jump naked over Poker Fisher's garden gate. On enquiring how the rest of his Christmas had been, and to divert attention from your own rather gloomy affair Fat Patrick vouchsafed the welcome information that his family had had a set-to almost before the celebrations began. His beautiful elder sister he said, as if he were her parent and not her younger brother, was proving immensely difficult these days, and seemed barely able to stay under the same roof as the rest of the family for more than five minutes. She had always been stuck up, like the rest of them at that bloody girls' school, but this first term at college had made her worse than ever. It was curious he said. His sister had made such a thing about coming back for Christmas and yet once home had taken no time in serving notice that their festive preparations bored her out of her tiny mind. For the first three days she had done nothing, *nothing*, not gone out, not seen her friends, hardly opened her mouth, just sat around the house all day looking at magazines. And then today, over lunch, as the turkey was about to be carved, surrounded by all those sausages and bacon-rolls and with seven different types of stuffing bursting out of it, she chooses that moment to announce that she's leaving the next day, going back to London, on *Boxing Day*. I mean, she could have waited until after the pudding. Someone was going to pick her up down by the Town Hall and no amount of pleading by her mother could stop her. She was leaving straight after breakfast. No, she wasn't going to bring him here. No, it wasn't a sudden decision. She had things to do, things to prepare for, and anyway what was there to keep her here? This information, delivered as Fat Patrick's father was sharpening the carving knife had driven him from the table and into his aircraft room, where he sat hugging his handkerchief for a good half hour before being coaxed back. You marvelled at the naivety of Fat Patrick for telling you such a thing, and the next day, on the Landing, while you waited for your washed father and your singed mother to emerge from the bathroom you wondered whether you should not supply your father with this little nugget, that Jim Liddle blubbed on Christmas Day, for it would be something he would appreciate, and undoubtedly, given his present form, would wish to incorporate into the rather faded music-hall act that he would present to the Muchmores over the forthcoming lunch. Like your father Mr Muchmore had no time for Jim Liddle and resented having him for a neighbour. Many is the time you have been with Fat Patrick in his home and seen Mr Muchmore in his garden, scowling over the garden fence, watching Jim Liddle as he mooched about the lawn, looking vainly up to the sky. According to your father, Mr Muchmore had recently admitted over one of their many pints of beer in the King's Arms (and which your father happily related the next day over breakfast) that he was convinced that having someone that was soft in the head lowered the price of his property. Not that he was thinking of selling mind, but should he want to, who would want to buy a house with a mental case for a next-door neighbour, let alone that he had a you-know-what for a wife? Mr Muchmore, it transpired, had written to the council over the matter, pointing out Jim Liddle's unsavoury habit of wearing pajamas in broad daylight and questioned whether such a person was a suitable member of what he chose to describe as a family community. Jim Liddle, he had concluded, should be removed once and for all and taken into care, a notion that your father had found so enticing that he had been quite unable to eat his bacon. But you did not tell your father, despite the fact that you would have *enjoyed* your father using some fresh material. You kept it to yourself primarily because there was a part of you that sympathized with Fat Patrick's beautiful elder sister and you wanted to keep the memory of her wish to yourself. It was only later, nearly a full year later, when you saw her again in such entertaining circumstances there in the pillbox, that it became obvious that what had brought his sister back to the grey enchantment of Rochester, and indeed what had drawn her so mysteriously to those long cold Saturday afternoons on the playing fields, was not her family, nor her friends, nor the varied collection of boys' legs, but the prospect of parading up and down before Mr Cooper, who on Wednesdays and Saturdays forsook his master's gown and tweed sports jacket and appeared on the playing field as a referee, dressed up in a pair of baggy blue rugger shorts and with a ridiculous whistle strung around his neck. But she was still at school then, still a schoolgirl! How was it done you wondered? How did a man like Mr Cooper get his hands on such a girl? Through parents' day? Did he perhaps ring up his opposite number in the girls' school and ask who was a likely prospect? Did Fat Patrick pimp for her, trade her in, in return for decent marks on his weekly essay? You couldn't have done that with *your* sister. No of course it wasn't like that. It would have been the school play, the *joint* school play, a recent departure set by an adventurous and forward-looking headmaster who thought having boys dressing up as Miss Prism or Ophelia faintly ridiculous and had harnessed the local girls' school to join forces in their yearly production (and in which your sister had played the part of Mistress Quickly in their recent rendition of The Merry Wives of Windsor) thereby depriving boys of the pleasure of dressing up as women, which they enjoyed and were often very good at, but ensuring that Mr Cooper, who was in charge of such events could jeopardize his marriage and his career in order to get his besotted leg over.

A fearful row had ensued. Fat Patrick continued, biting off the words, all through lunch and after, a *fearful* row. It was probably still going on. Look what you've done, his mother had said, look what you're doing by your selfishness, why did you bother to come down in the first place, three days, *three days* that's all, why even Mr Doughty stays in on Boxing Day and you admitted to Fat Patrick that it was so, except for one proviso, that it was a tradition, God knows how it came about, that on Boxing Day, and on Boxing Day alone, the five of you (the four of you now) trooped across the road at around twelve o'clock and had an unpleasant meal with the Muchmores. The SS girl, groaned Patrick, the SS girl *exactly* you said, *and* her drippy mother and you both giggled at the memory of Mrs Muchmore scurrying up and down their drive like a nervous mouse. There was a time, in the holidays, when you and Fat Patrick and anybody else that happened to be around, used to gather in your spare bedroom at half past six and wait for Mr Muchmore to come home and Put The Car In The Garage. You and your friends would practically cry with laughter at this event, crowding around each other, sticking your heads out of the window, listening to the loud and endless arguments that would come forth concerning wheel alignment, speed, direction, and gear possibilities, dancing around the room chanting. 'Faster! Faster! Forward! Forward! Straighten Up!' flapping your hands and shouting and swearing and falling about on the bed. There was no doubt that Mr Muchmore and family could hear this chorus of ridicule but not once did they complain. So regular were their appearances, so familiar were their cries, that it was almost as if they were something out of a Warner Brothers short, and this Putting-The-Car-in-the-Garage, your favourite routine. Mrs Muchmore in fact moved like a cartoon character, always nervous, always seemingly in danger, constantly jumping sideways to get out of the way. She had none of the grace of Fat Patrick's mother and none of the strength of your own. She was thin and jerky and not quite human, rather like a pencil drawing and when she stood alone, at the top of the driveway, with the garage doors behind her (they were of the modern variety which swung up and back) it was as if she were standing in front of some giant mousetrap primed to spring open and to devour her at a moment's notice.

There was a lot to sort out before you finally got to sit down to lunch. For a start there was the problem of your mother's appearance. The fire, or rather the series of explosions, coupled with The Battle for the Bag, had ruined both your mother's only good dress and a sizeable portion of her face. As she chased Carol into the house shouting Bring that back! Bring that back! and as Carol pushed passed you with the smoking remains of Mrs Briggs's Bag cradled in her arms, you noticed that while the right-hand side of your mother's head seemed perfectly natural, black and wiry and not a little unkempt, the left-hand side had undergone a radical transformation. Her hair had been replaced by a layer of unattractive stubble. You had seen farmers treat their fields in much the same manner. If that wasn't bad enough, both her eyebrows, prominent contributions to her facial expressions, had disappeared altogether. As for the dress itself, an olive-green monstrosity purchased at the height of father's career from a stuck-up store in London, it now sported more mud upon its dour colour scheme than a first fifteen rugger shirt, and its edges had all shrivelled up. The hem, which at one time had ended halfway down her calves now hung in blobs an inch above the knee. Your father, emerging from the bathroom looking guilty, as he did whenever he was forced to wash, hooted with laughter at the sight of your mother's face, for as he admitted later, she reminded him of one of those performers to be found in his favourite television programme, 'The Black and White Minstrel Show', but he was clearly unsettled when he saw the state of her hair. It was Carol who suggested the solution, Carol who had refused to come out of her room unless she could keep Mrs Briggs's Bag, and who threatened, as your father put it, to 'ruin the whole day' but who had shouted through the locked door, in answer to his pitiful cry of, What are you going to do Mary, what are you going to do? the reply, Why doesn't she put a hat over it. A Hat! he had exclaimed. Yes a Hat said Carol through her locked door. You mean she's going to wear a Hat throughout the meal? your father protested. On her head? At the lunch table? and Carol replied with the unanswerable rejoinder, Well, what *else* do you suggest she does? Go as she is? Actually, as you looked at your mother standing in a state of shock waiting for them to finish their discussion, you wondered why she couldn't go like that. Why couldn't she simply say that her hair had caught alight and leave it at that? What the bloody hell did it matter if her hair was singed and her eyebrows were all gone and she looked like something out of a bad performance of 'Oklahoma'? It struck you that was the difference between you and your sister, that, like your father, for all her indifference to other people, your sister *did* worry about these things, whereas you didn't give a hoot.

The problem was your mother had no hats, except for one which looked like a Spanish omelette perched on a fir tree and which proved too small to mask the damage. Again it was Carol who came to the rescue. I know who has *hats*, she said. Julia, Julia has hats. Her room is *stuffed* with hats, and she opened her bedroom door and, with Mrs Briggs's Bag in hand, pulled you down the stairs and across the road to the Liddle house where you stood for a moment, composing yourself before ringing the bell. Usually, because you were a regular visitor you would have gone straight round to the back door and poked your head round, but being Boxing Day you felt it was incumbent upon you to approach more formally. What an extraordinary pair you must have made arriving on the Liddle's doorstep that lunchtime, your sister filthy from her familiar wrestling match, holding that bag with shreds of clothing and charred drawing paper still stuck to its sides and you in your best bib and tucker, the two of you hovering about like a couple of self-made orphans. Fat Patrick's father answered the door and before you knew what you were saying, for in the heat of the moment you had quite forgotten about yesterday's fracas, after you had run through the gamut of breathless Christmas greetings and apologies for bothering them like this, you asked him if Julia was in. Fat Patrick's father turned back somewhat helplessly and you could see Fat Patrick behind him, glowering at you as if to say *how could you*, how could you ask such a question? Then Mrs Liddle appeared, dressed in a swathe of silk and easing her husband aside took one look at Carol and ushered you both in, saying Whatever is the matter Carol? You look quite out of sorts. Is your mother all right? and Carol replied that there was nothing the matter *really* but she, Carol that is, *not* her mother, needed a *hat* right away, a hat which covered her head *completely*. She was going out and as her hair was in such a state she wondered whether Julia might have one she could borrow. Mrs Liddle relaxed and smiled and said that Julia didn't keep many of her clothes at home anymore. No said her husband. She's flown, quite flown away, and Mrs Liddle had again had to calm him down. I tell you what, said Fat Patrick's mother to Carol, let's you and I go upstairs and see what we can find. Julia might not have that much, but you never know I might have something that could take your fancy. Now what do you want it for, some nice date? and with that she led your sister up the stairs leaving you with Jim Liddle standing awkwardly in his slippers and Fat Patrick still looking daggers. Curiously enough, although you had spoken to Fat Patrick only the day before, and had parted on completely amicable terms, this sudden excursion into his home unnerved you both. While you waited for your sister to return (you could hear them talking upstairs, laughing a little, Well what about *this*?) you were surprised to find that he didn't invite you to take a look at his telescope. You were just about to suggest such a move when his father shuffled forward and asked if you'd like to come and see what *he* was up to. *Dad*, warned Fat Patrick, but you said yes, of course, for you knew only too well it would be something to do with the Flying Boats, and you had often thought that if you played your cards right he might one day give you something in return, a badge, or book of tickets or even one of those caps with the golden insignia of Imperial Airways stamped upon it, something you could take down to the pillbox, something that would set you apart from all the others. You hadn't seen the back room for a couple of months, and when you walked in you were astonished to find that around the window overlooking the garden he had built a sort of cockpit with bucket seats and rudder sticks and a complicated looking dashboard set in front. Festooned around the walls were charts and diagrams, some of them navigation maps but others which appeared to be engineering plans. Sitting you down in what he called the first officer's seat he invited you to comment on the skill of his construction, that although there was nothing behind it, didn't it feel like the very thing? Not having ever known the very thing you were in no position to pass judgement, but you knew, from your own father's strange behaviour that on these occasions it was best to be as noncommittal as possible. Not that it seemed to do any good. To your dismay, after jamming one of those much coveted caps upon his head, he started to go into an elaborate flying routine, checking temperature gauges and fuel indicators, switching on the starter engine and generally preparing for take-off. I know it's all pretend, he told you, waving the rudder stick in his hand, and that there's nothing there, but it keeps the old Flying Boats on the move, and that's the main thing. Very soon he started to act like you yourself might have done about two years before, down at the pillbox with Fat Patrick and Nigel Cramphorn and Poker Fisher, making engine noises and shouting out Flaps! Rudder! and most embarrassingly of all, Lift Off! You were at a loss to know whether to take part in this charade or whether to pretend it wasn't happening, but you had to admit that the way he wore the hat and handled the controls and moved about in his seat was the most convincing performance of a pilot you had ever seen. It was only when he threatened to pass the controls over to you, that Fat Patrick came to your rescue and told you that Carol was waiting in the hall, but before you could leave his father had to wheel round and land you safely back on the water. As you made your thank-yous and walked back across the road with whatever Carol had chosen tucked into Mrs Briggs's Bag, you thought, Mr Muchmore is right. Fat Patrick's father *is* soft in the head. He *should* be locked away, and you resolved there and then to tell your own tale of Jim Liddle, to join forces with your father and Mr Muchmore and make the lunch go with a swing.

Where the bloody hell have you been, your father shouted as you both came through the front door. Do you know what time it is? You've been over half an hour! We're meant to be there in five minutes. You know what he's like, and while Carol commented with some justification that it was the last time *she* did anything for this family, you had to admit that he had a point. Mr Muchmore did have a thing about punctuality. He was a 'stickler' for it, and made as many bones about it as he could. Later, when you got to know Stella, you learnt more of the extraordinary regime that Mr Muchmore imposed upon his family, how his breakfast had to be upon the table at exactly a quarter to seven and his dinner at a quarter past, how he always made them brush their teeth twice a day for precisely five minutes, how he would stand outside the bathroom door listening (when Stella would run the tap and scrub *his* toothbrush under the rim of the lavatory bowl), how in the evening her mother had to account for every hour of her day. *Everything* it appeared had to be run on the lines of a clockwork Mrs Beeton. There was, she told you once, a clock in every room. All the bedrooms had clocks, the bathroom had a clock, the garage had a clock, even the downstairs lavatory had a clock. Everyone was expected to know the time and they were each assigned a number of clocks to look after. Stella herself was in charge of her own bedroom clock, the clock in the dining room, the clock in the kitchen and, most importantly, the clock in the hall (for she was the only one tall enough to reach its face), while her mother had to grapple with the carriage clock in the living room, the travelling clock in the bathroom, and the cuckoo clock in the downstairs loo. What about him? you asked and Stella looked at you in surprise and said Well, he doesn't do any, he just checks their accuracy, as if it was all perfectly natural. Like so many people you knew, like Fat Patrick and *his* father, like you and *your* father, although she thought her family life irritating she did not seem to think it abnormal, and it was only when you coaxed her into describing this life in detail, that she began to understand what a truly bizarre performance it was. Naturally enough you noticed more and more yourself. How Mrs Muchmore never seemed to appear much in the week except early in the morning at the front door to see Stella off and later, in the evening at half past six to help Mr Muchmore Park the Car. Once, coming back from school, you had passed Mr Muchmore's Rover idling under the chestnut trees near where the Spenser twins lived. He was sitting behind the wheel smoking a solitary cigarette, and it only dawned on you afterwards, when you saw him turning into his driveway a quarter of an hour later, that the reason Mr Muchmore was parked beneath the chestnut trees where the Spenser twins lived was not as you had assumed, so that he might have a quick undetected puff, but because it was not yet time for him to arrive home and that should he turn up early, unannounced as it were, the whole household would be thrown into utter confusion. What happened, you thought, when he came home *late*? When you added it all up, her father, your father, and any number of others, the two of you soon came to the conclusion that parents themselves were a deranged species, and later, when Stella vanished and Sergeant Weatherspoon was attempting to give you a hard time, when he hummed and hawed and tried to get you to spill the beans, asking you if you'd seen anything out of the ordinary, any strangers, or if anyone you knew *had been behaving oddly* you felt like pointing out that people had been behaving oddly for as long as you could remember and that as far as you were concerned the whole fucking street should be locked up, let alone poor old Jim Liddle.

Finally, with one minute to spare it was agreed that the two of you would go on ahead while Carol stayed behind to make mother look presentable. And don't take all day about it, your father instructed. I don't want to go there any more than you do. This was not strictly true, for Mr Muchmore was, after the closure of the aircraft factory and before the disappearance of his daughter, his principal drinking chum. They would meet up at least two or three times a week in the saloon bar of the King's Arms where they would balance their pint glasses on the brown and crinkled leather armrests of two uncomfortable armchairs and complain about the world. On Saturday lunchtimes you sometimes joined your father after a morning at the swimming baths (where Fat Patrick never went, unless forced to by the school authorities) and would stand next to him drinking a Britvic orange while he finished his pint. He would try and get you to sip his beer after taking a large gulp of it himself, but you always declined, not because you did not care for the taste of it (though you preferred Martini) but because in his eagerness to swallow as much as he possibly could, he always slopped a sizeable portion of it back into his glass, and the idea of drinking something that had been swilling around his rotting mouth filled you with revulsion. If he had offered you one of his cigarettes it would have been a different story, for he smoked a brand which you favoured, which came in an elegant red packet, and which, even from the money you stole from his trouser pockets, you could ill afford. Your refusal to sample his contaminated offering usually prompted Mr Muchmore to glower at you with obvious distaste. Today, shutting the front door, you wondered whether Mr Muchmore's manifest dislike of you would lead him to offer you nothing more substantial than Ribena, which is what you had been forced to consume the year before.

As you hurried to catch your father, rehearsing the moment when you would delight the company with your cruel and mocking account of Jim Liddle's inadequacy, you realized with some alarm that although a light snow had fallen earlier that morning, the precipitation had not been of sufficient strength to cover the traces of last night's memorable activity. Where the network of branches stretched across the front lawn, your footprints were as vivid as the scorch marks on the side of your mother's head. This created a bit of a problem. Although your father, now waiting by the gate and watching your progress with ill-concealed impatience, had not noticed anything out of the ordinary, any attempt to erase the evidence would only bring it to his attention, while if you left the markings as they were, and accompanied him across the road, then they were more than likely to be spotted by Carol or indeed your mother, both of whom were much more observant than your father (who took no interest in the garden at all but who bought armfuls of gardening magazines every weekend). The trouble was you could not afford to let these tracks lie undisturbed, for it was clear to even the dullest Girl Guide what had taken place. A couple of feet away lay the heavy indentation where you had landed, complete with the imprints where your hands reached out to regain your balance. With mounting alarm you could see that from there you could follow your footprints, with your toes, particularly your two big toes, clearly outlined in the snow. The implications were clear. Someone had apparently leaped out of thin air and disturbed the perfect stillness of the front lawn. Knowing Carol, it wouldn't take her that long to find out who, for looking up you were dismayed to discover you could even make out two indentations where the soles of your feet had curled over the edge of the bay window roof, where you had stood before jumping out into that fabled thin air, pink and naked and not at all cold. It was strange, you thought later, standing near the Muchmore's meagre fire trying to escape the chill of their gloomy and ill-heated room, how, when you were out there without the benefit of clothes, you didn't seem to feel the cold. You could run like that for almost ten minutes before suffering any ill effects. Last evening had been even longer. Last evening you had gone further than ever before, for being Christmas Day evening there was no one around at all. Apart from the odd display of twinkling lights set in an occasional front window and the ghostly glimmer of a lone freighter moving steadily up the Medway, nothing had stirred, not a car, not a soul, not a single cat on the loose. A complete silence had fallen upon the town as if it were in hiding. As you started on your journey, running towards Mrs Briggs's house and the path that ran down to the chestnut trees (an exceptionally risky route featuring an enclosed alleyway one hundred yards long), you had felt more like a Red Indian prowling round a settler's homestead than an English boy with a box of Christmas presents back in his bedroom. You were a savage here, a heathen born and bred, and though you wished no one any harm, you saw your body decorated in broad and savage colours, ready to pop up at any civilized window and scare the living daylights out of whatever happy family should chance to look up.

There was nothing for it but to take the matter into your own hands. You bent down grabbing a handful of snow and quickly threw it at your father, letting out a great whooping cry before jumping across into the danger area and fashioning three or more missiles, letting them off into his direction as fast as you could manage. All of these were wide of the mark, but no matter. By the time you had sent them on their way the area was quite obliterated and should Carol have marched out armed with a battery of tape measures and magnifying glasses, yeah even Fat Patrick's twelve-inch telescope, not even she could have read the signs now. You were well pleased. The expression on your father's face was another matter. He did not know what had hit him, or in this particular case, the several objects that had not hit him. It was a long time since anyone had thrown a snowball at him or had attempted to involve him in what he would describe as horseplay. It was quite out of your character too, this Christmas bonhomie, and you acted in the knowledge that its very peculiarity might arouse his suspicions. A look of sad astonishment came across his face and for a few vital seconds he was quite unable to move. It was almost as though he was unsure of where he was, as though he had been plucked up suddenly from his familiar habitat and set down upon a world that was utterly alien to him. He turned round to see if there was anyone else throwing these things at him, for he could not quite believe that his son, who had stood in the hall and rapped his fingernails against the brass bowl, as if to set the tone of this forthcoming lunch, was now chucking snowballs at him. He looked up, half expecting the street to be filled with all the children up on their lampposts again, laughing and giggling at this grown-up's misfortune, but the road was quite empty. By this time you had let off another volley, quite superfluous to your needs, but to lend a veracity to your sudden party mood. The final throw, before you dashed past him into the road, was more accurate than you intended, for it caught your father on the side of his head, roughly in the same area as your mother's burnt hair. With a cry equalling anything you had attempted, he rushed across the road in full pursuit and chased you up the Muchmore's drive, snatching at the snow as he ran. He called out to you. He threatened you in the most delightful manner. He was going to get you. He was going to get even. You were surprised. You had thought that your father would have been angry at this onslaught, that he would have shouted to you Not To Be So Stupid, What Did You Think You Were Doing, God What Did He Do to Deserve Such a Family, but no, here he was laughing and running after you in the clear Christmas air as if he were enjoying himself. For a moment you could almost imagine that this was a happy family, that it always had been a happy family, that this was how it could be if only . . . By this time you had your back to the Muchmore's front door and were watching him come up the drive, walking now, putting the finishing touches on his carefully constructed reply. He stood at the top of the drive, panting slightly and took careful aim. It was a surprisingly good effort. It flew across the garden at speed. There came a time, as it travelled towards you high and humming, when you debated as to the best course of action: whether you should stand there and let it crash against you, or whether you should duck and avoid it altogether. His intention was obvious. He wanted to hit you. There was a longing on his face, as if he hoped that this snowball would somehow break the long years of ice between you. It would hit you and he would run up and brush the snow from your cord jacket. You would make a joke of it and the two of you would carry this new found good humour on to the Muchmore's strange and secretive lunch table.

The Day Father Threw a Snowball would be a reference point for future (better) relations. But should you duck, should you out-smart him, he would realize that you had not been playing with him but simply taunting him, holding him up to ridicule. You had just about decided to stand firm when the expression on your father's face suddenly changed, and lurching forward he began to wave his arms about shouting Look Out! Look Out! It was all too clear to see that he was no longer looking at you, but directing his instructions past you, and that his outstretched arms were not just waving someone away, but thrust out as if trying to fetch the snowball *back*. You knew exactly what you should do and what had happened behind you and why your father now danced about in such a state of alarm. His snowball, gathered so hopefully was beyond his control. It had, by default, swiftly entered your sphere of influence. It was *your* snowball, flying to *your* arms, and you would turn it now to *your* advantage. It arced high over the Muchmore landscape, over rockery and lawn and concrete path and when it reached you, when it came within a foot of you, no, half a foot, you dropped to your knees exposing the bewildered face of Mr Muchmore to the flying air. Your father's snowball struck Mr Muchmore smack in the eye. As he staggered back, somewhere in the dark recesses of his house a clock began its long mid-day sequence. Twelve o'clock. You had arrived on time.

What did I tell you, your father shouted, pushing you roughly aside. Haven't you got any sense at all? I say Leonard, are you all right? Mr Muchmore was hopping about on one leg and howling like a baby. Why can't you bloody look what you're doing? he continued. Isn't it about time you acted your age? You could have blinded him! It seemed to you as you stood watching your father fussing over him, the snowball notwithstanding, that Mr Much-more must be blind already, for though it came as no surprise that your father should attempt to put the blame fairly and squarely on to your shoulders (*you* wouldn't be getting any sherry or bottled beer *whatever* happened) it would have been obvious to anybody with eyes in their head that you had nothing to do with the throwing of that particular snowball, especially to someone who had been standing not two feet behind you. However Mr Much-more did not correct him and indeed at every further denunciation your father cared to voice, grunted with reluctant approval. Hold still Leonard, your father was saying, and as he held Mr Muchmore's head and peered into his left eye you were struck by the fact that no one else had come out to see what was up, although any one with a pair of ears would have surely heard something. No eyes, and now no ears. This house seemed deficient in at least two of the five senses, and when you came to think of it, though you had been forced to dress up in respect of this long-planned Muchmore invitation, there was no smell of cooking either. No eyes, no ears, and it would seem no noses either. Let's get you to the bathroom and bathe it, your father said. Mr Muchmore was led up the stairs holding his head like a mustard-gas victim from the First World War. And clear that bloody mess up, your father shouted down as they disappeared from view. Do something useful for a change. God, you said to yourself, What's all this fuss about? It was only a bit of snow for Christ's sake. You looked down. On the doormat and around the tiled surface of the porch lay the slowly melting remains of the errant snowball. As you brushed it out on to the path and made to return into the hall you noticed one piece, somewhat larger than the rest, still in the far right-hand corner and though it went against the grain to follow your father's unreasonable orders you bent down to pick it up. It was only when you moved out into the sunlight to chuck it on to the lawn that you realized that in fashioning his totem to mend bridges, your father, who had chased you so handsomely, who had smiled at you so willingly, who had treated you to such an unexpected burst of familial friendship, had, in the short run up Mr Muchmore's drive, secreted into his precious and loving snow-ball a sharp and jagged stone picked up from Mr Muchmore's much admired rockery.

It was a long time before they returned, and for a good quarter of an hour you had the run of the Muchmore house to yourself. Or so it seemed. Although every now and again you could hear the odd distant sound of activity, the banging of saucepans perhaps? the oven door opening? bottles being uncorked? (unlikely) accompanied by a sudden burst of undefinable mutter, no one came to your rescue, no one opened a door and said, There you are Giles! Come in! The house was quiet. Although you could not remember the exact layout of the premises you remembered that the living room lay at the far end and you thought that while no one was about you might as well skirt into that and have a look around. If you moved quickly enough there would be ample time to help yourself to some of Mr Muchmore's cigarettes, which you remembered he kept in a large silver box on the table. Last Christmas your father had smoked about fifteen of them (though he later complained that he had never tasted such stale tobacco. That box, he had said. Never gets opened from one Christmas to the next.) and you were determined to get to them before he scoffed the lot. You had run out of cigarettes and so had he. Last night there were none to be found in his trouser pockets or his overcoat. You had gone out cigarette-less, which was a shame, for you liked to smoke while out on the town, up against a lamppost, sitting on a garden wall, flicking ash on to your feet.

Your father's overcoat was an interesting garment, for he often fell asleep in it, giving you the opportunity to rifle through his wallet, steal his small change, and add to your collection of driving-gloves. The tear in the upper reaches of the left-hand pocket meant that the lining of your father's overcoat often contained unexpected trophies: cigarette packets, coins, stray banknotes and most intriguing of all, scraps of paper that revealed to you a part of your father's life you were only beginning to understand. If you had to describe your father, if you were asked to *sum him up*, one of the last phrases you would use would be *He Has a Terrific Sense of Humour*, though you knew from reading the problem page in your mother's weekly that having a sense of humour was an essential requirement for any successful marriage. Here, amongst the fluff and torn betting slips you found evidence to confound this wholesome theory, for what these photostats of jokes and short stories confirmed was that your father *did* have a sense of humour, and so strong was his sense of humour that he was obliged to carry examples of it wherever he went. There were some jokes you did not fully understand but no matter, they would come to you in time. All appeared to be based on the twin themes of Race and Gender and there were certain characters who made regular appearances: Eskimo Nell, Rastus, and his favourite, Abdul the Arab. Many were illustrated with line drawings of grotesquely filled mouths and strangely spread legs. Limericks, doggerel, even iambic pentameter, he loved them all. You once discovered a small booklet, much the same size as one of Poker Fisher's train-spotting efforts, but where your friend's book catalogued particulars of the *Duchess of Gloucester* and *Queen Charlotte*, your father's little handbook featured, among others, *Yvonne* and *Marlene* and *Big Bertha*, whose number someone had ringed in red biro and who grinned at you in black and white holding a pair of huge breasts in her hands. Most intriguing of all, tucked into the centre pages of this guide you found a crumpled letter written in your father's hand and like no letter you had ever read before. It was not a business letter, nor a thank-you letter, but more a letter of intent, addressed to a Mrs M who he seemed to know very well indeed. In it he set out his requirements for your next visit, and though the finer points of the arrangements eluded you, you recognized the language well enough. Like the jokes he so treasured, the major preoccupation was again Race and Gender. You had never seen grown-ups write words like that, let alone with such vehemence. Every time he used one of those four-letter words (sometimes five-letter words) he blocked them out in crude capitals. The letter was peppered with them! You could practically see your father shaking with excitement. You could not stop reading it. Very soon you knew it off by heart. You would look at your father over the breakfast table and read the letter to yourself. You tried to imagine him thinking it, writing it, reading it out aloud. Where did he write it you wondered. In the car? In the privacy of The King's Arms? And who was he sending it to? Who was Mrs M? Not Mrs Muchmore surely. You had kept it. You had not known what it could be used for, but you had kept it. It was a dangerous thing to have in your possession, as unpredictable as a stick of sweaty dynamite, but you had kept it. You put it in a small tobacco tin and buried it in a hollow underneath the briar bushes. When there was little chance of your being disturbed you would prise it out of the earth, wipe off the soil that somehow always got through, and read again his elaborate instructions concerning one black girl and one white girl and the singular pleasure he would derive with Mrs M from the combination thereof. Now, standing in Mr Muchmore's porch, you remembered this treasure, and vowed that like the snow he so carefully wrapped around his sharp and jagged stone so would you decorate his little note one day and send it smiling on its way.

As you walked down towards the living room you couldn't help but notice that there were a lot of locks and bolts in Mr Muchmore's house. There were bolts on the top of every door and bolts on the bottom of every door, and out of each lock there protruded a large iron key. The bolts looked *cared for*, they were *oiled* for Christ's sake, and the keys were of a proportion that made them more suitable for a Norman keep than for internal use in a 1930s' suburban house. In all the cases, except for the living room, the bolts had been rammed home and pressed down, and a quick recce confirmed that all the keys had all been turned in their locks. How very odd. The house was shut up like a fortress. In your house apart from the front and back you couldn't remember *any* door that had a key in it, let alone one that was used. Even the downstairs' lavatory key was missing. When sitting on the lavatory you had to put your foot against the door to prevent anyone from coming in.

The cigarette-box lay, as you had remembered, on an ugly walnut table and on examination you discovered that Mr Muchmore had allocated eighteen cigarettes for the proceedings. Judging by your father's performance last year that would barely meet his needs let alone anyone else's. You took five, then another five, then replaced three. Seven. Seven cigarettes in your pocket. From the back window you could see across to the Liddle house, and the window where Fat Patrick's father had his room. You wondered whether he was there now, sitting in his crazy cockpit and you had half a mind to step out on to the veranda to take a look. A noise made you look back. Mr Muchmore and your father stood in the frame of the doorway looking at you intently. Both had pewter tankards in their hands. How long they had been standing there you had no idea. Had they seen you abusing Mr Muchmore's hospitality? Your father took a sip. From the froth on his lips you could tell they were drinking beer. Ah, said Mr Muchmore. There you are. While we're waiting for the food we thought you might have a little something to Wet our Whistle. I suppose you think that you deserve some too?

You looked at Mr Muchmore closely. His body expressed extreme satisfaction and permanence. It was squat and comfortable, dressed in a dark tweed jacket and light fawn trousers. Large feet settled outwards. His hands were thick and jointed. He looked like a bulldog waiting for his morning run, a thick jowl of flesh and bone jutting out into a stern, uncompromising stance which forced the bottom row of the Muchmore teeth out against the upper lip. He talked slowly but with great emphasis. He made statements rather than conversation, and each observation would end with a vigorous suck, a verbal full stop, a play of spit and tooth, lip and air. Your father's playmate. You had the impression that neither of them liked each other very much, but so what. They liked very little. It was their hearty dislike of things which drew them together. There was some bruising around Mr Muchmore's eye, but if you didn't know any better you would have said that he looked almost jovial. A glass of beer, you said, would be very nice indeed.

And what have you done with your good lady? Mr Muchmore asked your father, moving into the room. And what have you done with yours? he replied. The two of them roared with laughter. Mine is in the kitchen, Mr Muchmore answered. And mine is in the bathroom, your father countered, though it's a mystery to me what these women find to do in there. This much was true. Your father's knowledge of the ways of the bathroom was spartan. He was not a bathroom man and often needed to be reminded of where it lay and what its purpose might be. Your father had to be blackmailed into lowering his body into a bath and when he emerged from the few occasions when your mother *did* manage to herd him along the corridor to the poisonous dip, he scurried back to his little box-room to sit on the edge of his bed and light up a cigarette to recover from the shock. The number of times your father and the bathroom coincided could be counted on the fingers of one hand: Christmas (Eve, Day, or Boxing), The Evening of the Annual Works Dinner Dance (now defunct), The Day Before the Summer Holiday Car Journey (an expedition of nightmarish proportions) and two of his own choosing, The Last Night of the Proms, when he emulated Sir Malcolm Sargent and changed his shirt during the interval, and Robert Schumann's birthday, when he would line up bottles of imported German beer on the enamel edge and sing his favourite songs – *Spahend nach dem Eisengitter, bei des Mondes hellem Schein, steht ein Minstrel mit der Zither, vor dem Schlosse Durrenstein* – before going out on the piss. On average then, no more than forty minutes a year under warm soapy water.

The doorbell rang. That'll be them now, said your father. I'll get it, leaving you and Mr Muchmore to stare at each other. Neither of you could think of anything to say. Would you like a cigarette? No that's quite all right. You haven't many left. I'll have one of mine. I stole them from you only a few moments ago. And where's my glass of beer you old fart? A small scuffle started in the hall. Someone was fighting with your mother again. Not Carol. Your father. You couldn't hear exactly what was being said, but you could recognize the struggle of feet. It sounded as if he was trying to prevent her from coming in. No, he was saying, No you can't, *you can't*, while Carol whispered, Go on! Go on! Suddenly the door was flung open and your mother fell in, as if she had been pushed. Ah Leonard, she said, straightening up. I'm sorry to be late. No excuses I'm afraid. She held out her hand, but Mr Muchmore was too shocked to know how to respond. Although his eye was closing up, it did not prevent him from taking in every detail of the strange spectacle which confronted him. Carol had tackled the problem head on and had re-invented your mother, so that all aspects of her physical presence, her muscular arms, her thick eyebrows, the great top of black hair were accentuated to the point of caricature. The olive-green dress had been discarded and instead Carol had buckled her into the gaudy costume she herself had worn for her theatrical début. It was lucky, you supposed, that this rather over-elaborate creation had been cut to a full measure, for while Carol's frame was much the same as your mother's, there was a lot more flesh on her parent. Still it was not a bad fit. It was just that the heavily padded arms and shoulders gave your mother an aggressive, almost pugilistic appearance, and her biceps bulged out of the little lace stage ruffs in the manner of a prize fighter shadow boxing over a plate of cucumber sandwiches. What was more disturbing was Carol's solution to the problem of your mother's eyebrows, for here enthusiasm had got the better of her. Carol had painted your mother's eyebrows back on with what looked like boot polish (but which you assumed to be mascara) and in her haste had managed to join the two ends up so that it seemed as if your mother was sporting the top half of the Lone Ranger's black mask. As if that wasn't enough, instead of the customary Stetson that Clayton Moore favoured, Carol had brought back from Fat Patrick's house what looked like an exotic beach towel and wrapped it around your mother's head. Though it wobbled a little, and leant out at a dangerous angle, not a trace of the Great Hair Massacre could be seen.

That night your father raged around the house, cursing the four walls. You could hear him long after you went to bed, in the kitchen, in his study, in your mother's bedroom. What the hell did she think she was playing at coming dressed like that? Had she no sense at all? How dare she humiliate him so, wearing a bloody turban for Christ's sake from that wog across the road. She might as well have come shuffling in with the palms of her hands pressed together. Wait until I get hold of Carol. I'll give her hats.

The lunch had unfolded like a badly rehearsed musical, with characters missing their cues, fluffing their lines, and occasionally flouncing off into the wings. By the time the final curtain was drawn, both your father and your mother, and you suspect Carol, were completely drunk. You had never seen your mother drink quite like that before, gulping down what was on offer as if she were dying of thirst, banging her glass on the table as soon as it was empty, nor indeed could you remember Mr Muchmore being quite so free with his drinks tray. Sherry, wine, bottled beer, there were no limits to his generosity. Perhaps the spectacle of your father glowering across the table at your mother, whose eyebrows started to run at about half past one, and whose hat tipped over her forehead and threatened to fall across the table into the cold rice pudding at a quarter past two, drove him to unusual heights of hospitality. That of course was why you smelt no cooking earlier (though it did not explain the succession of crashes and bangs you had heard), for when the time for eating came, and you all followed Mr Muchmore into the dining room, you discovered that everything on offer was stone cold. Not a single item was hot or even warm. It was not surprising that the turkey was cold, or that the Yorkshire pudding was cold, (Yorkshire pudding?) and indeed although you had not expected to be confronted by a plate of cold roast potatoes they presented no real problem, but cold carrots? cold sprouts? *cold gravy*? The cold sprouts had been dipped in what you imagined was pickle but which turned out to be Marmite, and the Yorkshire puddings smeared with something Mr Muchmore described as 'Grandfather's Marmalade'. To your surprise both proved to be quite nice. You were not the only one who liked them. On lifting the lid to the lone vegetable dish, sprouts on one side, carrots on the other (and why you asked yourself later did it have a lid on if everything was cold), Stella, who sat opposite you peered inside and said Ah, sprouts! as if it came to her as a surprise, as if she hadn't spent half the morning banging about in the kitchen with her mother. Without offering them round she helped herself to a large, and rather rude helping. Mr Muchmore made no attempt to check this example of inhospitality, but looked upon his daughter with undisguised amusement. You must excuse my daughter's manners he said, helping himself to the very choicest cuts of turkey breast, but in this house one of our mottoes is Want Well What Others Will Waste. Have a carrot ma'am.

There were more mottoes attached to the Muchmore household than there were keys and bolts on the doors and before anything was allowed to roam free across the bare oak dining table Mr Muchmore had to unlock the topic with one of his manmade homilies. As you gazed upon the chilling spectacle of the boat full of congealed gravy, he announced that in *his* house they had a saying that Hot Meals Harden the Heart while Cold Cuts Calm the Colon, which stunned you long enough for the rest of the Muchmore family to appropriate the best of what was left. By the time you got to the meat plate there were no stuffing balls at all. Speak Plain, Eat Plain was another explanation put forward, though it failed to explain away the presence of the decorated Yorkshire pudding, nor the remark that accompanied it, that its inventor, Grandfather Muchmore, who had made the marmalade (*made* the marmalade? How old was it for God's sake?) had *Lived in Misery and Died By Poison*! It was unclear whether Mr Muchmore meant that he had died while making the marmalade or more worryingly had died because of the marmalade, but from the looks he gave his wife it was clear that for some reason Mr Muchmore seemed to think that she was somehow to blame. It was only later, when you and Stella had gone to several parties and you had appeared at least four times outside her window, when you could both laugh over cold sprouts and gravy, that she told you that Grandfather Muchmore had choked to death on a celebratory stuffed marrow, and that historically, the family had always blamed Grandmother Muchmore, who was never allowed out of the house again, nor indeed into the kitchen, for fear she might trot down to the chemist's for some tartar emetic or finish them all off with a dodgy Spotted Dick. Certainly the memory of this tragedy cast a gloom over the family that day, which was only deepened when your father blithely asked Mr Muchmore how business was. Considering your father spent hours with Mr Muchmore sinking pints of Best, you would have thought that he would have known a) how Mr Muchmore's business was and b) the sort of reception such a question would get, for after several minutes of bitter silence Mr Muchmore proceeded to tell him that a family business was a family matter. Keep it in the family and it will grow and flourish like one of your own children, he said, a thing to cherish. But let it out to play, let it indulge in unhealthy alliances, let others interfere, poke their noses where they don't belong and it will foul its own nest. A family business should have as its motto Mind Your Own Business As We Mind Ours. A little more Yorkshire pudding, *if* you don't mind.

As far as you can remember it was your father who first coined the expression the SS girl, and typically it contained as much malice as he could bear. The description SS did not, as you earlier suggested, refer solely to the manner in which she walked, but also the slight speech impediment she enjoyed, whereby Christmas was pronounced Chrissmass and Stella, Sscella. It was a particularly unkind remark of your father's, because everyone knew that the girl was unusually sensitive to her slight abnormality, which is why she refused to tread the boards under the direction of Mr Cooper (expressing complete contempt for school dramatics) and why, when the time came for him to read your essay, the name Muchmore meant nothing to him. He certainly would have recognized your mother's costume (and perhaps he knew it better than you imagined), but whether Stella realized the provenance of your mother's attire you could not tell.

Until Mr Muchmore went to fetch them, you had seen neither hide nor hair of Mrs Muchmore and her daughter that day. After the four of you had sat down and Mr Muchmore had opened four more bottles of beer and placed them in the middle of·the table he looked at his watch and informed you all that it was time to bring the womenfolk in. He left the room and came back a few moments later with his family in tow, Mrs Muchmore carrying the plate of cold meat, stuffing balls and Yorkshire pudding and Stella the plate of cold roast potatoes and the dish with the lid. They made an odd sight, small, shaky Mrs Muchmore followed by her tall strong daughter. Mrs Muchmore bustled and fussed but it was Stella, with her stubborn hair and her raven eyes that filled the room. She wore a plain black frock that hid her shape, but out of the cuffs, *out in the open*, came stern brown wrists, as thick and strong as your own. It was strange though. Although they said hello and Mrs Muchmore asked gently how your mother was doing, there was something reserved, awkward about them all, as if they were uncertain of what was coming next, of why you were all there. Indeed had you not known that Stella walked down to school with Carol every morning you would think that she never went out at all, that the way she lowered her face and snatched at her food while her mother sat patiently before an empty plate demonstrated that she had no experience of outside life whatsoever, that she was in a sense, a complete savage, a heathen. You wouldn't have been surprised if Stella had thrown back her head and howled, though in truth, it was your mother who was making greatest use of her neck. By this time your mother had finished her three sherries and was well into her second glass of red wine. Unlike your father or your sister she seemed as greedy for food as Stella and had a whole stuffing ball down her throat before she had even picked up her knife and fork. From the way she held it you half expected her to drink directly out of the gravy boat, and it was only when Mr Muchmore leant over and filled her glass up for a third time that she relented and let it go, swigging back the wine so vigorously that her hat caught the picture behind, knocking it askew. As luck would have it it proved to be a portrait of the murdered grandparent (without the marrow) and it took Mr Muchmore several anxious minutes before he managed to put it back on the rails. What an unusual hat that is, he had said grimly, straightening up the picture. Where did you get the idea from? The Ideal Home Exhibition? A lively bit of colour and no mistake. It certainly is, your father agreed, though there are those of us who think that there's a bit too much colour hereabouts these days. It was then, just as you were about to try a Marmite flavoured carrot, that your nose was suddenly assaulted by a wonderful smell of *cooking*, of spare ribs and barbecued chicken and great slabs of steak sizzling over some open fire. It made you squirm in your seat, you were so hungry. You looked to the door in the hope that all the banging and crashing you had heard earlier meant that this parade of cold comfort was Mr Muchmore's little joke, but from the looks on the faces of his family you could tell that they were as puzzled by the smell as you were. Where on earth could it be coming from? It was Stella who solved the riddle. Sniffing the air she turned round and drew back the curtain. There, across the fence, you could see Fat Patrick standing by the long charcoal grill that his father had built by the far side of their house, biting into an enormous hot sausage. The Liddles seemed to be giving some sort of outdoor barbecue with Fat Patrick's father dispensing chicken legs and baked potatoes and God, yes! Chump Chops! to all and sundry while his mother waltzed up and down with a great jug of punch in her hand. Everyone stood around holding something *hot*! Steam was coming out of their mouths, rising off their plates, flowing from their cups. A glowing fire warmed their outstretched hands. They were draped in scarves and mufflers and knitted gloves, sunny and happy, chatting to each other, drinking, eating, stamping their feet. And oh, the glorious smell! A nice crisp wing and a burnt potato. What wouldn't you give for that?

It's a bloody insult, your father said. They do it every bloody year, another bloody get together, and your father started, just as you knew he would. He would never forget that last Long Service Dinner as long as he lived, how Jim Liddle and a few others ruined it all. The expense the company had gone to to get those statues carved. Just so that Jim Liddle could smash them up. If it had been him, he'd have had him up before the law there and then, and saved every one a lot of bother, not least himself. Not many people seemed to realize that it was *he* who had saved Jim Liddle's bacon. If it hadn't been for him, Jim Liddle would be rotting away in that hulk across the water, instead of playing Biggles on government handouts. It was here, halfway through your father's story of Jim Liddle and the *Galway Bay*, flushed perhaps by the single glass of beer you had managed to extract from one of Mr Muchmore's brown bottles, that you felt it time to add your six pennyworth. Your story however did not go as planned. The more you attempted to ridicule him, the better Jim Liddle seemed to come out of it. The trouble was you could not rid yourself of the image of Fat Patrick's father swimming out into that dark and lonely current, of Fat Patrick's father hauling himself cold and dripping up on to that grey and distant hulk and living inside it without food or water or *anything* for five days. What had he done during that time? Had he just sat there, staring out over the water (which is what he was doing when they found him) or had he done what you had always wanted to do while squatting on the churned pillbox floor, peering through the fog and the rain and the sunlit gloom, had he *played* in it, had he wandered up and down the gangways in his peaked cap, conferred with the radio operator and the ship's clerk, chatted to the passengers, sauntered into the smoking cabin for a leisurely cigarette before turning in? *The Galway Bay*, the most magnificent, the most perfect (the most *intact*) of all the Flying Boats. Rumour had it that the *Galway Bay* was practically perfect inside with everything still in place, right down to the picnic hampers and the silver-plated cutlery. Nothing had been taken out, no seats, no wires, not even the bloody engines. In their haste to up their roots and decamp, the company had abandoned the *Galway Bay* (and her four sisters) and left her for the town to deal with. The last to arrive, they had simply sealed her up and moored her alongside the others. And Fat Patrick's father had been inside her! The truth was, you admired Jim Liddle for striking out to her. The truth was, and this is why you were so fickle to his overweight off-spring, the whole town admired Jim Liddle and Jim Liddle could wander around the town until his pajama-string *rotted* and *no one* would object, no one that is except your father and his squat friend, and in your eagerness to ingratiate yourself you had chosen the wrong story, not the one about Jim Liddle sitting in his study making improbable whizzing noises, but of him crying into his handkerchief on hearing of his wayward daughter's imminent departure. This did not go down well. This is not what your father and Mr Muchmore wanted to hear at all. They wanted to hear tales of idiocy, of incapability, of Jim Liddle losing his grip, not of Mr and Mrs Liddle raging over their daughter's behaviour, tears or no tears. Daughters should stay at home by God. If a few more stayed at home and did as they were told . . . This modern fascination for movement, Mr Muchmore observed at the close of your sorry tale, is all wrong. Too many teenagers spend all their days Sliding about on their Bottoms, bumping into each other and generally giggling, suffering under the delusion that Life is one Big Game of Dodgems. The youth of today, he said is a Great Heap of Arms and Legs. It has no sense, no purpose, just a great wriggling mass, writhing against one another for the feel of it. Look at all that dancing they get up to. Dancing! He had a maxim had Mr Muchmore, which if he could he would engrave on the heart of every girl and every boy in the land. Beat hard, beat hard you little beast, but *Beat Hard In Your Cage*. The very organ of life is trapped, bound by sinews and muscle, sentenced to life in a cage, A Cage of Bone. No prisoner suffers that length of sentence, no chain gang has to toil under such a strain. All its life the little heart must bulge and squeeze, pacing up and down in that tiny kingdom. That is where it is and where it must stay. *Must stay*! And it is our duty to teach our children that this is how it must be. *Must be*! Beat hard, beat hard you little beasts, but keep to your kingdom, or we shall all perish. No wonder the poor man is crying. Even with his limited hold on reality he can see how desperate the situation is. I'd probably be in tears too if I was in his shoes. Tears of Rage. For a moment you had managed to drive Jim Liddle's most implacable foes into defending him. Your father put them back on course. Well, he said, there're no tears in his eyes this afternoon at any rate. Probably glad to see the back of her. Wouldn't you be? he added. Not that we want to go into that here, but that's what comes of *mixing one's paintbox* Leonard, if you get my drift. He brought it on himself. That's what

I told him that night of the Dinner, when he went funny on us. You know what your trouble is, I said, don't you. You're too partial to . . . and here your father leant across and whispered into Mr Muchmore's ear. It was a large ear and had thick ginger hair sprouting from it and as your father's lips grew closer to it, Mr Muchmore licked his lips as if in anticipation of the taste to come. The trouble with you Jim, your father whispered so that you *all* could hear, is that you're too partial to *dark meat*. Mr Muchmore looked out across the way. Looks like he's got some on his fork now! he replied. They both roared with laughter again. And then! And then! your father cried, You know what I told him? You know what you should do with all that money? I said. Open up an Indian. You've had enough practice!

It took some minutes for their laughter to subside, by which time Stella had gathered up the plates and stormed out of the room. Carol looked to your mother for help but your mother was too drunk to know exactly what your father had said, a situation which your father, now firing on all guns, intended to exploit to the full. So there they are now, he continued, helping himself to another bottle, turning round in his seat so that he could see them, *Mr* Jim Liddle and *Mr* Peter Jackson and that other troublemaker, the one that had nearly hit him that night, the bald one, Gordon Mackenzie. From Scotland wouldn't you know. He suspected that it was Gordon Mackenzie who was responsible for all the trouble he'd had, all those threatening letters and obscenities on the walls, but of course no one could prove anything, least of all the police. Fat lot of use *they* were. What sort of man, asked your father, writes those sort of letters, full of the most disgusting filth? Runs a taxi service now, if you please. Sits outside the station picking his nose waiting for the 5.15 from Victoria. Doesn't mind living off the likes of us, now does he? Doesn't mind coming up to Gladstone Drive cap in hand when it comes to a Christmas Day Fry Up! *Boxing Day* Fry Up, Mr Muchmore corrected. Even Peter Jackson, your father continued, watching them with an agitated malevolence that could only be compared to his Dance upon the Landing, had the sense to sink his money into a corner shop. But what does Loopy Liddle do with his? Does he invest it? Does he take his wife on a world cruise? No. He waits until he finds a nice bit of marshland that no one wants and blows it all on that! It was true. Three or four years back, Fat Patrick's father had bought a tract of marshland somewhere on the Isle of Grain, where there was nothing but mud and grease and a massive tumbledown old boathouse with a few blackened ducks for company. A truly horrid place where no one would go for pleasure. Fat Patrick had told you his mother had gone spare when she found out. A bloody bog, she had shouted, What are we going to do with a blasted bloody bog? and she had boxed Fat Patrick's father's ears and for the only time in her life, called him a bloody *fool*. Can you imagine, your father said, waiting all that time to buy a bit of water! What good is water. Now beer! and he turned back and grabbed hold of his half empty bottle.

Stella returned with a bowl of cold rice pudding and cold custard. Your father fell silent. The atmosphere grew more relaxed. Your mother's hat and eyebrows were forgotten, the workers a thing of the past. Mrs Muchmore and Carol joined in. They kept to safe topics, how long the snow might last, whether there would be more, did we *want* more. Carol felt that Christmas was becoming very commercial these days and Mrs Muchmore was forced to agree. Mr Muchmore settled down and made a joke about home-made crackers for home-made mottoes, or perhaps it was the other way around. No one, observed your father grimly, reluctant to let the matter drop, is more crackers at home than him-next-door. Outside, the barbecue party had spread out on to the back lawn, where they were busy building a snowman. After the rice pudding you all moved back into the living room where, to everyone's obvious relief, more sherry was on hand. Stella passed a fruit bowl round. Mr Muchmore took an apple and bit into it. The morsel crossed his mouth once, twice and then he spat it out on to the carpet.

'This apple is rotten,' he complained. 'It is bad in the middle.'

You looked at the object with distaste. He moved forward and touched it slightly with his foot.

'The whole world is bad in the middle,' your father offered, after due inspection. 'You can always get another apple.'

'It looked perfect on the outside,' Mr Muchmore explained. He held it out and bit into it again. 'No, no doubt about it. It's bad all right.' He blew a second portion into the fire and stood before you examining the fruit closely. There was a sadness in his eyes, as if he had been betrayed by a trusted friend. He placed the apple on the mantelpiece and chose another. Another bite and a third section flew into the air.

'There it is again! Would you credit it!'

'Throw the lot out,' your father advised. 'That's what I'd do if I was in your shoes. Throw the lot out and start again. Change tactics. Get some pears.'

Leonard turned to his wife.

'Hear that,' he said. 'Get some pears.' He seized the fruit bowl and threw the contents in the fire. To his fury one or two bounced back on the carpet.

'That's the stuff,' your father applauded, looking down at Mr Muchmore scrabbling about at his feet. 'That's what we need in this country. Some weeding out. Let's have some more sherry.'

Mr Muchmore and your father moved towards the decanter. They held over the room the threat of real but unspoken anger. Leap down our throats if you dare. Brush your soul against our teeth if you have the nerve. Interfere with us at your peril! We are ready for you. Muchmore held the decanter to the light. He grunted and licked his lips. A small suck of appreciation seeped out from the tip of his teeth, then he remembered himself and turned his attention to his guests, filling each glass in turn.

'Sherry? Mrs Doughty, Mr Doughty, Carol, Giles, Stella.' Here he surveyed the room and finding everything correct poured a glass for himself. His wife, holding an empty glass vainly in her hand, gripped the side of her chair, twitched and stuck her arm out into the middle of the room.

'Just a little more sherry darling,' she said, and writhed again.

Leonard looked at her and then turned to his daughter.

'What does she want?' he asked, sucking in a great draught of air.

'Sherry. More sherry.'

Mrs Muchmore nodded. Mr Muchmore looked from his wife to his daughter and then jangled the keys in his pocket.

'I believe it is time for her to return from whence she came and leave us grown ups to talk in peace.'

The room became still. The brownness of the furniture, the cream of the walls seemed to become more intense. Outside you could hear Fat Patrick's mother shrieking with laughter but there was life here too. Such shameless monstrous life! Mrs Muchmore rose without a word and left the room. Her husband followed. You were acutely aware of every sound, the footsteps they made on the tiled floor while your mother suppressed an incipient state of hiccups. A door opened at the far end of the corridor, opened and then closed again. Then you heard another sound. You heard a bolt, a bolt shot home. First one, then another. *Oiled* bolts! They rang down the corridor as clear as any of their chiming clocks. Mr Muchmore had locked his wife in! Shut the door and locked her in! Mrs Muchmore was a prisoner in her own home!

He returned wiping his hands, satisfied by his day's work. He moved to the mantelpiece and turned to his audience.

'Yes,' he said, lifting his glass. 'It's a rotten old world all right.'

Your father clapped him on the shoulder.

'Aye,' he said. 'But nothing that a few pints of wallop won't put right.'

Ah yes. You could give them a few pints of wallop and your fingers trembled at the thought of it, of taking them by the scruff of the neck and marching them out into the garden for a good beating. You might even lean over the garden fence and ask Gordon Mackenzie if he'd like to join in. You looked across. Stella sat watching you. She had heard your every thought. You had said nothing but you had spoken to her for the very first time. Now came her reply.

'*I saw you the other night Giles. You were running across the road. I was going to call out to see if you wanted to come to Jessica's party but you were too quick for me. You'd better come better dressed than you were then though. Jessica's most particular.*'

In the days and weeks that followed, although there was much you remembered about that day (the locks and the bolts and Stella's reluctant replies as to her father's domestic habits), there was one small matter that evaded your memory – and it was only when strolling back home with Fat Patrick a few months later that you recalled it at all. Indeed had it not been for the fresh red-headed woman walking towards you, struggling with two suitcases held together with string, who knows, your father might be living there still, in his house overlooking the Medway?

'Why, hello,' Fat Patrick cried. 'I thought you'd already gone.'

Her face broke into a smile.

'Patrick!' She dropped the suitcases with relief and brushed the hair out of her eyes. 'And so we have. I've just been back for the weekend to collect the last of the things. I'm off up to Euston now, to catch the afternoon train. Probably have to stand all the way. Chock full of soldiers those trains are and do they give you a seat? They do not. Duffel bags and crates of beer all over the place.' She laughed at the prospect. 'Still we're well settled. Gordon's working with his brother now and we've just been given a place right round the corner. And how's your father Patrick?'

'Well enough.' He pointed to the suitcases. 'Would you like us to carry them for you?'

'Could you? That would be a blessing. I was hoping that Barratt might offer me a lift – Gordon used to work for him remember, not six months back – but would he give me one? He would not, the miserable old skin flint. So here I am, an ex-taxi driver's wife who can't afford the fare.' She laughed again. 'Are you sure you've got the time?'

Patrick picked up the heaviest looking case. 'Oh yes,' he said turning to you, 'we're in no hurry, are we? Do you know Giles? He lives across the road from me. Giles Doughty.'

She looked at you critically, as if trying to detect some flaw in your appearance.

'No,' she said quietly, 'we've never met.'

You trailed behind them as Fat Patrick and this woman, who he practically treated like a second mother, chattered their way to the station. The case weighed a ton. Every now and again laughter would peal back from them and you would stop and put the suitcase down, hoping that by the time you picked it up again they would be out of earshot. You did not want to hear Fat Patrick talking and chatting and enjoying himself with this unknown, lively woman with red hair and freckles on the back of her legs. And you did not care for the way she had looked at you, hard and with a deep-seated sense of mistrust. By the time you reached the

235

station she was busy queuing at the ticket office. You went up to Fat Patrick who was standing apart, re-tying the knot that held the lid down.

'Who is she?' you whispered.

'Mrs M,' Fat Patrick said. 'She's Gordon Mackenzie's wife. They've gone up to Glasgow to run a fish-and-chip shop. He used to work with Dad. A complete waste of talent, my dad says, him going up there. Should have gone over to Ireland with the factory *he* says. The trouble is', and he put his hand in front of his mouth, 'they're Catholics. He wouldn't get a job. Catholics can't vote there, did you know?'

No, you did not know, nor did you care, though you found it hard to believe. One man one vote that was how it worked. Your history master had told you that you should all be very proud of Britain's parliamentary democracy. There was nothing like it in the world. Fat Patrick must have got it wrong. But that was unimportant. You had found Mrs M. Not *the* Mrs M. but Mrs M. all the same, and suddenly your father's letter with the spidery handwriting and obscene exclamations had a home to go to. A good home. A home where the name of Doughty would mean something. She returned, stuffing her ticket into her purse.

'Well, I'll be off then,' she said. 'I can manage from here. Don't bother to wait.' She bent down and gave Fat Patrick a kiss. He appeared not to mind. Straightening up she stood back and looked at you.

'Well young Giles. That's the first time a Doughty has helped a Mackenzie and no mistake. Be sure to tell your father now.'

She held out her hand for the suitcase, and you acted quickly and without thought. Switching grip from one hand to the other, you used the movement to pull hard on the brown label that was attached to the worn handle. Mrs Mackenzie settled back into the case's weight. The label lay carefully hidden in the palm of your hand.

Later that evening, when everyone else was occupied, while Father was down at the pub, while your mother was watching television and your sister was out, you brushed your father's letter clean of soil and crumbled leaves and, placing it into one of the white envelopes he kept in a desk downstairs, took it into your sister's room where you rolled it through the black and ancient typewriter which always reminded you of a giant cinema organ. Using one stealthy finger you typed out the address from that label, a label that belonged to a suitcase which now lay open in a Glasgow hall, or a Glasgow bedroom, and which belonged to:

Mrs Gordon Mackenzie
15 Roland Rd
Glasgow

'Yes,' you thought, as you flicked the envelope into the post-box, 'it's a rotten old world all right.'

*

'So your father,' said Monica, easing back on her arms, 'was beaten up because . . .'

'Exactly,' I admitted, 'a little light revenge, a little schoolboy prank, a little letter from the mailman.'

'And if you hadn't . . .'

'And if I hadn't posted it to Glasgow my father wouldn't have been beaten up by Gordon Mackenzie nearly a year later, nor would he have had dog shit stuffed into his mouth, nor would he have fallen down in the gutter and I wouldn't have turned on my heels and he . . .'

'And he wouldn't have left home.'

'Maybe not.'

'Does Carol know this?'

'Of course Carol doesn't know. No one knows. Except you. And I don't quite know why I'm telling you. It's not as if you haven't got your own secrets, is it Monica?'

She looked at me, searching my face.

'We all have secrets, Giles,' she said. 'We all have hidden thoughts which are best left alone. Perhaps that is what you should do in this case. Perhaps you should leave Stella be, wherever she is.'

'No,' I told her. 'I can't. Stella blighted my life. Nearly everyone thought I had something to do with it.'

'Well they're right. You did have *something* to do with it.

There are not many girls of sixteen who make a habit of running around their home town with nothing on. If you hadn't encouraged her she wouldn't have been . . .'

'She wouldn't have been *what* Monica? You speak of her as if she's dead. That's what we all thought, that Stella had been murdered. That's what her father thought, that's what my father thought, that's what Detective Sergeant Weatherspoon thought, and they all thought I knew something. But she wasn't. She's alive and Carol saw her not seven days ago. So let's go back again. To that bar. Do you remember what she was wearing?'

'Something dark.'

'Black? Stella often wore black. Ordinary, sombre, black. Black?'

'Yes, black. Classy black.'

'A dress? A skirt?'

'A dress. Underneath a raincoat.'

'Well she would need a raincoat. The last raincoat of hers was found in the pillbox, with a rubber-band, an old bottle top and a box of matches in the pocket. We had smoked the last of the cigarettes the night before. Guards. Her father's brand. One before, one during, one after.'

'Sounds familiar.'

'No, nothing of that. One before the run, one while walking arm in arm down the road, and then, quickly, one later, in their garden shed. Amongst the geraniums. Before we went back to our separate beds.'

'Well she had something on underneath her raincoat this night, that at least I can tell you.'

'OK. If you had to describe her now, if you had to hazard a guess as to who she was, *what* she was, what would you say she did? Did she look like a woman up from the country, or was she more of a town dweller? What impression did you have of her? Was she married, single, wealthy, or what?'

'That bar is where people meet after work. It's not a night-out kind of bar. Office workers, people from the City, commuters waiting to catch a train from Charing Cross . . .'

'. . . and businessmen and their mistresses, I know. Which was she?'

'How do I know? Not a mistress.' She took another pull on the joint. 'She didn't look like she earned her living either. But she did look as if she knew the place.' She sat up. 'That's it! Go and ask the barman. She might be a regular. At the very least he'll remember her.'

I put my arms out in gratitude.

'Of course. I'll go tomorrow. God Monica, it's so simple. I just didn't think of it. Would you come with me? Can you spare the time?'

Monica leant forward and gave me a hug. Same old Monica. 'It's been a tough day or two for you hasn't it? Come on then. Lie next to me for a while.'

We smoked the last one in the dark, lying side by side. That's what we all do when we are adults. We lie in the dark, side by side, wondering what the other is thinking. I thought of Eric and Michael and their two ridiculous huts, stationed like two railway engines in a children's picture book, side by side. Is this what joins Eric and Michael? Is this what I would have to do to join the human race? Is this what Monica desires with her fisherman friend? Was it this that drove my wife to marry me, to lie *side by side* and was it the sterility of this proximity which drove her to the abortionist's clinic, the attempted suicide, and the successful separation and divorce. Cutting free at last. Here I was lying with Monica, as I had done so many times, and as I looked at her now I realized that there was nothing within her that I knew, and that there was nothing within *me* that I knew to be within *her*. It was not simply a feeling that we were two separate beings, from two separate sexes, but we were two separate *species*, that the language I spoke and the language she spoke were different languages, that the world she saw and the world I saw were different worlds as different as the eagle's from the hare's. Touching her skin, I realized that there was not one living thing that had anything in common with me. I was alone, as are we all. Perhaps it is only by knowing this that we can possibly be together. But I was not going to be together, was I? Not with Monica. Not if she had anything to do with it. Monica wanted to be together with her sailor chum. I remembered his picture on her bedside table and had the horrid suspicion that if I bent down and looked inside her handbag, I would find a replica tucked away in its folds. It struck me then, that I had some unfinished business to complete. I placed my hand inside her dressing-gown.

'Time to go,' she said, pushing me off.

'Go?'

'We've a long day ahead,' she said.

'But I thought . . .'

'I know what you thought. I always know what you think.' She put out her hand. 'See what I mean?'

'What *is* all this Monica,' I said.

'It's called misplaced affection, Giles. If you were a less selfish man, I might . . .'

'You might what Monica, sleep with me?'

'No, I've done that. I might *like* you better. As it is . . .'

'As it is, I'm not quite up to standard am I? Is that why you never let me make love to you properly Monica?'

'You know perfectly well why Giles.'

'So I do. Got to keep those mucus-lined walls scrupulously clean for old salty cock. Swab the decks! Here comes the navy!' I leant across, spitting the words on to her face. 'What I would like to do Monica, *dear*, is to stretch you out on my sister's bed, which you have appropriated without my permission, and Fill You Full of Doubt, right now, Up To the Very Brim!' I grabbed the back of her neck and kissed her, kissed, it seemed to me just like Stella must have kissed those two men, with my heart surging with rage.

Monica took hold of me and threw me to the floor.

'You're drunk Giles. Go now before you do anything stupid. Go now, before I chuck you down the stairs. I'll see you in the morning.'

I got up unsteadily and moved towards her again. 'Monica?'

'It's all over Giles. Go home.'

I stumbled downstairs and walked unsteadily to the door. Monica was throwing me out of my sister's house. After she had lulled me into thinking that I did mean something to her! I drove home cursing her name. Let Johnny Oates fuck her, let Johnny Oates get her pregnant. What did I care? I had cunt aplenty. I parked the car. I knocked over two or three dustbins on my way in and I knocked over the Woman from Spain's bicycle when I tried to shut the door. By the time I got up the stairs I could hear someone stirring in the spare room. I went in. Clare was fast asleep. The Woman from Spain was next to her, rubbing her eyes. I beckoned to her. She shook her head. I bent over and pulled her arm. No, she whispered. Bedtime. It's all right, I said and hauled her to her feet. I didn't want to look at her and I knew that if I didn't get it over with quickly I might well pass out. I brought out a couple of mint chocolates that I had pocketed from the dinner table. Look, I said, I brought you these, but she didn't want them. I stuffed one in her mouth and led her out into the hall. It's all right, I said and made her get down on all fours. I lifted up her nightdress, but each time I tried I lost my balance. I hung on to her shoulders, I grabbed her hips. I clutched at those great swinging breasts of hers, but it was no use. *Mummy?* came a small sleepy voice. *Mummy?* I leapt up and pushed her away. It's all right I said and held on to the doorframe. It's all right I said and did up my trousers as best I could. It's all right I said and went back in. Clare was sitting up, half asleep. It's all right I said, I'm here. I fell over something. It's all right I said and pulled myself up on to her bed. I thought I heard *Mummy*, she said, I thought I heard someone crying? Crying? No one's crying I said. You're not crying are you? No. I'm not crying either. *Someone* was crying, she said. I heard them. It woke me up. It's all right, I said. Everything's all right. No one's crying now. I leant over to kiss her and lost my balance again. I knocked over her bedside lamp and slid to the floor. It's all right, I said, it's all right. No one's crying now. I lay there a minute to get my bearings. It's all right, I said, it's all right. The Woman from Spain returned and helped me back to my feet. It's all right, I said, it's all right and she led me to my room. It's all right I called out, it's all right. I'm here. The Woman from Spain sat me on a chair. Would you like a chocolate? I said. I saved them specially. I looked in my pockets but could not find them. All gone, I said. All gone. I'll get some more in the morning, but she had left. It's all right, it's all right, I said. I'm here, and thankfully fell asleep.

Four

AND THAT WAS THAT. Apart from the futile visit to the barman under Charing Cross Station, who remembered the incident, remembered the two men, remembered the scowling woman, remembered even Monica open-mouthed at the scene, but who could add nothing, who had never seen Stella before, until the night I danced with the nurse with flat feet, until the night I took her in my arms and waltzed her up and down the ward, passed the snoring and sniffling beds, passed the shrouded ones, the shifting ones, passed the one who tried to kill herself and who lay at night with headphones clamped over her unruly head, until that night, when our feet slipped up and down the polished floor, when all I could hear was the sound of her squeaking heels turning to the rhythm of the radio, apart from that night when the nurse with flat feet and I conspired together, when we unstrapped my sister and, with her radio playing some foreign music station, bathed my sister by the light of the slatted moon, when I was reminded of other lights, shining through other windows, bathing another body (so similar, so different), when I was reminded of that moving window in that midnight train, with Fleur half sitting, half lying, spread out before me, soaked by the station's empty light, apart from that night, when the nurse with flat feet stood on the other side of the bed and raised my sister's arms as I soaped my sister's pungent hair, raised my sister's legs as I squeezed soap down my sister's stolen calves, apart from that night when we bent down close over my sister's body, when our hands met across the barren reef of my sister's chest, when we brushed past each other on our journey around my sister's keep, apart from that night when everyone else in that ward was asleep, the first time I had ever known such a thing, even the woman who had tried to kill herself, who gulped down their sleeping draughts and chewed on their sleeping pills and who sat up every night crunching her teeth listening to God-knows-what, when even she lay asleep on her side with her mouth open, the music dead in her ears, apart from that night when the nurse with flat feet and I waltzed up and down the ward, me in my stockinged feet, she in her regulation shoes, singing snatches of the Blue Danube and Drink to Me Only With Thine Eyes and any other maudlin and sentimental tune that came into our heads, apart from that night, when I arrived late, with half a bottle of whisky inside me, on my way to spend a night with Fleur in some hotel in Knightsbridge, she just back from Gloucestershire, a good two weeks since we had seen each other, apart from that night, when, after we had bathed my sister and had sprinkled her body with talcum powder, white flakes falling on my sister as the snow falls in the dead of night, turning her sickly skin into a silent landscape, empty of life but possessed by a strange and remote beauty, I, flushed with expectation and in huge good spirits, turned the music up softly and told the nurse with flat feet that I no longer wanted to look at my sister lying there, and I was fed up with it all, that all I wanted to do was to lift her up and dance with her, hold her, dance with her, breathe some life into her, *didn't she understand*, and the nurse with flat feet came over and put her finger to my lips and told me to be quiet, to hush now and be quiet or I would wake the others, apart from that night when the nurse with flat feet said Is it she who needs the dance then? Is it she who is asking for all this attention? apart from that night when I bowed my head and told her No, it was me, *I* wanted to dance, *I* wanted to be held, Would she dance with me? I promise to be quiet, Look I'll even take off my shoes, apart from that night when without warning, as if on cue, the 'Hilton Balcony' swung out on the radio, as if Speedy Bec had set up underneath my sister's very window, apart from that night when I asked the nurse with flat feet, Do you know this? Do you know this? and she nodded and I said, Isn't it wonderful? Doesn't it just make you simply float? and I bent down, removed my shoes and moved across, took the nurse with flat feet in my arms, and in a classic ballroom hold took off, round my sister's bed and out down the corridor and into the ward, when I rested my head on the nurse with flat feet's shoulder, when, out of hearing of Speedy

Bec's melody, I sang the sweetest songs I could remember, songs of self pity and adoration, apart from that night when we turned and danced past those lifeless shrouds, when I kissed the nurse with flat feet on the neck, and fell in love, when I forgot, when I could have danced all night, apart from that night when my sister sat up alert and alone, when my sister sat up suddenly with eyes blazing and jerked those tubes out one by one and had us running back down the ward, me slipping in my stockinged feet, clutching on to beds and curtains, lurching from side to side (no one chasing me this time, no wheezing caretaker with a torch in his hand coming up the stairs), when my sister sat up and jibbered and jabbered out those spare-room instructions four months after the tree had knocked her cold, four months after the puma had licked the blood from her bruised head, four months after Stella had led her to her open grave, apart from that night, when my sister awoke for her one and only time and started it all off again, I had done nothing to solve the mystery.

That of course is not *exactly* true, but what with one thing and another, and despite the encouragement of Dickey Dove, who had invented a cocktail in my honour which he called Deep Depression, I had no time (and for that read inclination) for much detective work. The night with Monica had seen to that, that and the drive down the following morning when we followed a line of refugees down the length of rubble-strewn Kent, our faltering route guided by regiments of red and white traffic cones. It seemed to me as Monica stared out of the window with nothing to say, despite my apologies, that the way my car was handed over to these conical dwarfs, who led it over lanes and boundaries, who danced ahead with all of us following in tow, was how the rest of my life was going to be. How different from that brief moment the day before when we tore across the road of our own volition. Overnight, everything had suddenly changed. No more overtaking, no more flashing lights and deliberate bad manners, no more slugs of whisky, no more joints and most definitely no more gratuitous sex in the front seat. What use four-wheel drive and five-speed gearbox now? What use two point five litre engine and the urge to top one hundred and twenty? What use an ounce of dope, two bottles of champagne and a hotel forecourt? None.

Those mad minutes with Monica on the motorway had been a last desperate fling. Excess had gone. Excess had gone clean out the window. Excess had been scoured and scrubbed away, and the last time I had attempted it (admittedly under difficult circumstances) with two bottles of Barolo, several stiff whiskies, and copious lungfuls of Monica's finest under my belt I had blown it and revealed myself as a victim of *I knew not what*.

Of course I had not abandoned *all* intentions of finding Stella but until that moment when Carol spoke I had let the matter slide. There was so much for me to do, so much that occupied my time, that I could not, would not, dare not explore any other territory. I did go down to Ashford a couple of times to hang around Wye, but as I told Dickey Dove in the evenings, I was not sure any more whether I wanted to find Stella. Somehow the stuffing had gone out of me. What Monica had said about leaving well alone rang true. I had Clare to attend to and Carol to visit. I had breakfast to eat, suppers to cook, books to read and a household to keep. A quiet life is what I craved. The idea of the unknown was something I wished to avoid.

'I know what you mean,' Dickey Dove said as he handed me another potion of his vile concoction. 'It was a feeling I often found myself in the grip of when surrounded by acres of the ocean blue. The overwhelming desire to shut yourself in your cabin and see nothing, to *limit your horizons*. Hearthrug over Hammock. That's what I keep telling my daughter who insists on seeing this fellow who has an earring stuck in his buttock and reads *On the Road* out loud to her. He is, if you pardon my French, all pose and no pouch. What he needs is a little less Kerouac and a little more Horlicks. Less Panavision and more Brownie 127. I mean what sort of man is it that writes down his own dreams? And then tells you.'

'That's pretty bad,' I agreed.

'It gets worse. Only the other day he told me, after asking me to rustle up a Margarita, rustle up, *rustle up*! he told me that he was sick of Kent and that he wanted to see the world. He said, and here it gets really grim, "*Travel broadens the mind.*" "Broadens the mind?" I said, "BROADENS THE MIND! Look at me, I've been everywhere. Everywhere. Can you look me in the eye and tell me that travel has broadened *my* mind?"'

'What's his name?'

'Norman Morris. I call him Norman the Nomad.'

'You should have taken a shotgun to Norman there and then,' I said. 'Saved Thomas Cook a lot of grief. Are you sure you put anything in this drink?'

'That's the whole beauty of a Deep Depression sir. You can never be sure that it has any gin in it at all. Just when you've decided that you're going to drink something you like, the mercury falls out the bottom of your barometer and you find yourself wallowing in an unnavigable melancholia. Recovery is not easy. Two days to find the compass, two days to work out how to use it and two days to make port.'

'Give me another,' I said, forgetting Monica's strictures.

I had become quite attached to Dickey Dove. It was he who helped me over those first dreadful days, who stopped by the hospital to see if I was all right, who put me up in his front room while we waited to see if she would pull through, and who sat up with me until dawn, listening to the story of Stella Muchmore.

'We had people disappearing all the time,' Dickey said. 'But none who turned up twenty years later. We lost a chap in Aden once though and picked him up in the same place a year later. Tried to change the date of his boarding-pass would you believe. When he was confronted with his misdemeanour he claimed he'd been drugged and kidnapped and then forced to play cricket month after month by a deranged potentate with an obsession about the MCC. Talk about hookah eyes. Captain took pity on him though and had him on board washing glasses. Blow me if he didn't bunk off again two weeks later in Singapore.'

'I wish Stella had turned up within the year with hookah eyes,' I said. 'It would have made my life a lot easier.'

Dickey reached out.

'If it hadn't been for Stella Muchmore sir, your sister would not have followed her to Wye and if your sister hadn't followed her to Wye you would not have checked in to The Post House and I . . .'

'And you?'

'And I would still be an odalisque to Ashford, serving drinks to the unworthy. I have a stake in this too sir. If you want any help in running this Stella to ground, then Dickey is your dove.'

There were two other people, however, who I had sought out once Carol was stable and once Clare was safely installed. Michael Mulligan and Fat Patrick's beautiful elder sister. Michael came first.

When I rang there was a thunderous noise in the background, as if a freight train were running through the back.

'What in God's name is going on?' I shouted.

'Giles,' cried Eric. 'Where the devil have you been? Lady Bracknell is fit to bust, I have been without sleep for the last four days and Michael is the happiest man alive. He holds the two of us directly responsible by the way. Come over at once do you hear. The place is awash with celebration.'

'Someone's birthday?'

'Birthday! This has nothing to do with mothers or fathers Giles. Black Monday Giles, Black Monday. What a day.'

'Forgive me Eric, but I've been a little out of touch. What's happened?'

'What's happened? Where have you been? Only the greatest stock market crash since the nineteen twenty-nine. Billions wiped off the stock exchange. Catastrophe and ruination abound.'

'And you're celebrating?'

'You don't understand Giles. The Monday before the storm, a week *before* Black Monday, Michael took a stroll down into the financial section of his citadel and stopped outside nineteen seventy four. April 30th to be precise. There he sought the advice of one Graham "Gilt-Edged" Garmondsway who was much concerned about the forthcoming General Election. Anticipating a Labour victory and the debilitating effect this would have on the market, Gilt-Edged Graham (the man they call Mr City) told his readers to get out or expect heavy losses. It would be safer he wrote to keep your money *under the mattress*. So that is what Michael did. There and then. Thanks to his incisive instructions all our money now sleeps with us. Actually we take it in turns. Sometimes Michael takes the money to bed. Sometimes I take the money to bed. In the daytime we hang it out on the clothes line and pick at it at will. Hence the champagne and Guinness. Come over at once do you hear.'

'But the noise? Is Michael roller skating again?'

'Michael, Fleur, Jago, all of us,' he explained. 'Jago is very light on his feet you know. Quite balletic. All we need is you.'

'This wouldn't be the nude roller skating I have heard so much about?' I asked. 'You sound oiled enough.'

Eric laughed, 'No. That is a summer activity. Though if it would ensure your presence I could insist upon it. I don't suppose anyone would object.'

'I fear my days of appearing in the nude are long gone,' I said, 'anyway I am not in the mood. Listen, I don't want to spoil your party, but I have some bad news. And I need Michael's help.'

By the time I turned up the place was empty and there was not a roller skate, champagne bottle, nor banknote to be seen. Eric and Michael were standing in front of their huts, waiting.

'This is a terrible business,' Eric said.

'A terrible business,' Michael repeated. 'Fleur sends her sympathies. Says to get in touch if you need anything.'

Fleur and I had never been sure whether they knew or not. I let it pass.

'What I need now Michael, is for you to put your papers to work. I need to refresh my memory, to read it up again. I need to do some archaeological digging in this landscape of yours.'

Michael held out his hands. 'I have been working at it from the moment you put the phone down. The trouble is not everything is hanging out *on line*. There's mountains of stuff laid out at the back. A vanishing schoolgirl you say? Back in the Sixties?'

'It made the nationals,' I told him. 'I could go down to Rochester and go through the archives, because the local papers covered it extensively, but I'd rather not expose myself to their scrutiny. The name of Doughty is still remembered there I'm sure.'

Michael looked immensely pleased with himself.

'I've got *boxes* of vanishing acts,' he boasted. 'Drugs, communes, Greek Islands, India. Everyone was leaving home then. Everyone is leaving home now too, only no one gives lifts anymore.'

'I don't think it was written up like that,' I told him. 'It was more to do with . . .'

'Sex?' asked Eric. 'If it's to do with sex we'll never find it at all.'

He's got simply masses on sex. Too much really for one mortal to contend with.'

'Not sex either. At least, it wasn't then. It was murder Michael. People thought it was murder.'

It took us half an hour to track the story down. A number of papers had covered it, principally the *Daily Express* who had taken up the story a few days after her disappearance. It was strange reading about it all again, reading about Gladstone Drive and the pillbox down by the river, stranger still seeing those pictures again, pictures I had never seen but which were so familiar to me, one of Stella, smiling stubbornly in her school uniform, one of her house with her mother and father standing in front of their rockery-lined drive, one too of Detective Sergeant Weatherspoon, standing on the towpath, looking grim. It was almost a year since the day of the Boxing Day dinner. We had had a spring and a summer of it, and the night before she vanished we had met up long after everyone else had gone to bed and walked hand in hand down Gladstone Drive smoking a cigarette without a stitch on. The last time I had seen her. It might sound improbable to you, that in October we should be able to do such a thing, but the truth is that in exposing ourselves regularly to the elements we became immune to them. Wind and rain and the mantle of an autumn chill did not penetrate our skin as it would yours, and in bad weather it would take four or five minutes before we began to feel any ill effects. Had anybody taken the trouble to look they would have discovered how unusually brown our bodies were, tanned not by the sun, or by lotions and cream, but by the midnight glow of the weather, by the rays of the moon and the breeze coming up the estuary, by the hard driving rain and the late river mist clinging to our limbs. There was depth to our colour, a deep shining resonance, and when I lay awake at night on the top of my bed it was as if I glowed in the dark, and when I lay awake at night on the top of my bed I knew too that across the road Stella lay on her bed and marvelled at how she shone. How we loved to dance, to roll on the grass, to leapfrog through leaves, to race down the alleyway, to chase each other round trees, to run naked through the place where our elders and betters slept.

Needless to say, none of that was in the papers. Stella Muchmore was last seen in the late afternoon of October 15th, setting off along the towpath towards home. Although her father was at home nursing a nasty dose of flu, she had gone to school that morning as normal and according to her schoolfriends and the headmistress had sat through a perfectly ordinary day. There had been nothing odd in her behaviour, and though her form mistress remarked that she had been a little withdrawn, that in itself was not unusual. It was part of Stella's character. In the afternoon however she seemed to perk up and when school ended she walked down with Jessica Mann and Poker Fisher's sister, Elspeth, to the boys' school where the three of them helped to paint scenery for the forthcoming school play. Elspeth and Stella left at about five fifteen, when the caretaker, old Lewis, came to lock up. Together the two girls walked up through the town. It was a mild evening, with rain forecast and though it was near closing time the High Street was still busy. They were seen by several people, most notably by Arthur Spackman, who ran the newsagents on the corner, who sold Stella a bar of chocolate, and, he later admitted, a packet of ten cigarettes and a box of matches, and by Ralph Barratt who remembered shouting at them when they ran out in front of his taxi without warning. At this point Elspeth and Stella parted company. Stella wanted to take the long way home along the towpath (where it would be safe to break open her new packet of fags) while Elspeth was in a hurry to get back and start her homework. 'She was in no rush to get home, even though we had a lot on that night,' Elspeth had told the police. 'She asked me to go down to the river with her, just for a half an hour or so, but I said no. I had to get back home. She said, "Please yourself", like she would, a bit huffy but not really bothered, and walked off. She wanted to hang about.'

That last remark, widely reported in the papers, and headlined in one, served as a warning to young girls not to wander about unaccompanied. Our school rules were changed; we all had to be home by four thirty instead of six; the towpath was proclaimed out of bounds. However a development came a few days later which led the police to believe that Stella had not simply run off or been abducted by a stranger, but was killing time *before meeting someone*. Four days after Stella vanished, Judith Spenser, one of the Spenser twins, came forward and told the police that she had seen Stella, or someone very like her, waiting up by the chestnut trees in the alleyway at around a quarter past six, nearly three quarters of an hour after she had left Elspeth Fisher. Judith had been up in her room with her sister doing her homework, when she looked out of the window and saw a girl in school uniform standing back from the road. The light was fading rapidly, and as the street lamp was broken she could not be exactly sure if it was Stella (which is why, she said, she did not come forward in the first place), but she described whoever it was as a tall, dark-haired girl, who kept on looking at her watch. 'It was obvious what she was doing,' she said. 'She was waiting for someone. Like everyone else.' The chestnut trees was a favourite place for us to meet, and many a young school romance started under those leafy branches. After a few moments Judith went back to her work and when she looked out again, about ten minutes later, whoever it was had gone. Was this Stella? The police quickly established that no other schoolgirl was out at that time, and although they could find no corroborative witness to Judith's testimony, they put this down as the last probable sighting of Stella Muchmore. Had she met someone? Someone she knew? Someone we *all* knew? We never found out.

This sighting had always puzzled me, for had Judith Spenser, then a sensible girl of fifteen, said that she had seen Stella hanging around at eleven or twelve o'clock, rather than six, I would have said that it *was* Stella she saw, but that Judith had got her dates wrong, for the night *before* Stella disappeared, the last night I saw her, Stella had been hanging around the chestnut trees *waiting for me*. Although Stella and I usually set off from her garden, on occasions we agreed to meet up some distance away from our homes, sometimes by the old shed in the allotment, or down by the pillbox but as often as not underneath the chestnut trees on the waste ground at the end of Gladstone Drive. I would bring Mrs Briggs's Bag, borrowed for the occasion from the downstairs cloakroom, and when we had decided on our route we would undress, stuff our clothes in the brown safety of that precious cast-off, hide it carefully and then set off. Although more open, and therefore more dangerous than the other two locations, halfway down the alleyway split in two. One path led to the main road and the town centre, the other cut across to the road leading to the playing fields. When we were not playing our secret games, when the weather was at its most generous, when we wanted simply to *run*, the playing fields were of course our natural habitat, for there we could run and skip and bowl along without a care in the world. The only danger was getting there and back. You may ask why did we not wait and undress under its protection. Certainly it would have been safer, but the truth is, it would have made our task too easy. Running naked on some playing field was a fool's trick, a dare a young man might undertake with a little drink inside him. What we were doing was reclaiming ourselves, redefining our town, establishing our own lives, and though the playing fields gave us a freedom we could not find elsewhere, we needed, above all things, to defy the laws that governed us and to place ourselves *at risk*. And risk, danger, discovery, is what the *other* fork, the one that led to the town, provided in technicolor. Theoretically it was possible to follow a circular route, down the alleyway, out into Fairfield Street, across the main road, down to the river, along the towpath and back up to Gladstone Drive and the alleyway via the allotments and the adjoining gardens. It was the outdoor replica of my indoor run, with a hundred corridors and a hundred doors to choose from, and a hundred mothers and a hundred fathers waiting at the end of every one. We longed to run it. We would walk the route in day time looking for safe locations. And we tried it once at the height of the summer, when the heat seeped out of the gutters of the town long after the sun had gone, and only the cold ribbon of the river brought a freshness to the evening ahead.

We had met as arranged by the chestnut trees around half eleven. In the afternoon a sullen south-westerly had come in, irritable and restless. There was electricity in the air and on the ground, and as we ventured out that night under cover of the swollen clouds it was clear that soon the lightning would crack and the thunder would roll, and we would be drenched with the sweet smell of steaming rain. I nodded in the direction of the Spensers' house. What about their swimming pool? Wouldn't it be great to be swimming when the storm broke. Stella said No. We don't know our way around there. We'd make too much noise. We'd end up getting caught. But a swim, I said. I really feel like a swim. Haven't you ever wanted to go in there? No said Stella and I'm not going to go now. Why don't we do what we've always wanted to do? Why don't we try it tonight? We stuffed Mrs Briggs's Bag high up in the tree nearest the air-raid shelter and set off, down the alleyway, peering around the corner before dashing across the first road and leaping into the safety of a gloomy gravel drive. I have a feeling about this, I said to Stella. Where to now? Stella pointed to a tree forty yards down. Behind it was a tall wooden fence. If the worst came to the worst, she said we could probably scramble over it, though God knows what might be on the other side. That's all very well, I said, but after that there's *nothing*. Stella turned to me. Her face was fierce. Sweat ran down from her hair and I could taste the strong smell from her arms. We're here now, she said. And we're going to do it. Down to the tree, and then as fast as we can down the road to the car park. If we hear anyone coming we've got enough time to get back to the fence. After that it's just a dash across the road and then the river. OK? As if in answer, a first low peal of thunder broke a couple of miles away. The wind blew a little. It was heading our way. Come on, she said and ran forward.

We nearly did it too. Once by the tree we waited while a lone car drove into town. The wind blew again, brushing past us, telling us to hurry down to the river before the storm broke above us. Before us lay the longest and most dangerous stretch, when we had to venture into the thick body of the town and dance across the coils of Rochester's guts. There were no trees now and precious few drives. Small houses with small, bare gardens and peppered amongst them the outposts of Rochester's trade; a bicycle shop, a bankrupt milliner's, the crumbling walls of Medway's neglected commerce. This was the gauntlet we had to run, though run is the wrong word to use. Running was a temptation, but a risky business, for it is hard to alter course in full flight. So we stole along, half bent, hugging at what little protection the warm pavement afforded us, Stella in front, her eyes on the refuge up ahead, me glancing back for any sign of headlights in the pregnant sky. Three-quarters there we heard footsteps, clear steel-capped footsteps ringing out from around the corner. No time to dash forward! We would fall into his arms! I looked back. There, illuminating the aerials and the roofs above, came the slow sweep of a car about to crest the hill. Soon it would tip down and catch us in its lights. We looked around. There was nothing to protect us, no driveway, no garden wall, just those tall grey walls and their meagre shadows. Only a small black car, parked directly in front of us, gave us any hope. Another burst of thunder, nearer now. The first light speck of rain. The footsteps quickened. The lights started to sweep down. Naked and trembling we crouched down behind the car hoping that the lights and the footsteps would disappear, but we knew we were caught. At any moment the car would bear down illuminating us in its full glare, and as it slammed to a halt the man with the steel-capped brogues would look about him and exclaim, What the Devil! What would we do? What would our parents do? What would the schools do? Terror gripped us, shocking, trembling terror. We were not in Gladstone Drive now playing in the safety of our neighbours' gardens, nor were we roaming the playing fields at will. We felt like wild animals, let loose in a hostile world. We were there to be hunted and trapped. A cry would go up! The chase would be on! I groaned. Lightning split the sky. Stella turned blue. Thunder broke the air. Stella swore. Lightning and thunder. Lightning and thunder. Lightning to split the trees, thunder to shake the plates, lightning to strike us down, thunder to wake our mothers and fathers and have them scurrying around in their dressing-gowns. Stella banged on the window and swore again but I could not hear her. There was no car and no footsteps now, for now the rain started in on our backs, beating on the road, splashing us from below, roaring in our ears. Stella swore and banged on the window and pulled on the handle of the black passenger door, pulled once and pulled twice, and pulled it open. Jesus, she said, and scrambled on to the floor. I dived in after, throwing myself on the back seat, before rolling down on top of her. We lay there wet and trembling, with our heads down. The lights swept past. The footsteps quickened and then swiftly faded. We lay there, frightened, listening to the heavens dance upon the roof. We were inside now, but we were not safe and oddly enough, although we had stood in the rain many times, now, when the danger had passed we could not go out again. We could not simply open the door and resume our journey, for our journey had come to an end. We had to lie there, waiting for the rain to pass, and for the first time, stuffed down the back of this dog-smelling car we became strangely conscious of each other. We had touched each other before, we had lain side by side and thrown our arms around each other in mutual delight. But not like this. Before it had been a leaping back, or a wild laughing arm. Here it was close and still, panting with repression. We had come too far. Oh we had come too far! The rain passed quickly. We disentangled ourselves and ran back to Mrs Briggs's Bag and our hasty, crumpled clothing. We ran home and prayed to God when we learnt that we had not been discovered. We had taken on the town and had nearly been snared. We had done the best we could and felt each other's heart beating. We never tried the trip again and indeed it was some time before we ventured out beyond Stella's garden, let alone visited the chestnut trees. We understood that we had been wrong, that our wild forays were an illusion, that we were no different, but more free than exhibits in a zoo. *Beat hard you little beasts, but beat hard in your cage*! And so, beaten, we turned Gladstone Drive into our park, and like the tame beasts that graze so forlornly around those stately homes, we grew bolder in our sheltered grove. But that night we did not run, we did not jump and leap about, we did not kick our way through the dark gardens of our neighbours, we did not clamber over the bonnets of their cars, stand arms outstretched in the middle of their lawns, we did not borrow their bicycles, nor play croquet on Mrs Briggs's back lawn. That night, October 14th, we picked up Mrs Briggs's Bag and strolled hand in hand down Gladstone Drive as if on an Easter Parade, bowing royally in greeting to our sleeping neighbours. Good Night Fair Fishers! Lie happy in your beds! Sweet dreams Brave Deerings! Rest awhile in your slumber! Be still Kind Cramphorns! Sleep tight Gallant Greys! Be boundless in this endless quest! We owned the drive that night, we walked down it as if it was ours, to do with what we liked. This was the way it was always going to be. We had found out a secret way of doing things, the only way to work this world, to have a secret, to keep it well, and when the opportunity came, to live this secret, to roam its boundaries and touch its very walls, to preserve a special way of being that released us from our parents, our family, our friends and the deadening weight of our inherited past. When we got to the end of the road we smoked our last but one cigarette and when it was finished and after I had pushed the stub into the soft grass outside her garden wall, we kissed and discovered ourselves freezing. We kissed and drew back in cold amazement. We kissed and I never saw her again. And why Stella was hanging around the chestnut trees early the next evening, while Judith Spenser watched her from her bedroom window, and who she might have been waiting for, I had no idea.

It wasn't until half past seven that Mr Muchmore raised the alarm. Up until then he had assumed that Stella was still working on the school play, and it was only when Elspeth rang to talk to Stella about some work they had to do, that he realized that something was wrong. Things moved swiftly after that. By half past eight a full scale search was already in operation, with members of staff from both schools searching the grounds, while police and neighbours toured the area. They found nothing. By ten o'clock, with a heavy rain adding to the difficulties, the operation was stood down until morning. Daylight saw the police drafted back in heavy numbers, frogmen searching, wading through the dripping riverbanks, dog handlers let loose amongst the cold and windy buildings of the deserted factories and cadets from the training centre at Maidstone on their hands and knees crawling through the sodden scrublands and flattened nettlepatches of our scattered wastes. By the end of the morning they had levelled the allotment, and the area outside the Spensers' house, and left them shaved and bleeding, and in the afternoon they found Stella's mac, wedged into a gap between the concrete wall and the concrete roof of the waterlogged pillbox.

According to the newspapers, Stella's macintosh (unlike my father's) revealed few significant details. I knew a little more than that, for Sergeant Weatherspoon had laid out the contents of Stella's macintosh pockets before me on the fourth of the seven interviews that I had attended. As usual Policewoman Andrews had escorted me to the interview room. After waiting a minute or two Sergeant Weatherspoon appeared, carrying a wooden tray covered by a white towel. He sat down and placed the tray, very delicately sideways on, in front of him, folding his hands, priest-like, over its lumpen shape. He smiled benignly at me.

'I am glad you could come today,' he said. 'You could be a great help today. Would you like to be a help?'

I nodded. He pressed his hands together, as if in prayer and continued.

'Not all of us are in the position of performing services to the community Giles. Some of us find ourselves doing it as part of our job. Others join organizations specifically designed to help the less fortunate. Meals on Wheels, the Rotary Club. I expect your parents belong to one or two.'

I shook my head.

'No? Well, they're not alone. Most people are prepared to let the world go hang. Sometimes they find themselves in the awkward position of having to choose between doing something for the benefit of all, and doing something for themselves, but as often as not they choose the latter course. But in this context of service and sacrifice I was heartened to note, when examining your school records, that you had been a scout.'

'What', I asked, 'has that to do with anything? That was long ago. That was before . . .'

'Yes?'

'Nothing.'

'That was before your brother drowned, isn't that right? You dropped out of the scouts just after he drowned, isn't that right? You tried to save him though didn't you? You pulled him out of the water and gave him the kiss of life, like you'd been taught. You tried to get his heart going, pushing on his chest. You broke two ribs in your anxiety I believe. But it didn't do any good did it? Didn't bring him back to life? I am surprised in a way that you can bear to go down to the river at all, after all that.'

'It was my fault, not the river's,' I said. 'He left the climbing frame before I was ready. He should have waited for me. I just didn't want to go right then. He should have waited for me. Anyway, what do you want to dig all that up for?'

'I'm afraid Giles,' Sergeant Weatherspoon said, 'that digging is what it's all about. That's what we are here for, to dig. That's what makes our lives exciting. Digging is in our blood, and in our bones, and in our feet. *These Boots Are Made For Digging*, Giles, to paraphrase a popular song. You may not be able to see them, but all of us in the force carry little shovels over our shoulders, even our young friend who drove you down here, who wears his uniform as though he were patrolling Carnaby Street rather than the outmoded Medway towns. We are all diggers at heart. There's nothing we like better than cutting into history and pulling out a nice wedge of damp, buried life. The things you find! Well, when I discovered that you had been a scout I thought, well perhaps I have this Giles all wrong. Perhaps he can help us after all. Scouts are trained to observe! They spend their waking hours following footprints and tying the countryside up in sheep shanks and great reef knots. I was never a scout. My father disapproved of scouts, if you can believe it. My son is a scout and my father, being a humorous man, told him as he stood before him in his bright new uniform, that he would have preferred it if he had upped and joined the Mau Mau. My father has an aversion to uniforms, which made it difficult for me in the early days, when I was still living at home. I had to take the bloody thing off outside, in the garden shed and fold it into a carrier bag before I was let back into the house. But enough of me. I did not bring you down here to tell you my life story. Nor am I intentionally rambling on like this in order to make you nervous and unsettled. You are not a nervous sort of boy. Indeed both Andrews and I concur that of all the boys and girls who have come in here over the years, you are the most *un*-nervous, if there is such a word as *un*-nervous, we have ever seen. Is there such a word as *un*-nervous Andrews? Andrews says no. Andrews know best. Now for a boy not to be nervous, to be *un*-nervous, is one thing, but for a boy, an *un*-nervous boy to be at the very *centre* of an unusual and inexplicable mystery, a mystery which the police are investigating, is, to say the least, *interesting*. It is interesting to me and it is interesting to Police-woman Andrews there, who will find the lessons to be learnt from this case extremely useful should she wish to further her career in the force. It is interesting, because in my experience, young boys and young girls who are suddenly thrown into the arms of the law through no fault of their own, usually become unaccountably afraid. Their hearts race, their speech tumbles out, they want to know where mother and father are. They fidget, they put their hands under their bottoms, they jiggle their legs, they ask to go to the lavatory and can they have a glass of water. Should you acquiesce and bring them a cup of tea or a glass of orange juice, or *a pint of urine from the old people's home*, they grab hold of it and gulp it down as if they had just spent a weekend camping out in the Valley of Death. And if you tell them a joke they laugh hysterically, and if you fix them with a big brown eye and say, "I don't believe you. I think you've been telling me a pack of lies", they start to sweat most horribly, even if they have been telling you the gospel truth.

'But you. You are different. You are all calm. You are all serene. No perspiration on the upper lip for you. No wind to ruffle your sails. *Giles, King of the Doldrums*, that's what we should call you. And yet, it is *your* girlfriend who has vanished and it is you, if you don't mind me saying so, who are under the greatest suspicion. And not just by me, or by young Andrews here, who is most eager to learn and who is *as hungry as a wolf at the door*, but by your teachers and your neighbours and even, dare I say it, by your friends. What a burden for a young boy to carry, wouldn't you say? And don't you carry it off well? And that, Giles, is the rub of it. You carry it too well.'

He turned the tray around and pushed it out into the middle of the table.

'Isn't this fascinating?' he said. 'Don't you find it fascinating? Consider this then. In most interviews, or interrogations as I prefer to call them, I try and get the subject to talk as much as possible. I give him a cup of tea, a cigarette and a long piece of rope. Have you ever watched a dog on a long piece of rope? No matter how bright, how docile, how well trained that dog is, sooner or later he will become hopelessly entangled, unable to move, strangled by his own inability to recognize the rope's true nature. All he can do is wait for someone to come along and sort him out. That's what happens when you get people to talk. Eventually words snare them. And do you know why? Not because I ask the right questions, though that helps. Quite simply, like the dog and the rope, people aren't used to words. They don't understand that the true nature of words, is not to *communicate*, as philosophers and marriage guidance counsellors and fancy linguists would have us believe. They are there *to trip you up*. The more you use, the more you'll be found out and everybody, *everybody*, has something to be found out. You know this, which is why I haven't asked you to say anything today. I haven't asked you for a word. And I'm not going to. I've heard all you have to say and I don't need to hear it anymore. I want you to listen. I want you to listen to the words coming out of my mouth, see how calm I am, how patient I am, how Policewoman Andrews sits in the corner over there with her arms folded and her breath nice and even, watching your every move. There's an EP my daughter brought back from France the other week. She was over there staying with her French pen pal in Vichy. It seems she had a good time. Anyway she brought all these records back, Johnny Halliday, Richard Anthony and one by a tarty looking piece called Sylvie Vartan. The thing about Sylvie Vartan's song is that she sings part of it in English, pretty dire English, but English nevertheless. Most of it is incomprehensible to me, but the main refrain goes *I'm Watching You*, and as I shaved this morning . . . do you shave every morning yet Giles? No, let that pass . . . as I shaved this morning and heard this Sylvie Vartan song coming out of my daughter's battery-operated Dansette record player, and knowing that you had been invited down to visit us *yet again*, I thought, that's it. That's what I'm doing with Giles. *I'm watching you*. And that's what I'll tell him. And it's not just me. We're all watching you. Your neighbours are watching you. Your school is watching you. The whole town is watching you. No! Don't say anything! Don't utter a word! I don't want you to tell me anything! Bottle it up Giles! Keep a tight lid on it all! Let that pressure grow! You can do it! But one day someone will come along and give you one shake too many, and then, whoops, out it will all come. You know what I'm talking about don't you Giles? At your age you spend half the night waking up to find that whoops, out it has all come. No control over it whatsoever. Nocturnal Emission is the technical term for it. The colloquial expression is, I believe, Wet Dream. Don't look like that Giles. We're not trying to embarrass you, are we Andrews? It's all perfectly normal. The point I'm making Giles, is that telling the truth is, I acknowledge, a large and unpredictable thing, but when one goes to great length to suppress it, one day, quite unexpectedly, just when you think you are safe and sound, whoops out it all comes.'

He stood up and walked around to my side of the table. Leaning over me he pulled the tray towards me. When it was directly in front of me he straightened up and put his hands on my shoulders.

'And now,' he said, 'I have a little surprise for you. A little game you can play for me. A variation of what the scouts used to call Kim's game. We have found Stella's coat, a coat I am sure you are familiar with, inside and out, no doubt. I am not going to tell you where we found it, not yet, but what I am going to do is to show you what we found in her pockets and while you look at them I will be watching you very carefully. Policewoman Andrews will be watching you very carefully. Look at the tray. Maybe there's something not there that should be there. Maybe there's something there that should not be there. Maybe you'll tell us. Maybe you'll make it up. Who knows? We'll leave you now. Do you see that mirror over there? It's a two-way mirror. Our chief had it installed last year. He likes watching people when they think no one can see them. I'm different. I like watching people when they know that every move they make is being noted down, scrutinized, and generally put through the investigatory mangle. Come Policewoman Andrews. Let us go then you and I and sit in the other room where we can deliberate our findings over a strong pot of voyeuristic tea.'

It was several minutes before I did anything. The towel covering the tray smelt of chlorine, as if it had been used recently at a swimming pool. It was one thing Stella and I had never done, gone swimming, although we had promised ourselves that one day we would – steal over the Spensers' garden wall or break into the municipal open-air pool, or, like Fat Patrick's crazy father, strike out for the Flying Boats, for the *Galway Bay*. I wondered whose towel it was, not Sergeant Weatherspoon's certainly. Policewoman Andrews's? The young chap who drove me down, who had done a lot of the house-to-house enquiries, what was his name? I studied the mirror to see if I could detect any change. Were they staring at me as I was staring at myself? There was nothing to see on either side. I turned back and lifted the towel. There were four things on the tray: a watch, a box of safety matches, a green rubber band and the metal top from a bottle of beer. I can remember that, but whether I can remember *everything* about them . . .

'I can,' says the boy.

He is sitting there as pleased as punch, dangling his legs from Michael's trestle table. He has a horrid superior air about him. I am in half a mind to pick him up and throw him in the Thames.

'I thought I had seen the last of you,' I told him. 'I thought you'd gone back into hiding.'

He shrugged his shoulders. 'Nowhere to go,' he said. 'You have the Bag now, and . . . the other thing.' He shivered.

'I do have the other thing, that is true. I have everything now. The Bag, the other thing, and . . .'

'And?' the boy asks quickly. 'What and?'

'A head start,' I said. 'I know that Stella has been spotted. She doesn't. The chances of finding her are in my favour.'

The boy snorted.

'You won't find her,' he sneered, 'not unless you fall over her. Stella's too clever for that.'

'It's not just me anymore,' I explained. 'There's others now. There's Carol and Monica and Michael here. There's Dickey Dove down in Ashford. Pretty soon there'll be Fat Patrick. And in the last resort, there's . . .'

'Yes?'

'Detective Sergeant Weatherspoon. Above all, there's Detective Sergeant Weatherspoon.'

'He didn't find her then. He won't find her now.'

'He didn't find her *then*,' I tell him, 'because little boys like you didn't tell him everything. Take those objects. You didn't tell him everything about them did you?'

The boy pats his pockets for a cigarette. He has run out. It is so often the case when buying a packet of ten. A boy runs out too quickly. Another trip to the sweet shop. Another risk.

'I told him about the bottle top,' he argues. 'I helped him with the bottle top.'

'You thought you helped him with the bottle top,' I told him severely. 'You were safe with the bottle top, for the bottle top was the only item you did not recognize, the only item you could not account for. In itself a bottle top was not unusual. You and Stella often found things like that scattered thoughtlessly about the pillbox, cigarette packets, sweetpapers, other disgusting items left by people who didn't know any better, schoolchildren, the idle youth of the town, courting couples. It made you so angry, that they should disturb it so, and before they could do anything else, you and Stella would clean the place up, stuffing what you found in your pockets or satchels to dispose of later. Although it was an ugly and friendless place, cold in the winter, damp in the summer, to you the pillbox was as graceful and mysterious as the Flying Boats it looked out upon. The two were somehow connected, so implacable, so silent and so empty were they all. There was nothing in the pillbox at all, just rough concrete walls and a low ceiling which let the rain in on to the mud floor, but in harmony with its companions, it was dark and broody and had seen life. Like the Flying Boats the pillbox had windows which had looked out upon an uncertain world and though it had sat there, immobile, while they flew low, hugging the open water to protect their naked bellies, it had always seemed to you that the pillbox was in some way the Flying Boats' anchor, that the pillbox was watching, ever alert, ever on guard, waiting for its flock to come home. Now they lay not four hundred feet apart and in the late hours, when the mists rose and the Medway moon was upon you, you would call to the Flying Boats, you and Stella, call from the shelter of that lonely outpost, hoping that they might hear you, hoping that they might turn, hoping, against all hope that one of them, the *Galway Bay* would break its moorings and drift across so that you might clamber aboard and fly away. When Fat Patrick's father had returned from the sanatorium you had tried to get him to talk about the *Galway Bay*, tried to get him to describe what it was like inside, whether it was true that everything was still there, but Fat Patrick had told you that it would only get him worked up and it was better not to mention it, pretend it had never happened. It was a shame, for if you could have had your way, if you could have somehow kept the pillbox to yourself, you would have liked to deck it out in Imperial Airways colour, with carpets and seats and huge ashtrays all around, made it the *Galway Bay*'s equal, where you and Stella could lounge around, smoking cigarettes, drinking tea, looking out through the travelling window while planning your next expedition. But you could not. All you could do was to keep it clean. Which is why the bottle top did not surprise you at first. It merely confirmed that Stella had been in the pillbox, and that, as usual, she had tidied the place up.

'However as you looked upon the tray and this solitary beer bottle top, it struck you that it was strange that this was the *only* piece of litter that Stella had collected. On his return you asked Sergeant Weatherspoon whether the pillbox was clean when they searched it, and when he replied *no more than usual* indicating that there was the usual sort of mess lying around, you replied that you found that odd, that if Stella *had* been cleaning the place up, then you would have expected her pockets to be filled with other matter as well. What an observant boy you are, Sergeant Weatherspoon had replied. Didn't I say Andrews that this boy would do the business, and already, with one little bottle top he is pointing to things that would never have occurred to us. As a matter of fact, Sergeant Weatherspoon continued, lowering his voice in a manner that convinced you not at all, We did find the wrapper from the chocolate bar she bought that afternoon, but somehow it has gone missing. I expect Andrews here, who is a stickler for neatness, threw it in the rubbish bin without thinking. No matter. I do not lay much store by the sweetpaper. But the bottle top is quite a different matter, you are quite right. Sergeant Weatherspoon stopped. He wanted you to go on. In fact you wanted to go on yourself for out of all the objects on the tray, the bottle top gave you the most opportunity to establish that someone else was involved, that you had nothing to do with it. It seemed to you, you said, that the absence of sweetpaper or some such litter in her pocket could mean two things. One, that she had started to clear up the pillbox, but had been interrupted, or that she hadn't picked up the bottle top from the pillbox at all. Sergeant Weatherspoon got up out of his chair at that and started to pace about the room. That is precisely the sort of thing I want to hear, he said. It starts to take us away from the pillbox, away from her home ground. For if it is true, that she didn't pick up the bottle top from the pillbox it means that she didn't pick it up at all. A beer bottle top is not the usual sort of thing that girls of sixteen pick up off the street now is it? We know she didn't buy a bottle of beer that night and now we know, or we think we know, that she didn't pick the top up. Which means . . . *she was given it* you added. Exactly, cried Sergeant Weatherspoon. She was given it.'

I look at the boy. He is interested in all this. He likes objects. He would like a world filled with objects.

'Of course, although the police established that Stella didn't buy such a bottle, that doesn't mean to say she couldn't have *had* a bottle of beer in her possession. She could have taken one from the sideboard in the dining room.'

The boy looks at me with some contempt.

'Stella did not like beer. We all knew that. No someone else drank the beer.'

'And Sergeant Weatherspoon thought that the someone was you.'

'I suspect he did. I said that this was not the case. I told him *I* did not like beer.'

'And?'

'He didn't believe me. He said all boys of sixteen like beer. Even if they don't like it, they like beer.'

I nodded.

'So that is the story of the bottle top. The bottle top introduced a third party, a third party who opened and possibly shared a bottle of beer with Stella, perhaps down by the pillbox, perhaps somewhere else. Let us leave the bottle top for a moment. Let us concentrate on the other items, the Watch, the Box of Matches and the Green Rubber Band. *The Watch*.'

'The Watch was Stella's wristwatch, a birthday present from her father. She hated it and she wore it as little as possible. When she got up in the morning she would wear it down to breakfast, and when she came back from school it would be on her wrist when she sat down for tea, but at all other times, when she was not at home, when her father couldn't see her, she took it off and kept it in her pocket. I hate time, she would say. When I get out of here, I'm never going to wear a watch ever again. I'm going to ignore time. Time can go to hell.'

'There was nothing wrong with this watch then? The glass was not cracked. It hadn't been broken in a struggle?'

'It was in perfect working order,' the boy replies. 'It had come to no harm. And why should it? It was where it always was, safe in her pocket.'

'And did everyone know of Stella's dislike of her wristwatch. Did Carol for instance? Did the rest of the school? Did her mother?'

The boy considers this for a moment. It is clear that it is a question he has not confronted before.

'I would have thought', he said, after a while, 'that as she never used it, not many people knew she even *had* a watch let alone disliked it. Stella was not one for confidences.'

'All right. Let us leave the Watch. Let us look at another of these trophies. The Box of Matches for instance. It is, on the face of it, no different from any other box of matches. A small, flat box concealing a little tray. It has a picture of Rochester Castle on the front. Inside are between fifty and sixty matches, all waiting there, ready to be struck. A boy buys matches mainly for one reason, and that is to smoke cigarettes, for matches and cigarettes are for him the first entry into the adult world. But he is still a boy nevertheless and though the matches lie there, waiting to be cupped in the hand, to be pressed against the tip of his precious cigarette, so that he may inhale the bitter wind of sulphur as well as the cruel taste of tobacco, it is not the only reason to have matches, for he is still a boy and for a boy, a box of matches can be put to other uses, to propagate illicit bonfires, to introduce live bangers into letter-boxes, to set fire to the back seat of your local cinema, and most importantly, to burn down your school. All these things cross a boy's mind when he has in his possession a box of matches, for a boy is both adult and child and while he may yearn for the nicotine-stained fingers of his father, his childish delight in destruction still lies vivid in his soul. What freedom, what opportunity a box of matches affords. Like the alleyway some boys know so well, it offers you two paths, one leading to the grim reality of an ordered world where adults work and ruin their lives, and one to the uninhibited expanse of empty, uninhabited space, where you can range at will. It is more dangerous than its companion, the packet of cigarettes, for the cigarette packet is silent. It does not signal its presence in unguarded moments (though it can, if you are not careful, leave a distinctive smell in the inside of your pockets). But a matchbox rattles. It rattles when you fling your school coat across the hall, it rattles as you stand to attention in your classroom, it rattles as you plump down in front of the kitchen table, ready for your evening tea.'

I place the box before him.

'*The box of matches*,' I say.

He begins, 'The trick to carrying a box of matches about is to stuff a small piece of paper inside, so that the matches don't rattle. Not paper from an old envelope or a sheet of paper torn out of a notebook, for they do not mould themselves exactly to the contours of the box. Tissue paper, toilet paper, that is the answer.'

He pushes the box open. There, stuffed inside, is a torn piece of white tissue paper. He smiles. He lifts the tissue.

'It is nearly full this box, but see . . .?' He closes the box without the tissue in it. He lifts it up and shakes. It rattles. He turns it over in his hands. 'This is what I taught Stella. So this is Stella's box. We always carried matches with us. Most of the time we bought Swan Vestas for they were non-safety matches and if the box got damp, chances were you could still use the matches. When I saw these on the tray I assumed that the shop had run out of stock and she had bought these instead. We did not buy them only for cigarettes. In the summer we would light small fires of dried grass and twigs. We would light them on the top of the pillbox and by the pile of grass cuttings on the playing fields. On one or two occasions we lit them in other people's gardens, and left them to smoulder through the dawn. But primarily the matches were bought for cigarettes. We would sit on the pillbox and strike them against the rough concrete. We would sit on garden walls and strike them on the brick.'

He pauses for a moment.

'There are two striking sides to this box. Only one has been used. The marks are quite clear. Three broad strokes. That would indicate between one and three cigarettes smoked. Not an excessive amount.'

'Do you remember the brand?'

'If we could get them, Guards. Long gone. We got a taste for them when we stole from her father. They were strong. "Change over to Guards" the adverts used to say. And that is what we did. You need a strong cigarette to smoke in the open air.'

'So, out of a packet of ten bought at around five thirty, Stella smoked between one and three cigarettes. She tore a small piece of tissue from a paper handkerchief, of which there is no other trace, and put the box back in her pocket. But not the cigarettes.'

'We came to an agreement, Sergeant Weatherspoon and I that although she could have smoked three cigarettes on her own, it was more likely, if three cigarettes *were* consumed, that she had shared them with someone else. And when we took into account that the cigarette packet was not there, it seemed certain that she must have met up with someone.'

'Someone who smoked.'

The boy looks at me wearily.

'We *all* smoked then,' he said.

'Why,' I said, 'if this someone else took the cigarette packet, did he not take the matches?'

'There is no clear answer to that,' he replies. 'Not one we could agree on. Detective Sergeant Weatherspoon put forward the proposition that whoever it was didn't need the matches. That he had a lighter, or a box of his own.'

'And you?'

The boy shrugs his shoulders.

'I put up no explanation. But there did seem to be another, to which Sergeant Weatherspoon seemed oblivious.'

'Being?'

'That all this theorizing about a box of matches and a missing cigarette paper was irrelevant, that whoever Stella had met up with had simply disposed of the mac as quickly as he could. The cigarette packet could have been anywhere. It could have been dropped up by the chestnut trees. It could have been picked up by a passing tramp. They could have been thrown away, lost in a struggle. *Anything*. All he really wanted to do was to hide the mac. To give him a bit more time.'

'That is all very well,' I say. 'That is what you thought then, when you were all imagining she had been abducted, raped, murdered. But we know that she was not murdered. We know that Stella Muchmore is alive and well. As she is alive and well, the chances are she disappeared of her own accord. *Her* coat, *her* cigarettes, *her* matches. Why leave the macintosh at all? It was October. It was raining that night remember, suddenly, sometimes heavily. She would have needed a mac. *Unless she had a better use for it.*'

The boy stops swinging his legs.

'You know what I think,' I tell him. 'I think she made fools out of all of you. I think she went to the pillbox, as Elspeth suggested, to kill time. I think she sat there, waiting, and while she waited she smoked a couple of those cigarettes. She would have been nervous, for at six fifteen or thereabouts she was due to meet someone, someone she had arranged to meet secretly, someone who was going to take her away. So she smoked her cigarettes, looking out over the Flying Boats, those imprisoned craft which besieged your mind so, knowing that in a few hours she would have left them, would have escaped that town, would have been set free. She smoked the cigarettes and walked up to the chestnut trees as arranged. And why the chestnut trees rather than the towpath? Because whoever it was, *was driving a car*. He would drive up the road, flash his lights or poop his horn and she would step out of the shadows and get in. The car arrives. Stella gets in. They are both nervous, excited. It isn't all over yet, but to set them on their way, he opens up a bottle of beer, balances it between his knees and opens it up, handing her the bottle top to get rid of. Without thinking she puts it in her pocket. Perhaps she has another cigarette then, cigarette number three while he finishes the beer. Perhaps they *both* have a cigarette, cigarettes three and four. He lights them with his lighter. Now they have one more thing to do. Lay a false trail, a trail which will suggest that she has been taken against her will, that her life is in danger, that she is most probably dead. They drive down to the centre of town, down the side street where the path and the narrow steps and the towpath lie. Quick he says, give me your raincoat, and Stella leans forward and pulls it from her back. Is the watch in there? he says, don't forget the watch, and she says don't fuss, it's there, in the impatient way of hers, and hands him the coat. He wants this to be over now but he knows what he's doing. He jumps down the steps and hurries along the towpath. He reaches the pillbox where he intends to hide the mac. It's cold and wet, there's no one around. He ducks in, and before he stuffs it between the wall and the ceiling he goes through the pockets to make sure she hasn't left anything there that will incriminate them. There's the watch, left as planned. She doesn't like it, and to her parents, who don't know how infrequently she wears it, its discovery here will indicate a *stripping* of some sort. What else? A rubber band, a packet of cigarettes and a box of matches. He shakes the cigarettes. They're nearly full . . . *Shame to waste them* he thinks. He puts them in his pocket. He shakes the box of matches. Nothing. Empty. He's in a hurry now. He stuffs the mac away and is back in the car in three minutes. They drive off. They've done it. The goosechase is about to begin.'

The boy looks down at his knees and his shoes hanging in the air.

'If this is the case,' he asks, 'why did she not leave her mac there in the first place? Then they wouldn't have had to risk going back into town.'

'Yes, that must have frightened her a little, going into the heart of the town like that, when she'd nearly been caught there a few months before with you. They probably *had* planned for her to leave it there before joining him. But, there was one small problem that night. It was raining. She would have had to wait for him in the pouring rain. So she wore the mac for an hour or so longer.'

'She could have taken it back there herself.'

'She could, and maybe she should, but we know she didn't. If she had she wouldn't have taken the cigarettes and left the matches. Only *he* would have done that.'

'He?'

'Her new friend. Perhaps leaving the mac was his idea. Perhaps she'd told him of your meetings there. Perhaps he used the pillbox himself. Knew of its connotations. Yes, leaving a schoolgirl's mac stuffed inside the pillbox, where Rochester's reluctant virgins take their cure, would have been just the job. A theatrical touch. Which brings us to *The Green Rubber Band*.'

He picks it up and, placing it over his two hands, pulls it apart. It is thick and strong.

'When the green rubber band was not in use, Stella wore it around her wrist. It was the only thing she wore around her wrist. Although it had a practical purpose, she wore it as a snub to the watch her father had given her. Carol once told me that the other girls often made fun of Stella and her green rubber bands, for most of them were into bracelets and rings and a green rubber band was decidedly unfashionable. Stella didn't mind. It suited her arm, thick and strong. But it was not there simply for decoration. The green rubber band was used to tie Stella's hair back. She would use it when she climbed out of the window at night, for otherwise her hair would get caught up in wires and branches. If we had any climbing to do, or if we had to crawl under fences, she would put it on then. She had very wild unmanageable hair. It was a liability. The rubber band was her protection.'

'And did she wear it at other times?'

'I wouldn't know. I believe she wore it at school when she was in the chemistry lab, or the art department. Anytime when she had to keep the hair out of her eyes.'

'So she would have probably worn it that night, when she went down to paint the scenery at your school?'

The boy agrees.

'Which brings me to a puzzle which must have worried you,' I said, 'for I know it worries me. *Why* did she go down to paint scenery that night? You know as well as I do that Stella had never shown any interest in the school play. Indeed both of you ridiculed such activities, and even these newspaper reports suggest that Stella's decision to go down that night with Elspeth and Jessica took both of them by surprise. True, as it now appears that she had time to kill, painting scenery in the relative warmth of the boys' assembly hall was probably better than hanging about in the cold, and it is also true she had told her parents that this is what she was going to do after school, but even having told them, there was no reason for her to do it. No one was going to check up any earlier. So why get involved in the school play where all your friends and acquaintances are, where something unexpected could happen to bugger up your timetable? Wouldn't it have been better to wait somewhere alone, somewhere where no one could interfere with her plans? Unless of course the someone she was meeting was down there at the school play as well, someone with whom she had to make last minute arrangements, someone who could drive a car, someone who knew the pillbox, who knew you, someone who smoked, who liked a drink, and who you now know, showed a weakness for young girls in school uniform. What had you heard that night with Fat Patrick's beautiful elder sister who had come down to see him unexpectedly, when he couldn't use the car, when perhaps he dare not use the car, when he told her it was being cleaned, when he was so nervous, *it's a bit different now she said, a bit different from my school uniform, Oh I don't know I rather liked your uniform, rather liked getting it off you mean, not always, he said, I didn't always take it off, no, and you bloody should have done, all down my front it was the first time, I'll catch my fucking death like this, why couldn't we have used your bloody car, it looked all right to me.*'

'George Cooper,' says the boy.

'George Cooper,' I reply.

*

I WAS ON HER DOORSTEP five days later. Julia Savage lived in graceful comfort, in a large mock Tudor house that stood back from a broad and secluded road. It was a dinner-party house, with a dinner-party gravel drive and the maid who showed me into the dinner-party drawing room probably got paid in dinner-party tips. It had one of those drawing rooms with matching sofas and gilt-edged mirrors and a great whirring clock on the mantelpiece. A pair of bay windows looked out on to a large, but now distraught, garden. At the end of it two young men were grappling with a fallen willow.

The last time I had seen her was at her mother's funeral four or five years back and even then it had been a very brief encounter. Julia hadn't stayed long. She came down in some chauffeur-driven car and sat with Fat Patrick and his poor father while the coffin trundled towards the flames. It had been the first time I had been to a cremation since the death of my baby brother (Mother had been lowered into the ground. We could not face another cremation, one of the few things we ever agreed on as a family. Coming so soon, just under the year it would have seemed almost like a *production line*), and I had forgotten, after the service and the hymns, what a heartbreaking noise that machine makes, how industrial it looks, how industrial it is, with its churning cogs and dangling rubber curtain, and the hidden roar of the furnace so rudely intruding, turning what is meant to be a place of remembrance, and dare I say it *prayer*, into a brutal waiting room for extinction. If you must burn someone, if burning is the thing to do, then why not place the body on a bonfire in the open air, cover the wood with scented oils, surround it with dried flowers, put a match to it and watch the lot go up in flames, up to the sky, *towards heaven* for example. How strange I had thought that this is all that is left of Britain's furnaces, how those hard houses of fire that once fashioned hulls and funnels and aeroplane wings, cars and bicycles, *knives and forks*, have themselves become extinct and the only way the furnace lives on is for them to feed on the dead.

Julia had sat with her brother and father in the front row, her trim black hat and rather too attractive black dress a marked contrast to Patrick's dishevelled appearance, but each time she sat down after a hymn or prayer she inched a little further away than the last time, as if to impress upon the rest of us the great divide that lay between them. For all her poise and obvious wealth, she had not changed. She was still as eager to show herself off now, in that knowing, off-hand manner of hers, as she had been all those years ago up on the rugger pitch. Seeing the two of them side by side I thought yet again how marvellous it was how one could be so ponderous, so awkward, so singular, while the other, for all her haughty elegance was stained with a sexuality that could never be erased. I never knew if Fat Patrick knew about George Cooper (for I never told him) and when I picked up the phone in Eric's hut and explained everything to him that was the one thing I left out. Though I had Julia's address from Carol's will I wanted to sound him out first.

'The thing is Patrick,' I said, 'I have to talk to your sister.'

There was a pause on the end of the line. He was on his guard.

'My sister,' he said slowly. 'About the will you mean? She's terribly posh these days, what with her husband being such a high flyer. She doesn't want to know dad and me. Thinks we might get into trouble and spoil his chances.'

'How is your father?' I asked.

'Dad's fine,' he said slowly. 'We're off soon.'

'Off?'

'Leaving the Medway behind.'

'Abroad?'

'Possibly abroad. It's difficult to say with Dad. He's so pig-headed. What do I know? He was only talking about you the other day.'

'Really?'

'Yes. Said he never gave you that trip you always wanted. The trip we all always wanted.'

'Well, send him my best will you? Perhaps I could come down to see you?'

'Giles,' his voice grew suddenly urgent. 'Why don't you come with us? It's going to be so memorable. You could bring who you like. What about that friend of Carol's you brought down once. Monica somebody?'

'That's not quite as hot as it was. What about the Germans?'

He laughed, 'I am a tolerant man Giles, but no, not the Germans. And not Monica then. I'm sure you've someone else. If she likes adventure . . .'

'This all sounds very mysterious and wonderful, and God knows I am in sore need of a break, but how can I, with Carol in hospital and Clare to look after? Besides, there's Stella. I was hoping you might help me.'

Patrick, like Monica before him, sounded a note of caution.

'Is this wise? Stella did for you. Stella removed what little faith you had in the human race. And look what she's done to Carol. Stella is not good news. And is it any wonder? Remember that father of hers.'

He went into Muchmore's Putting-the-car-into-the-garage-routine. '*Am I straight? Are the wheels in line. Look at the wheels woman!*'

'*Forward, Forward,*' I came back, '*Straighten Up!*' There was a pause while we laughed in memory of those boyhood evenings.

'Find her then,' he agreed. 'Find her and bring her along too. Bring them all along. You needn't stay the whole course.'

'Patrick what is this? Not some dreadful outward-bound thing surely?'

'No, no. It's a sort of cruise.'

I was not convinced.

'I can't quite see you as the cruise type. I've a friend who knows all about cruises. Actually in a perverted sort of way I could see him enjoying a cruise. I could invite him I suppose.' I paused for a moment. 'What am I saying? This is ridiculous. Of course I can't come on a cruise. I've got a job to do among other things. And so have you.'

He sniffed. 'Work and I have parted company. I have become excess to requirements. Government savings you know. Forthcoming privatization. They got rid of me three months ago.'

'God, I had no idea. You should have rung and told me. Still, I'm sure something else will turn up.'

'Giles,' he said, in a reproachful manner, as if it were almost my fault, 'I'm an overweight, unattractive, over-the-hill, unmarried man who for the last thirty years has done what he was told. I have no offspring, no one close to me, I look after my father with little outside help. I am not even allowed to be uncle to my nephew and niece although I would be a good uncle. I live alone with my collection of French glass, my collection of stereoscopic photographs and the thing that started me off, those cigarette cards of mine and sometimes when it is hot, or when it is cold, or when it is exactly *in between*, I feel like throwing the lot into the canal. I should have followed your example.'

'I wish you wouldn't keep reminding me of that episode. It was one of the worst things I've ever done in my life. It still makes me feel terrible just thinking about it.'

'The trouble is you should have torn them *all* up, then I might have been defeated. Perhaps if you'd done that I would have been forced to consider normal pursuits: pop music, girls or perhaps boys. Who knows? I don't. Instead I kept my head down and plodded on, rose silently through the ranks, board examiner, school inspector, deputy head of region, job-for-life, home at night with another example of eighteenth-century French glass or a perfect set of Franklyn Davey 1924 Boxing Instructions tucked under my arm, and grew up, if not gracefully, then without ripples in my life. And then there was you Giles, whose life was nothing but ripples, the way you mistreated that poor wife of yours, your wild drinking, the days you came down here hardly able to stand, when I would listen to you on the radio thinking Giles is pissed out of his mind again, your dead brother and your murdered girlfriend, your indiscriminate and at times loathsome lust, and though why can't I have some misfortune like that, why can't I teeter on the edge of some terrible self destruction, why is my life so settled, and then I would look at you again, reeling under a terrible delusion that you were enjoying yourself and I thought, actually Giles is the last person I wanted to be. What I wanted to be was me, *only more so*. More *me*. And that is what I am going to do with my redundancy money. I am going to be me and father is going to be father. I am going to sell my collection of French glass and I am going to sell my collection of stifling cigarette cards and Victorian camera work, and I am going to take the bulk of my generous pay-off and we are going to indulge ourselves. We are going on a cruise. A very special cruise. Come with us why don't you. The trip of a lifetime. It's all paid for. All you need is pocket money.'

I was getting angry with this. It was a typical Fat Patrick speech, slow and matter of fact, with a horrible logic to it all.

'It seems fairly ironic to me that you should be attempting to persuade me to abandon everything just when I am trying to live up to my responsibilities. I wonder what the court would have to say when they learnt that I'd whisked Clare off on a world cruise, leaving her mother to die alone in hospital. I wonder who would get custody then? Your sister that's bloody who.'

There was a sharp intake of breath on the other end.

'No, no. You're right. Anything but that. Keep her well away. Stay here. Fight the bloody will. God, I don't know. Perhaps you *should* do a runner, smuggle Clare out of the country. Set up in Turkey where there's no extradition. If it comes to that I'll even perjure myself and tell the court what an upright member of society you are. Anything but my sister.' He stopped for a moment. I could hear him thinking in that fussy way of his, fidgeting, pushing his spectacles back. 'I tell you what Giles. Before you go and see her. I'll send you something. A good luck charm. A going away present. Don't go and see her until you've got it. It will bring you luck. Promise?'

I promised. It arrived three days later. He had constructed a special book for it, with forty-eight separate Cellophane pockets. The 1938 Ardath sectional set of the Empire Flying Boat. Forty-seven were in perfect condition. One, smack in the middle, had a single tear running from top to bottom. It had been pressed together over the years, so that it no longer looked quite as brutal, as final, as when it had happened, but it was still there. I showed Clare the set when we got back from the hospital that night. We took them out of their case and began to lay them out.

'When did you get them?' she asked me, folding them down carefully on the kitchen table.

'They're a present from an old friend,' I told her. 'Someone who went to school with me. He collected them. This was his favourite.'

She placed another two side by side.

'If it was his favourite,' she asked, 'why has he given it to you?' She dropped a card and turned to me with a frightened look on her face. 'He's not *dead* is he? I don't want to touch them if he's dead.'

'No, no,' I reassured her quickly, 'he's not dead. It's just that he's selling them now, and I was his *best* friend. This was my favourite too.'

I knelt beside her and put my hand on her head. As she bent down once again over the blue and green set, her hair fell away to reveal a long scar running across the back of her neck.

'How did you get that cut?' I asked.

'Daddy threw a spade at me on the beach, when he was . . . when he was . . .'

'. . . getting ill,' I suggested.

'*Dying*,' she said, still intent upon the picture, 'when he was dying.' She looked back up at me. 'He didn't mean to hit me. He couldn't control his arms and legs very well by then. The sun made him angry.' She reached back and touched it with her tiny hand. 'It's there now,' she said. 'It won't go away.'

'Scars never do,' I told her.

She wanted to take the set to school the next day to show all her friends but I wouldn't let her. Perhaps I didn't want it out of my sight after all those years, perhaps Mrs Briggs's Bag and the brass bowl were turning me into some sort of Proustian jackdaw. Anyhow I had it out on the front seat when I drove over to Richmond to see Patrick's sister, Julia, Julia Savage (née Liddle).

She hadn't changed much over the last four or five years, in fact she hadn't changed at all. The gym club and the sauna and the twice-weekly appointment with the masseur had seen to that. The mouth was a little older, the eyes were a little harder, and the fingers a little bonier but the clothes were still carefully chosen, colour co-ordinated, designed to flatter. Expensive too. We sat on opposite sofas, and for a moment I couldn't help wondering how many times she'd lain naked on them, fucking to her heart's content. These things, I am sorry to say, come into a man's mind without a moment's thought. They are no less important for that. It is the chaos of sexuality, the lure of nature calling him back to the wild, the wish to see order overthrown. I cannot speak for women (I cannot speak for men) but I have seen them under this weight too.

She was under the impression I had come to talk about Carol and Clare, so for a while I played on that fiddle. She listened to me politely, but held everything in reserve. There was no warmth, only suspicion. I knew of Carol's will I said, and frankly, I didn't agree with it. Clare was going to stay with me for the time being. I hoped she would understand. I hoped she would support me. Of course she was free to come round and have a look, and of course if Clare wanted to live with her, that would change things completely.

'As it is,' I said, 'if you were to ask her now she would most certainly elect to stay with me.' Julia scowled and looked at her fingers, as if she were waiting for something. 'I have to say,' I added, hoping to bring some light relief into the proceedings, 'that I find looking after a child a very wearing business.'

'Don't we all, Mr Doughty. That is why some of us employ nannies.'

'I don't believe in nannies,' I snapped back quickly. 'I'm not sure I believe in mothers and fathers much, but I certainly don't believe in nannies.'

She looked at me and then over to that fat clock with all its insides showing and spoke as though I was not in the room. 'No? And who do you believe in then? One of your many young lady friends?' She turned. 'Don't look so surprised. Carol tells me everything.'

'Yes, and how is that?' I asked. 'You were never close at school. You didn't go to university with her or anything did you? How come you kept in touch with her?'

Julia smiled. It was a smile someone who knows everything gives to someone who knows nothing.

'We didn't. Carol and I met up again through our husbands' work.'

'The Home Office?'

'Exactly. They first met at some conference or other, discovered they lived near each other, played a couple of rounds of golf, and then he invited us to dinner, and who should be there but . . .'

'. . . my sister.'

'Your sister.'

'And then we discovered that Clare went to the same school as my daughter, though Beatrice is a couple of years older. Which is why, amongst other things, Carol always felt that should something happen to her, Clare should come and live with us. Not the main reason of course.' She looked at her watch. 'The main reason was you. That's why I've asked my husband to be here. He shouldn't be long. I think you'll find, once my husband is here, you'll see the folly of trying to go your own way.'

As she spoke there was the sound of a car door slamming. A side gate into the garden opened and through it stepped a trim looking man in his late forties. He had a camel-hair coat over dark blue, rather military-looking trousers. He turned and waved to her and then indicated that he would just walk down to the bottom of the garden and talk to the two men. Damn it! This wasn't what I wanted at all. I wanted time alone with her. She wasn't going to talk about her past exploits in the pillbox with hubby perched across the room.

'The thing is,' I said, 'we can talk about Clare if you want, but that's not what I've come about. The reason Carol is in hospital is that she was following Stella Muchmore, the girl who disappeared, remember?'

Her face froze. Her body stiffened.

'That's right, Stella. The girl we all thought was murdered, the girl who some people thought I killed. You remember that last sighting by Judith Spenser, by the chestnut trees under her bedroom window? I know who Stella met there now. I've worked it all out. It's someone we both knew, you rather better than me I fear. George Cooper.'

She got up and moved towards the window. Her husband was still talking.

'You mean the English master at the boys' school?' she said. Her voice was dreamy, far away. 'What makes you think I knew him?'

I got up and stood beside her.

'Julia, I saw you. I saw you one night about a month after Stella disappeared. It was late. You were in an alleyway with him and then a little later on down by the river.' I tried to make it easier for her. 'I heard you rather than saw you. I couldn't help it. I was hiding behind the hedge. It was me who drank that bottle of whisky you lost, remember?'

I was watching her closely now, and her eyes jumped with the memory. I blundered on, 'I didn't recognize him at first, not in the alleyway, but then, with the light from the fire I could see . . .' I stopped. I had just trodden on my little lie. 'Well yes,' I admitted, 'I did see you together. You can look in as well as out of a pillbox.' I hurried on. 'I don't want to go into all that, but you must understand. It was George Cooper who met Stella that night, I'm sure of it. Think back. Don't you remember how nervous he was. How he wouldn't use his car. And what he said about your clothes, *your school uniform.*'

If I had expected her face to blush at the thought of me seeing her half naked in the mud with my English master on top of her, I was to be disappointed. She was cold and angry and in control. She had come a long way since Fuck me George, fuck me.

'You're even worse than Carol made out you were. Get out

before my husband has you thrown out. And if you think you're going to keep Clare . . .'

I was surprised by her vehemence.

'There's no need to get all worked up about it,' I said. 'I'm not trying to embarrass you. All I want you to do is see if you can remember anything about him that would help me. Did you keep in touch at all?'

Julia looked at me scornfully. 'That's very likely isn't it? That I should keep in touch with a man whose penchant was for young girls in school uniform.'

Outside we both watched her husband directing the workmen. He looked out of place there in the ruin of the garden, so well groomed, smoothing his hair back with his kid gloves, moving from one foot to another trying to prevent too much mud getting on his polished brogues.

'Look Julia,' I said, 'I know my sister didn't trust me, and there is no reason for you to, but Carol is where she is because of all this. I must find out what happened to Stella. And George Cooper is the key. Four weeks before he met you, he met Stella up by the chestnut trees outside the Spenser twins' house. What happened then I have no idea, but they must have been in it together. That meant that she was with him, or had been with him, when he met you.' I felt for this woman then, standing in her perfect drawing room with her perfect husband outside, listening to me raking up a long dead adolescent fling.

'I'm sorry,' I said, 'I understand how you feel and I don't want you to get unnecessarily involved. We don't have to talk about this now. I'll meet you wherever you want. There's no need for your husband to know.'

She turned to look at me. For the first time she appeared unsettled.

'You must never tell him anything, understand?' she insisted, '*Anything.*'

She was more than unnerved, she was worried, slightly frightened.

'Why?' I asked. 'What's the matter? What's your husband got to do with it?'

She grabbed me by the arm and led me back from the window.

She started to speak very quickly, her eyes never off the man in the camel-hair coat. He had finished his chat now and was picking his way through the debris as only a man who has never gardened can.

'I'm not going to see you later,' she said, 'because there is no need. You've got it all wrong. Yes, George Cooper liked his schoolgirls well enough and yes, irritatingly enough you are right, he did drive up to the chestnut trees that night, the night Stella disappeared and yes he did pick someone up. But not Stella. It was me who was waiting for him. I'd been up in London since September and I was desperate to see him. I'd told him I was coming down for a long weekend and he said that he couldn't get away Saturday or Sunday but that he was free Monday night after his bloody theatre practice. Of course I wasn't down for a long weekend. I hated home. I just wanted to be with him again. I didn't tell anyone I was coming down, but I was terrified that someone would recognize me, and then I had this brilliant idea of dressing up in my old uniform. It killed two birds with one stone. I wanted to please him. I wasn't there anymore and I thought, with all those other girls about . . . and then if by any unlucky chance I did see someone who knew me, as I was dressed up as a schoolgirl, and as everyone knew I'd left school two years ago, no one would cotton on as to who it was. So he drove up, and there I was, dressed just like the old days, and we drove out to the Isle of Grain, did the best we could, then back I went on the last train to London. And that month away from him, with him in charge of another bloody school play, which is how we got together in the first place, drove me nearly out of my mind. So I came down unexpectedly a month later. Pretended I wanted to see the family. He wasn't best pleased, though he was happy enough when . . .' she looked at me straight in the eye, as if that old familiar gene that lives in men was there, swimming in my retina, '. . . when I got him going. Funny you should remember the car, for although his car was in the car park for some reason he wouldn't let us use it, said he was worried someone might see us, though it was much safer than hanging round Rochester High Street in the freezing cold. I think he'd got someone else in tow by then and there was something in the car that he'd forgotten to clear out, something that might have aroused my suspicions, something that might have brought the likelihood of him getting his end away that night to a full stop.'

I grimaced. It could have been Monica speaking.

'But why didn't you tell the police all this? You knew they were convinced you were Stella.'

'Well why do you think? He begged me not to that's why. Said it would ruin his career. And I was in love with him. The little shit.'

'But later on you could have. When you fell out with him.'

'You don't really know anything do you? I couldn't later on, for by that time my life had changed. I'd started going out with my husband.'

Her voice changed suddenly. She broke into a sweet and composed smile.

'Darling,' she said. 'How good of you to be on time. You remember Giles Doughty don't you?'

He came forward, a vain man, with a vain tan upon his face. He had left his camel-hair coat out in the hall but his regulation brass buttons and his regulation epaulets did nothing to hide his posturing elegance. He came forward holding out one of his manicured hands.

'Mr Doughty,' he said. 'The last time we met, you were sick all over my boots.'

Police Constable Savage had come a long way since then. He had met Julia Liddle in the last round of house-to-house enquiries, when the case was almost on its last legs. He had taken off his helmet, placed it on his lap, and noted down her lies, her evasions, and her half truths and taken stock of this young beauty who up till then had evaded their nets and thought this is the one for me. Perhaps he could sense in her the poise, the ambition, the longing desire to shine that lay in him. From that moment on they became inseparable, she travelling down to Rochester for weekends, he catching the train up to London on the odd evening off. How that lie must have grown in her in those early days, when he would tell her of the case, how the trail had ended up there in the chestnut trees, how frustrating it was for all of them. How she must have longed to tell him. No no, that was not Stella, that was *me*. And as each day passed, as each hope was dashed, as each interview was consigned to the wastepaper basket, her lie would have grown hard and cold and lodged deep within her. How could she prise it out without leaving an open bleeding hole? How could she tell him, the man she wanted to marry, that she had misled them, that she could have pointed them away from the chestnut trees, back to the pillbox, and the raincoat. Why she could lose him. Better to keep quiet. What difference does it really make. They still *have* the raincoat. They have found nothing else.

Naturally, Commissioner Savage remembered the Muchmore affair, a commonplace occurrence now, he offered, but in its day, unusual. A salutary case he added. Missed opportunities brought about by old-fashioned thinking.

'And do you still see Detective Sergeant Weatherspoon?' I asked.

'I see you understand my point Mr Doughty. No, no. He retired many years ago. We'd lost touch anyway, when I moved on.' He flicked the subject away with a wave of his hands. He had come home early for another matter. 'But enough of the past. I'm sorry to hear of your sister's accident. This must be a trying time. My wife tells me that there's some difficulty in the interpretation of your sister's wishes. We were very close to your sister, particularly when her husband was alive. I was sorry that I couldn't be at his funeral. We were attending a conference on policing in Miami that year.'

I saw my opening now, an opening to keep Clare and damn the lot of them.

'I was hoping,' I said, looking rather pointedly at Julia, 'that we could clear this all up with the minimum of fuss. There's been a bit of a misunderstanding.'

'Indeed?' He looked at his wife. 'A misunderstanding? Have you called me away for a misunderstanding dear?' His voice suggested that neither misunderstandings nor minimum sorts of fuss came into his remit.

'Yes, I've just discussed everything with your wife and for the time being, while Carol is alive, we both think it best if Clare stays with me.' Julia nodded in reluctant agreement. I got up. 'I'm sorry, but I have to go. This storm has thrown us into complete chaos.'

I left with both of them looking distinctly off peak.

'The thing is,' Eric told me later the next day, over a lunch-time whisky, 'she won't touch you now. You could be caught desecrating Roy Plumley's grave and drummed out of the BBC and she would do her best to hide it from him.'

'Eric,' I warned. 'You're on the air in ten seconds.'

'Sorry,' he said. 'Did you ever meet Roy Plumley though?'

He was right. By December, when the time came for my trial guardianship of Clare to be formalized, Julia Savage raised no objections. Monica acquiesced too, albeit reluctantly, telling me that she would be keeping a watchful, distrustful, eye on me. Despite all my protestations, by this time Monica and I had ceased to function. I had seen her often enough at the hospital and we had spent a few evenings together, but she would have nothing more to do with me. The last time she had stayed over at Carol's I had left her with a chaste kiss and returned to the flat. We never mentioned that last dreadful evening but the knowledge that when she went to bed with him she was trying to get pregnant and when she went to bed with me she was simply having . . . having what exactly? still seemed not only obscene but logistically uncertain. I tried to talk to her about it once down at Brighton, walking along the promenade.

'Did you not find it a difficult thing to do Monica?'

'Did I seem to find it difficult?' she asked.

'No, no, what I meant was didn't you think it was a bit, a bit *risky*. I mean if it had happened, how could you have been sure whose it was?'

'The only way I could have been sure,' she said turning the tables neatly on my question, 'would have been to persuade you to have a vasectomy. But you wouldn't have wanted that, would you?'

'Oh I don't know,' I said, falling straight into the trap. 'I can't see myself as a father can you?'

Monica turned round and put her arms on my shoulders. 'That Giles, is exactly what Carol thinks.'

Fleur had suggested (one of the few pieces of practical advice she ever gave me) that I get Jago to do the legal work for me, but I did not want to put myself in Jago's hands. The less Jago knew about me the better. Jago would have been good at it, of course.

'Breaking up families,' he told me one evening at Eric's, 'is what I do best. There she sails, the family boat, calm upon the waters. But throw a little money into the hold and you'll have a mutiny on board before the sun goes down. Which is where I come in, pitching the family overboard.'

'Not all families fall out,' I said.

He looked at me.

'Not all families are given the chance,' he replied. 'Was yours a happy family?'

I told him it was not.

'No. Was Eric's? Not that I know of. Was mine? Not exactly. Was Fleur and Michael's? God. Imagine Fleur and Michael as kids.'

'Who were their parents?' I asked. 'Fleur . . .' I stopped.

'Yes,' he said quickly.

'Never talks about them. Neither does Michael,' I added over hastily.

Jago looked at his fingernails.

'Never talks about them? I don't remember you talking about yours. I don't remember Eric talking about his. I don't remember me talking about mine.'

'No.'

Jago got up and went to the hatchway that looked out over the river. I should have thrown myself in there and then. How could I have been so careless? In an unguarded moment I had sown a seed of doubt in his mind, offered up the suggestion that I might be seeing more of Fleur than these chaperoned meetings at Michael's. And Jago was a suspicious man. One night he had confided to me that he knew that everyone fancied Fleur, that the way she dressed and acted and held herself excited men, and I, drunk, played myself for a clever bastard and agreed saying Well you must admit, she does look very . . . Very fuckable? he suggested, and I said Well, I wouldn't put it quite like that and he squeezed my hand hard and said, Wouldn't you? Well how would you put it? Fascinating, I said. Attractive, and Jago said Yes? Well who do you find fuckable then? There's me and there's Fleur and there's Eric and Bonzo over there, but we never see you with someone in tow do we. Why is that? Been neutered have you? and I laughed and said No, that I did see someone, but that she lived down in Brighton and . . . And? And she wasn't exactly footloose and fancy free. Ah, said Jago. Breaking up a happy home are we? Not content with your miserable past you're consigning someone else to a miserable future, and I replied, No it wasn't quite like that. No, Jago answered sternly. It never is, is it? And now he stood with his back to the river looking back at me.

'Well,' he called out, 'you're a family man now, now that you've got a little cuckoo in the crow's nest. You'll be needing a wife before long. I could fix you one of those Vietnamese refugees if you like.'

*

So CLARE AND I were home, not home and dry exactly, but I knew that the longer she stayed with me the greater the chance that I would be able to keep her. And after those first two months that was what I wanted. Come December and I was determined to make her first holiday with me a memorable one. I did not want us to stay in the flat, nor could we go far away in case Carol's condition changed. But I wanted us to leave the city behind, to escape the cold streets of London, and the cold walls of her mother's hospital. Then I had the idea of the bungalow. I would turn the bungalow into a surprise Christmas palace. I rang up Patrick. I'm coming down for Christmas, I told him. I thought you and your father might like to come over the day after Christmas Day. Just me and Clare. Possibly someone else.'

'Someone I know?'

'No one you know. But he doesn't live far away.'

Dickey thought it a great idea.

'You think presents,' he said, 'and I'll think food. Some of the presents can be food, but conversely none of the food can be presents.'

'You've lost me,' I said.

'Presents which you can eat sir, must not be regarded as food, as doing you good. In fact they must be seen as doing great harm, rotting teeth, upsetting stomachs and ruining meals.'

'And I must get some.'

'You must get an armful sir.'

'And you'll think the food.'

'Exactly sir. Turkey, pork, ham, pâté, Christmas pudding, sausage rolls, stuffing balls, cranberry sauce, ice-cream, brussels, cabbage, Christmas cake, jellies, trifle, dates, figs, crystallized fruit, nuts, raisins . . .'

'Dickey, Dickey. It's Clare I'm bringing down not the Licensed Victuallers Association.'

'Very glad you mentioned them sir. Claret, brandy, port, cognac, Armagnac, rum, pop, fizz and of course . . .'

'Gin,' I said.

'Crackers,' he said. 'Crackers, streamers, poppers, whistles, fireworks and . . .'

'And?'

'Sprouts. No Christmas is safe without sprouts. When we spent the festive season on board sir, if they didn't get sprouts the passengers often turned quite nasty. Sulked in their cabins. Made Father Christmas walk the plank. And who *is* going to be Father Christmas sir?'

And so, leaving Clare with Mrs Delguardo, I drove down there and with Dickey's help decked the place out with holly and ferns and fairy-lights. Dickey brought an enormous Christmas tree from some market.

'You should have got a smaller one Dickey,' I told him as we tried to bend it into the corner. 'It's far too tall.'

'When we were at sea sir, if the going was rough, and it usually was at Christmas, we would put the Christmas trees in at different angles, so that the passengers were never quite sure whether the ship was rolling or not. Saved a lot of Christmas puddings that way. Talking of food, sir. I couldn't help noticing that there are two fridges in the kitchen.'

'I had to buy the second one for the food you've brought,' I explained. 'The other . . .'

'The other?'

'Has other things in it.'

'And a chain around it.'

'And a chain around it.'

All that last week I seemed to be shopping and hiding things and driving down secretly to meet up with Dickey. We had the place looking pretty good though by the time we finished. It was dark and green inside, like a cave, with candles stuck in pieces of driftwood. The draught from the wind outside made the ferns and the holly rustle and it struck me when we had finished that we had made a safer, prettier version of my room that night in The Post House. Somehow that seemed right. Standing back, with Dickey at my side, admiring our handiwork, I caught myself thinking that I was glad that it had come to this. Not glad that Carol had suffered, but glad how things were turning out. Carol would not recover. She would never speak again. Her life was over. Now it was my turn. Mine and Clare's. Stella could remain hidden. I no longer cared. I had better things to do.

We piled the presents under the tree. For Clare I had bought a kite for the beach, roller-skates for the road, a dress for parties, a paint-box for rainy days, a book of poems for bedtime and a video of the great Ub Iwerks. For Fat Patrick and his father, two gifts for their forthcoming journey; an old-fashioned ship's compass set in an oak box, and a gleaming sextant with which to write to the stars. For Dickey I had found a rare recording of Speedy Bec and Max in the late forties. Max was on the cover and though one trumpet looks very much like another I had a feeling that the one Max was holding was the one that now hung behind Dickey's bar. At least I hoped it was.

We drove down on Christmas Eve. Dickey was waiting at the door, a silver tray in his hand, and upon the tray a key.

'This is *your* key miss. Yours to unlock. Once in there, you can do whatever you like.'

Clare picked up the key and turned it, with some difficulty, in the lock. She pushed back the door and there it stood, a green cave flickering before her. She clapped her hands and ran in. In the corner stood the huge tree and from its sparkling branches hung toffee apples and chocolate animals and hundreds of liquorice allsorts.

'This is a Help Yourself Tree, miss,' Dickey explained. 'It is impossible, under the rules of engagement, to be told that you have had enough or that you must wait until after supper. And only you miss, *only* you, may eat from it.'

She stood underneath and bit into a large chocolate rabbit. The tree shook and shed a vast quantity of pine needles.

'This tree is as bald as a badger,' she announced.

Dickey clapped his hands over his eyes.

'I knew it,' he cried. 'I knew I shouldn't have bought it in Ashford. As I told your uncle once miss, they simply don't understand fresh.' He bent over. 'Kick me miss. Break off one of its horrid branches and beat me with it.'

'Dickey. Dickey,' I said. 'It's the best tree in the world. Let me give you a hug you old fraud.'

We spent Christmas Day opening presents, flying kites, eating, walking and larking about. Dickey had bought Clare a second-hand accordion.

'Everyone should be able to play a musical instrument miss,' he said, as she struggled to put it on. 'It should be compulsory. And not any old music. Bugger Brahms miss. Ellington is what this country needs. No A Train. No A level.'

'You can tell that to my guest tomorrow,' I told him. 'See what he thinks. Tell it to Fat Patrick. Perhaps that's where he went wrong. No jazz on the curriculum.'

Patrick came with his father as arranged. The wind had dropped and it was a bright morning, and as we walked along the sands before lunch I was conscious of how content Jim Liddle appeared. He had lost that distracted, troubled expression which had haunted him all those years ago. Back in the bungalow, watching him and Dickey walking up the beach, I told Patrick how well I thought his father looked.

'It's the cruise,' he explained. 'It's put a new lease of life into him.'

'Ah yes, the cruise.' I handed him my two gifts. He unwrapped them solemnly, and placed them on the table.

'Not really the ideal thing to take on holiday I suppose,' I confessed, 'but I couldn't resist them.'

Patrick beamed.

'They are simply marvellous,' he said. 'Simply marvellous. Dad will be over the moon. It is just what we need.'

'Need?' I questioned.

'They reflect the spirit of the enterprise. Dad,' he called out as they came through the door, 'Look what Giles has given us. What could be more appropriate.'

I explained to Dickey. 'Patrick is taking his father on a cruise.'

Dickey wrinkled his nose.

'A cruise? A winter cruise? In *winter*? Are you sure your family ties are strong enough?'

'Dickey's little joke,' I explained. 'Dickey used to work on cruises. He has only recently left the sea.'

'I have given up all things with salt in them by way of celebration,' Dickey said, reaching for a bottle of champagne. 'And where are you embarking from? Southampton?'

'No. From around here.'

'From Dover? I didn't know any cruise line went from Dover.'

'Not Dover,' Patrick explained. 'It's a private trip with some friends of ours.'

Dickey popped the cork, smiling.

'Not a cruise at all then. That explains your enthusiasm. Shall I pour?'

So we drank our bottle while Clare examined Fat Patrick's present to her.

'Would that be chickens I see before me?' Dickey asked, peering over her shoulder.

Patrick came over. 'Ogdens *Poultry Set*. 1915. Two sets were issued in one year. One with "Ogdens" on the front, one without.'

'Patrick,' I admonished. 'I thought you were selling all the valuable ones?'

Patrick smiled that slow shy smile of his.

'Not all.'

'This is very educational I must say,' Dickey continued. 'It appears that two of my daughter's chickens, Dibby and Gob, are Plymouth Rocks, while the other one, Sidney is a Dorking.'

'Old-fashioned breeds,' Patrick added. 'I have saved other collections too. Wills *Merchant Ships of the World*, 1924 and a rather splendid one called *Life in a Liner*. Would you like to see them some time?'

'I would indeed sir, particularly the latter. I often wondered whether there was life on a liner and if so where it might be hiding.'

Dickey walked them back to their car. He came back running.

'Quick, sir.'

'What's the matter,' I said. 'Someone drowned?'

'It's horrible sir. Horrible. Draw the curtain, before Clare sees.'

'What is it? A corpse?'

'Worse than that sir. Morris Dancers. Dancing along the beach sir. A whole crowd of them. Can you see them sir?'

Indeed I could, bells clanking, handkerchiefs waving.

'You can almost hear their stomachs from here sir. If only we had a portable sheep dip.'

'Sheep dip?'

'For their beards sir.'

'We don't have a sheep dip, Dickey. But we have something better. Something most appropriate.'

I called Clare and took them both through to the kitchen.

'Did you never wonder,' I said, removing the chain, 'why this fridge had a chain around it?'

'I thought you might have someone frozen in there sir, someone you didn't want to get out.'

I swung the door back and there, set out on silver foil, stood rows and rows of perfectly formed snowballs.

'I modified this fridge to keep it at the exact temperature, so that the snow would stay just so. See . . .' I picked one up. 'They are still light, still fluffy.'

'How old are these snowballs sir?'

'They are a year old,' I told him. 'I made them last year.' I held Clare before them. 'Look Clare, there has been no snow on the ground for nine months and yet we have snowballs. Why don't we take them out and creep up on the dunes and give those Morris Dancers a pounding.'

'Can I lead the charge?' Dickey asked. 'I've always wanted to get my own back on Morris Dancers. Morris Dancers are almost as bad as . . .'

'Sailors?' I suggested.

'Cockneys,' came the reply.

*

AND THUS IT WAS I came to my dead end, a dead end which neither Clare's brimming eyes nor the sight of my sister wasting away on her cast-iron bed could unblock. Until that night, when I danced with the nurse with flat feet, when I swooned and cried in her arms, when I fell in love with flat feet and dangling wrist-watches and sturdy starched arms only to be woken by the voice of my sister crying out, a voice I thought I would never hear again, crying out loud and clear, waking the slumbering patients, the sick and the dying. Even the young woman who tried to kill herself, pulled off the headphones and sat up, as if this were the better music, this shouting, this high pitched shouting. We careered down the corridor the nurse and I and though I was in my stockinged feet I must have pushed past her as I slid towards the door. There was my sister sitting bolt upright, blood pouring down her arm, pulling the drips and wires out, kicking her legs, flapping her arms, screeching for help. I ran round and took hold of her, I ran round and shook her, looked into her eyes and shook her and suddenly I saw my sister again, saw all the depths of my sister swim to the surface. I pressed her shoulders tightly. I was squeezing my sister out and as I did I knew that my sister knew that she was my sister. There were questions in her eyes, silent questions bubbling up, questions she would never ask, and knew that she would never ask, questions about Clare and questions about me and the long life we would have together, and I answered them all. I kissed my sister on the cheek and all the sorrows of our childhood floated clearly in my tears. If only our brother hadn't died, if only I hadn't pushed him away, pushed him off his climbing frame, if only I hadn't told him that he was a boring baby brother, that I was fed up with his stupid games, fed up with him spoiling everything, fed up with him always hanging round the pillbox trying to butt in, that I didn't want him around and why didn't he push off, go and do something useful for a change, using a favourite expression of our father's, instead of always hanging about, why don't you do something useful if you want to play at Flying Boats with us, go and get one or something, and hadn't I pushed him off, so that he fell on his knees my baby brother, and didn't he pick himself up and trot away down the garden without once looking back, me watching him out of the corner of my eye, sitting high on his climbing frame, indignant, fuming, hoping he would soon come back. And didn't I sit there for what, an hour, waiting for him to crawl back, waiting for him to beg forgiveness, to plead, to promise me that he would not spoil my games, that he would do whatever I told him to, that he wouldn't get in the way again, promise, and didn't I sit there, the sun hurting my eyes, wishing he would hurry up and then when mother called, when she walked out with a towel slung over her shoulder, pulling her hair back and asking calmly at first where's Josh, didn't I lie, suddenly realizing that I hadn't even heard him, not a sound, not even that half baked whistling of his, nor his whirring helicopter noise, no footfall, no creaking branches and *that I had no idea where he was*, by saying he was here a minute ago, he must have just gone down to the bottom of the garden, *What* she said, *What*, Have you no sense at all, Can't I trust you to keep an eye on him for a minute, and didn't I jump down, feeling annoyed, feeling guilty, suddenly realizing the terrible thing I had done in banishing my brother on this lovely day, and didn't I call back to her, telling her not to worry, he's only gone to the allotments or something, he'll be there, and didn't I go down through the allotments in a haphazard sort of way, expecting to come across him, squatting in the framework of the old shed, or standing in the midst of the wild raspberry canes reaching up for the raw fruit, having forgotten all about our quarrel, and when he wasn't there didn't I call again, slightly louder now, trampling my way over to the pillbox, where Poker Fisher or the Cramphorns or Henry Deering and his dog might be, and Wasn't it empty, Wasn't it cold, Didn't it stink of nights of old, and wasn't I afraid, afraid of the great emptiness that was welling up inside me and didn't I run out on to the footpath calling his name, calling his name, and didn't his name ring then, the name I have never spoken since, can never speak again, didn't it ring over the water to where the grey and silver machines lay, and didn't I look at them and think, No he wouldn't have, *couldn't* have, and didn't I look up and down the towpath, all leafy and green and happy in the sunlight, Wasn't it warm, Wasn't it bright, Didn't the world seem such a delight, with the water lapping and the clouds floating peaceful in the sky, and didn't I start to trot then, first one way, then the other, fifty feet up, fifty feet down, calling his name, *Joshua, Joshua*, called his full name, I never knew why, I never could explain, why I called *Joshua, Joshua*, as if I already knew he had passed into history, that he was no longer a boy called Josh, a hundred feet up now, a hundred feet down, hoping that someone would come along, a couple of the old men from the works perhaps, or Mrs Briggs, Have you seen my brother, in a blue shirt and shorts? Why yes, he's down that way playing with some dog or other, Isn't he small, Isn't he sweet, Doesn't he make your life complete, and didn't I start to race then, and didn't I start to pound down the towpath, following the flow of the water, fright leaping in my throat, Didn't I call, Didn't I shout, Didn't I know there was no one about, and didn't I see him as I turned the bend, see him straight away, as if my eye was guided directly on to his body, and didn't I know from the way his arms floated lazily in rhythm with the river that he was dead, gazing with drowned eyes at the muddy bottom, and Didn't I jump, Didn't I slide, Didn't I flounder up to his side, gulping water, grabbing him by the back of his baby collar, and didn't I haul him out of the water, haul him up the slippery bank, didn't I bend my legs and pull his body up the slope. Wasn't I strong, Wasn't I bold, Didn't my grip take a good hold, didn't I pull him up on to the towpath, his arms slack and his shoes dragging ferns and weeds and an old crisp packet in their wake, with his little head lolling about and didn't I place him face down as I had been taught at scouts, with his elbows out and his face on one side and didn't I push down on his shoulders, Didn't I press, Didn't I count, Didn't the water bubble and fount, water from the Medway, our river, our town and didn't my brother groan, didn't I hear him groan, I did! I heard him groan, and didn't I turn him over, thinking it's all right, he's going to be all right, and didn't I open his mouth, where there were no fillings, only perfect teeth, Look at them shine, Look at them white, Didn't he brush them every night, and didn't I press my lips to his and didn't my lungs breathe into his, and didn't he groan again, into my mouth, and didn't I taste it, didn't I swallow it, didn't it fill me up that groan, not a boy's own groan, but the dread sound of a dead soul groaning in the dark, Wasn't it foul. Wasn't it vile, Wasn't it just the bitterest bile, and didn't I cry his name, for the last time, saying Oh, please no, Please come back, I'll do anything, and didn't I pound his chest, bang on his heart, beat him with the palms of my hands, crying his name, beating his body, breaking his ribs, my baby brother's ribs never to mend, never to heal, never to grow, broken like the rest of us, while he rose into the air. And didn't I sit astride him, and wasn't I found by a couple of old workmen, walking up the path for an evening smoke, and didn't one run to Dr Morgan who lived just down from us, and wasn't he in and didn't he come running with his bag, a little crowd forming around me now, and didn't he push past the lot of them and Wasn't it plain? Wasn't it clear? Didn't he whisper into my ear?

> Your baby brother is altogether
>   But all together
>   He's all together
> The most inanimate lifeless boy
>   That I have ever seen
>
> These eyes of mine at once have noted
>   His lips are livid
>   His legs are bloated
> The hands are blue and the body is
>   A ghastly shade of green
> Ghastly shade of green!
>
> The coroner has to convene

Oh my sister I am sorry for what I have done, and for what I am about to do, for now there is no time to make amends. I didn't mean to destroy what little was left of our family, to render it utterly impotent. What was in the air that day? Where did it come from? How bleak the wind had blown since. You have found the only person who truly liked me and look what she has done. Carol stared into my eyes and all that night rose up again. I could see her telephoning, jamming the coins in while she watched Stella out of the corner of her eye, I could hear the urgency in her voice. I watched her as she boarded the train, following Stella at a distance, sat with her at the back of the carriage, while Stella stared out of the window up ahead. The wind was starting up now, the rain falling against the windowpane, but it was the noise of the train, the darkness, and the unknowing that would have increased my sister's agitation. How she must have wanted to walk forward, to seat herself across from Stella Muchmore and watch her reaction. Was that it? Was that what she did that night? My sister's eyes swam again. I'm telling you, they said, I am telling you, and I followed her again into the wet and the cold as she set off from Wye station to struggle up that hill. She gripped me hard my sister out there, gripped me as we bent into the furious wind, as we tugged our coats around us, and entered into that long dark climb with the broad trees starting to creak and moan and bend like bamboos. And when we reached the top, and below us we could see the world helpless under the blackening sky, she summoned all her strength and opened her mouth. I could not hear her at first for all the noise that was around us, for all the branches tearing and splintering one another, as the hill began to shake, so she clung to me harder and shouted again, her lips very white and very close but with every syllable extended, as if I were some distance away, peering through the gloom. Forward! Forward! she cried. Straighten Up! Straighten Up! and with that, her hands still beckoning she went slack, and lay back on her bed.

*

THIS TIME I TOOK Fleur's advice. She lay across me with her legs in the air while at long last I recited the story and the reason for my sister's demise. What I needed was simple enough. An address. An address would end the riddle. 'Go and ask Jago,' she said. 'He'll know how to find it.'

'Ask Jago? Are you mad?' and Fleur leant across and reached for a peach, biting into it so that the juice fell on my shoulder and told me she was not mad. It was the obvious solution. He has lots of contacts with the police, she said. He even gets invited to the annual Policeman's Ball.

'But what about us?' I said.

'What about us?' she replied, and rolled back to extract what little there was left.

I did not like the idea of having to humble myself before Jago but I was desperate now. He had chosen to establish his offices above one of those East End boxing clubs, those criminal equivalents of Sandhurst, where their young men learn not only the delights of the padded glove, but more importantly the etiquette of the criminal class: how to dress smart, what rings to ease over what fingers, how to sit polite at table what with the prospect of blood later on, and above all, the correct attitude to flesh, some what may be smacked playfully, some what may be beaten senseless and some what comes to them by right of ownership. I was reminded of that night when I first saw Fleur and Jago together, when he held her aloft, as a fighter might stand in the ring, holding the spoils of his victory high above his head. Glory to the victor! As I mounted the stairs I could hear the sounds of exhortations, of squeaking shoes, of punches coming from below and though once inside the noise was less apparent what was unmistakable was the smell of men's sweat. Waiting to be shown in I had the odd feeling that I was here for an exam, rather than to make a request, and as I sat there quaking in my shoes, I thought back to those dreadful driving lessons I had undergone, when I had agreed to take to the wheel for my sister's sake, so that I could help her ferry her dying husband and had suffered all the humiliations that a man in power could heap upon me. My instructor did not like me and did everything he could to make my life miserable. I found co-ordination difficult, and on occasions I would put my hand on the gear stick and leave it there, not absolutely sure that it was mine. Hands on the wheel dimwit! Hands on the wheel, he would scream, And don't look down. Don't you know what your hand looks like? and would bring the car to an ignominious halt. I could teach a monkey better than you, he would add, smirking as he folded my latest cheque into his top pocket. I promised myself that on the day that I passed I would find Mr Horne and kick him verbally in the balls. Sure enough clutching my signed certificate in my hand I did find him, leaning up in the doorway of the Test Centre, picking his teeth with a copy of the Highway Code, but when it came down to it, I found myself thanking the man, taking him by the hand and bloody thanking him. As I waited to be shown in I wondered what price Jago would extract and whether I would find myself thanking him too.

I was ushered in by a woman who appeared to have a very broad and very broken nose. Jago was on the phone and waved me down with an enormous hand, raising his eyebrows in mock despair of his conversation. Around the walls were pictures of fighters with their hands held up in that half bent, crouching stance that boxers seem to think attractive, fists held in front of their faces, their stomachs sucked flat against the top of their sweet little trunks, shadow boxing their own image. I recognized only a few, British boxers mostly, some current hopefuls, but in the main fighters from the Fifties and Sixties, Brian London with his famous glass chin, and naturally enough Jimmy James. Jimmy James's picture was signed. *To Little Tommy Jago*, it read, *A right little scrapper*. He sat before a huge slab of bare marble. On it there was one sharpened pencil, a loose leaf of unlined foolscap, the telephone, a video handset, a bowl of fruit and a pair of red boxing gloves. There was a door to the left of him, with a frosted upper half, and on it were engraved the words, Erskine Brothers, Slaughterers to the Meat Trade since 1889. By its side stood a giant television screen with a video recorder stacked with tapes. They were all labelled with big names from the fight game. Marciano, Ali, Johansson. I was still reading them when eventually he put the phone down.

'It's all fights here,' he apologized. 'My dad used to run the place downstairs. You a fighting man?'

I told him I was not.

'No. Thought not. Well you have to be born into it really, grow up in it. Boxing mad our family is. Satellite up on the poop deck gets practically any fight in the world, if you know how to tune in. I get Mrs Lonsdale in there to get me all the foreign papers, just so I know what's on. I expect you think that strange being a friend of Michael's, buying a paper, reading it the same day, *throwing it away*. That's not her real name of course, Mrs Lonsdale. We call her that because her husband, Gordon, belts her so often.' He paused. 'Nah, didn't think you'd find that funny. We may live in a modern world Giles, but when all's said and done, what's mine certainly isn't thine nor anybody else's, which is why I'm in such demand and that's why Mrs Lonsdale or Annie Erskine as she is legally known, finds trouble keeping her looks about her. Her husband doesn't mind a little blood. That's his grandfather's door over there, and this marble here,' he ran his hands over it, 'was where they skinned everything. He used to hold them down as a young boy while they slit their throats.' He nodded back to the television. 'Get's a bloody good picture don't you think?' He pressed the handset.

I turned. To my dismay the familiar tune of 'Planetrain' came up, and sure enough, standing in the centre of a school playground, surrounded by children, stood Fleur, looking up at the camera.

'Ah,' Jago said, grinning. 'That's blown it. I *do* watch other things you see. Good programme "Planetrain". Trouble is she records it any old place. On my tapes, her tapes. I've even come in here for a night with the boys – we come up here after the pubs are shut and put a few fights on, and halfway through watching Floyd Paterson getting the stuffing knocked out of him, who should pop up but you know who. I never used to watch television when I was a kid. Didn't know what I was missing.'

'They weren't like this then,' I said, feeling on dangerous ground . . . He smiled, a knowing smile and gave me a wink.

'You're right there. Don't know how she gets away with it frankly. Producer fancies her probably. They're all poofs down there, did you know? All the children's presenters. I don't mind poofs in boxers. But I don't like them on telly, in Fair Isle jumpers, mixing with kids and looking wholesome. Know what I mean. That's why I like watching Fleur. Do you watch her at all?'

'Sometimes. She's very popular with my niece,' I explained.

He nodded. 'Well, it's the age isn't it. Mind if I keep it on?' He pressed a button so that the sound went down. 'You said you wanted some help. That sister of yours died or something?'

I looked quickly at the screen. Fleur was talking directly into the camera. The screen was full of her hair and her lips and those dazzling demanding eyes of hers. She had a way of opening her face wide, of bending forward and opening her face to the world, mischievous, inviting it in, and she was doing it now. Although I knew it was a recording it was as if she knew we were both in the room together, watching her. There was the sound of raucous laughter coming from below, and though I tried to explain as quickly as I could, what with that and the sound of Fleur's voice in the background, I began to falter along the way. I was sweaty, and nervous, and for some reason afraid. Suddenly I felt very alone. Jago sat there, half listening to me, half watching the screen, his enormous hands roaming over his desk, playing with an apple, picking up the pencil, testing its point against the back of his hand. I had just explained why I needed to find Sergeant Weatherspoon, and why I thought he might be able to help me find him, when I was aware that there was something terribly wrong about the sound coming out of the television set, terribly wrong, and terribly familiar. I looked across and though the light was not perfect, there was no doubt as to what was being played. We were in my bungalow and it was early evening. The windows were open and Fleur and I lay underneath them on the near edge of one brass bed. The other had been pulled back to accommodate the camera. The curtains were billowing out and as Fleur raised her legs round my back and stretched her arms out she caught one of them in her hand and twisting it round her arm, used it to raise herself up to get a better look.

'See what I mean,' Jago said, staring at the screen. 'Hopelessly disorganized. Always leaving the car keys somewhere, forgetting to turn the gas off. Just like her brother really. What a thing to leave lying around eh, especially when she knows I like watching her shows.' He pulled out a video box from the drawer and examined it. '"Planetrain" August 1990, this one reads. Weymouth and Devizes. And so it was, but just as I was getting into it, what should appear but this.'

'Look . . .' I said.

He held out his hand.

'Not yet. There's a bit coming up, pardon my French, that I'm quite partial to. Swing the chair round why don't you. It's on rollers.'

The picture wobbled and changed abruptly. The room flew by, snatches of floor and ceiling and a pair of feet, and then, the picture changed. It was brighter, lighter and there she was again, her face in close up. She smiled into the camera, with that wide open, expectant look of hers and we could hear the creak of the first bed as I climbed over it to get to her. Then she turned slightly, to face me and to place the thing that was mine and should not be mine between her lips.

'Nice and roomy, that little craft of yours,' Jago remarked. 'Don't mind if I turn the sound up for this bit do you?' He pushed the fruitbowl across the table. 'Have a grape,' he said, stuffing a handful into his mouth.

We had thought it funny at the time, for her to do an obscene parody of her show. 'I can't help it,' I had said. 'Whenever I see you on television, see your face close up, I just imagine that mouth on me.' Fleur had laughed. 'So you *do* want to appear on television,' she said. 'So why imagine?'

She held it out now and waved it in front of the camera. Why had we done it? Why had she *kept* it for Christ's sake? Why hadn't *I* kept it? As a matter of fact I thought I *had*. Had Jago got one of his henchmen to go through my belongings? Unsure of the exact protocol on such an occasion I found myself doing as Jago suggested and settled down in my seat to look upon the scene as if I were an innocent spectator, and that the object singled out for so much attention had *nothing to do with me*. And in many ways it *was* nothing to do with me. It was like standing in front of the mirror wondering who you are. That wasn't me there. Not really me. I wasn't *there* any more. I was here. When I came to think of it, looking at this thing playing peek-a-boo at the camera like some grotesque glove puppet, all blue and purple, it didn't even *look like* mine. Indeed had it not been for that first episode, with both of us lying full length on the bed, there was no way that Jago could be certain that it *was* me. I began to wonder if I wasn't safe after all, if in fact you *could* tell it was me from that first shot. *I* knew it was of course, but thinking back on it, all Jago had of me was a side view of a naked man with his head down screwing his wife in the fading afternoon light. Fleur was clearly in the picture, but as for the bloke *well it could have been anybody*. I quickly ran through the various bits of my body showing, whether there were any distinguishing marks on my legs or arms, an unfortunate tattoo on the buttock perhaps that might give me away. Nothing. The film had also been taken a few months ago, when my hair, thank the Lord, had been a good deal longer, so not only did I look different, *but my hair had been hiding my face too*. All that connected me to what we were watching was the voice, similar to mine, but here consisting mostly of unintelligible utterances emanating from the back of the throat, and the location which Jago had never visited, but which undoubtedly belonged to me. Not perfect, but only circumstantial. I could have lent it to her for instance. Things were beginning to look up. For a moment I weighed the possibilities of an outright denial. God Jago, it may *look* like me, but I can assure you that it isn't. The thing is too bloody ridiculous for words. I looked at him out of the corner of my eye. He was chewing on his grapes almost as noisily as Fleur was feasting on the thing she had in her hand, though unlike her he did not pepper the proceedings with a perceptive running commentary. Brazen it out that's what I would do. I was just about to take the bull by the horns, when Fleur took the thing which was mine but which I was about to deny any knowledge of, out of her mouth and started talking to it very rapidly, egging it on, encouraging it, cajoling it, and what's worse *talking to its bloody owner*. By name! By bloody name! I hadn't remembered any of that. I closed my eyes for what inevitably came next.

'Well,' said Jago, switching off the set, 'she seemed pleased enough to see your handsome face again. She'd be good on the Food Programme don't you think?'

He pushed the red boxing gloves over towards me.

'You can get changed in that room over there,' he said, nodding in the direction of the glass door. 'Gordon will help you on with the gloves. Gordon!'

One of the men who I had seen with him at Jimmy James that night came in through the door and raised me to my feet. I do not remember whether it was he alone, or whether Jago helped me, for I had no hold on reality. What I had seen was not real. It wasn't me there, not really me, and if it was not me there, how could it be me here? I tried to tell that to Gordon, as he led me into the other room, and he was kind and solicitous and said that he understood and told me to pull off my shoes. He raised my shirt over my head, undid my belt and asked me to step out of my trousers. He held out the gloves and I thanked him as he helped me on with them, tying them tightly to my wrists. He led me down the back stairs to the gym. It was empty save for the four of them; Jago, Mrs Lonsdale, someone with his back to me and a man in red shorts, skipping in the ring.

'The thing to remember,' Gordon said, as he took me across to them, 'is keep your arms up, keep light on your feet and keep out of reach. Duck and weave, duck and weave all right? He's a Southpaw and a quick bastard at that.'

Jago came up and greeted me. He seemed so pleased to see me, so polite. I felt timeless, standing there in my underpants with those absurd gloves stuck on the end of my arms, helpless and childlike. I looked at him as if he were my protector, with his hand-cut suit and silk tie. He led me over to the ring.

'You remember Giles here, don't you Olga?' The man with his back to me turned and waved his fat fingers.

'Certainly I do,' the man sniffed. 'A natural comic. Very humorous about the jazz era. Pleased you could make it. Appreciate it.'

Jago helped me to the steps. 'Olga's part owner,' he explained. 'Busy man. When I told him you were showing, he dropped everything though. Nice that, don't you think?' He lent in and put his hands over my genitals. 'You are a lucky man,' he whispered, 'for these things which I hold here, which are very precious to you it would seem, will probably be the only things of yours that will remain the same colour this afternoon.'

'Jago,' I pleaded. He put his fingers to my lips.

'Shh,' he said. 'Don't thank me. It's nothing. You'll get your address. You'll have it before you leave. But you have to pay the going rate. This', he indicated to the dark man above, 'is your first instalment. Four rounds.' His mouth brushed my ear. 'The second is your undertaking never to see her again. Ever. You're not to talk to her, write to her, nor meet her secretly at some chromium-plated spermatic hotel for afternoon tea and muffins. It might be an idea to throw your television into the Thames, just in case word comes to me that you switched on *the wrong channel by mistake*. Now go up there and do your best. He's under the impression you don't like niggers. You'll find your legs will go first.'

I groaned. Jago patted me sympathetically on the shoulders. 'This is nothing. If I had been my old man, you'd be driving home with your fucking head rolling about on the back seat.' He looked me up and down. 'Gordon!' he called out. 'Gordon! He hasn't got any fucking boots on. Get him something for his feet for Christ's sake. Annie, you be ready to sluice him down. I'll do the bell. Muttonleg?' The man in the ring looked down. 'Have you got that shield nice and warm now?' The man stopped skipping, raised a hand and spat with difficulty into the cupped glove. Something white flew through the air. Jago caught it. 'Open up,' he told me, and pushed it in my mouth. It was wet and slippery and bit into my gums. 'There,' he snarled. 'That's the last fucking favour I'm doing you. All right Gordon, let's get on with it.'

*

OUT ON THE DECK there is nothing, only heaven and the pounding sea. Below men are shouting at you, laughing, offering playful advice, but you cannot hear what they say. There are times now when you sit alone, when you feel the water squeezed on your brow, when words of encouragement, words of sympathy, words of hope are whispered into your ear. Ah sweet is the water, trickling down your back and soothing too the hands which knead your shoulders, pummel your legs, and cup your breasts, breasts you have possessed for years but never knew, how unhappy you are to have such breasts, they are heavy and sore, how uncomfortable and *unlike* you they are, they hang like bags of wet sugar on your frame, is this what it is like to have breasts? they make you agitated and unsettled, make you feel what you are not, you wish you could get rid of them, they should not exist. They have told you to sing, a tune, a whistle, a snatch of something, it will help you for you must hold on to what you can, the ropes, the railings or you will fall overboard. Soon the bell will call you from your resting place, and you will step forward and face the Moorish captain again who sits opposite, smiling. He has a red costume, his boots are laced and he looks like a pirate. He dares you to walk the deck with him, but for the moment all is quiet, you could so easily go to sleep, lay your head on mother's lap, and ask her to unbutton herself, *Ah meinem Herzen, an meiner Brust, du meiner Wonne, du meine Lust,* here spit into that she says and you look dully into this bucket of water, shaking your head, she grasps the back of your neck and pushes you down, you gulp and gasp, you are lifted up again and shoved under again. Two bells sound and you are pitched forward, the deck is tilting, your legs are unprepared, you are not a sailor, not even a stowaway, only a boy, a lonely boy without a home, thrown from his mother's arms, tossed in the air, you lift your hands but these are not your hands, these are huge and useless, you hold them before you swollen and heavy, you lift them up and they are knocked aside, if only there were someone here, someone to help you, Fat Patrick perhaps, can't he stop this, Not me, says Fat Patrick, pushing his glasses back on his nose, You were my only friend, you stood around me with such a crowd as this to wound and hurt me, *help you*? Monica then, perhaps Monica can, Not me says Monica, pulling on her little white socks, Not me, you have used and humiliated me, *help you*? Not me says the boy perched high on the lamp-post, not Jack Grey, not Henry Deering, not Poker Fisher, we are children, we have our own future to think of, what about your *sister*? if only she were here, she would rush to your defence, she would not shun you, she would duck through the rope and haul you away, explain that it was not your fault but she is not here, just the Moorish captain, he leaps up and swipes your head, slams into the depths of your stomach. You fall to the wallowing deck. You roll around, clutching yourself, you beg and plead, all gone, all gone, but now he stands above you and though the light hurts your eyes you are surprised to find that no thunder comes. He hooks his thumbs into his costume, his stomach ripples, it is flat and dark and surprisingly smooth, you could rest your head upon it as Stella rested hers, hear the muscle work his breath as she must have heard his, he starts counting, they all start counting, these ruffians, these jolly salt tars, *one, two, three, four*, you look up, surely the time for thunder is here, but they laugh and shake their heads, *six, seven, eight, nine*, and still there is nothing, only the wet deck and the sluice of water, the Moorish captain standing, no wonder it is all wrong, he has been stripped of his uniform and he has no fingers to count with, only those hands with bloated thumbs which he holds above his head, pull the shield out he orders, and a man with fat fingers lifts you to your knees and grapples with your gums. Open wide he says and your jaw hangs slack, your lips are bleeding, your mouth is suddenly full and you cannot breathe. Fill her up the men cried, Fill her up! To the very brim!

*

THEY THREW MY CLOTHES in the back and me in the front and stood on the pavement to wave me off while I bent over the steering-wheel squinting at the address taped to the inside of the windscreen. Apart from a slight swelling around the left eye, Muttonleg had left my face alone, but by the time I got home I could barely move. I ran a hot bath and I lowered myself in with a large whisky by my side. Later I rang Mrs Delguardo downstairs and told her I was down with influenza and would she mind looking after Clare for the night. Good woman that she was, she told me she'd send the Woman from Spain up to see if I was OK but I told her not to bother, that a couple of aspirins and a good night's sleep was all that I needed. Just take care of Clare I said, I'll rest easy if you can do that. When I woke again the light coming in through the window was from an afternoon sun and when I managed to focus my eyes I could see from the date on my bedside clock that I had slept for nearly a whole day.

Someone must have come up to my room because my clothes were neatly folded, Monica-style, on the back of an armchair and the bottle of whisky that I had taken to the bed, stood on the small table by its side. I felt like I had been put through a mangle, every part of me was squeezed flat, drained of energy, lifeless. I hung limp and heavy and as dead as any corpse. I stood up and went to the mirror. Overnight a colony of colours had sprung up, great bursting blooms of bruises and blood and battered skin crowding in on one another, a blossoming blue on my breasts and a blotchy rotten yellow about my stomach, and from my kidneys a ghostly touch of green seemed to be working its way through. I could not recall him hitting my legs but they too suffered from this blight and were mottled with patches of an unnaturally vivid red. I tried to raise my arms but I could lift my elbows no higher than my chest and when I let them fall they banged into my sides as if they could fall off at any moment. I turned in the mirror to see what else they had accomplished, and as I did so I heard a sharp intake of breath.

The Woman from Spain stood in the doorway, her hand over her mouth. She came up to me and held my arms out, and looked at me, trying to ask the questions she could not form in English with her eyes. I shrugged off my appearance as best I could but she shook her head and quickly left the room. I heard her run downstairs. When she came back she was carrying a towel and a small plastic bottle and she led me back to the bed and bid me lie down again. She worked on my back first, her thick blunt fingers working their way up from the base of my spine. She had good fingers the Woman from Spain, fingers with instinct, despite their rough hew, and as she ploughed her way across my fatty rolls I must have drifted off, for I could have sworn I heard the piano start up, one of those infernal tunes my father used to play, 'It Cannot Be', yes that was the title, *Ich kann's nicht fassen, nicht glauben, es hat ein Traummich berucht, wie hatt' er doch unter Allen, mich Arme erhoht und begluckt? Mir war's, er habe gesprochen: 'ich bin auf, ewig dein!' mir war's ich traume nich immer, es kann ja nimmer so sein*, but when I awoke and looked back, half expecting to hear those ghostly notes drifting up the stairs, it was only the Woman from Spain rocking on her haunches, singing me childish melodies that I had been playing to Clare. There, she said, there, there, and she turned me over tenderly, as though I were a partly cooked confection that could well break in two. Bad men, she said and shook her head. Bad men, she repeated, adding, All gone, and for a moment I thought that maybe Jago and his friends had brought me back themselves, but then I remembered the drive back, and how I had clutched on to the steering-wheel while I heaved what little was left inside me out on to the dashboard and my lap. My car, my beautiful silent, metal blue car, all covered with blood and vomit. Christ! I tried to sit up but the Woman from Spain shook her head and pressed me back and, looking behind her, leant forward and gave me a conspiratorial smile. I shook my head, now was not the time but although I did not ask for it, the Woman from Spain reached up and pulled off her dress. She was big and brown and she took me in her arms, your young Spanish arms which smelt of sweat and floor polish and massage oil and she cradled my head while she sang those precious songs. That is how mothers calm their children, show them love and security and that is what she was doing for me. But she knew me did the Woman from Spain, and after a while it became obvious that there was another way to make me feel better. It was not that she wanted to, or indeed that

I wanted to, rather that this is how it was done here, upstairs. Under the circumstances I was surprised I had the ability to respond at all, but the Woman from Spain was simplicity itself. She put her fingers to my lips. Quiet! she said, and it was true. I could not hear another sound. I knew what I was doing, but lying there so weak, so battered, in such disorganized pain I felt as if there was nothing there that belonged to me. It was a strange, awkward occasion, and as we progressed a bastardized version of the R & B hit 'Ain't got no home', one of Clare's current favourites tumbled into my head. Almost at once I heard the voice of Mrs Delguardo calling her, and not only calling her, but talking to Clare, telling her to wait downstairs. Panic makes you forget many things, and for an instant, as I pushed the Woman from Spain off and dragged her shaking across the room into the cupboard, stuffing her clothes under the duvet before appearing at the door fumbling with my dressing-gown, I forgot my aches and pains altogether. You're up I see, said Mrs Delguardo, Are you all right? and Clare rushed past me and began to jump on the bed. Mrs Delguardo stood in the doorway looking in. Everything is all right, she said, Clare had a good night, slept with my niece. Where is she by the way, have you seen her this morning? She was downstairs a few moments ago and now she's simply vanished into thin air. Hiding probably. Hiding? I said. Surely not. Perhaps she's gone out shopping. Oh, no, said Mrs Delguardo, I don't let her go out alone. You never know who's out there these days. Mrs Delguardo, I admonished, Your niece is a grown woman. Surely she can go out on her own? How else do you think she's going to learn the language? She won't learn anything if you keep her locked up all the time. Mrs Delguardo looked at me. Don't be silly, she told me. How could I let her out on her own? Why it would be safer to let *Clare* out on her own. Safer? I said. But Clare's only a child. Yes, said Mrs Delguardo, but a bright one. While my niece, poor thing . . . She shrugged her shoulders. Some days I am fooled. Some days I think that the doctors are wrong, that she will change. Some days I take her to the shops to buy her some clothes and I look at her and think, she is a good looking young woman, surely there is nothing wrong with her, of course she will have boyfriends, of course she will marry and have children, and then she stamps her foot, or sulks, or wants an ice-cream and I realize, no this cannot be. In years she may be an adult, but in her mind she will always be a child. I worry what will happen to her when I am gone, for I do not think the rest of the family will look after her. Now you, you must get some more rest. You look terrible. Clare can stay with us another day. Clare loves to stay with us. She is teaching us funny English songs.

Mrs Delguardo took Clare back downstairs. I pulled the Woman from Spain from the cupboard and got her dressed. I sat her down on the bed and handed her her bra. I watched her pull her pants on and handed her her dress. I stood her up and brushed her hair with my fingers. I knelt down and tied the laces on her shoes. My hands were shaking so much I could barely tie the knots. When she too had gone I went back to the whisky bottle and sat in the armchair and watched the light fade. When it was empty I walked down the stairs and found Mrs Delguardo in the kitchen. Mrs Delguardo I said, I am going to bake some biscuits this evening for Clare and I wondered whether I might borrow a few things. Certainly Mr Doughty she said. What will you be wanting? Some greaseproof paper and a rolling pin I said, and she said certainly again and fetched them out of her larder. Back upstairs I took off my trousers and underpants and walked into the kitchen. It was not cold. I took the bread board from out of the drawer and laid one of the layers of greaseproof paper on its uneven surface. Then I laid the thing that was mine but which should not be mine on the top of it covering it with another layer of the greaseproof paper. I smoothed the paper down over the thing that was mine but which should not be mine. I could see it quite clearly. It didn't look as if it could do any harm. It looked small and like me, not a little scared. I don't know why I put the thing which was mine but which should not be mine between two sheets of greaseproof paper but I did. Perhaps I had seen something similar on a cookery programme or was conscious of the need to be clean and tidy. Perhaps I had been brought up properly after all. I took hold of the rolling pin and started to sing that song again, appropriating the words of Mr Clarence Frogman Henry who was born in New Orleans on the nineteenth of March 1937 and who could sing like a girl and sing like a frog and who had a hit with this tune in 1956. This is how it goes. As a matter of fact this isn't *quite* how it goes but this is how it went then. *I ain't got a mother, I ain't got a father, I ain't got a sister, not even a brother, I'm a lonely boy, I ain't got a home.* I raised the rolling pin high and brought it down hard, down on the bread board, down on the greaseproof paper, down on the thing that was mine but which should not be mine, which had no right to be mine, which meant nothing to me. Oo-oo-oo-oo-oo-oo-oo-oo-oo! Oo-oo-oo-oo-oo-oo-oo-oo-oo-oo! Oo-oo-oo-oo-oo-oo-oo-oo-oo-oo! Oo-oo-oo-oo-oo-oo-oo-oo-oo! *I'm a lonely boy! I ain't got no home!*

*

Mrs Delguardo drove me to Casualty. Try as I might it was impossible for me to keep the screaming in, and after she had turned her television off for the night she heard me rolling about on the floor, biting the bed covers in an attempt to stave off the pain. God knows I hadn't meant to cause myself that much harm. I just wanted rid of the thing. By the time she banged the car against the hospital car park wall, the only way, she later explained, she could stop it from going forward, with me curled up, howling in the back, blood leaking out of me on to the seat like water from a rusty garden tap, my car's near perfect body work was as bruised and battered as its owner. It could only have been a twenty-minute drive, but when Eric came to pick me up three days later I hobbled down to find that added to the minor dent from the storm, there was now a long deep gash running the length of the passenger's side, both wing-mirrors had gone, and the rear bumper was sufficiently dented to prevent the boot shutting properly. In the heat of the moment, it appeared that Mrs Delguardo forgot that she couldn't drive, which is why she left it there, rammed up between two industrial dustbins, rather than drive it home.

'What in God's name has happened here,' Eric cried. 'We can't drive back in this. It stinks to high heaven. She could at least have left the windows open. Or got someone to come and clean it out for you.'

'Mrs Delguardo will do no more cleaning for me,' I said, 'nor any of her relations. Under the circumstances I think she did rather well.'

My car is a dodgem now, burnished with the clashes of the age. Once it was silent, with nothing in it but an empty presence. Once my car was like the hotel room, spacious and clean and without any trace of me at all. It was like me, and so, in a curious way, is it now. What must we both look like, both limping along. I have become a different driver now. I do not care if I scrape the side or let my cigarette drop to the floor. I do not care if there is mud and gravel on the carpet or whether the seats bear the marks of scufflings from small shoes. There are, I am sorry to say, still traces of blood and vomit to be found, and it is these, rather than anything else which I am preparing to erase. I open all the doors, so that the car stands in the road ludicrously wide, inviting them to be torn off by a passing milk float, and if I were alone I might be tempted to drive off with all four doors flapping, to break them off on lampposts and oncoming lorries, leaving pieces of my car scattered across the countryside, *leaving me exposed*. I open all the doors and return to the empty hall, bereft even of the Woman from Spain's dread bicycle, from which all our trouble stemmed, gone with Mrs Delguardo and her niece, gone God knows where. I had to tell her, once I had returned from the hospital, once the tubes had been taken out of me, once I could piss properly again without leaning up against the wall, weeping into my folded arm. I had to tell her what I had done, and why I had done such a thing to myself. Making biscuits in the nude indeed! Mr Doughty she had said, You don't beat biscuits you know, but even though she didn't believe the reason for my little accident, she had kept her mouth shut when talking to the doctors, good woman that she is. They were under the impression, thanks to Eric's regular visits that it was all the work of a jealous boyfriend, or that I was part of some frenzied homosexual ring, something that Eric's unflagging interest in my penis only heightened. 'And how is it today nurse?' he would ask, sauntering in with his wide brimmed hat in his hand. 'Swelling *going up* I hope?'

'Tell me,' Eric asked, sitting down on the edge of the bed, lifting up the covers every now and again to annoy me, why *did* you do it? Rather a drastic way of becoming celibate, n'est-ce pas?'

I outlined the grim details, of both Jago and the Woman from Spain, to him first, and then confessed a shorter and probably less convincing version to Mrs Delguardo the day I came out. They did not keep me in long, but what an age it was. How thoughtless I had been. Perhaps Carol was right. Clare was so worried, so frightened when she saw me in a bed like her mother's, surrounded by sick, unfriendly men like her father. She was trembling when Mrs Delguardo brought her. I will be out soon, I told her, it is just a minor thing, and the Woman from Spain was there too holding Mrs Delguardo's hand, her head cocked to one side. It was so obvious to me seeing her there, but I could not tell Mrs Delguardo then, nor could I look the Woman from Spain in the eye. It would have been good for Clare, and easier too if they had stayed, for Clare has an affection for both of them but under the circumstances I expected no less. I was only glad that the Woman from Spain would never have to see me again. But to desert Clare at such a time. To damage myself and desert her! How could I? What sentiment, you will say, What self seeking, self pitying sentiment, and yes it is true, I do feel sorry for myself, but it is sentiment that brings tears to my eyes, not pity. I am coming to realize there is nothing wrong in being sentimental.

So the hall is empty of their belongings, their bicycles and their boots and their raincoats, and all that remains in the downstairs flat is the stark furniture that was there when they arrived. Even the beaded curtain that divided the kitchen from the dining room has gone and I stand in the doorway, looking at the empty table I rode around that drunken evening. But the memory is as bare as the cupboard. I have told Clare that we are going down to the coast this weekend, down to see our friend Patrick, and in truth we are, but we are also doing something else. We are tracking down Stella, for I know now where she is and who she is with. My sister told me, sitting up in bed shouting out those spare-room words. I would prefer not to take Clare really, for I cannot say what the outcome will be, but who could I leave her with? She does not know Eric and Michael and of course Julia is out of the question. So Clare and I are on holiday. It is all right. She will come to no harm. I can leave her with Patrick while Dickey and I drive across to do what we must. Dickey has agreed to come and we are to pick him up this afternoon outside the hotel. I have told Monica that I am taking Clare down to see Patrick and that we will spend a couple of days down by the sea. While we are away Monica will stay in Carol's house (with Johnny Oates she intimated, would that be all right?), so she can visit Carol, who since that night has not spoken another word.

Mrs Briggs's Bag is packed with all the things we need. Carol was right to keep it. It is a marvellous bag, seemingly limitless in its ability to envelop. Clare has two warm dresses, four shirts, three tops, six pairs of trousers and an armful of socks and knickers and woollen tights. Her shoes and wellington boots lie scattered in the boot. I have packed books and crayons and two or three games. Her favourite tapes are stacked in the rack.

When the car is washed, I change into a clean pressed pair of jeans, a clean loose shirt and a thick woollen jumper which I have never used – a present from my wife. It fits perfectly. It is warm and comfortable and looks good and I wonder why I have never worn it before. I pack a torch, a length of rope, a tape recorder, and about four hundred pounds in cash. I have no idea if I will need the money, but I will leave it in safe keeping with Patrick, while I go in search of Stella with Dickey by my side.

I pick Clare up from school. We have over a week now, the weekend and her half term. We might stay down there all the time, for Patrick is due to go on Monday or Tuesday he says (as if he doesn't know when his cruise starts!). I have been thinking that come summer, Clare and I could spend a couple of weeks down there. Could we bring a television this time? she asks, I don't want to miss it, Miss what? I say, my heart sinking, What do you think? she answers, 'Planetrain' and I reply, No, I would not want to miss it either. I tell her not to worry, there is always the video and it is true, there will always be the video. Without Clare prompting me, I have set the video to switch itself on, on Saturday, between the hours of nine thirty a.m. and eleven thirty a.m., and again on Monday and Wednesday mornings from ten to ten thirty. And should these fail, should I have programmed in error, and should some football match or the morning service or some wretched snooker championship lurch on to the screen, we will always have others to watch. I have thrown none of them away. I cannot. Last week, holed up in my bed, hardly daring to drink for the agony it would cause me, I videoed her three shows, watched them time and time again, the shine in her eye, her smile, her breathless laugh. I looked closely to see if I could detect any difference, any trace of sadness, or loss, or guilt, any *emptiness* there. I sat up in bed and went through the programmes sequence by sequence. I pressed the play button and saw her burst into life, looking as she always looks. I pressed the slow motion button and watched her body turn. I pressed the freeze control and studied her laughing face. I ran through them time and time again but there was nothing. I sat back as she tumbled and writhed and came up smiling and I thought only a few days ago, with only a few changes in the weather, and all has passed. Three months ago I would have played them in trembling anticipation. Now they are as my father's postcards, messages from the dead. They are empty, as empty as that moving platform, bathed in a hollow light. I am nothing to her now and every time I sit with Clare, my arm curled round her and watch the television, every time Clare selects a 'Planetrain' tape and stuffs it into the machine I see how much I am nothing to her. How did it get like this? Why could it not have been proper? Why couldn't I have *told* her how I felt, asked her to *choose*? Was the sight of Camber Sands so fatal?

Michael Mulligan suggested to me a horrid thought, on his only visit and one which I cannot believe to be true.

'I will not forgive that sister of mine for this,' he said.

'For this?' I replied. 'Fleur had nothing to do with this.'

'Not directly,' Michael said. 'But thanks to Jago you were already in a certain frame of mind. I mean do you really think that Jago saw that little film by *accident*?'

'But, that doesn't make any sense. Why would she do that?'

'Because Jago is dangerous,' Michael explained. 'And when he's dangerous, he's exciting. I saw them last night. They're having a marvellous time. Do you think they'd mind if I took some of those old magazines away with me?'

So I am withered and cast aside. I was hopelessly in love and never thought to be. I never wanted it like this, never wanted to ache so, to feel so empty and so unloved. No unloved is not the word. There is someone who loves me, who is beginning perhaps to love me and she sits behind me watching me in the mirror, watching me drive, watching me take her away on a holiday.

Perhaps it is wrong of me to take her away like this, perhaps we should go somewhere else but I have no choice. Not since my sister sat up and spoke those spare-room words. Clare is eager to be off and finds the traffic through London a great bore. She kicks the back of my seat in frustration and asks me When will we be there? She leans forward and hands me a tape. She wants to sit in the front, to sit up with me, but I tell her No she can't, She is not allowed. It is against the law (it is not) and besides, that seat is already occupied. He is small like she is and can barely see out of the windscreen.

'I am glad you could make it,' I say, 'for this may be our last trip together.'

He looks at me.

'Something has come into my view,' I say, 'something which we both should have known, had we looked a little harder. Had we thought it all through. Had we told Sergeant Weatherspoon all we should have told. We would not have been caught, for there was nothing really to catch. I have been so wrong. I am glad you have come I told him, for I know what happened to Stella Muchmore and where she is.'

The boy leans forward and grips the dashboard.

'You have been wrong before,' he says.

I look in the mirror. Clare has fallen asleep.

'Do not smirk about this,' I tell him. 'True, I have been wrong before, but now I am right. Our sister told me.'

'Our sister? I thought she . . .'

'She spoke some words the other day. Not many but enough. For a moment I did not understand why she should say those words, perhaps she was simply living in the past, playing in the spare room, bouncing on the bed, *looking out the window*, but looking into her eyes, I saw that she was telling me something important, something she had been saving her strength for, hanging in the very bottom of her life to swim up and gasp out. Quite suddenly I knew. She had seen Stella, and she had heard Stella speak those words.'

'What words?' the boy asked.

'Words you are well familiar with,' I said. 'Do not worry I will tell you. But first I want to go through everything again, to make sure I am right. When we get down there I will write a long letter and we will send it to Detective Sergeant Weatherspoon and it will explain everything. And this time it will tell all the truth.'

The boy shifts uncomfortably.

'In many ways I don't blame you. If the police had known everything about you, I think you might have confessed to something you hadn't done. First we have to clear one thing up. First we have to get to the bottom of your lying, and your evasions, for they in themselves are not so very bad. Let us go back to the climbing frame and your baby brother and the way he left you that day. You did push him off, you told him to go away, not to pester you, that you were fed up with him and he wandered off, rubbing his eyes, and you sat there, aloof, waiting for him to come back. You were annoyed when he did not, for secretly you would have liked to have played the game he wanted, to ride down on the coach to Southampton, to get your tickets clipped and to play the captain of the Flying Boat and he the steward or navigator and later you would take him down to the pillbox and sit by the slit window and get him to do what you wanted. But he did not return and when your mother came out with a towel slung over her shoulder, you were furious with him for spoiling the whole afternoon, for getting you into trouble. He was not in the allotment, nor was he sitting on the pillbox and you started back up the track in some alarm, thinking my God, *if anything has happened to him* but as you rounded the bend, you saw him sitting on the bank, as happy as Larry, throwing bloody twigs in the air, whistling that stupid helicopter noise of his as they twirled down into the water. How annoyed you were that he had not sloped off as you had thought unhappy and dejected, but was quite content idling the hours away by himself, that he cared nothing for you and those stupid childish games which you should be outgrowing anyway. Isn't that what your father had said only the other week? Isn't it about time you stopped playing those bloody stupid childish games Giles and did something useful for a change? Isn't it about time you grew up a little? in front of that overweight friend of his in the King's Arms when you came in with Fat Patrick after school swimming, fighting over some memento you had, what was it, a matchbox, a matchbox with the Imperial Airways stamp upon it that Fat Patrick's father had given the two of you. You were arguing as to who should have it, for you were going to be captain that day, and the captain should have to light the passengers' cigarettes when he walked down the length of the craft, asking everyone if they were all right, if they were enjoying the flight, and would they like to step forward into the captain's flight deck and Fat Patrick was saying No, no, that's the *steward*'s job, *He* lights the cigarettes, *I* should have it, and your father snatched it out of your hand, saying Give it here, Isn't it about time you stopped playing these bloody stupid childish games and did something useful for a change? Isn't it about time you grew up a little? and he tore open the box and rudely struck a match to his own cigarette (which is when you started to carry matches and smoke seriously yourself). And here was your baby brother, spurring you as well, getting you into all this trouble, and you decided to give him a fright, to do that thing that your father did on the rare occasions when he tried to be playful. They were always cruel, your father's games, always designed to worry or humiliate, and this creeping-up game, when he would come up behind you when you were standing on a rail, or looking out over a cliff or balancing on a parapet, and seize your shoulders and *push*, push while gripping tightly, so that it only *felt* as if you were going to fall, was a good example. How you hated that trick, every time he did it you told him how much you disliked it, and he would laugh. Your mother too disapproved. He might fall she would say, It's so *stupid*, and your father would wave her away impatiently and tell her not to be such an old woman. You didn't have to be too careful, he was quite oblivious to his surroundings your baby brother, throwing his little collection of twigs into the air, watching them fall into the swirling water below, and so, for perhaps one of the few times in your life you consciously emulated your father, played your father's hand and rushed up and grabbed him by the shoulders, to your consternation you found your hands were not big enough, that as soon as you *pushed* you discovered that you could not *hold*, and that baby brother was falling forward into the air, clinging on to nothing, scraping the sides of nothing, screaming into nothing and the long splash below. He fell head first, just like you had learnt how to dive in the school swimming pool, sitting on the edge, your arms outstretched, falling, head down, into the chlorinated water. You clutched at his coat, and grabbed it, did you grab it? if you did it soon was torn away and he landed in the water your baby brother, face first, face and then knees, curled up, a terrible dive really, all splash, his arms out, all splash and cries. There was a low branch in the water, a broad branch, a branch that you had stood on many times, stood while the water lapped at your feet. Sometimes when the river was in full flood, the water covered it completely, but here it was not so much underneath as lying on the surface. Your brother met the branch as he fell. He splashed into the water, then smacked his head hard. You heard it, it was like slapping water with your open palm. You heard it and heard a kind of burbled moan as your brother rolled over and started to twist about. You lost no time. There was no time to lose. You slithered down the bank. You jumped forward and slithered down the bank, a little too fast perhaps, a little too hasty, for when you reached the water you went straight in, not controlled but straight in, losing your balance in the process. You fell backwards. The bottom seemed to be nowhere. You fell backwards and couldn't get up. He was so near your baby brother, had you been standing you could have grabbed hold of his arm, but you could not regain your balance, and by the time you had, by the time you had flailed about in the water, struggling against the tow and the slippery mud underneath he was ten or twelve feet away and moving along quickly, turning and drifting and bobbing up and down. The river was not so very fast here but you knew you could not reach him, that you had a better chance to reach him if you got out and raced down the towpath to overtake him, he was a good little swimmer your brother not as strong as your sister, who had strong arms like her mother, but if you could not get to him quickly, meet him as he came along, it would be all right, so you turned and tried to get up out of the river, to climb the bank, but you could not. Every time you hauled yourself half out you would grasp at a clump of grass or a thin branch, but the grass would simply come away in your hand and the branch would slither out of your fingers and you would slide back. How long it took you to get out you do not know, one minute, five minutes, but somehow, by clawing and pleading and digging your hands hard into the bank you managed to haul yourself up. You chased after him hard down the path but could not see him! You ran and ran but he was nowhere in sight! He couldn't have gone this far surely? You were in a panic now. You didn't know what to do. You must have passed him. You turned and ran back, screaming for help, calling his name and screaming for help, why wasn't anyone else here and before you knew it you were back to where he had fallen in! For an incomprehensible moment you danced on the spot, looking this way and that, hoping that someone might come down the path, that a rowing boat might appear, calling for your mother, wanting above all to run back and tell her, but knowing you shouldn't that it would only waste time, cupping your hands and calling her, calling her, knowing that she most likely had gone back inside and couldn't hear you, wasting precious minutes as you stood and called, why did you do it? before charging off again. It was bad now, you knew it was bad and you ran and you ran and you ran, you ran knowing that there would be no end to your running, that no matter how hard you ran, how quickly you covered the ground, the race was lost.

So when Stella disappeared, when her raincoat with the watch and the rubber band and those other things were found down by the pillbox, next to the river, you could not tell them everything, indeed you could hardly tell them anything, for would not one curious involvement and entangled improbable tale lead to an investigation into the other. First baby brother, then Stella. Why they might even have thought that it was you who cut the Flying Boats loose. A dangerous boy altogether. And that is why you did not tell Sergeant Weatherspoon the other thing about that last night you spent with her, the other thing which now seems crystal clear to you, thanks to your sister babbling those frozen words.

'It was always possible,' says the boy, in a vain attempt to stave off the final demand, 'that they *were* connected. That somehow the Flying Boats' disappearing act was somehow linked to Stella Muchmore.'

I am ready with my reply.

'I think not. The release of the Flying Boats was probably the work of a couple of men from the old work force, disgruntled with

323

their lot. They wouldn't have sought to sink any of them, least of all the *Galway Bay*. Think of it. If she were alive now, she would be the star attraction in an aviation museum some place. She might even still be working. You could have realized your ambition. You could have walked the length of her and sat in the captain's chair. But the *Galway Bay* is gone, never to return. Gone the same way as your baby brother and the schoolboy essay. But Stella has returned. So let us go back once more, one last time to that last night, and what you never told Sergeant Weatherspoon, why you truly couldn't tell him, terrified boy that you were. If you had, all this would never have happened. This storm, this wreck, is all your fault.'

'What do you want to know?' he asks.

'It's too late to prevaricate now,' I tell him. 'You know what I want to hear. I want to get it exactly right, so that I can tell Dickey and Fat Patrick and the man in retirement. We will meet them and then we will drive to Wye station and then we are going to find Stella, for if I am not mistaken she is still under the same yoke that she was all those years ago. Nothing has changed, nothing has changed. If only you had listened to your Detective Sergeant Weatherspoon. You didn't tell him everything, did you? You did not tell him the worst thing about that night.'

The boy folds his hands in front of him. He is resigned to his fate.

'I was afraid,' he says simply.

'Of course when you look back on it now, and take yourself through the things found in Stella's raincoat, it seems perfectly obvious who put them there. It was not the box of matches or the lack of cigarettes that give it away, though the disappearance of the cigarette packet points to a smoker, but it is the watch that is the real clue. The watch. The watch she loathed. The watch she rarely wore. That is why, if you had thought about it, it could not have been Stella waiting under the chestnut trees that night, for according to Judith, the girl in the school uniform, standing around in an agitated fashion, looked at her watch *all the time*. Had it been Stella, it would have been more likely that she would have had the watch in her pocket, that if she was interested in the time, she would have taken it out and looked at it, surely something Judith

Spenser would have remarked upon. But nevertheless the watch was left in the raincoat pocket. Why? Why was the raincoat left at all? Consider this for a moment. The last time we talked, knowing that Stella was alive, we argued that she had taken part in the deception herself, that the mac was not stuffed away, hidden by an abductor, but planted by Stella and an accomplice in order to give the impression that some harm had come to her. The same interpretation of the mac's presence was also true before we knew she was alive. Abducted or absconded the mac meant only one thing. That something bad had happened, and as we have already said, as Sergeant Weatherspoon asked you, if it *was* the work of an abductor, a kidnapper, a rapist, a murderer *why leave the mac at all*. A foolish thing to leave behind a mac. Who knows what clues it might have thrown up. Pieces of hair, skin, a thread of cloth caught in a button, a spot of blood? And found too in such an obvious place. Better surely to take it away, to burn it later on, to destroy the watch, throw it in the Medway, destroy the watch and burn the mac. Now, knowing Stella is alive we assume that this was a charade in which she took an active part. She said "We will leave my mac, We will leave it by the pillbox where I spent so much time. It could mean many things. It could mean I am abducted. It could mean I am raped and dead and floating down the Medway. However, given the weather conditions, it is unlikely to mean that I left of my own accord. So we will plant it and we will plant in it something which probably should not be there, something that both my parents and my teachers know I wear. We will put my watch there, for it was a present from my father and my parents believe that I am fond of it, that I wear it all the time. I would not take it off." So the watch points to a deliberate attempt to pull the wool over our eyes. You were one of the very few, perhaps the only person who knew that Stella did *not* like her watch, that she would take it off whenever she could and stuff it in her pocket. But why would you be asked? The police would ask her parents about the watch, they would bring them the watch and ask Does this belong to your daughter? and they would reply, Yes it does, She wore it every day, and there would be a terrible silence as the ghastly inference was made, that somewhere along the line she had been made to take it off, *to strip*. Her parents' testimony would be enough to strengthen the police's darkest fears. Absconding girls don't leave their raincoats and watches behind. Raincoats protect them from the cold. Watches, at the very least, can be pawned. But unusually, because you were such a strange, composed and silent boy, the police did ask you, and you told them nothing. You did not elaborate. You did not tell them Stella's feelings. And if you had, if you had leant over and gathered the watch in your hand, toyed with it and told Sergeant Weatherspoon of Stella's deep antipathy towards it, he might have pondered for a moment on the watch, which according to her parents was Stella's *beloved* watch, and according to you was her *despised* watch and perhaps then, with her watch leading a double life, a life in the pocket and a life on the wrist, Sergeant Weatherspoon might have supposed that there was an interesting discrepancy here, just as there was an interesting discrepancy in the finding of the mac itself, and with her little wristwatch ticking away, niggling in the back of his mind he might have doubled up his two premises, that the mac meant abduction, but also the mac could have been left deliberately, and that what was in it, was meant to tell him *the wrong thing*. She wasn't murdered, as we assumed, but *neither did she disappear of her own free will*. She was captured and held prisoner, and the mac is the clue. The mac was hidden by an abductor but hidden deliberately, knowing that the police would find it, knowing that the inference would be that she had been taken by force (all of which was true), but implying, that she most likely was dead. And what was in it? A rubber band which she wore around her hair, a match box which we have come to assume was left by a second party because a) he didn't need it or b) he thought it was empty, a beer bottle top which she could have picked up in the pillbox (unlikely) and a watch which according to her parents gave the mac a bad name, and which according to you did nothing of the sort. So consider this. That the watch was planted, planted by someone who wanted to indicate that Stella had come to some harm, by someone who believed it to be one of her most precious possessions. And why should he not think this, this smoker of Guard's cigarettes and drinker of bottled beer, this man of keys and locks and bolts on the door, *this keeper of time*. He has seen her wearing it every day. He even gave it to her.

'He was home that day remember? He rang in to say that he had a sore throat and wouldn't be coming in to work. October, a lot of flu about. Perhaps he did have a cold, but he also had other plans in mind. He had been dreaming them up all night. Something had to be done. It couldn't go on any longer. *Not after what he had seen the night before.*

'There was more truth to your essay than you care to remember. It wasn't just the running naked, there was something else that you had done that night, something that you had done and someone else knew you had done. Something which you never admitted, and why you were so thankful that no one else had admitted. You had met as agreed by the chestnut trees. It was getting cold and you knew that this would be one of the last nights for some time when you would be able to take your time. You had had a wonderful summer with Stella but tonight had been strange, walking hand in hand down the length of Gladstone Drive smoking one of the last of her father's cigarettes. It was almost a final act. You had reached, quite literally, the end of the road, and a new phase of your two lives was about to begin. By the time you reached Stella's drive and stubbed out the cigarette you both realized that you were absolutely freezing and you quickly took out your clothes from Mrs Briggs's Bag. You pulled on a thick jersey and a pair of trousers, Stella a flannel shirt and some jeans. Despite the fact that it was late and getting colder by the minute, neither of you wanted to leave. There was something else in the air now, something that you had first felt shaking with fright in the unknown car. You lingered by the gate, and upon Stella's sudden suggestion agreed to go into her greenhouse at the bottom of their garden to smoke the very last cigarette. She said she would buy some more tomorrow and replace them, though unless he was entertaining (Entertaining! That made you laugh) he only used the cigarette box when he ran out himself, which was a rarity. The greenhouse was warm and sweet and you leant back amongst the flowerpots and seed boxes breathing a languorous and seductive breath. You felt close to Stella here, closer than at any other time and you pulled her towards you. Stella, you said and bit into her neck. She held you apart and looked questioningly. Mind the geraniums, she said. For Christ's sake don't knock any plants over. He'd have a fit. She brought her hands to your face and kissed you. It is good in here though isn't it. Pity we didn't come any sooner.

'A sudden stream of air flooded over you. You looked up. There in the doorway stood Mr Muchmore wrapped in a thick grey overcoat, carrying a flashlight in his red, swollen hands. Although the path to the greenhouse was clear there were leaves on his shoes, as if he had been waiting for you, hiding beneath a tree, sheltering under the eaves of the garage. He shone the light on to you and your bodies glowed for a moment full and confident, and then as the beam of light travelled quickly up and down you fell apart and grew cold again. He came within five feet of you and sprang forward, hitting her hard on the side of her head. She swayed, gasping at the blow, knocking plants askew as she staggered back. He lunged again, an open hand on to her hair, he grabbed her and pulled her head down, tucking it under his arm as you stepped back from the circle of light. What huge fantastic shadows were playing now! How larger than life they were! Larger than your life. You were hardly there. You stood back, waiting in the wings. You could see her arms around the back of his thighs, her left ear revealed as he held her head in a tight bun. You could see her breasts hanging down out of her shirt, see his face all crimson and hot. With his free hand he snatched a bamboo cane out of its pot and shaking the earth free he dragged her shirt up over her head and began to beat her bare back with slow, regular strokes. You could see how his mouth worked, like a juggler in the ring, concentrating hard, mouthing words of self-encouragement, see how her throat swallowed, how the veins moved in her neck. You could hear the cane fall, catch the drop of her breath. You stood in the dark with your heart gulping, your hands by your side, a true spectator. The blows came quickly now. They landed on her neck and shoulders, they landed on her kidneys and on the base of her spine, they fell on the length of her back. And all the while he sang into her ear. Is this what you like my little gutter girl. We'll have it like this then. Every day if you like.

'A wetness came to his lips. He began to shout, formless things bred in your father's car and in the brown leather armchairs of the

King's Arms. But his desire was stronger than his ability, and his arm grew quickly tired. Stella tried to twist out of his grasp and as she did so, the flashlight moving wildly in his hand, you were caught up in the dance. Her legs caught against yours and the light fell upon you and you found yourself standing in the ring. That's it, he said, Come closer. Have a good look. Is this what you want? Is this what you want? You turned your head away. He reached out and pulled you nearer. How your shadow loomed with the rest of them! You were part of this now. His breath was on your breath, his lips were near your lips. There was just the two of you and a bundle under his arms.

'"Giles? It is Giles isn't it? Good. Here you are then Giles, you and me, you with your shirt undone and she with her shirt undone and me all buttoned up in my overcoat. This wasn't what you wanted at all. You wanted to feel her didn't you? You wanted to look at her didn't you? But not like this. Well, this is how you should look at them Giles, this is how you ought to learn to look at them. Those eyes of hers for instance. What do you think they are saying? What do you think they were saying when she waved goodbye to her mother this morning? What do you think they were saying when she put her hand up in class? And what do you think they were saying when she reached round and unclasped that little hook for your benefit? Is this what it's all for Giles? to become naked, to undress in the dark, in a glass house full of mildew, and mew in a stank wet hole? Is this what your mother and father have trained you to do, to come around and put your hands on such a girl, who would lead you in the dark and settle down like some beast on a bale of straw? Is this what fathers do when they bring daughters into the world, to raise them so that they might stay out all night and take their blouses off as soon as their fathers' backs are turned? Is this what you will strive for in later life? Will you marry this one and see it reproduce? Will you have a little daughter and will you raise her and clothe her and feed her and then come home one night and see her all grown up, lying on the carpet with her tongue hanging out?"

'He stopped to catch his breath. He was wheezing and panting. He looked at you.

'"I'm going to do you one very good favour Giles, a very great favour indeed. I am going to hand you this cane and watch you raise your hand and strike back at the wrong you have done. I am going to make you understand that you are as shamed by her as I am. For what is she? Nothing. Worthless. Unshaped. You must repudiate her Giles. Take this and strike her out of your life, beat her down so that she might never raise herself up again. Strike her for my sake and for your father's sake, strike her for all our sakes, but above all, strike her for *your* sake. Let the night ring with it, let the glass in this greenhouse shake loose in its frame, let the roof tremble and crack, and let her mother, tucked up safely in her white nightgown, see her sweetest dreams curdle. And if you don't strike her for any of these reasons, then think on this. If the length of this cane does not find its mark, if her back does not flinch, if I do not see her eyes start to roll or her breath cry out, if you hold back on me, if you do not put your spleen and your spirit into this blow, then this hand of mine, which now holds out this bamboo will tomorrow morning pick up such phones to call such fathers and will unscrew such pens to write to such headmasters as to see an end to you all. I will destroy you Giles, destroy your prospects, crush your hopes and send you out of this town a leper. You will not be wanted here, like the rest of your family. You will be like your father, a pariah, an outcast, a man who looks out upon the water and sees nothing but a cold and unremitting solitude. And your mother will look upon you in your isolation and wish that it had been you rather than your baby brother. You tried to save him I am told, tried to save his life. Well, save your life now Giles. Save yours as he lost his."

'You hung your head. You told him you could not do it.

'I don't care if you can't do it, he said. Just do it anyway. Would you rather touch her again? You said no, but you could not look up. What do you want to do then? he asked and you replied that above all you wanted to go home. And never speak to her again? he suggested. And never speak to her again, you replied. And never talk of this or utter this to anyone, to lock it away, to lock it and bury it so deep that it will not surface for a thousand years, and you said Yes to lock it away, bury it deep so that it would not surface for a thousand years.

'So then, said Mr Muchmore pushing Stella forward, there is

just this one more thing to do, to seal this pact, to make sure that I can trust you, so that I know that you mean what you say, and while he waited you thought that if you stood there, if you could hold that moment tight, then it would be yours. You could pick this moment up and take it out of this place and bury it, like he said. It would be as if it had never happened. You could bury it alongside that other thing that had never happened. They could keep each other company, and you wondered how many other things would occur in your life that had never happened. There was nothing in the world really. You could feel yourself coming to an entrance, a sort of gate, something you could walk through unscathed. You had stood too long, not coldly exactly, but as a statue forged and immobile in the kingdom of air. If you held your ground and gave nothing, if you only protected yourself, sought no solace, no friendship, returned to the mirror and looked upon your silent and lying face then you would survive. Tell no one, tell nothing, keep silent, not only about this, but about *everything*. Your place was not here, not now, nor was it in your room where at least you could collect your thoughts. Only in the air were you safe, only in the kingdom of air. Five minutes ago you could have stopped Mr Muchmore's hand, sprung to Stella's defence, stood your ground and taken the consequences. All that had gone. All that remained was your passage from this place. For now you were roped to this man and he could hurl you off, send you spinning down, but soon you would have climbed this height, you would be raised up, high above him. Mr Muchmore and Stella were not there any more. The tree groaning outside had greater life, the wind that was blowing through the door a greater soul. Outside was where you wanted to be, outside, safe. You had not been caught. She had. You drew your breath, raised the bamboo in the air and brought it down. That was not correct, Mr Muchmore said, That was not a blow of repudiation. That was a caress. You raised your arm again, and brought it down once more. That is not correct either, Mr Muchmore said, for you closed your eyes and that is not the way to be counted. Stand up and do the job properly. You stood up and opened your eyes. It was green in there, with green leaves rustling in the swinging light. Stella was quite still. In the reflection of the glass you could see her face looking straight ahead. Her eyes shone out.

'That was the end to it. You never saw her again. The next day, after a full day's school Stella vanished, and though the rivers were dragged and the nettles along the footpath cut down you knew what had happened, you thought that you had driven her away. Like your baby brother before her, you had pushed Stella in and she had gone, gone where, down to the river perhaps, to step into the water, to drown herself. Gone to London to escape her parents, to run away from her only friend. And when you were told that her mac was found, you thought then, perhaps it hadn't been you, perhaps something else *had* happened to her, something bad, and later, when Judith Spenser came forward, you thought that Yes, Mr Muchmore had been right, she was a dirty deceitful girl who had been meeting others on the sly. But whichever it was, how close you were, how dangerously close you were to it all! You were terrified at what people might say, about what Mr Muchmore could say. You saw him of course a number of times, usually in the company of your father or his pale and trembling wife, when he would take almost no notice of you, and it was only when you were walking back from school a week later, when you met him coming out of his drive that he told you that although he had been appalled by what he had seen that night, as he did not believe that you had anything to do with her disappearance, he was not going to mention it to the police. It would serve no purpose, he said, somewhat reluctantly, to blight *two* lives. You could have kissed him you were so relieved. You wouldn't get into trouble after all. You were safe. Safe from Stella and the other thing. And you had to keep it that way, for you felt sure that if they ever knew what you two had got up to, the police would grab hold of you and throw you in the water and watch you flounder and turn and twist in despair, and that when at last they decided to haul you out and laid you gasping on the side, there would not just be Stella Muchmore wound round your ankles, but around you both would be the tender arms of your dear, dead, baby brother. Stella had gone and whether by hook or by crook it was nothing to do with you.'

'I don't understand,' says the boy. 'You're saying that *her father* . . .' He stops. He is lost for words.

'I am saying,' I tell him, 'that I now believe that the reason why the police never found Stella was that she never really went missing. I think she was at home all the time. I think her father did it. She didn't want to go back that night not because of what had happened the night before. She probably would have taken off altogether had she known what was in store for her. I think her father spent all day preparing for her return and when she came home, around six, he led her somewhere, perhaps down to the cellar, perhaps up to the loft, who knows? put her in a coal hole, a dark and hidden room, drugged her first probably, and kept her in that state while the heat was on. And there she stayed.'

'But not for ever,' the boy protests. 'You can't keep people in cellars for ever.'

'Why not? As long as there are no prying eyes you can do whatever you like. And who is going to suspect him, her father, of doing such an outrageous thing? He reported her missing. He rang up in high agitation. He had the neighbours out touring the streets until midnight. He helped cut down the nettles by the allotments. It is not surprising any way girls running off. They do it all the time. Family quarrel, bust up with the boyfriend. And then the mac was found. With the watch she loved so much, the watch her father identified. That's her watch he would say. Yes that's hers. She wore it all the time. I gave it to her. Don't tell her mother you have found the watch. It would only upset her. Who is going to look for Stella Muchmore now? She is dead. A body is all they can hope for.'

'So all the while afterwards, while we still went to school and went on holidays, while we had Christmas and Easter, while spring came and then that long summer, when we all took our exams in our shirtsleeves, Stella was locked up there, *all the time*?'

'Very likely, yes. Though maybe he transferred her somewhere else later on. Somewhere safer. Somewhere quieter.'

The boy leans forward. He has an objection to make.

'But her mother? What about Mrs Muchmore, wouldn't she . . .' He stops, remembering.

'That's right. She's dead. Like her daughter really. The only difference being that in the case of Mrs Muchmore there's a body for Dr Morgan to examine. She hung herself. In the garage.

Perhaps she didn't know at first, perhaps he managed to keep it from her. Perhaps she knew and went along with it, poor cowed woman that she was. Perhaps she couldn't take it and killed herself. Or perhaps in the end she tried to stop him, and he half strangled her, or filled her full of pills like he did Stella, strangled or drugged her and dragged her across to the garage and lifted her up on the rope he had prepared. And who watched her being cut down, took her down and had a good look? That old fart Dr Morgan that's who. She's hung herself. He can tell by the rope marks on her neck. What a ghastly business. We don't want to put you through any more than we have to Mr Muchmore but . . . Yes I understand. Yes, she had been taking sleeping tablets. And anti-depressants. Dr Morgan prescribed them remember. And stupidly I told her about the mac and the watch you found. I told her only the other night. I didn't mean to of course and it upset her dreadfully. I shouldn't have done of course. It just seemed to come out. Mr Muchmore buries his head in his hands and watches the police drive away. Now there will be no one to pry into his secret. Just him and that big house.'

'But wouldn't they have searched the house to begin with?'

'Only cursorily. And if they weren't really looking . . . When the police searched Christie's garden they failed to notice femur bones *propping up the fence*, let alone the six or seven bodies tucked away under the floorboards. A doped up girl, locked away in a cellar room, the door hidden by chairs, coal, all manner of junk . . .'

'But wouldn't she scream? Cry for help?'

'Perhaps she did at first and no one heard her. But one quickly gets used to things. And then, what, nine months later he moves out. The house with such unhappy memories is put up for sale. If I remember rightly, he moved out *before* the house was put up for sale, so that any prospective buyer would look round an *empty* house. No one really remembered him going. He was like the Flying Boats, an embarrassing piece of history which Rochester preferred to forget. But I know where he is now. I went and got his address.'

'But how can you be sure?' he asks.

'My sister. Your sister. *Our* sister. She grabbed me and

shouted those words we knew so well, the words we used to hear echoing around Gladstone Drive every evening around half past six, with Stella balancing on the rockery and Mrs Muchmore standing by the entrance to the garage. *Forward*! *Forward*! *Straighten Up*! *Straighten Up*! The only words she has spoken since the accident. Why? Why did she use up all her strength to mouth words I had not heard for over twenty years. Was it simply a bang on the head talking? At first I thought so, but riding in the taxi to the hotel . . .'

'Hotel? What hotel?'

'Just a hotel. Nothing special. Where I used to live my life. Gone now. But riding to this hotel I thought what if she wasn't dwelling in the past? What if she was trying to tell me what she had seen that night, what she had heard, after following Stella up that hill? There are lots of houses tucked away up there, and over the other side, secret hidden houses with steep narrow drives, where someone who is not very good at driving would still need help to park his car, would need his daughter to help him, a daughter who has been trained over the years to do her father's bidding, a daughter subdued, a daughter regained, a daughter under his thumb. *Beat hard beat hard you little beast, but beat hard in your cage*!'

'But she wasn't in a cage when Carol saw her. She was in a wine bar. Alone.'

'Alone, but still under the yoke. Who knows how many years she stayed under lock and key? Three, four, five? Perhaps she was allowed out after a while, allowed into the kitchen and then the garden. She would do his bidding now. He had her spirit locked up like something in a bottle, like an essay in a bottle, all written out, fading fast. Perhaps after a while he would allow her to go down to the shops to buy food, to become the housekeeper he still needed. As the years grew perhaps she was trusted to go further afield, to Ashford, Canterbury. She might even hold down a small job locally, where he could keep an eye on her, where she could come back regularly at night. A little risky? Yes, but maybe not so very much. Maybe he has grown complacent, maybe he has let things slide a little. Maybe in some way he has forgotten what exactly he has done, that he's got away with it for so long, he believes nothing can happen. Maybe she comes and goes now more or less as she pleases, even to London where she can experience a little more freedom, but only so much, looking at her watch, taking it out of her pocket, looking at it, careful not to miss the train, the train home, where her father would be waiting. She is perfectly normal now. She lives in a perfectly normal world.'

'But surely she would have broken free. A spirit like Stella's?'

I looked at him, this boy, hoping that it was not so.

'And have you broken free?' I ask. 'Have I?'

I reach back and dig into Mrs Briggs's Bag.

'Here,' I say, 'I've written something for you. Nothing elaborate. Just an old boy's essay. Accurate in intent. Fanciful, no doubt, in execution. Who knows? Perhaps we'll find out the truth later on this weekend. Let's just call it *The Third Bad Tale of Mr Muchmore*.'

The Third Bad Tale of Mr Muchmore

Mr Muchmore gets up. He has slept well, though he feels as if he has barely had forty winks. Last night he saw the most disgusting thing in his life. He knows he ought to wake Martha and tell her everything, but seeing her lying there, wrapped up in her orange flannel nightgown, dreaming of her dead Dodo, he feels nothing but disgust. They are all the same underneath. That it should come to this. The Liddle girl was bad enough, parading up and down the garden with practically nothing on, but to think that his own daughter . . .

He had been in half a mind to ring Doughty last night and give him a piece of his mind, but now he is glad he hadn't, for if he had, all hell would have broken loose. There would have been conferences and conflabs all over the place and then the wives would have poked their noses in saying, What are we going to do now? and running down the road to have a word with the school and he doesn't want any of that. He knows exactly what he is going to do. If she can't be trusted to behave herself when out of his jurisdiction, she won't go out at all. She can stay inside, all the time, *under lock and key* if necessary.

The phrase under lock and key encourages him. He likes it. *Under lock and key*. The more he thinks about it, the more it trips off his tongue, the more it makes sense. *Under lock and key*. Not out and about hobnobbing with every Tom, Dick, and Harry in long trousers doing God knows what, but here, *under lock and key*. What is the point of sending her to school, of wasting good money, if this is the result? It's all the school's fault anyway, filling her head with half-baked nonsense about self expression. See what happens? *Under lock and key* that's the answer.

Still, there is a difficulty. If he simply refuses to send her to school, if he insists on keeping her here, at home, where he can keep an eye on her, the school will present all sorts of difficulties. He will have swarms of teachers and social workers and other namby-pamby do-gooders crawling over him before he can say Doctor Barnardo's. Unless of course, no one knows she is here. Unless everyone thinks that she has disappeared, run off with some spiv or been grabbed by one of the unemployed while walking back from school, *murdered* perhaps. That's it. Dead! No longer living! No longer *any bother*. If only he hadn't lost his temper in front of that wretched boy. If only he'd let them get on with it and then caught her when he'd left. Still, he'd already cooked part of his goose, and it would be a simple matter to stuff his rear end with a further portion of the Fear of God. Under the circumstances that boy wouldn't be too keen to go into all the sordid little details, he'll be bound.

What he wants to do now is to unlock Stella's door, march in there and give her one of those examinations, to see just how sordid those details are, but the truth is he doesn't quite know what to look for. He could ask Dr Morgan he supposes, in a roundabout sort of way, but it would be a strange topic to bring up over a casual pint. Tell me Peter, what do you look for to see if a girl is, you know, I mean do you need a *magnifying glass* for instance? and although Dr Morgan might look like an old soak, fit only to watch drunks walking the white line down at Rochester Police Station, he isn't quite the fool everyone imagines.

He unlocks Stella's bedroom and walks in. She is staring out of the window. She looks as if she hasn't slept much either. Good. She'll be quite exhausted come the evening. He looks at her and smiles. He will bide his time. He will wait until the moment is right, when the coast is clear and then, pounce! Stella shrinks back. She is not used to him smiling and it unnerves her. He scowls. She is visibly relieved. He tells her gruffly that he is ashamed of her, that she is a bad, wicked girl but he does not want to upset her mother with this. He tells her that he hopes she has learnt her lesson, and that if she promises not to do anything like it ever again, he will say no more about it. She is to go to school and behave properly.

He rings work and tells them, in a funny voice that he has come down with the flu. He feels so powerful putting on this funny voice and talking through his hat. They believe every word. They tell him to 'take care' and 'get better soon', the fools. If he had his way he would sack the lot of them.

He brings his wife breakfast in bed.

'Porridge,' he says and places it on a tray in front of her.

His wife looks at it. What on earth has possessed him to cook her porridge?

Half an hour later Mr Muchmore returns. His wife is lying there breathing heavily. Her eyes are open but she is not exactly awake. The spoon has fallen out of her hand on to the floor.

'Have you eaten it all?' he demands.

She points to the empty bowl.

'I think the milk was a little off,' she says slowly, as if she had some difficulty in forming the words.

Mr Muchmore smiles.

'That was not the milk Martha. That was the sleeping pills. You are now quite confused and even more unable to think on your own than usual. You will become disorientated and quite incapable of focusing on the fact that I am about to take our daughter in hand. Later, when the hue and cry is on, tonight in fact, I will get Dr Morgan to prescribe you some of those really big knock out drops he's so fond of handing out, and they will keep you under for at least a week. You can get dressed now and do something useful.'

Mr Muchmore looks out over the lawn as she struggles to raise herself up. She can wander about the house in this half conscious state for the rest of the day. She might as well get used to it. That's the way it's going to be for her for some time to come. No one will think anything of it. They'll expect it in fact. How many times has he read that phrase in the papers. *Tonight Mrs So-and-So is at home under heavy sedation.* He'll sedate her all right. He'll sedate her so she won't know what day of the week it is. The trouble will start in about a month's time, when he has to go back to work again. As she drags her thin white legs out of bed he realizes that before all this is over he might have to attend to her as well.

The cellar is divided into two, the main cellar and a small damp room at the back where he keeps his old copies of *Investor's Chronicle* and the *National Geographic*. As luck would have it there is an old mattress propped up in a corner, and an old fashioned mangle which Martha used to use before he caved in and bought her that washing machine. What he has to guard against is Stella banging about and making a noise, especially in the first week or so, when the police will be in and out of the house like fair weather men. He will have to build something for her, to keep her in, a sort of box. It wouldn't necessarily have to be a very big box. For instance he'd once read in the *National Geographic* that in order to keep their chickens from running way, certain tribes in Africa stick their beaks into the ground. It stops them in their tracks. They don't squawk. They don't move. They don't know what to do, and he imagines that it would be much the same for an errant daughter, if she suddenly woke up with a large box on her head. A *Headbox*, that would give her something to think about. He will make a Headbox, a large and cumbersome Headbox. It has many advantages, a Headbox. It will take less time to make than a body-sized box, it will cost less money in materials and if she starts screaming or shouting for help, no one will be able to hear her! He'll fix it so that she'll a) have enough room to breathe, and b) can't stand up in it. He will also tie her hands together, turn the mangle on its side and rope her feet to it. If she starts to behave herself, he will think about taking them off.

He finds Martha in the garden, washing the rockery. He hands her a nice cup of cough mixture.

'I am going out for an hour or so. When I get back I expect something nutritious for my lunch.'

Mr Muchmore drives over twenty miles, whistling to himself. He parks outside the hardware store in Faversham and strolls in to buy padlocks, chains, and some lengths of stout wood. The hardware store smells like every other hardware store he has ever known. He goes to the back, and is dismayed to find the young man in charge idling about consulting a magazine devoted to women's breasts. Is there no end to it! He wouldn't be at all surprised if that Liddle girl ended up posing for such pictures. He shudders at the very thought. He is about to remonstrate with the young man, to pull the book out of his hand and report him to the manager when he remembers that he has driven all the way over here to be *inconspicuous*. He holds his temper in with great difficulty. He explains to the young man that he needs some strong, pliable wood to build a rabbit cage and hands him the diagram he drew over breakfast. The young man looks at the drawing with an air which suggests that he would much rather be looking at his previous reading material and then has the nerve to remark, in the most insolent of manners, that in his opinion this construction is far too small to keep rabbits and that apart from a small flap at the front which he presumes is to stuff lettuce leaves through there doesn't seem to be any light coming in.

'You ain't got no windows in this here rabbit hutch,' he tells him. 'You ain't got no wire mesh. What's more,' he adds, without any sense of shame, 'how are you going to get the rabbits *in*?'

Mr Muchmore looks at him with increased venom.

'It is not for *rabbits*,' he explains. 'It is for *a* rabbit.

A very old and infirm rabbit. A *blind*, *arthritic* rabbit who moves hardly at all. And I do not have to get him *in*. I intend to build the hutch *around* him.' The youth puts down his copy of *Health and Efficiency* and ambles off into the interior. That told him!

He drives back slowly and passes a number of cyclists on his way home. They are dressed in shorts and are bent over their handlebars in a most unsightly manner. He tries to recall if his daughter has a bicycle, but remembers with some glee that after tonight she wouldn't be needing it even if she does. Let her mother ride it if she must, but the thought of his wife with her bottom extended in the air made him feel quite ill.

It is later than he thinks when he gets home and Martha has a warm broth on the stove consisting of carrots and spinach. He dips his spoon into the bowl and pulls out a long straggly green thing.

'What in heavens name do you call this?' he asks her.

Martha looks at the weed intently.

'That is a nettle,' she says at last. 'Nettles are very good for you.'

Mr Muchmore lays it across his plate.

'That is not a nettle Martha,' he tells her. 'That is a thistle.'

He pours the soup down the sink, telling her that time and tide wait for no man and that he has work to do even if she hasn't. Back to your knitting patterns, he declares, not that his wife has ever knitted anything in her life. *Why not*? he wonders. Why should he have to buy cardigans and sweaters and expensive pairs of socks when she has a perfectly good pair of hands on her? What does she do all day anyway? Gossiping with those schoolmarm friends of hers, idling about with her shopping trolley, exchanging tittle tattle. She could start knitting him something right away. So could Stella soon.

He goes into the garage and makes the Headbox. It is much more difficult than he imagines to get six sides of wood to stick together. What is more he discovers that the idle youth in the hardware shop is perfectly right. Stella's head does not come by itself. He has forgotten all about her neck and it takes him several hours to work out how to fit the two halves at the base together. Luckily his garage is well equipped. He lines the box with foam rubber torn out from Martha's sun lounger. This will sound proof the box as well as ensure that she does not bang her head unduly on the hard surfaces. By the end of the afternoon he has everything in place.

'What is that?' Martha asks when he comes in and puts it on the kitchen table.

'A rabbit hutch,' he tells her. Martha squints at it. It does not look like a rabbit hutch. It has no windows, no wire-meshing.

'A rabbit hutch?' she asks. 'Why have you made a rabbit hutch? We don't have any rabbits.'

Mr Muchmore looks at her with a certain degree of contempt.

'Of course we don't have any rabbits,' he replies. 'If we had rabbits we would already have a rabbit hutch. This rabbit hutch is for the forthcoming rabbits.'

'Forthcoming rabbits?'

'Angora rabbits,' he tells her. 'For knitting.'

'Knitting?' Martha asks. 'You aren't thinking of taking up knitting are you?'

'No,' he answers. 'You are.' And before locking her in the living room he pours her a large tumbler of sherry.

Stella comes home at about a quarter to six. She hangs up her raincoat. He is ready with a thick drink of hot chocolate and after she has drunk it he grabs her and pushes her down the cellar stairs. It is black and dusty down there and as he hauls her along she struggles and kicks. Her cries and pleas are soon overtaken by the sedative, and when he opens the door to look he is pleased to see that she has had the decency to slump down on the mattress. The next part is the most difficult, manhandling the Headbox down the stairs, into the room and over her head. It takes much more physical strength than he thought possible. When her head is safely in it he checks to see that none of the air holes are blocked and that the latch is on tight. Then he binds her hands together and ropes her feet to the mangle lying on its side. Now he piles against the door all the junk he can find so that the door is quite hidden, an old bedstead, carpets that should have been thrown out years ago, five rotten deckchairs, a radio that can only get Vera Lynn, Stella's discarded sledge, and, he is pleased to discover, her bicycle.

He goes upstairs to the hall. Now comes what he considers the most dangerous part. The planting of the evidence. Stella's raincoat. As a precaution, so that no one will see him carrying it, he decides to wear Stella's raincoat underneath his own. It is a little tight around the shoulders but no matter, his own mac soon covers it. He checks the living room. Martha is sitting there blinking blindly at the television. His work is nearly done, but his heart is racing and his lips are terribly dry. It has been thirsty work. He goes into the dining room and opens up a refreshing bottle of beer. He catches the top in his hand and stuffs it in his pocket. As he does so he feels a packet of cigarettes in the lining. He doesn't remember them there. He looks down. His hand has slipped inside Stella's pocket! So that's where his cigarettes have been going all this time! The little minx! He rummages about but there is nothing much else. An empty box of matches, a rubber band and chocolate wrapper. Inspiration hits him! He was going to leave the mac as it was, but finding all this muck in her pocket has given him an idea. He will leave something of hers, something that she cherishes, something that will make the police think the worst, make them think she is most probably dead. And they will be right. Stella will be dead. This Stella at least. Dead and buried. He is going to kill this Stella off and raise a proper *Muchmore* Stella, raised on Muchmore principles and Muchmore lines. No gadding about for Stella Muchmore Mark 2. No flights of fancy for her. He'll keep her tied down, just like those blessed Flying Boats they keep out on the river. He'll see to that. He goes back downstairs, pulls aside all the junk and pulls the watch from Stella's arm. It is a good watch, an expensive watch and he is loath to let it go, but then he reasons, it won't be for very long. The police will hand it back to him after a while! He smiles at that. They will hand it back to him and later, when she has learnt to behave herself, he might even allow her to wear it again, as a reward.

He doesn't have much time now and as he hurries to the garage he is worried about the return journey, for tonight, for the first time in many months, he will not have either his daughter or his wife to guide him back in. As he drives down the road he gets the most terrible shock of his life. Standing under the chestnut trees he is horrified to see a young girl in school uniform hanging around looking at her watch. For one terrible moment he thinks it's his daughter, that somehow she has got out and it is only when he remembers that *he* has her watch, in *her* coat pocket that he calms down. As he passes he can see that indeed, it is not Stella, how could it be? This girl is a little taller, a little fuller in the chest by the looks of things . . . My God! He momentarily loses control of the car. It's the Liddle girl! Dressed up in a school uniform! But she left school last year! What on earth is she playing at! Some fancy dress party no doubt. And why's she hanging round this Godforsaken spot? Up to no good he'll be bound. What in heaven's name is happening to Rochester? Is there no teenager in this town with any sense of decency? The Liddle girl hanging around the chestnut trees like a common little tart. Probably wearing suspenders under that dress if he knows anything about it. How Doughty would love to hear of this, but he'll have to keep this one to himself. Pity. Worth a couple of pints of anybody's money.

He drives down and parks the car. It is windy now, and cold, and there is a mist coming up from the river. Lucky that. Well not lucky perhaps. Ordained. This is going to work. He knows it. There is no one on the towpath and he hurries along it so fast that he almost passes the pillbox in his eagerness to get there. He stands before it. It is squat and ugly and he can hear it breathing through several of its nasty mouths. He ducks inside and switches on his torch. It is one of the most disgusting places he has seen, with seven different kinds of muck on the floor. He can just imagine what tricks they get up to in here! Filthy beasts! He shines the torch up and down to see where he can put the coat. Should he lay it on the floor, trample it around in the mud and squalor, or should he hide it away somewhere. For a moment he favours laying it down, like a couple might do before they . . . but no, to add to the sense of mystery reason tells him to hide it, not too cleverly, for then they would never find it and all his hard work will have come to nothing. A gap in the ceiling and the wall is just perfect.

He is back in his car within three minutes. He starts back up the hill. As he rounds the bend by the chestnut trees he is just in time to see a pair of brake lights come on and a door shut. He squints ahead of him, wondering if he can recognize the blighter. The car turns round and speeds off in the other direction. He is home before he knows it. He parks the car in the drive.

He is amazed how easily his plan works, how gullible the police are, how helpful are his neighbours and how pleasant it is to keep Martha in a state of complete ignorance. Barring the odd time when Stella wakes up and starts to whimper, thanks to Dr Morgan Martha does not have a clue what's going on. On the few occasions she does hear something he tells her it's the rabbits he's bought and such is her drugged state she nods as if to say, 'Of course, the rabbits.'

Later on of course it becomes more difficult. Stella quickly learns that if she is to be allowed out of her Headbox, if she wants her hands to be unchained, then she will have to be quiet and do as he says. The need to eat and the need to go to the lavatory, and not to soil one's clothes quickly takes precedence over other considerations. Sooner or later he will reveal to Martha that Stella is alive after all. She will be so grateful she will do anything. He will be able to involve her in the conspiracy as well.

She is taking the tablets and drinking of her own free will now. So when he tells her, one breakfast time, he is not surprised to find that she has difficulty in forming the words.

'Alive?' she says. 'My Stella is alive?'

'Yes,' he says. 'She is alive. I have saved her. I have kept her from harm.'

She is pathetically grateful, falls on his feet and hugs his legs.

'Where is she?' she cries. 'Where is my darling?'

'She is safe,' he tells her. 'I have kept her from harm. And we must keep her here. Out of their grasp.'

Martha nods and wipes her eyes.

'Where is she Leonard? Let me see her.'

He takes her down to the cellar. Martha collapses by the door. She looks at him without understanding.

'Why is she here, Leonard? Why is she down here?'

'She was weak,' he explains, 'weak like you. Do you want her to end up like you?' he asks.

She shakes her head.

'But where did you find her?' asks Martha. Mr Muchmore strokes her head.

'No need to worry about that now. She is safe. That's all that matters. She would have been dead had it not been for me.' And it is true. Had it not been for him she might as well be dead.

Martha pleads to see her and with great reluctance Mr Muchmore opens the door. Stella is lying there with the Headbox around her head, her hands behind her back and her legs tied to the mangle. Martha starts to wail.

'It must be like this,' Mr Muchmore urges, '*Must be*! We must keep it a secret. If they find out she is here they will take her away and we will never see her again.'

He opens up the Headbox so that Martha may see her daughter's face. Mother and daughter's eyes meet and then Mr Muchmore pulls her aside and shuts the lid again.

Martha is terrified. He has tied her to his conspiracy but he knows as the days go by her facade will start to crack. She will not be able to keep up the pretence to outsiders. She is weak. If they were simply left alone, maybe Martha would be all right, but here he is sure that she will give the game away. Perhaps he should have waited. Perhaps he should have waited until they moved away, somewhere quiet and secluded where no one could interfere with their lives.

Martha is drinking a good bottle of sherry a day

now but far from calming her down, it is making her more irrational and unpredictable by the hour. One morning he wakes to hear Martha scrabbling at Stella's door with a breadknife, trying to prise the lock open. She turns round. There is a mad fury in her eyes and she starts to hiss at him. It is all over. He grabs the knife from her and hauls her upstairs. He stuffs three pills in her mouth and washes a tumbler full of sherry down her throat. He leaves her in the living room and locks the door. Bringing a chair from the kitchen he walks over to the garage, takes out the hemp rope he keeps in the back of the car for breakdowns, and throws it over the rafter at the back, tying the end in a loose, but effective knot. He unlocks the living-room door and drags Martha out through the french windows round to the garage door at the back. Once in the garage he closes the door and switches on the electric light. It is almost impossible to lift her, so he has to ask her to stand up a bit. He walks her across to the tap and runs a rag under some cold water.

'Come on Martha. Wake up old girl,' he says, and Martha blinks and tries to use her legs.

'That's better,' he says. 'It'll be all right. You'll see.'

He has to get on the chair with her.

'What are we doing?' she says. 'What's happening?'

'The car,' he explains. 'You can see the car better like this. We're going to take Stella out of here. I need your help to get the car out.'

She nods, stupidly. He is standing up with her now, wobbling about with her, struggling to maintain their balance. With one hand he holds her against him and with the other he reaches out for the rope and pulls it over her head. Now she can struggle all she wants to. He lets her fall against him while he quickly tightens up the knot. He jumps down. Martha drops to her knees, her back swinging wildly against the bamboo chair. She straightens up, holding her hands out like someone balancing on a lurching ship and for a moment sees herself standing upright looking out over the car. *Over the car?*

'Leonard,' she says. '*Leonard?*'

He kicks the chair away from her and watches her to make sure the rope doesn't break. Back in the house he goes upstairs to wash and shave. As he stands on the landing he sees a police car draw up on the other side of the road, but to his immense relief the two officers have come to question the Doughty boy again and that danger has passed. He mounts the rest of the stairs. He'll give it half an hour before he rings Doctor Morgan. Time enough to feed Stella and put the Headbox back on.

'Do you know sir, I am getting rather addicted to this detective lark,' Dickey said as he settled into his seat. 'Before you turned up nothing ever happened, apart from the odd sales manager being kicked across the conference hall and the regulation spot of after hours hanky panky. But since your arrival Ashford has taken on the aspect of an Adventure Theme Park. Are you sure we shouldn't be dressed up in funny hats or something?'

'You *are* dressed in a funny hat,' I said. 'Unless you're Swiss. Not many men walk about Ashford in their leisure hours dressed in Tyrolean headgear I'll be bound. All you need is a pair of lederhosen to make the picture complete. And don't call me sir, Dickey. It doesn't suit us.'

'There was a rule at sea, if you don't mind me bringing up the subject, that you only called those passengers for whom you nurtured the utmost contempt by their Christian name, the ones who bought you drinks and told jokes, and talked about getting their sea legs. As I always said, if you want to survive such rites of passage the thing to do is to leave your sea legs at home, by the fireside, stuffed into a pair of pom-poms, but it's pitiful what a breath of fresh air can do to people. I couldn't call you by your Christian name if I tried sir. It would be, how can I put it, an unnatural practice.'

'Well, we don't want any of those,' I replied. 'I've done with unnatural practices.'

'So have I sir. The other day I threw out half the bottles from behind the bar. No more balms made out of coconut matting, no more syrup of cough mixture, and no more swizzle sticks. If they want a cocktail and it isn't made out of two parts gin, one part gin, with a touch of, you know *gin*, then I'm not the man to make it sir. An entirely reasonable stance I think you will agree. I had been thinking about it for some time but the other day my daughter's young man sidled up to me and demanded one of those drinks with a *double entendre* and it was all I could do to stop myself from reaching back and battering him over the head with the golden horn. I mean guess what he asked for?'

'You remember Clare,' I said, changing the subject as fast as I could.

'Indeed I do,' he turned round, 'I am very pleased to see you again miss. What a Christmas eh? I have a young relative to look after too miss. She's a sensible girl though and takes no notice of me at all. All she thinks about these days is her chickens, her young man and her muscle tone, something in which the young man in question is singularly lacking. I've seen friskier bollards. I would have thought', he said, turning back to me, 'that under circum-stances which come all too readily to mind, given the peak of her condition he would barely be able to get off the starting block let alone last the distance. Particularly as he's carrying the baton.'

'Dickey,' I warned him. 'Remember the company. And what's in the basket? We're not going on a picnic you know.'

'Actually sir, you *don't* know. A picnic is the very thing which we could be going on, and this, I am happy to say, is, as you surmised, a picnic basket, appropriated from the kitchens of the Queen Elizabeth herself. It has a number of things which would interest the serious picnic-goer. A collection of hard-boiled eggs. A display of tinned peaches and evaporated milk. Titanic gob stoppers. Multifarious packets of crisps. Four kinds of fizzy drink. Six bottles of champagne. Twelve balloons, seven penny bangers, three rockets, six roman candles, a bowl of olives, a bag of cashew nuts, four toffee apples, half a pound of Stilton, a stick of bread and two and a half pounds of raw steak.'

'Raw steak?'

'Just in case we decide to hold an impromptu barbecue.'

'Barbecue?'

'Barbecue sir. It is a modern invention imported from Australia. You all stand around in someone's garden swallowing tinned beer or sucking on an alcoholic cucumber, something which passes for a drink anyway, watching the host throwing lumps of raw meat in the air, a bit like a juggler sir. Shorts are in strong evidence. As are paper plates.'

'A sort of dinner party without trousers.'

'A sort of dinner party without a great many things sir. Chairs for one. Soup for another. Lavatories too are often dispensed with. When all the drink is consumed everyone troops to the end of the patio, lifts up a portion of their shorts and urinates over a nearby flower, or, if they are organically minded, on to the nearest compost heap.'

'That's if you're a man,' I said to him. Dickey shook his head.

'I am afraid to say sir, that the women also wear shorts. I wrote a melody after one such occasion entitled "The Ship's Barbecue". A very melancholy piece sir.' He sniffed.

'Which reminds me,' I said, pointing to it, sitting on his lap, 'why have you brought your trumpet?'

'The Walls of Jericho came tumbling down with such an instrument,' he reminded me. 'And you might be in need of some walls tumbling before the night is through. If you do, then I will be . . .'

I put my arm on his shoulder. 'I know,' I said. 'I know Dickey. You will be my Joshua.'

We arrived at Patrick's twenty minutes later. He was expecting us.

'Well,' I said, as we went through into his small room at the back. 'Are you up to all this? Looking after Clare for the night I mean?'

'Clare and I will have great fun,' he said. 'I still have some more cigarette cards left. I thought she might like to look at them. And Dad will be back later. He's busy making some last minute preparations. I'm afraid though there's not much room for you tonight. One of you will have to sleep on the sofa.'

'As long as it doesn't move about,' Dickey said, patting the cushions, 'I can sleep anywhere. Round windows are my only problem.'

'That's OK,' I added. 'If the worst comes to the worst Dickey and I can drive over to Camber and spend the night there.'

'And when do you think you'll be back?' Patrick asked.

'I don't know. By morning at the very latest. I'll give you a call.'

'Morning? We might be off by morning.'

'I thought you said you wouldn't be going for a couple of days.'

'Circumstances change,' he said. 'Have you not noticed the change in the weather?'

It was true. The high pressure centred over the Balkans, which had been firmly established over Europe for most of late December and January was beginning to break up. A slow moving front had brought rain and strong winds to north-west Britain, but elsewhere, for most of this month it had been mild and dry, and down here, in the south east, the days had been almost springlike, warm and sunny and light. On the sixth I had taken a reading of 15.8 centigrade up on the Weather Centre roof, while at the same time at Kinloch Hourn in the Highlands 306 millimetres of rain had fallen in forty-eight hours. The weather divides us as surely as culture. The weather *is* culture. But now the pressure was falling and a depression was forming to come up the Channel. Tonight could be the last fine night for some time.

'Be back by daybreak if you can,' urged Patrick. 'If we miss this spell we might have to wait another week.'

The evening was still clear when Dickey and I set off. We got to Wye half an hour later and wound our way up the hill. The road had been cleared now, but the raw stumps which lined the route reminded me of that raw, bruising night. I stopped three quarters of the way up.

'That is where I found her,' I told Dickey. 'Where the clearing is.'

Dickey corrected me. 'That's where the puma found her sir. I often wonder about that puma you know, where she is now, how many sheep she's eaten. I'm sure if you hadn't fed her the eggs she wouldn't have found your sister. It was her way of saying thank you.'

'I didn't know you were so fanciful, Dickey.'

'Animals know best, sir. That's all.'

We rode along the crest of the hill, took the long left-hand bend down and then turned left again. We were running parallel to the other road, but on the other side of the hill. The trees were thick now.

'There,' I said, pointing to a small road, fit only for one car, off to our right. 'It's down there I think.'

'It might be a good idea if we parked here,' Dickey suggested, 'and walked the rest of the way.'

Halfway down on the left-hand side we came to it. The house stood back in a damp hollow, behind a tall straggling hedge which hid it from the roadside. There was a steep narrow drive leading to an outside garage. The garden, though not wild, was untidy, as if someone chopped it back every month or so, but not much more than that. It was a younger house than it looked, probably built in the Twenties, but it was large and dishevelled and dirty white. It was built for privacy and kept that way. There was a light above the front porch and a light somewhere around the back, the kitchen I assumed. Apart from that it was in darkness.

'There it is,' said Dickey. 'What's our next move?'

'I don't know,' I said. 'What do you think?'

'You could try ringing the doorbell.'

'I don't think ringing the doorbell is quite the thing. I'd like to know the set-up before announcing myself. He might come up with a crowbar or something.'

'Not to worry sir,' Dickey said, 'I could aim one of our champagne bottles at him.'

'This isn't a cartoon, Dickey,' I reminded him. 'I'm not up some bloody lamppost now.'

We were standing at the edge of the drive wondering what to do next when we heard the grinding of a badly driven car coming down the road. The engine was shuddering, as if the driver were a novice and uncertain how to use the gears. I pulled Dickey in and ran. We were opposite the front door now, standing on an overgrown path. A thick tangle of old briar rose ran down both sides. There was a large evergreen by the garden gate and we crouched behind that. Almost at once the car appeared, poised on the lip of the drive. The two beams from the headlights shone down on the front of the house, illuminating the front door and the pale brickwork above. The man inside the car was short, his head barely coming up to the dashboard. He was peering over the wheel, tapping his hand impatiently. He revved the engine once, twice, then brought his hand firmly down on the horn, breaking the stillness with the shrill sound. Almost at once the front door opened and a woman came out, shielding her eyes from the glare. We were twenty yards away, no more. So close. She wore a plain black dress down to her ankles, and her thick black hair hung long and loose. As if in acknowledgement the driver dipped his lights and put the car into gear. She moved across the front lawn, past the unlit windows of the downstairs rooms, picking her way across the damp grass until she came to the garage doors. Pulling them open she turned, framed in that dark, gaping mouth. The driver rolled down his window and leaned out into the night. The head was square and bald, and though I could not see it, at the end of it hung a loose and belligerent jaw.

'Well?' he shouted. 'Am I right?'

The woman nodded and beckoned him down.

'Come on,' she cried. 'Come on. Forward! Forward!'

The car jerked forward and stopped, jerked forward and stopped, jerked forward and stopped. Halfway the blunt head appeared once more.

'Are the wheels straight?' he cried. 'There's not much room this side. Look at the wheels! Look at the wheels!'

She bent down, as if to reassure him, and then, using both hands, drew him down again.

'Straighten Up!' she cried. 'Straighten Up!'

If there had been any doubt in my mind that this might not be Stella they were dispelled by those four words, with those strong S's singing out into the evening air. They were like bell chimes calling across the slumbering countryside. They ran up and down the hill, they echoed around the dirty walls and the broken slate roof, they rose up to the canopy of bare branches and hung there above our heads. *Forward! Forward! Straighten Up! Straighten Up!* It *was* Stella who I saw before me, the Stella I had watched from my spare room with Fat Patrick and Poker Fisher and my own dear baby brother, the Stella who had sat across the table from me that Boxing Day, and who had climbed naked out of her bedroom window, who had jumped down and played leapfrog with me, the Stella who was pulled from the very hum of life, to live in a secret twilight world in this dark damp hollow in the woods. I wanted to cry out. I wanted to step forward into the circle of light and stand before her.

'Dickey,' I whispered, 'while they're parking the car, I'm going to try and get in. If you can distract them long enough I can probably slip in the front door.'

'What do you want me to do?' he asked. 'Blow my trumpet?'

'Pretend you're lost or something. He probably noticed the car parked up the road. Try and get them away from the house for a second. Then go back to the car and wait for me. If I'm not back by . . . I don't know. Give me an hour. No, that's too short. Give me till ten.'

As the car manoeuvred slowly into the garage Dickey ran back up to the road. By the time they had closed the garage doors he was standing at the top of the drive, arms akimbo. His hat was in his hands. A supplicant's pose.

'Ahoy there skipper!' he cried. 'Is that a harbour light before me?'

Mr Muchmore stopped in his tracks and peered up the drive. His arm went out, across Stella's stomach, as if to prevent her from moving forward.

'Who is it?' he said deliberately, squinting into the night. 'What do you want?'

'I was wondering if you could help a poor mariner to his port of call,' came Dickey's voice. 'I'm fixed to be meeting some mates in a tavern hereabouts and I seem to have lost my bearings. Could you steer me back on course?'

Bending down low under the cover of the wild roses I ran down the length of the path, through the front door and into a large and dimly lit hall. It was tiled and covered with old, tired carpets, and lit by a bulb of very low wattage. I had the impression that this was a constant light, that no matter what, this hall would be lit in such a fashion day and night. It was a spacious hall, a bare hall, with a dark recess down one end, a small round table in the middle, and an old-fashioned hatstand near the entrance. To the left of me were two closed doors, both unpainted, and to the right of me was another door and a corridor which ran to the back.

There was a light coming from the other end and a warm smell, a smell of something cooking, something hot and meaty. There would be an Aga in the kitchen and an old-fashioned pulley for hanging washing, and on the wall there would be a broken bell-box and the names of the rooms it no longer served. Directly in front of me lay the stairs, and the dark safety of the unknown. I could see landmarks there, the landing and the railed banisters where I could settle while I gazed down upon the landscape below. I had taken a gamble. I had leapt into an unknown, unmapped house without a thought of dogs, escape routes, or third parties lodged beneath its roof, but as I ran up the stairs I knew that this was where I should be. Oh vigilant hall! I know your tricks, how watchful, how tenacious you are! The hall would tell me. The hall would speak. I gathered myself into the gloom and let the air from that hallowed place rise up and envelop me.

Although it was quiet enough, there was an underlying rhythm to the house, a sort of murmuring which I could not place. All houses have noises and smells and creaks of their own, but this sound was not the wind in the eaves, nor the rattle of water pipes, nor anything internal, and yet the house was humming. It was everywhere; behind me, below me and above me. I shivered. I was too old for this sort of thing, to go stealing about in other people's homes, to place myself in the hands of God knows what. This house was no friend of mine. I did not know which rooms I could enter safely, which windows I could lever open, which ledges I could jump from. Would it give me away as soon as its master returned?

There came a scuffling, as though someone was wiping their feet, and then she came into the hall and stood in the centre, waiting. Mr Muchmore followed. He turned to face the door and shut it slowly, as if squeezing the last vestige of the outside back into the night. He reached up and slid the top bolt home. He bent down and grappled with another. He straightened up and dealt with the two locks and the thick, dangling chain. Each one was tested, and at every turn there was a grunt of satisfaction and a warm suck of spittle. We were all in here now, the three of us, locked in together.

'Lost his way, indeed,' he was saying. 'What was he looking

for in the first place, *that's* what I would like to know. *I've* never heard of a pub called The Sailor's Knot.'

'Not to worry father,' she said. 'He's gone now.'

This was the first time I had heard Stella speak for over twenty years. Her voice, not surprisingly, had changed. It was still strong but there was a gentleness to it as if the edges had been sanded down. Not weary, or cowed, but serene and peaceful, almost in control. I crouched forward. The two of them were standing there, her with her arm stretched out waiting for him to hand her his coat. She was taller than him still, still straight and strong, with a silver streak running through her jet black hair, and though I could not see her face clearly, her skin had that same olive complexion that I remembered. He was red and breathless, and moved awkwardly.

'He is old now,' said the boy. 'Old and infirm. You did not expect him to look so decrepit.'

He was sitting there holding his knees. He seemed most unconcerned to be in such a place.

'How did you get in here?' I whispered. 'This is no place for a boy.'

'This is exactly the place for a boy,' he replied, leaning back. There was an insolent calm about him that I did not like. 'A boy knows what to do on such a landing. The question is', he added, smirking into his sleeve, 'do you? Just look at him, puffing and grunting like a walrus out of water. What are you going to do with such an ancient relic? Kick him down the cellar steps?'

He was right. In my mind's eye I had expected Mr Muchmore to be as he was when I last saw him, but now I saw how stooped he had become, how low his head hung, how uneasily his feet shuffled on the tiles. She helped him out of his coat, and as if she had read my thoughts, said, 'You look tired tonight Father. You should not have gone out today. You need some rest. You have not been yourself since the night of the storm.'

He held up his hand as if to silence her and turned his back on her. She brushed the back of his shoulders, and then, as he turned to face her, the lapels of his tweed jacket. I was watching a routine. What was wrong with it? Anything? For a moment I wondered what I was doing there. Perhaps I had got it wrong again. Perhaps she *had* run away, and he had found her later. Perhaps *he* had saved her. What use would I be under those circumstances? Then I remembered Monica had described her, how she had trembled at those words she had heard and I recalled the last time we had all been under one roof.

'Only dead men rest, Stella,' he said. 'Dead men and Dodos.' He lifted his face and sniffed the air. 'What's for supper?'

'Your favourite,' she said.

He moved across to one of the doors and pulled out a thick set of keys, turning them over in his hands. He found the one he was looking for and opened a door. Light flooded out on to the hall carpet.

'Hurry up and light the fire,' he complained. 'And where is my sherry? Is it not time?'

As if by answer the whole house started up, whirring and clattering. Now I knew what that humming sound had been – the chatter of a hundred clocks, clocks whispering in locked rooms, in studies and morning rooms and *cupboards under the stairs*. Below me a grandfather clock started its long journey towards seven.

He moved about the drawing room. I could hear the rustle of papers, the strike of a match, someone poking the coal. Then came the clink of a decanter stopper.

'I may have one myself Father?'

He grunted his approval.

'Sit down Stella. Come and sit down and tell me what use you've been all the day long.'

And so she sat down and I listened to her day in this damp hollow as she unfolded it by the light of the gathering fire. I heard about the work she had done in the vegetable garden and the argument she had with the man who came to chain-saw the fallen trees, and lastly her trip down to the jewellers to see if her watch was fixed.

'That jeweller ought to be struck off,' Mr Muchmore informed her. 'He's worse than useless. I should have taken it up to London, got someone decent to look at it.'

'I was thinking I could go up there myself,' Stella began, 'perhaps next week.'

A hand came down hard upon the leather armrest of an armchair.

'No!' he said. 'Never again! Look what happened the last time.'

He stopped suddenly. His voice took on an accusing tone.

'You were very helpful to that man just now,' he said. '*Too* helpful to my mind. Helpful is as helpful does, they do tell. You haven't done something foolish today have you? He didn't follow you here as well did he?'

'No, no, Father. Nothing like that. I have been down to the shops, that is all. I saw no one.'

'Never seen that man before?'

'Never Father.'

'Never talked to him?'

'No Father.'

'You know what I do to errant daughters, disobedient daughters?' His voice was trembling and I could hear the sound of jangling keys.

'Yes Father.'

'Yes Father,' he sighed. 'Will I never be rid of it?' he asked, 'To live in misery and die by poison! The Curse of the Muchmores. Well we have lived in misery, have we not Stella?'

'We have Father.'

'We have. And who caused it?'

'I did Father.'

'You did. And who suffered for it?'

'You did Father.'

'I did. And what were the consequences?'

'The capitulation of Mother, Father.'

'The capitulation of Mother. And why did she capitulate?'

'Because Mother was weak, Father.'

An uneasy mutter came from his lips. The catechism was over.

'And are you any different? I had hoped to make you strong Stella.'

'That is why you should allow me to go to London again. I have not been there for *months*. I enjoyed my visits. I enjoyed . . .'

'Yes?' His question was loaded with suspicion.

'I enjoyed being alone,' she said simply.

'You can find all the solitude you need here, in your home,' he said, sucking in his breath. 'I have become soft in my old age Stella. You do not need to go to London. Look what happened the last time. It nearly cost us everything. The house crashing down over our heads, strangers knocking on our door . . .'

'Not so very strange,' Stella offered. 'I would have liked to have talked to her. We could have become friends perhaps. What is strange is that she hasn't got in touch again. I thought she would. She seemed so thrilled to find us.'

'Those Doughtys never were a trustworthy bunch,' her father replied, 'I doubt whether the passing of the years has made much of a difference . . .'

He got up. I could hear him helping himself to a second glass of sherry.

'Ten minutes,' he said, 'I'll be ready in ten minutes. Exactly mind.'

Stella came back into the hall and turned into the tiled passage. She trailed her left hand along the wall, and then the kitchen door opened, and I was alone again.

'So they had seen Carol that night!' I whispered to the boy. 'Spoken to her! Carol had knocked on their door and talked to them!'

The boy looked at me scornfully.

'You should listen more carefully,' he said. '*I would like to have talked to her*, is what she said. Which means *he* talked to her, *not* Stella. Once back in the house Stella does as she's told. Or at least that's what he thinks.' He smiled.

'What do you mean?' I asked.

The boy raised a finger. 'You should be more observant, more watchful, *more suspicious*. Like your old adversary down there, you have become complacent. She might look like the Stella of old, but the Muchmore years have taken their toll and Stella has learnt from her father and from her house, just as you learnt from yours. This is a distrustful house, a wary house, and Stella has lived under its roof for nearly twenty years. It is not all one-way traffic now you know. Did you never wonder what she was doing up there, why her father let her go up to London at all? When your sister called you that night she said that Stella looked as if she had done the journey many times before, and indeed your sister was correct. Stella goes up to London once a month, catching the first cheap-day return to Charing Cross. During the rest of the month Stella only walks down to the shops. On Saturdays she accompanies her father to the market in Hastings, where he grumbles while counting out from his unwieldy collection of pound coins. He carries as much change as he can. Money should weigh heavy on one he says. Notes he tells her are for nincompoops.

'There are other markets she could go to, the one in Faversham for instance, and a rather unpleasant one in Ashford, where everything is broken and soiled, but she is not allowed to go to those, and so, naturally, she does not, even when she could when Father is not there, for Father is always there, Watching. Even when he is not there, he is there Watching, which makes her monthly trips to London even more exciting. After the first time, when she went of her own accord, when she suddenly found herself on a train to London, not quite knowing why she had got on and what she was going to do when she got there, she came back that evening to find Mr Muchmore sitting in the garage, his head buried in his hands, ragged with grief and rage. He had locked her in her room for over a week. She didn't care. She had had a wonderful time, a marvellous time. The things she had done! She did not regret it. It was worth the risk and she would do it again. She would make Father see sense, tell him that all she wanted to do was to walk around, to watch people, to see how foolish, how contemptible they were (which was true in part), and she reminded him that whatever else he thought about it, there was no denying the fact that *she had come back*. He relented, reluctantly at first, but gradually her trips have become part of their routine, and routine is one thing her father hates to disturb. Of course the real reason he relented was that he had hardly eaten that whole week, some slices of bread and dripping, the remains of a half-eaten sherry trifle, and several tins of cold pilchards, and though her range is limited, Mr Muchmore depends on Stella's cooking. Stella's cooking is perfect. She cooks his favourite. So an arrangement was made, that on the fifteenth of every month, she travels to London, to do as she pleases. As often as not she buys a pair of shoes, black and sensible, which she will place alongside the other pairs gathering dust in her wardrobe and Mr Muchmore will remark that he can't for the life of him understand why she needs so many pairs, but that the Ways of Women will forever remain a mystery to him, and Stella is happy enough to fool him with this, her only visible folly. Of course that isn't the whole story. As well as buying the sensible pair of shoes she always buys another, more flamboyant pair, a pair of high heels or sling-backs or felt boots from Turkey, telling the assistant to put them both down on the bill as one, and these she wears for the day before throwing them off the train when nearing home. She has a favourite spot now, on a slight embankment, and she often wonders whether anyone has come to expect these quite unexpected gifts, someone who hides behind the long straggly bushes on the appropriate date, waiting for the next surprise to come flying through the air. It is not her only deception. The years have made her quiet but wily, and when she acts, she acts quickly. On the rare occasions when he drives her down to the station for instance, she can barely wait for the train to leave before getting up and walking down the carriageway to the toilet. *Engaged* it says when she is inside, and indeed she is *Engaged*, *Engaged* applying the Estée Lauder Lipstick and Eye Liner and Impalpable Powder Blush which she stole from a fashion store in Bond Street. She is a confident thief now and stored underneath the floorboards in her room are trophies from her local expeditions, old doughnuts and Cornish pasties from the baker's (presents for the mice), pencils, Sellotape and balls of coloured string from the stationer's, and cheap earrings, bathsalts and tasteful packets of contraceptives from any number of chemists'. She saves her greatest skill (the skill London has nurtured) for the general store in the High Street where, near the cash desk, the owner keeps the wines and spirits and the items she is after, the bottles of beer. She has a whole row of such bottles now, hidden by a line of tottering flowerpots on a shelf in the garden shed and when she is alone, when Father is out, she marches down there, strips, and drinks them one after the other, sometimes as many as four in a row, standing there among the rusting gardenware, gulping them down while rubbing her breasts. Sometimes when Father comes home, she feels quite elated and drunk, but she is careful to disguise her breath, and talks to him in a slow and careful manner. In any case he does not notice things as much as he used to, and she does not have to be so much on her guard as she had when . . . when she was younger.

'The make-up is not the only item she carries in her handbag unbeknown to her father. She takes the contraceptives as well, for she has found over the months, that these can come in handy too. She has no favourite stalking ground, for she is careful never to go to the same place twice and her chest-of-drawers is stuffed with the different notepapers she has taken from the hotel lobbies, *The Argyll*, *The Salisbury*, *The Dorsetshire* all printed in elaborate fake handwriting and on which she writes her letters, addressing them to Mother, Wherever She May Be. These hotel bars, often decked out with feeble names of their own, The Regency, The Dickens, The Fireside Chat, etc., are fitting places to go after a good morning's shoplifting, somewhere quiet and anonymous, where she can sit at the bar with a gin and tonic in her hand, sizing up the opposition. If only her father could see her now! As well he might! He might walk in and ask her What The Hell Does She Think She's Playing At, sitting there with a bag of stolen property at her feet! In truth she doesn't care what she steals for once it is in the bag, so to speak, she has no further use for it, and indeed knows that she has to be rid of it all before she steps off the train back at Wye Station. To begin with she left the bag on the luggage-rack above her head, but once, some interfering busybody stuck his head out of the window and handed the wretched thing to her right there on the platform. Luckily Father was late, and by the time she heard his car coming down the hill she had tossed it over the bridge into the river. But what if he had been there? How would she have explained that lot away? How would she explain *any* of it away, particularly the Spider Hour when she would strike up intelligent conversation with unknown men, acting worldly and mysterious, while all the while her heart was beating furiously as if it may break out. *Beat hard, beat hard you little beast but beat hard in your cage*! As often as not she is quite happy to leave it at that, to have a drink or two and move on, leave them with a hint of regret in their eyes, Bye Bye Boys, and if they behave themselves that is all she does do, but there is always the off chance that someone will elect to make a fool of himself, who will look at her in her only expensive black dress, and draw the wrong conclusion. Her father believes that dress to be exactly the same as the others, but he only sees it under a raincoat or when she is standing stiffly at the door, carrying in his birthday cake. He does not see it sitting on a bar-stool with red lips and a gin and tonic in front of it, does not see it with the sleeves pulled up ever so slightly, does not see it over the black lace brassière she stole from Marks and Spencer's without looking at the size and which, to her surprise, fits her perfectly. These encounters have never come to anything, and if one did Stella thinks she would have to kill herself quickly, there and then, with a razor blade in the bathroom, or perhaps on the train back, getting out at Paddock Wood or Sevenoaks and jumping in front of the next express. Usually the afternoons pass peaceably enough, and she is content enough with that, but there is a part of her which likes the confrontation, and when the opportunity arises does not hesitate to act. How many times has she heard a whisper to a willing (or unwilling) accomplice, 'Quite fancy that over there', or 'Wouldn't mind giving her one', at which point she downs her gin and tonic and walks over with the broad smile on her face that takes him quite by surprise, Well come on then, she says in a nice voice, loud enough for all the bar to hear, and he says Sorry? lifting his head out of his drink, I said well come on then, Why don't you, she repeats, I've got all afternoon and he looks away embarrassed, mumbling, No, No, It's OK, looking in vain for help. Why, what's the matter, she asks, concerned, not belligerent, *never* belligerent, always kind and thoughtful, Did I hear you Wrong, Did you not say that? Did he not say that? she adds and as often as not the barman or whoever is around looks on with wry amusement and shrugs his shoulders, she is not drunk, not causing a disturbance, not swearing (and she never uses *those* words, those words he would want to use in private, the words *she* sometimes wants to use, to spit in his face, then she *would* be thrown out, or the police might become involved), and it is a damn sight better than listening to the old fart in the corner talking about the Common Agri-cultural Policy, so he turns and looks in the man's direction as if to say, You got yourself into this mess old chum, You talk your way out of it, The thing is, Stella adds brightly, sitting down next to him if she can, A Man Who Knows His Own Mind is a rare commodity these days, one to be encouraged, rewarded even. Are you a guest here? Or shall I book a room in my own name? and the man's eyes would swivel helplessly around the room, Don't tell me, Stella admonishes, fishing in her handbag, You're worried about, you know, *your health*, It's not as if you've ever met me before, Not to worry, and she draws out one of her stolen contraceptives, pulled out of its packet for just such an occasion, transparent and dangling. *Will this fit?* she asks politely and kisses him full on the lips as he shrinks away, Too bad, she would sigh, Too bad and drops it into his beer before walking away. She always tells herself as she sits on the train thinking of her day's exploits that it is the best way to leave her stolen goods behind, for no one remembers the carrier-bag she came in with, they're all too busy looking at the floating contraceptive and her purposeful, elegant exit. An hour and twenty minutes later she is met by her father at Wye station.

'"Did you have a good day?" he asks, grudgingly as he drives her back up the hill.

' "Yes Father, I did. Look. I bought a new pair of shoes," and shows him yet another pair of black shoes. Mr Muchmore grunts and drives on. He will never understand them.'

'You cannot be sure of all this,' I tell him.

The boy pointed down to the drawing room, where Mr Muchmore could be heard reading the newspaper.

'No more can you be sure of his wife's death. Or how exactly he incarcerated Stella. She must do *something* up in London. It is her revenge. There is steel in Stella. Hidden steel. There always was. But do not imagine these visits to London are solely her salvation, a way of preparing the ground. They are not. They are dragging her in deeper.'

'What would you do?' I asked.

'A boy would walk down that corridor and open the kitchen door,' he told me. 'A boy would take this opportunity to talk to Stella while her father was reading the evening paper. A boy would not be afraid to come down from the landing into the hall. A boy knows that we all have to come down from the landing and into the hall whether we want to or not, and this boy knows the moment to choose. Come down at the wrong time . . .' He wiped his finger across his throat.

'Perhaps,' I ventured to suggest, 'perhaps you could go for me, to sound her out, to see how the land lies.'

The boy shook his head. 'If she were the Stella I knew, then I would go. But she is not. She would not listen to me now. She would not even acknowledge my presence. She would pretend she could not see me.' He gripped my arm. 'Get her out. Get her out *now* while you still can, before . . .' He stopped. 'Too late. You have missed your chance. She's coming back now.' He jumped to his feet and skipped down the stairs.

'Look,' he said in a sing-song voice. 'Look what she is bringing him for supper.'

The far door opened and Stella came back down the passage. 'Father,' she called out, 'Father, it's ready now.'

Mr Muchmore came out of the room and walked over to where Stella was waiting by another locked door. Her hands were held together, covered by a white napkin, and on the napkin there rested a golden, glistening pie. It was wide and deep and through its carefully positioned slits came an unmistakable smell. A steak and kidney pie! Mr Muchmore could not stop looking at it. His eyes travelled back and forth as he tried to locate the correct key. I too was transfixed by its aromatic power. How luxuriant it seemed in these surroundings, how sensual and opulent. I could touch such a pie, dip my fingers in and lick the juice. My stomach began to turn.

I had to come halfway down the stairs to watch them eat their meal. Mr Muchmore was half hidden from my view, but I could see Stella sitting at the other end of the table. It had been laid out with table mats and rolled napkins and a salt cellar at each end. Behind her, dangling from one of the light brackets hung the remains of a Christmas decoration, one of those paper chains you can make yourself. Clare and I had spent a whole afternoon sticking them together. We had taken some over to her mother, and hung them over her bed. So they celebrated Christmas here. I had not expected that.

They ate in silence. Every now and again Stella would lift her head and stare out across the room to the door and the hall where the boy waited. Why couldn't he simply walk in and tell her that it was time to leave, that he had come for her at last? Then they could leave, never to return. Stella would take his hand and follow him up the road to where Dickey was waiting in the car.

With his food nearly finished Mr Muchmore began to comment on the value of Stella's pie. It was a good pie, he declared, a *very* good pie, a better pie than ever your mother used to make. It was just . . .'

'Just what Father.'

'It is a *steak and kidney* pie, Stella.'

'Yes Father.'

'Yesterday was a *steak and kidney* pie, Stella.'

'Yes Father.'

'And the day before that.'

'Yes Father.'

'Indeed I cannot remember a day that has gone by without a steak and kidney pie Stella. I was hoping . . .'

'Hoping *what* Father?'

'Hoping that perhaps we might have something different soon. A pork chop, a plate of bacon, a little fillet of plaice.'

'But Father,' her voice sounded shocked, but there was a deliberate coldness to it. 'It is your *favourite*. I cooked it specially. Now have another spoonful, before it gets cold.'

'Stella, in truth I could not.'

'Father!' The voice was stern now. Stella got up and crossed over to the other side of the room. 'Eat it!' she commanded. There was a rattling sound as the spoon chased round the plate. I could hear him chewing and swallowing, chewing and swallowing and felt the gorge rise up in my throat.

'Waste Not Want Not, is that not one of our mottoes Father?' Stella's voice asked. 'You must eat it all, every bit. It will make you strong again.'

What sort of madness was this? Did they feed on each other then, Stella and her father, one with keys and locks and threats from the past, one with gentle words and kidney pies and hopes to the future? I could hear Stella breathing now, but it was not Stella's breath that came from her lungs but her father's. I could hear his inherent belligerence, his indignant purpose, his hostile implacability, all of it coming from her. The boy was right. It had to stop.

I walked down the stairs and stood in the doorway. She was standing over him with the spoon in her hand, watching him while he tried to swallow that last mouthful. He had a napkin around his neck and it was stained with gravy and pastry and little bits of meat.

'Stella,' I said, 'he has had enough.'

Stella screamed. Mr Muchmore pushed her aside and jumped to his feet. There was nothing awkward in his movements now.

'Who the devil are you?' he demanded. 'What do you want?'

I looked at him evenly.

'You know exactly who I am, Mr Muchmore. I haven't changed that much over the years. But I am not a little boy any more and you have no bamboo cane in your hand and we are not in a glass house either. But here we are again. The same three people. Me, Stella and your goodself.'

Stella stood with her hand against her mouth. Now she spoke.

'Giles?' she said, 'Giles? Is that you?'

I came forward.

'Yes, it's me Stella.'

'Father, it's Giles! Giles Doughty! Carol's brother!'

Mr Muchmore stepped forward.

'I know who it is well enough. What do you mean by this intrusion? How did you get in here?'

I took no notice of him. I was looking at Stella.

'Do you remember me, Stella?' I asked her. She put a hand to her face.

'Of course I remember you,' she answered. 'But what are you doing here?'

'The same reason my sister came. To find you.'

'We do not need finding,' Mr Muchmore threatened. 'Leave us alone.'

'I knew that my sister had followed you,' I continued. 'I did not know that she had come here.'

Stella nodded. 'That was months ago. She appeared at the door one night. Said she'd spotted me on the train and followed me home. Father answered the door. Such a surprise to see her after all these years. And still the same bossy Carol.' She looked pained for a moment. 'She said she would get in touch. She never did.'

'My sister is in hospital,' I told her. 'She was struck down very near here. She never got back.'

'Struck down?' Stella asked quickly.

'The night she was here. The night of the storm. A branch hit her. On the road leading down to the village.'

She looked at her father.

'That was her? I thought you said . . .' she began.

'Take no notice of what he says,' he cried, moving round the table. 'Remember what happened the last time you followed his advice. Remember what it cost.'

'You should have taken the car like I suggested,' Stella persisted. 'You should have given her a lift.'

I turned to him. 'You walked with her?' I asked.

'Carol and Father had a long talk in the study. I was hoping to have a word with her myself, it was so many years, but Father said she had to catch a train. He walked her down to the station, didn't you Father?' She turned back to me. 'But what are *you* doing here?'

I could only tell her one thing.

'I have come for you Stella, to run away with you if need be. Like we should have done.'

Stella looked shocked.

'But I don't want to run away. Why should I run away?'

What could I say to her? You *must* come away, away from a man who locked you up, who murdered your mother and struck my sister on the head with a branch and left her for dead? All so that he could watch over his errant daughter, a daughter he once found half-undressed in the privacy of his greenhouse. I stepped back and swung the door back on its hinges.

'No? Do you want to stay here, with all these locks and bolts and with your father watching your every move? Do you want to live in this house with all these clocks ticking away?'

I took hold of her wrist. 'Don't you remember Stella how you hated this watch, how you would never wear it? Don't you remember telling me how you hated time, that as soon as you left home you were going to ignore time, banish time, that time was going to go to hell? Isn't it about time you sent it on its way? I last saw this watch in a police station when the whole of Rochester was out looking for you. Where were you then, Stella? When did you get the watch back?'

Stella looked at her father.

'I earned it,' she said, lowering her eyes. 'I had been bad. And you were too.' She raised her eyes to me. 'If it hadn't been for you, my mother would not have . . . And father wouldn't . . .'

'Yes?'

'Father wouldn't have had to . . .'

'That's enough!' cried Mr Muchmore. 'Leave us! If you have any humanity within you, you will go now. Let us live here in peace.'

'I cannot leave Mr Muchmore. I am locked in, the way you like it, the way Stella is locked in. We are all locked in together. You are used to locking people in. Many years ago you locked Stella up. Isn't that right Stella? Weren't you locked up for a very long time? For months on end? In a sort of cell? *Beat hard, beat hard you little beast, but beat hard in your cage.* Remember?'

Stella began to tremble. Her eyes darted to her father. Her hands were shaking.

'Don't listen to him Stella!' Mr Muchmore spluttered. 'I had to be firm with you.' He turned on me. 'You talk of bolts and chains and locks on doors. Does not every home have locks on the door? Does not every household bolt itself in at night? When darkness comes, and you cannot see what is out there, don't you praise the Lord that you have keys to turn and locks to oil, so those villains who would break into your life and steal your most precious possessions might be thwarted. Isn't that why we submit all we hold most dear to us to imprisonment, to protect them from the grinning thief. And you were the thief! You! With the easy look and the come-on. You were the thief! Here to steal my thunder! I saw everything that night. And I thought houses were secure! I thought once I had locked the front door and the back door, my wife and daughter would be safe. But I was wrong. I looked out of my window and saw you standing there with that bag in your hand. Aye I kept Stella hidden. Stella knows it. Hidden from prying eyes and hand-wringing busybodies. Harsh punishment maybe. But look at her now Mr Doughty? Do you see anything wrong? Do you see her in chains with shackles on her legs? When your sister saw her and started in on her meddlesome ways, was Stella blind-folded or handcuffed? Did she look afraid? Are you brow-beaten Stella, are you caught and captured and wanting for growth?'

'No Father. That was long ago. Before I got better.' She turned to me. 'Father *had* to keep me don't you see? He had no one left after Mother ran away . . .'

Mr Muchmore sank back in his chair.

'Ran away?' I said.

'For what I did. For what we did. She ran away . . . from the shame.'

Oh Stella. How could I tell her that her mother was dead, that twenty-three years ago she died in her childhood garage, that a hemp rope strangled the life out of her, that Dr Morgan cut her down. How could I tell her that while she was bound and gagged and roped in the basement, the body of her mother was taken to the mortuary and found to be the body of a suicide, that she had taken her life when the balance of her mind was impaired? I could not. I could not. Not yet. Not right away.

'No one expects *you* to run away Stella. You are not the type to run away. Your father has seen to that. You are not weak, like your mother. You are strong. Your father knows you will not run away, like he said your mother did and I am not asking you to run away. It was a foolish thing for me to say. I have come to take you on a journey, a cruise, with Fat Patrick and a few of my other friends. Just like old times. We are all going to meet up like we used to down at the pillbox and from it we will see the craft that you will board. Only this time it will not be pretend. This is no Flying Boat without wings, without engines, without pilots. This is a ship that will bend its will, set its rudder and move to the wind. This time you can climb aboard for real, Stella. Your father knows you are strong and that when you are ready you will return. It would be good for you, to go somewhere, with your friends . . .'

'Father is my friend,' she said.

'Father *is* your friend of course, but there are other friends, friends you have not seen for years, friends you have never known.'

'Your sister?' she asked. 'Will your sister be there?'

'You can see my sister when you return. You *must* see her. It will do my sister a power of good, to see someone associated with that night. *Wouldn't you agree Mr Muchmore?*'

He rose to his feet once more. In his hand he held his bunch of keys. 'To your room Stella!' he cried. 'I will deal with you later. As for you . . .'

He turned to throw me out the door, but I was no boy he could lead by the ear. The boy was on the landing, watching, listening, learning, seeing what *he* should have done all those years. But I would teach the boy, teach him and Mr Muchmore, yeah even Stella. I was angry now, angry for myself and for my sister, angry for Mr Muchmore and those missing years, angry too that Stella had not rushed into my arms and thanked me for coming to her rescue. I pushed him with my hands and he staggered back against the table. I pushed him again, harder, and this time he tripped over his chair and fell to the floor, pulling the white tablecloth and the salt cellars and the unfinished steak and kidney pie with him. It smashed against the floor, and for a moment the spell was broken. We all looked at the great white oval dish cracked in two, with the pie's guts spilling out on to the floor. It could have been him with his brains spilt, or with blood gushing from his stomach. We all knew it and Mr Muchmore put his hands across his belly, as if to hold in his precious, vulnerable life. I bent down and grabbed him and pulled him towards me and there was a moment when he hung there, his face close to mine while Stella stood motionless beside us. I don't know what I would have done, what I was going to do, but at that instant we heard a great screech outside like a bird of prey in pain. Stella let out another cry.

I let him fall back to the floor. 'You are lucky,' I told him. 'That is Dickey Dove. You met him earlier this evening. He is calling Stella and me on his trumpet, like a ship's siren calls its passengers back on board. Would you wish to lock him up here as well?'

He looked at me and then at Stella. There was fear in his eyes.

'Come on Stella, help me up with him.' We lifted him up and put him back in his chair.

He slumped down. 'I have lived all my life for you Stella. I moved house for you. I took early retirement, sold my share of the business, all for you. I could have gone to prison for you! Don't leave me now Stella. What will I do without you?'

'It's all over Mr Muchmore,' I told him, not letting her reply. 'Stella is leaving tonight.'

I led her into the hall. 'Go upstairs,' I told her, 'and pack what you will. But hurry. We haven't much time.' It wasn't so. We had all the time in the world, but I had to get her out quickly before she realized what she was doing. She was as much in a daze as he was. If I could only keep her moving along . . . She started on the stairs and then hesitated.

'I have no bag,' she announced. 'I cannot go. In truth I cannot go. Only father has a travelling bag, and he would never let me use that. He uses it himself on the rarest of occasions.'

I brushed past her and went up on the landing. He was sitting there with the blessed thing on his lap.

'It's no use sitting there clutching it to your bosom,' I said. 'It isn't ours any more. It belongs to someone else.' He handed it over without a word.

'Here,' I said, holding it out to her. 'Pack them in this. This is yours now.'

She took it slowly, turning it round in her hands. 'I never thought I would see this again,' she said. 'Mrs Briggs's Bag.'

'Mrs Briggs's Bag,' I replied. I walked up with her to her room. She took out three piles of clothing from her chest-of-drawers and on top of each laid a black dress. She was looking at them as if she had never seen them before. They were identical to the one she had on.

'I have seven of these dresses,' she said. 'And one special one.' She reached out and took another seemingly identical dress from her wardrobe. 'See,' she said, holding it up to the light, 'it *is* different. Pure wool, and so . . . so comfortable. But I shall not be needing it. Carry it downstairs for me Giles.'

I followed her. At the foot of the stairs she turned and took the dress from me. 'Wait for me here,' she said, and ran down to the kitchen. I watched her as she opened the door and then, as she disappeared from view, I heard the sound of a metal grate being opened and the roar of a fire.

'There,' she said on her return. 'That's that.'

We stood for a moment in the hall. It would be the last time she ever stood there. I took her hand.

'You *must* come away, Stella. You see that don't you?'

'Yes,' she said, 'I see that. But I may return mayn't I? If I should wish it so.'

'Of course you may, Stella. You are free now, to come and go as you please. But you must come away with me now. You have no choice.'

We left that house in the damp hollow with Mr Muchmore standing in the doorway. Stella told him not to worry, that she would take care of herself, and that he was to take care of himself, did he hear. She buttoned up his coat and brushed his collar and kissed him tenderly on the cheeks.

'Do not fret Father,' she said, 'I will not be gone for ever.' She picked up the bag and started up the drive. Mr Muchmore cried out.

'Stella! Stella! Stella my own!'

She looked round and faced him.

'I must go Father, you know I must,' and with that she turned her back on him and walked up the hill. There were tears in her eyes by the time she settled down in the front seat beside me, with Dickey behind us.

There was still no change in the weather. What wind there was was slight and there was no sign of the promised rain. I rang Patrick from Wye station. He was in a high state of excitement himself, never mind my news. A crowd of people was already there, he said. It looked like it had to be this coming morning. *Everything* was happening down there. Well everything has also been happening up here, I told him, and I don't think Stella needs extra company. Tell you what. I'll take her to the bungalow. It's a bit cold and damp but a fire will soon put that right. I'll take Stella there and drive over later. Patrick paused and talked to someone at the other end. That wouldn't be necessary, he said. They'd call for us at the bungalow in the morning. He giggled. What about Clare? I asked. Is Clare all right? Clare is having a whale of a time he said. Clare will come with us. I will deliver Clare safely in your hands. She is with Dad now, trying on his cap. He never let *me* wear his blessed cap, I replied and Patrick laughed and told me that was because I never asked nicely enough.

Where are we going? Stella asked when I got back in the car, and I told her patiently that I had a bungalow down by Camber Sands. Surely she remembered Camber Sands, didn't she ever go there as a child? Hadn't she ever gone there with her father and she replied Camber Sands, Camber Sands and nodded her head, but whether she meant she knew it as an adult or when a child I could not tell. How long will it take to get there? she asked and I replied Not long. It's not far. Is it Dickey? and Dickey said, No, though if you look in your mirror sir, I think you might wish you had made that phone call a little further on, and I looked up, and there he was, right behind me, swerving from side to side, trying to overtake me. In his haste Mr Muchmore had somehow left the interior light on, and in the mirror I could see his face, crouched over the wheel. It was a mad face, full of fury and determination. It did not seem possible. We had left him so forlorn, so helpless, but here he was again. As I watched him now cursing us, running the car as close as he dare, I could imagine what he had done to my sister. This was no frail old man on our trail and there would not have been one that night either. What had he said to Carol? Probably a perfectly plausible story, told over a glass of sherry or two (Sherry? Mrs Doughty, Mr Doughty, Giles, *Carol*) to put her off her guard, how the Salvation Army had found Stella in London six years ago, and how, despite the depths to which she had fallen, he had taken her under his wing again. He hadn't contacted anyone from the past, for naturally enough he didn't want to reopen old wounds. It was a little thoughtless of him perhaps, but she would surely forgive a father for being over-protective to his only daughter. He would have been polite, solicitous, even downright friendly, and Carol would have listened to him, nodding her head, maybe not believing it all, but with no sense of the danger she was in. Of course you may come again, he would have said, And bring your brother too. Just let me know in advance so that I may prepare her. Bring him tomorrow if you wish. We are not going anywhere, and he would have laughed a little. But now you must be getting back. It's a filthy night out there. I would offer to take you in the car, but I'm afraid the damp has got to the engine and I haven't been able to start it all day. I'll walk down to the station with you and although Carol would have protested, he would have said, No, no, I insist, I am not so old as to be unable to treat a lady properly! and secretly Carol would have been glad, for it was indeed no night to be out alone. So he would have put on his coat and helped her with hers and after saying goodbye to Stella, they would have started out on that filthy night. The wind would have been strong by then, devilishly strong, no question of conversation, no time to watch what the other was doing, head down into the battling wind, first up the narrow lane, then across to join the steep climb down. And there, when it was darkest, with the rain lashing against them, and the wind screaming, he would have stepped back quickly, picked up a fallen branch and clouted her hard over the back of the head, maybe once, but probably two or three times, first on the road where he had room to swing, the second and third as she tried to stumble away into the undergrowth, falling into the tangle of the wood. And he would have stood over her as she lay with the rain falling on her and the trees rocking crazily above her, groaning and creaking and ready to crack, thinking Well this is a stroke of luck, and would have returned back to his home, where he flopped down in his chair, never to regain his strength. Until now.

The boy leant over. 'I think,' he said, 'for all our sakes, you'd better lose him before he starts hooting his horn and bashing us in with his bumper. If Stella finds out that he's behind us she'll probably jump out of the car here and now. This is an empty road and yours is the faster car. So put it to some good use for a change. Get us out of here.'

I changed gear, and put my foot down. The road was narrow and foreign to me and as the car rocked from side to side, great cascades of low branches arced over us.

'Faster! Faster!' the boy cried. 'Straighten Up!'

It did not take me long. Once out of Wye, Stella began to relax. It was as if the house had as much hold on her as her father and once out of its grasp she could begin to explore new territory. But she was uneasy sitting in the front with me driving and a complete stranger in the back and it was clear that she had not yet fully grasped the fact that she had left. She would start to talk, ask me questions, wonder at the passing of our lives and then she would look at her watch and exclaim, I must go back, I must go back. It is all right I told her. There is no need to go back. He is not expecting you to go back for at least a week. A week! she said and held her hand in front of her mouth as if to indicate what a preposterous, unbelievable prospect a week away from her father might be. A week will do you good I told her, knowing that within a week she would have discarded her watch and her other black dresses, thrown them and everything else that went with them to the wind. Oh Stella I wanted to say, you will be all right. I know you will, for that night when my sister saw you, when those men blurted out their little phrase, something deep within rose up, the real Stella long buried. How right and brave you were that night to spit on the faces of those two men, not your Spider Hour but simply to rage at them, even though you probably could not work out why you were so incensed. Throwing insults in people's faces is good for you! Sending time to hell is good for you! Running naked down the street is good for you! We drove on, through the lanes still lined with fallen trees, past fields still scattered with rotting broken branches. When will we be there? Stella asked. In about half an hour at the most and Stella looked at her watch and fussed, I must get back, I must get back. But we did not turn back. We drove down over the marshes, speeding along the military canal towards Rye and the singular outpost of Camber Sands. I was glad I had spent my youth there now, glad that my parents had built that dread bungalow, glad that I had started my summer days on a creaking cast-iron bed with my head upside down playing games of escape with my baby brother. Up to Rye we went, up over the bridge, past the roundabout, and then out of town, out on the road to Lydd Airport and then right, to the bending road which leads to the spare beauty of the sands. He is not here then? she said when she walked in and I asked Who? and she said Father of course, and looked in every room to see where he might be. He is not here! she said, in a surprised tone, adding, And there are no clocks here either! What will Father do without clocks? What shall I wind if there are no clocks? and she looked at her watch and said I must get back, I must get back. It is soon time for bed, time to wind the clocks, and I took hold of her hand, and said there is a bedroom here you may use, and you do not have to worry about the clocks, there are no clocks here, Look, I held her hand in the palm of mine and drew her watch over her wrist, You do not have to wear it, see, you can take it off, put it in your pocket, like you used to when you were alone. And she looked at the watch and put it in her pocket and told me that she was not used to being alone, that Father was always there, He follows me everywhere, He will be following me here no doubt, and I said, No Stella, he has not followed you here, and he will not follow you where you are going. And where am I going, she asked and I said in faith that I did not know, that I had no plan, only that Fat Patrick was going away, on a boat and I thought in my foolishness that it would be a pleasant change for her, to go with someone she knew, an old friend, and Stella looked at me as if I had stolen her, as if I were responsible.

'Are you kidnapping me then?' she said. 'Would you lock me up too?'

I took hold of her arm.

'No, no Stella. I want *nothing* from you Stella. Nothing. Only that you may be free.'

Stella reached out and touched my face. 'Oh but you do Giles, you *do* want something from me. You want me to erase this.'

She leant out and touched my face. She touched it again. She touched it three times.

'Father is a strict father but he is my Father and he loves me *and I love him*. He did not betray me to others. You did that. You betrayed me. You betrayed me to him. You gave me up to him, delivered me into his arms. Without you there would have been none of this. And I . . .' She buried her face in her hands and as quickly raised her face up again. 'Yours was the cruellest act Giles. I *never* recovered from that. All the time . . .' she shivered, 'all the time I was inside, I remembered your face and how hard it grew, so unloving, so selfish. You raised your hand not once but *three times* Giles, *three times* you struck me. Think what would have happened if you had not struck, if . . .'

'. . . if I had struck your father . . .' I suggested.

She looked at me with anger.

'If you had stood up to him, if you had stepped in, if you had simply pushed him away. But you did not. You struck me, *and then you forgot me*. I knew no one would come. I knew I was alone. I knew why Father was doing it, I knew why, but you?

377

Why had you struck me? Why? What had I ever done to you that wasn't . . .'

'. . . good,' I said. 'Oh Stella it was. It wasn't bad like your father says it was. It *was* good Stella. It was *wonderful*. I know I did you a terrible wrong. And not the first I have done to someone, and maybe, maybe, not even the worst. I was a boy then Stella, a boy alone, a boy adrift. Like the Flying Boats.'

'Ah,' she said, 'the Flying Boats. Are they still there on the river?'

'No, no,' I told her. 'They have long gone. But Fat Patrick is here. It is he you will go away with.'

She began to look around wildly again, and said But I do not know him, I do not know *you*, I do not know where I am, nor where I am going, I must be going back now, I *must* be going back. I did not know what to do now with this frightened woman. I had torn her away from her father, I had torn her away in the dead of night and driven her across the county in the dark alone with a man she hardly knew and another who she had never met before. She took the watch out of her pocket and started to wind it, reciting as the spring wound tighter, Take me back, Take me back, I *must* go back, and I looked at Dickey and at that moment we both thought we would have to take her back, that there was no alternative, that we had done wrong, and then I heard it, we all heard it, a huge humming sound which filled the air, a huge humming sound which was carried on the dancing waves and the mystery breeze, which turned the world and spoke our names. We ran out on to the beach. We looked but there was nothing to see. We held our hands to our eyes but there was only the gentle lap of the water and the pale mist rising slowly from the sea. What was it this sound and why did it stir our hearts so? What was it this white crescendo and why did we search for it so eagerly? There it is, cried Dickey, Look there! no *there*! and we followed the length of his arm, and saw her coming low across the water. She came from the east, with the morning sun blinking in her eyes. She came low and level, grey and lovely and hugely hulled, with men at her windows and as timeless as the silver sand she ran alongside. There were lights on board, and little flags fluttering and down her prow I could read her name. The *Galway*

Bay. Stella turned and gripped my arm. It was true what you said then she said. This is no Flying Boat without wings, without engines, without pilots. You always said that one day we will ride the Flying Boats. And here it is Giles. You have brought it to me!

A boat was lowered into the water and two men and a smaller figure settled unsteadily aboard. I recognized them all, Fat Patrick, Jim Liddle and Clare. They were soon ashore. Clare was jumping up and down. It's great she said, it's just great. It has got *everything*. 'Planetrain' has got *nothing* on this and Patrick smiled and said that Clare was right. It's all there Giles, he said, all there. It always *was* there, every scrap of it, down to the wicker baskets and table napkins. They would have destroyed her, cut her up, hawked her on a bargain pavement.

'There are others still on board,' Fat Patrick explained, 'the others who were part of the long secret. They had stolen the Flying Boat that night. It had been Dad's idea, ever since he had swum over to the *Galway Bay*, broken in, and found it with nothing but the ignition key missing. Those three days inside had been a revelation. He had walked up and down the length of it, he had laid down upon the damp cabin beds, he had sat in the cockpit and peered out through the window streaked with rusty tears. It had come to him when they had sent him away, the months he spent in the sanatorium. All he could think of then was the *Galway Bay*. She was a caged bird. He was a caged bird. Everywhere he looked there were caged birds. And so for eighteen months he made plans. He scrubbed around, collecting discarded diagrams, old maintenance books, he had wandered about the town in his pajamas, the eccentric collector of Flying Boat memorabilia and plotted while the town sniggered. He had sat in his study at night with his captain's hat on and planned while cruel laughter came drifting over the fence. At first it was almost an exercise in fantasy, but gradually it came to him that he *could* do it. He could set her free. He would make her surge forward, rise up in the air. Just like you! For he had seen you those nights. When he sat alone in his room with the lights off and the moon shining on the garden, he had seen you come jumping over the fence, only later did he tell me, when we were working in the hangar one day, standing on her wings, reliving that night, only then did he tell me how he saw you racing round our garden with nothing on, how he watched you run and leap into the air. That Boxing Day, the day your sister came round to borrow one of Julia's hats for some date or other, all the old crew who worked with him on the Flying Boats, who knew their workings better than they knew their own cars, had come round, Peter Jackson, Gordon Mackenzie, et al. His father had built a barbecue out the back, and although it was cold with snow on the ground they had all stood outside drinking punch and eating sausages while his father told them what he intended to do. My mother had nearly dropped the punchbowl, *Do what*? she said, *Do what*? and he had told her, I intend to take the *Galway Bay*, to let it run on the Medway again. I'm going *to teach this town a lesson*, and I want you all to help me and they had clapped him on the back and said we'll help, we'll do it, but shouldn't you be a bit more, you know, discreet, nodding their heads in my direction. Oh no, said my father, I meant *all*. Patrick can help too, if he wants.

'That night it had nearly all gone wrong. Peter Jackson had come round early, and Gordon was due to come up from the station with one of Mr Barratt's taxis. My mother had made them thermos flasks of hot tomato soup and individual brown paper bags full of sandwiches, they were lying there on the kitchen table, my father and Peter standing waiting, when the front door opened and in my sister walked dressed up to the nines. They nearly called it off that night, for we didn't want her hanging around, but luckily she went out, went out to meet some girlfriend or other, not that my father would have minded, he was so pleased to see her, why she had only been away a few weeks and here she was again, but no sooner had she arrived and kissed them briefly on the cheek than she was out again. Do you think it's safe to let her go out, my father said, and my mother had held out her hands and said, You try and stop her. So we were free to go then, my father, Peter Jackson and me, my mother had tried to keep me at home, saying don't you know what you're doing James, she always used James when she was angry with him. What do you think you are doing, involving a boy in this mad scheme? and my father took my mother by the arm and said That's just it, I want him to see that I'm not mad, I want him to see his father as he was, as he should have been, and he will, do you hear, and besides, how many madcap schemes do you make coffee and biscuits for, and then twenty minutes later Gordon Mackenzie came round and we were off, down Gladstone Drive, down the High Street out to where Peter Jackson's old pilot's boat lay. I sat in the back, behind the driver and as we drove down the main street I swear I saw my sister duck into the alleyway with someone I knew, who was vaguely familiar to me, an elder boy at school perhaps, but then she was gone and we had passed the traffic lights and were turning down to where Peter Jackson's boat lay. It was not difficult at all to set the Flying Boats free, to lean out and cut the wires with the great industrial shears that Gordon had picked up, and nor did we have much difficulty in attaching the *Galway Bay* to the boat. Flying Boats were built to be towed. By the time we had secured the line the other craft had begun to drift downstream turning and twisting in a carefree ballet, describing huge careless circles. They moved swiftly, arbitrarily, and there was a time when we feared we would crash into one, that the current would draw one of them across our lines and snare the whole venture, and though one came close, looming up in the dark, the current caught her again and she drifted away into the mist. We hadn't meant to steal the *Galway Bay* exactly, we hadn't meant to hide her away all these years, the intention had been to climb aboard, to turn the engine over (Gordon could have done that. Gordon could have practically willed that engine to start, he knew it so well) and to race it up and down the Medway, *to wake the town*. But since Dad had climbed aboard, metal plates had been riveted over the hatchways. We could not get in. And so we carried on, pulling her down the river, past the Naval Dockyards, and the hemp factory and the silent anchored ships, it was so quiet that night, there was nothing moving on the river, just the mist and the shadows of the low moon, at times we could not see the shore, just hear the dim hoot of a foghorn, and once out we simply continued, towed it round the head towards father's land out on the marsh and that great hangar of his. We couldn't get it in the hangar that night of course, for we had no winch there, and there were not enough of us to push it up, and so we had to leave her there while we got help. Someone is bound to see it, we thought. Someone will report it before we have time to do anything, we will be caught for sure, and we turned the boat and chugged back up the river. It was early in the morning now, the sleeping river so empty, no one knew how empty, only us, the mist had risen now and I remember looking back along the towpath, where you and I had spent so many hours, looking across to the pillbox. Someone had lit a fire there earlier in the evening, the embers were still glowing, and I wondered if they had seen what we had done, whether it might not have been you and your ever present box of matches, whether the police would be waiting for us when we drew alongside, but they were not. It was quiet and still, with only the noise of the water lapping and our low, muttering voices. What we need, my father had said, is a strong vehicle to pull her up. A tractor would be best, or a truck of some kind, and Gordon said What about a Daimler, a bloody great black Daimler that's as strong as a hearse. I don't want to use a hearse my father said. I didn't say that, replied Gordon, I said *like* a hearse, Barratt's *Wedding Car*, that's what we'll use, and we jumped back into the taxi and drove down to the lock-up where Mr Barratt kept his fleet of cars. You'll get into terrible trouble for this, my father said, Terrible trouble, and Gordon laughed and said that if they played their cards right Barratt would never know and besides the old skinflint was going to give him the chop as soon as the Christmas season came to an end, he just knew it and with that he jemmied open the door, and there she stood, black and gleaming, with white ribbons decked out across the bonnet and a pink bow on the radiator. What a beauty said Gordon, running his hand along her flank. This will bring the *Galway Bay* home, and so we climbed into the wedding car in our muddy boots while Gordon lifted the bonnet. It was so quiet when she started, just the faintest shudder told you that he had done it, and we drove out, along the main road again. Do you know, said Gordon, as he picked up the peaked cap lying on the passenger seat, Only he is allowed to drive this bugger, he's terrified that one of us might scratch it or get it dirty, and with that we all broke out laughing, three men and a boy in this huge black car, God knows what would have happened if the police had seen us, out along the coast road we drove and then turned off on to the dirt track which led to my father's scrubby marsh. Oh it was wet and slippery that track with deep ruts and half frozen puddles, twice the Daimler sank and spun in the snow and twice we had to get out and push while Gordon leant out of the window and watched the wheels scatter slush, how we had to push, how the car slithered, how we shouted. Dawn was coming up and at last we dropped down into the hollow and there she lay, the light playing on the silver wings. Gordon hooted and pressed his foot down, the mud flew up, the wheels slipped and then we were down there, with ropes and guide lines and wooden rollers across the ramp. It was harder than we thought, pulling her up, for though the Daimler was strong enough, it was hard to keep the *Galway Bay* straight. Forward! Forward! we would cry. Straighten Up! Straighten Up! and I remembered all those afternoons in your spare bedroom, while we watched Mr Muchmore park his car. We got her in at last, a few bumps and a few scratches, and then, with her standing there, water streaming from her bow, we realized the enormity of what we had done. We had stolen a Flying Boat, we had stolen *the* Flying Boat. The *Galway Bay*. There she lay and though we had not yet gone aboard her we knew inside there was *everything*, waiting. We cannot give her back now, said Dad. We must keep her, keep her and tend to her, and perhaps one day, if we are good, if we treat her right, we will be able to take her out and let her fly, and so we made a pact, three men and a boy, to do just that, to keep quiet, to work and preserve her. Now our race is run, now we are going to take her up, she will fly now and with us inside. Now it is time to throw caution to the wind, for me and my father and Peter Jackson and all the other caged birds on board. And me said Stella. And me.

They rowed out an hour later after we said goodbye. Dickey stood on the shore and placed the horn to his lips. They rowed out with Stella sitting calmly in the middle, the boy at her side. He had tugged at my sleeve only minutes before. Can I go too, he had asked. I was going to admonish him. I was going to tell him that I needed him with me, now that Clare was here. Then I remembered. Stella had the bag now. He would have to follow it. I looked at him with his brown eyes and his brown hair and his large boyish head looking out over the water. Of course you can go, I said, Go with Stella. Go with Stella, and don't come back. And don't come back. So they rowed them away, Fat Patrick and his father, one passenger and one stowaway, rowed them to the *Galway Bay*, to the promenade cabin and the smoking cabin and the tubular adjustable chairs. I saw them dock alongside. I saw them clamber aboard with other wiser arms to steady them. I saw Stella in her black dress stand in the forward entrance and dig her hand into her pocket. I knew what she was taking out. She held it in her hand, looking at it and threw it out towards me, high in the air. It rose up, glinting in the sun. I wanted to reach out, to catch it, to hold it in my grasp. If only I could! Surely I could! But then it fell, lost into the sea. Then the doors closed and the engines started and the beast turned and faced the wind. The spray, the great spray of their future was thick now and they were hidden from view. See the windows strange and low! Imagine the huge angles that mark its height, that speak for its breadth! Now it races! Now it thunders! Now it lifts! Now it roars! Into the kingdom of air! Into the kingdom of air!

'It's over then,' I said to Dickey, repeating a phrase he had once said to me.

'Not quite sir,' he replied. 'Look.'

Half a mile away over the brow of the dunes, with his engine screaming, came Mr Muchmore. How he had found us I will never know. I can only imagine that he remembered my father telling him about our bungalow. Perhaps he had even come down here with him. The car lurched over the top of the hill and slid down the sandy slope. There was no chance of him catching them, for the *Galway Bay* was almost out of the water by now, but that didn't stop him. The car raced across the beach, bumping and lurching from side to side, smoke pouring from its exhaust, out over the bay and into the sea, where it began to sink in the soft sand. The tide was well out, while up ahead lay a series of sand-banks and when he could go no further Mr Muchmore flung the door open, jumped out and began to run forward, sending clouds of seagulls clattering into the air. From one bank to another he ran, until he stood on the last, his arms outstretched, watching the huge boat climb into the sky. And standing there, watching the Flying Boat rise up, he seemed to realised that Stella had gone from him forever for suddenly he hung his head and his arms dropped down to his sides. He had lost.

The tide is swift at Camber Sands and when it is time for the sea to return it does so with frightening speed. As he stood without hope, I became aware of the sea creeping around us, flowing over the ripples of sand. We were far enough out ourselves, but Stella's father was a good hundred yards ahead.

'Quick,' I said to Dickey. 'Get Clare back to the hut. I'll attend to this.'

I began to run forward and shout at him. At first he did not hear me, could not hear me, for the sound of the *Galway Bay* still rang in our ears. Only when it had gone, when there was nothing left in the sky, did he realize the predicament he was in. The water was swirling round the sandbank now, growing ever deeper around him, and I think it was this vision of being on an island that made him hesitate. If he had stepped off and waded through quickly he might have made it, but he did not. He walked its length, as if to find the safest route and then tested the water gingerly with his foot. It went up to his knees.

'Quick! quick!' I cried. 'Before it's too late.'

He hesitated again and lifted his leg, as if to remove his shoes and trousers.

'There is no time,' I cried. 'Hurry! Hurry!'

This time he heard me, saw me splashing through the waves, but the strength of the oncoming tide was making it hard for me. He tried again and stepped off into the sea. Almost immediately he was up to his waist with his arms stretched out, as if attempting to hold the rising tide down. The sand was soft and treacherous. He fell once, he fell twice and the third time when he rose again he was no longer walking. The water was up to his neck and he was sinking fast. I could see his head turning from side to side, I could see his mouth gasping for air, I could see his arms flail above him, see his body twist and turn. Then the undertow began to take hold. Again he slipped, again he fell, again he was pulled and each time he came up I could hear him call *Stella! Stella! My Own!* Was it on the sixth or seventh time he did not come up. I do not know. But suddenly he was gone and I knew that the current had taken him.

They found his body an hour later, floating up the Rother to Rye Harbour. Later that morning, while Dickey took Clare to the Sealife Centre over at Hastings I wrote a long letter to Sergeant Weatherspoon and sent it to him, via Scotland Yard. We lit a fire that night down on the beach and ate baked potatoes, while Dickey draped raw meat over the garden fence, in the hope sir that the puma might sniff us out once again. The next few days we walked the sands, ate fish and chips and visited a number of pubs while Dickey composed abominable tunes on his trumpet. I rang up the hospital every morning. I talked to Monica every night. We were staying longer than we intended but that was all right. There was no change and we were on a holiday. The first proper holiday I had ever had.

We stayed late on our last day, running races and eating too much bad ice-cream and got back to London around midnight. Clare was asleep in the back of the car. I carried her up to bed. I kissed her sleeping head. I thought, I will kiss you tonight and every other night you sleep.

I picked up the mail from the hall and went back upstairs. There was nothing much. An invitation to some meteorological gathering in Fife, a couple of bills, a postcard telling me that I had missed my last dentist's appointment, and a small brown package with a letter Sellotaped to the outside, from an old-aged pensioner in Devon, Detective Sergeant Weatherspoon, late of the Rochester Constabulary, he thanked me for writing him such a full and illuminating account. He had always hoped I would get in touch with him, and he was heartened that he had not waited in vain. It is not in a policeman's nature to give rewards, he said. We do it grudgingly and to people we hold in the lowest esteem, but this he was giving gladly with the best of wishes. They had found it a couple of months after she had disappeared, on one of their regular trawls of the river banks, and though there was no reason to suppose it had anything to do with it, he had kept it nevertheless. On his retirement he had taken it with him as a memento of those fruitless days. He never knew who had written it, or what it had contained, but, like the case itself, *I felt that there was something there which I could not read, something in front of my eyes but which was like a blank sheet of paper. If only I could discover what it was and what it said I would have learnt everything.* I opened it up. The top was a little rusty, and yes, the salt water had long lifted the writing away, but inside the half whisky bottle were four folded sheets of foolscap, marked with a ghostly wash of blue.